SCALE

THE BLAZE LEGACY
BOOK TWO

L.R. FRIEDMAN

Scale

Copyright © 2022 by L.R. Friedman

This book is a work of fiction. Names, characters, places, brands, and incidents are the products of the author's imagination or used fictitiously. Any resemblance to actual events, locales or persons, living or dead, is entirely coincidental.

ISBN: 979-8-9862079-3-3

Cover Design by Eternal Geekery

Map by Darian- Instagram: aareli.art

Edited by The Editor & The Quill

2
THE BLAZE
LEGACY
SCALE
L.R. FRIEDMAN

AUTHOR'S NOTE

The Blaze Legacy is a slow burn enemies to lovers fantasy full of dragons, shifters, delicious tension, and spice that builds with the series. It has dual strong female leads with each having their own romantic storyline, one character developing into an MF relationship and the other into a sapphic one.

A curated playlist as well as a list of content and possible triggers can be found at the back of the book.

Grymm Mountains
Inverno
Silent Woods
Alucinor
Spuma Sea

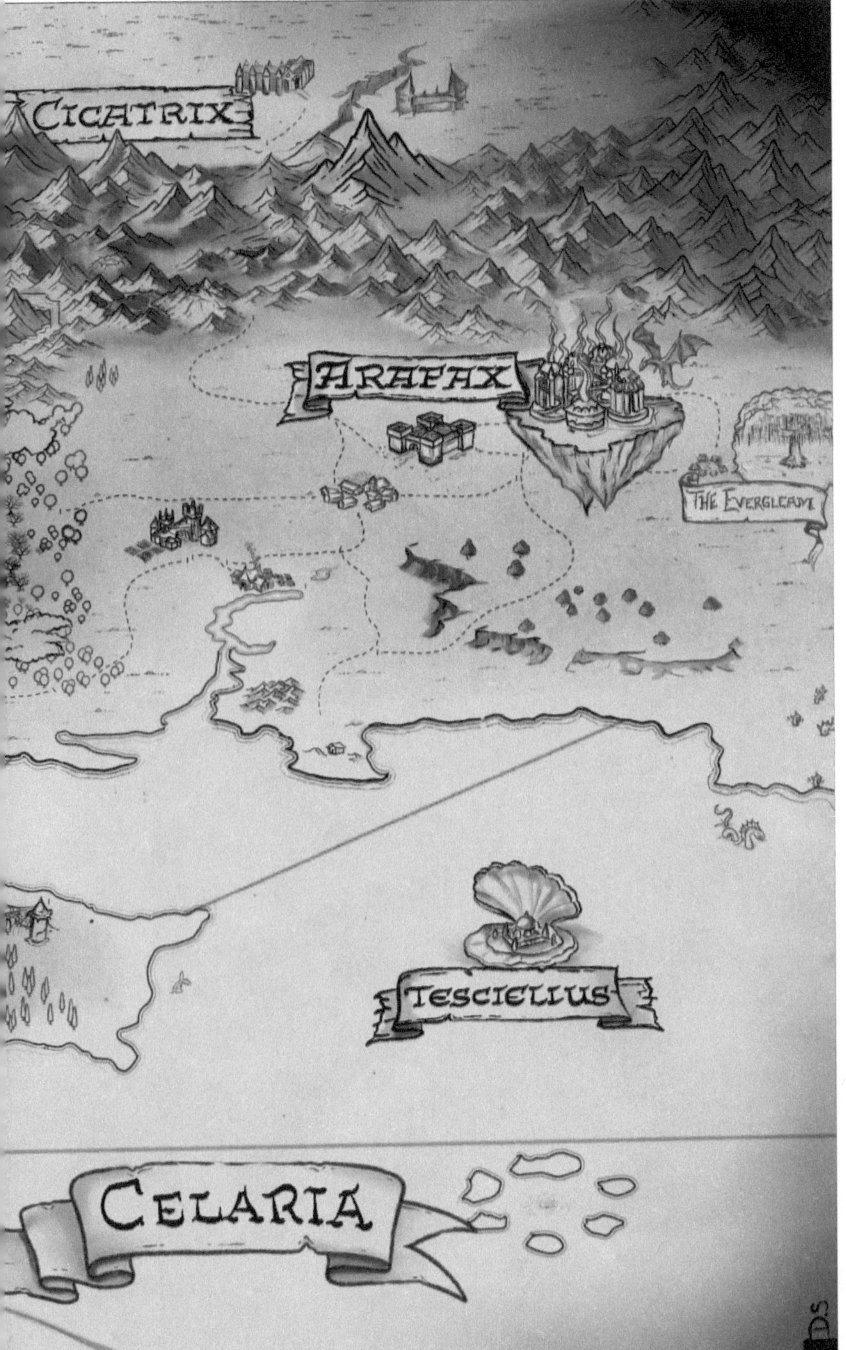

CICATRIX
ARAFAX
THE EVERGLEAM
TESCIELIUS
CELARIA

CONTENTS

To the ones still uncovering their worth
—this is for you.

PROLOGUE
AISLIN, AGE 10

"Roar!"

Black silhouettes flickered against the swaying sheet, bathed only by the dim candlelight illuminating the bedroom. Huddled inside our small blanket fort with our shoulders pressed together, my brother and I held out our arms, twisting our hands into shadowy figures.

I let out another roar, my knuckles parting, my creature snapping at him.

"Ca-caw!" Anders crowed, scrunching his face, brows knit in concentration. His thumbs crisscrossed while the rest of his fingers beat against the imaginary wind. "Take that, dragon! Caw!"

I shook my head, laughing at him.

"Phoenixes don't caw," I stated matter-of-factly. Anders was still little—only six—and it was my duty as his big sister to teach him these things.

"Well, what sound do they make?"

"They screech," I said, before my dragon gobbled up his phoenix with a roar.

"Hey!" Anders pouted, crossing his arms over his chest.

"Sorry," I shrugged. "Our dragons are always victorious."

"You never let me play the dragon." He rolled his eyes, a mischievous glint streaking through his emerald irises. His tiny fingers prodded my side as he giggled like a maniac.

"I'm not ticklish," I said, holding up my hands in makeshift claws facing him, "but I know who is!"

He grinned as I attacked, my fingers flitting over his ribcage. His legs jerked uncontrollably, twisting his body away from me, gasping between giggles.

ROARRR!

Our eyes snapped to the window.

I scrambled out of the blanket fort, helping my brother up, and we scurried to the windowsill, peering up at the purple night sky. Trailing across the moonlight, three scaled silhouettes soared above the clouds, small figures outlined on their backs. The scarlet and sapphire dragons climbed higher, the third one flaring away from the group, diving right toward our house. Anders gasped, and I gripped his small hand in mine. "It's okay."

His face lit, and he ripped his hand away, waving at the man standing on the back of the emerald dragon. Its glowing eyes locked with mine, dipping its scaled snout lower and giving us a clear view of its champion.

Our father.

Pointing into the bedroom, Father closed his eyes and brought his hands to his cheek, pretending to snore—signaling us to get to sleep. We'd already stayed up past our bedtimes, and I was in charge since our parents were out. My mother was teaching some new water wielders who'd just come of magic age, and my father had training and important meetings with the King.

"Come on, Anders," I said, ushering my brother away from the window after blowing my father a kiss with a final wave. "Mother will be home soon. If she catches us still up, she'll spray us with ice water."

It wouldn't be the first time.

"But I wanna watch Father fly!" Anders whined, dropping his shoulders and dragging his feet toward his bed like they were stuck in a pool of taffy.

"I'll tell you a story," I offered, pulling back the blanket and giving him a boost when he struggled to climb under the covers. I sandwiched him in, tucking the bedding around him until he was nestled in tightly.

"Fine," he huffed.

I pressed a kiss to his forehead. "I love you, sprout."

"Yove you too," he yawned, giving a small smile.

His eyes fluttered, a realm of dreams awaiting him, then they jolted wide a moment, fighting sleep.

"Story," he reminded.

I tucked a few brunette strands of hair behind my ear. Looking out the window, I watched the dragons fly out of view, carrying our father off with them.

Clearing my throat, I turned back to Anders. I knew he'd be asleep before I finished, but I started one of his favorites anyway. It was a story our mother had told and retold many bedtimes before.

"Once upon a time, there was a great warrior who was a military advisor to the King and a chosen champion of one of Arafax's Revered..."

16 years later

1

DRU

The Revered have returned.

I thought back to the Queen's chilling words while slitted, silver orbs blinked up at me in quick succession.

"Are they back to normal yet?" Kyleigh asked, pushing up to her elbows on the bed.

"Not yet. But I'm sure they will be soon." I stroked her cheek, trying to reassure her. She needed me—needed me to be the steady voice of reason. But I didn't know if I could be that for her.

I'd try my damnedest.

Aislin sat in a chair in the corner, legs swung over its arm, hugging herself, completely silent. Her skin was pallid, eyes still brilliant emerald with onyx sliced through the centers. She hadn't said a word since everything happened earlier in the throne room. While I carried Kyleigh to the fort's guest chambers, the Queen sent a few guards to help Aislin as well, but she'd kicked at them, refusing their assistance.

The Queen sat on the other side of the bed, hands clasped

in her lap. "No one can know," she'd whispered to me, before escorting us to the room. "It's not safe for her."

Kyleigh.

Her *daughter.*

Arafax's *princess.*

Heir to the throne.

How could I have been so blind? So stupid. What would happen to us now that Kyleigh was royalty? Would she still want to go back to Vermont with her mother now in Celaria?

Hundreds of questions poured into my mind, crashing into the clarity I desperately tried to cling to. I'd spent the last hour scouring the royal library, combing through its texts for anything that could tell us more. There wasn't much to go off of since so many texts had been destroyed by The Blaze. I needed to understand what was happening to Kyleigh to keep her safe.

I couldn't lose someone else.

Kyleigh cleared her throat to get my attention. "What is happening to us? What are the Revered?"

"Dragons," Aislin rasped, voice barely above a whisper. Her eyes snapped to their usual shape and glow. "The dragons...they're people. They're us."

"Yes," the Queen confirmed. "It would appear so."

Kyleigh sucked in a breath, and I brought her to my chest, holding her close and stroking her hair. I wanted to be able to explain it all, but I was still at a loss. Still shocked. The Queen's eyes narrowed on me, making my throat constrict.

The obedient part of me felt as if I should let go of Kyleigh, not wanting to displease the Queen I'd served for years. But her daughter needed me, so I'd comfort her and deal with the consequences later.

Aislin scrutinized herself, tugging at the fabric of her

clothes so she could inspect any other surprising changes to her body. "My parents. They knew about this? My mother—"

"Your mother had to have been a dragon. Your father, her chosen champion," said the Queen, looking impassive. I knew her steadied disposition was an illusion, considering she'd panicked when she discovered her daughter had the same ability.

"I don't understand," the overwhelmed assassin muttered under her breath.

"Dragon magic is passed down through the bloodlines of Arafax's founding families. When someone with the dragon magic passes, the next one deemed worthy within their bloodline gains the ability. But we can talk more about this later," the Queen said, making it clear that was all she would share right now.

Aislin swung her feet off the chair, boots hitting the floor before she rested her elbows on her knees. Lightning flowed from her fingertips, and she began throwing the iridescent bolts back and forth—a tic she tended to do when she was anxious. "They just kept it a secret from everyone? Even from their own families?"

"Yes. Even from them." The Queen nodded.

Aislin gave the monarch a pointed look. "Seems like all parents have their share of secrets."

Coming to terms with the facts being presented had me stumbling off my axis.

The two women in front of me were descended from the founding families of Arafax. They were dragon shifters with magic meant to protect the realm. And one of them—the one I found myself falling for—was also the heir to the throne. The scaled dragons that I remembered flying over Arafax growing up, protecting our kingdom, were people who had entirely separate lives from that duty. Families.

I'd spent years after The Blaze reading and researching the leftover contents of the royal library and had no clue about this.

What else was I in the dark about?

"How come *you* knew about this?" Kyleigh directed the question to the Queen, pulling back my attention.

"My oldest sister was one," she said, tone clipped. "The trait must have passed on since the gem's return."

"So, what happens now?" I asked the Queen. I had no clue how to proceed; how to navigate this *situation*.

"No one other than the people in this room can know Kyleigh's true identity."

"But M—"

"Both identities," the Queen said, cutting her off, silver eyes flaring.

Kyleigh snapped her mouth shut, closing her eyes tightly. She squirmed against my chest, as if trying to find a way to get comfortable. After she'd settled, she opened her eyes.

The slits were gone.

Ruby light flickered from within the Queen's clenched fist, lips pressed in a thin line, eyes snagged on Kyleigh in my arms. It didn't seem like the Queen was thrilled about our relationship.

She is one of Arafax's Revered and its princess.

I pressed a kiss to Kyleigh's forehead, reminding myself that she was more important right now. I could prove myself to the Queen—there's already so much I'd done to serve her and Arafax. She'd eventually come around.

"Everything's going to be okay," I whispered. It could've been a lie, but it was one I desperately needed to believe.

"Doesn't fucking feel like it. I'm a damn dragon," Kyleigh muttered back up at me.

"Technically we are revered, not damned." Aislin let out a frustrated sigh before standing and crossing the room, heading for the door. "As enlightening as today's been, I'd like to return to The Lavender so I can process this shit from the comfort of my own bed."

"Wait," the Queen commanded, and Aislin halted in the doorframe. "I'll have my servants pack some things for Kyleigh, and you two will head to The Lavender together."

"What?" they questioned in unison.

"Kyleigh can't stay here. If anyone figures out who she is, they could tell the Enchantress. I can't take that risk." She looked at her daughter, face pressed into hardened lines as if trying to douse any flare of emotion. "I'm sorry. It has to be this way. At least for now."

"Fine." Kyleigh chirped in reply. She swung her legs over the side of the bed and got to her feet, tugging at the seams of her dress. "Let's go, Dru."

We walked along the corridor, her fingers laced with mine. Tears dragged down her cheeks, but she kept her gaze pinned forward. I knew how much she hated crying in front of others, so I remained silent, skimming her knuckles with my thumb, trying to offer her some sort of comfort. The suddenly empty conversation uncorked all the questions I'd plugged out of my mind, letting them flood in and saturate it.

How could we keep this a secret and also keep everyone safe?

Would I be allowed to continue seeing Kyleigh now that we'd discovered who and what she was?

Would she still even be interested in me with all that had transpired tonight?

She had the potential to become the most powerful

wielder in Celaria and could have anyone in the realms that suited her. By some strange miracle, our paths had crossed without this knowledge. Even stranger, she was interested in me—the son of peasants who preferred to tinker with contraptions and abstract concepts rather than toys. A man who'd been taunted as a boy. Someone who was nothing more than a null.

Other than my work for the Queen producing technology to help us recover from The Blaze and strategizing ways to keep our kingdom and its citizens safe, I really had no other true value to Arafax. To Kyleigh. Not yet, at least.

Those things might not matter to her today, but they might once she realized all her available options.

After all we'd gone through together, the idea of not being good enough for her terrified me; therefore, I'd do everything in my power to prove my worth.

"Dru." Kyleigh stopped in her tracks, gripping my shirt.

"What is it?"

"If the two of us are dragons," her eyes flitted back and forth like she was sifting for something in her mind, "then who's locked away in Inverno's dungeon?"

2

REDMOND

Shadowy tendrils climbed up my spine. A feline chuckle vibrated against my chest, grating my ears. My eyes remained transfixed on the heap of ashen husks beyond the window. I'd seen the pile before but never gave it a second thought. Now that its pinnacle was visible from the windowsill, it nagged at me.

What's their purpose?

A warm, wet tongue slithered along the curved scar just beneath my hip bone, the sensation rushing straight to my cock.

I attempted to keep my wings splayed behind me, trying to heave the injured one up to match the other's height. The healers said it should only be a few more sessions to get back to normal. A few sessions *too fucking long*. I'd been summoned, and now looked broken in front of the Enchantress.

That was never good.

She preferred to be the one to break me.

The smoky fingers of her own wings tested them,

reaching up and primping them into place before one grazed the cage dangling from my neck. Despite being empty, it somehow felt heavier than it did when the gem was locked inside.

I held my breath knowing tonight had nothing to do with pleasure.

Tonight was about punishment.

"You failed me, then had the audacity to ignore my summons."

She wasn't wrong. I had failed. But I hadn't failed the Enchantress.

I'd failed Neve by not seeing what was right in front of me. By letting my hurt drive my actions. Blind me.

I'd failed my own people, taking their ability to bond familiars, something sacred to Inverno.

"I couldn't fly while my wing healed."

"Hold still," the Enchantress purred through crimson lips, ignoring my response. A soft demand from her was no less threatening.

Her wings ghosted the edges of my mine, causing blue and white flames to ignite, rippling out from my back and covering their span. The Enchantress's black eyes pinned me in place, and she moved up my body, running her taloned fingers along my feathers, folding deep into the roots. She took her time, twisting, pulling, plucking a fiery feather.

It took all my willpower not to flinch while she repeated the slow torment a few more times, sticking them in the glass jar full with the others she'd collected over the years. A reminder of all our visits and the power she continued to strip away from me.

She could pluck at me all she wanted. This pain was

nothing compared to the things I'd done. The devastation I'd inflicted.

I deserved it.

Just not for the reasons the Enchantress believed.

With two quick claps, she summoned her wisps. They'd been buzzing around the cabin, vacant shells flitting aimlessly in their spectral covens. They always left me feeling unsettled. It was hard to know if they understood anything outside of their mistress's orders.

"That one," she said, pointing to an ornate, purple box sitting high on one of the shelves in the corner of the bookcase.

Two wisps flew up and pulled it down, bringing it to their master.

"Thank you, darlings," she said, before giving another pair of quick claps, dismissing them.

Cranking the small gear attached to the back of the box five times, she lifted the embellished lid. Music crooned from its depths, a tune I'd never heard before chiming from a series of various-sized gears filling the base of the box. Along the inside of the lid was a mirror reflecting midnight eyes back at me.

"Don't look away or I'll make this worse for you," the Enchantress whispered, placing the hand not holding the box on my bleeding chest. She lapped at the blood seeping from the four shallow scratches she'd gifted me when I'd arrived.

What sort of punishment was this?

Digging her nails into the already torn flesh, she smothered her fingers in blood, then dribbled it on the mechanisms. They turned, spinning in an odd pattern, separating the layer of gears until only a talisman and a handful of them remained.

"Have you ever seen a clockwork talisman before?" she asked, bringing its chain over my head. The gears bumped into the empty cage and set of rings already situated there.

"I haven't."

My eyes didn't budge from the two dark irises staring back at me. I tried listening to the Enchantress's incantation, but I physically couldn't look, trapped in the spell she cast. My heartbeat's unsteady pace countered the rhythm of the music cranking from the purple box, the clanging of gears scraping against each other reverberating through my chest.

The cogs of my mind twisted and warped, everything beginning to swirl, until I no longer stood in the Enchantress's cabin.

I was standing at the epicenter of Arafax's village, staring at my father's back.

A terrifying *roar* swallowed up the sounds of swords clanging behind me, snapping my attention to the sky. A blue dragon towered over us, razor-sharp teeth bared, puffs of white escaping its bloodied maw.

"It took her!" my father shouted, crossbow aimed at the giant beast—one of Arafax's Revered. A few arrows were lodged in its sides, heavy iron chains attached to them. "It took your betroth—"

No.

It's not possible.

I'd just seen her. She couldn't be...

I refused to even say the word.

My hands shook. *I knew what happened next but could do nothing to stop it.*

Hundreds of icy daggers rained from above, driving into my father and sending him crashing to the ground. A pit formed in my gut like I'd been punched there, the air ripped from my lungs.

"Father!"

I scrambled to him, pulling him upright, shaking him. Bloody shards of ice covered and filled his body, his insides spilling onto the ground.

Onto me.

Tears burned my eyes. "No, no, no. You can't fucking die on me. Not yet."

I wasn't ready.

My body trembled, a chilling fire rippling through my veins, head bursting in throbbing pain.

My entire vision filled with blue flames and all I could hear were screams.

Until I found myself standing at the epicenter of Arafax's village, staring at my father's back, a terrifying roar swallowing up the sounds of swords clanging behind me, snapping my attention to the sky...

HEARING THE BOX SHUT, I BLINKED, FINDING MYSELF CURLED on the ground in a pool of my own vomit, ignited wings cradling me.

I lost track of how many times my father's death replayed in my mind.

It felt so real.

The anguish, the overwhelming power of my uncontrolled shift, the heat of the flames ripping through my body, the melting ice seeping through my bloodied clothes. The compounded loss of Neve and my father strangling my heart, choking out my words.

It was as real as it was that night over a decade ago.

I gasped for air, fumbling for my throat.

An icy numbness swept through me, seeing the dragon kill my father.

Neve killed my father...

The thought had drifted into my mind but I'd brushed it away, not wanting to believe it. Not wanting to tarnish the relief I felt that she was alive. But it was true. After repeatedly witnessing the worst moment of my life, there was no denying it.

She'd killed him right in front of me.

"What the fuck was that?"

"Just a piece of magic collected from a memory weaver who had the misfortune of visiting me," the Enchantress said, lifting the chain over my head and placing it back in the box. She handed the trinket off to her wisps, rolling her shoulders. "One of the few positives of your failure is I now have more power at my disposal. Usually a weaver's magic would take too much out of me."

The thought of Alucinor's fabled weavers made my throat dry, clogging my ability to breathe. Everyone knew to steer clear of the peninsula that ran between Arafax and the sea.

Leave the weavers alone, and they'll leave you alone.

If the Enchantress now had access to their abilities, what else had changed with the gem's return?

She clapped twice, her wisps hurrying to help me off the ground, a few others cleaning up the mess I'd made. The winged phantoms carried over washcloths, sweeping them along my body until I was clean. The Enchantress watched from her chaise, pitch eyes glittering, scanning me intently.

When all the wisps had been dismissed, she stood,

walking to me, her sultry voice especially low. "I think you've had enough punishment tonight."

She reached down and gripped the base of my shaft, tugging me in long, unmerciful strokes.

My stomach roiled, my mind fighting to redirect my thoughts while my traitorous body responded, reflexive to her possessive touch.

I'd come to the Enchantress a lost, young prince suddenly thrust into kingship without my queen. All I had was my anger at Arafax and the need to feel anything other than loss.

It had taken me some time to discover where my father hid the gem that he'd promised her. A thousand steps beneath my castle in the belly of a sapphire beast.

What I thought was *just* a sapphire beast.

"I don't like when you're distracted," the Enchantress said, frowning.

Removing her copper claws, she pulled the last talon off her pinkie before letting it drop to the floor. Twinkling onyx fingers skimmed up my chest, grazing over the open slashes. She slipped a fingertip into her mouth, sucking off the crimson smear, and my cock twitched in response.

I hated that it did.

But we were both monsters, and monsters like us dwelled in the realm of dark and bloody promises.

I understood what happened when vengeance wiped away the shreds of your humanity.

That's why the Enchantress couldn't know that Neve was alive. Her elemental abilities compounded with being able to shift into a dragon would be too alluring to someone desiring power. I'd caused Neve enough pain—even if it was unintentional. The least I could do was keep her safe.

If that meant going along with a marriage of alliance

forged between two vicious hearts that craved revenge, so be it.

"Soon, everyone will bow to us." The Enchantress's silky sable hand grazed the bond mark on my hip. Her mark; her claim over me branded into its ugly scarred lines. "It's all finally coming together."

Her words echoed in my mind, sending a shiver through me while she stroked me with possessive precision. My body trembled, still shaken by what I'd relived over and over again. The terrifying prospect of what other horrors the Enchantress could conjure with the right combination of magics flew through my mind.

Clenching my fists at my sides, I fought the knot building in my stomach.

Play along.

Then, bring her down.

3

KYLEIGH

"**G**lowing brightly for twenty-one years, Ky!"

I stood atop a table made from a lavender-whiskey barrel, staggered cheers echoing against the tavern's walls. A few dozen criminals sang me a birthday song I'd never heard before with lyrics that would make a sailor blush. The drunken patrons raised their glasses, clinking them in celebration. Meanwhile, the still-sober ones sat wide-eyed, sipping at their drinks, mumbling quietly along to the verses they didn't know so they looked like they were participating.

"It's not my birthday!" I shouted to the crowd, directing my attention to Aislin and Sweeney who stood smugly behind the bar of The Lavender Leigh Inn & Pub.

"We know, but we weren't exactly in the place to celebrate then," the snarky former assassin yelled back at me.

Sweeney waved his arm, the motion whipping around the musty smell of ale and booze. Patrons tossed coins into the floating tornado until Aislin whistled, clenching her fist in the air. The coins spun, following a path right into the register as Sweeney pulled out shot glasses in a straight line, filling each with a different concoction, creating a rainbow gradient of colors.

It was amazing getting to meet the air wielder who'd taken Aislin under his wing. She'd claimed his power was elegant, but now that the Evergleam's gem was back in play, his skills went way beyond his famous *breezetending.*

Aislin placed her hands on the bar and hopped over it with both feet, planting her combat boots on the pub's wooden floor. Turning to Sweeney, he handed her six shot glasses full of vibrantly colored mixtures that she carried over. A few patrons helped me off the tabletop they'd placed me on minutes before the serenading began.

"How did you even know it was my birthday?" I asked Aislin.

She ignored my question, spreading the glasses out on the table. Sweeney walked over with another six, rounding us out at a full dozen rainbow shots.

"Want to do the honors?" She glanced down at my hands with a smirk. I snapped, igniting my pointer finger like a personal lighter before torching the shots one at a time. It was a new facet of my power I'd finally been able to harness.

We each grabbed a shot glass, Aislin holding a brilliant blue while I lifted a golden yellow, flames spilling out from them until a blast of wind turned them into nothing but smoke. We gulped down the next set of shots, the alcohol warming my throat, spreading through my chest.

"You still haven't said how you knew it was my birthday. I never mentioned it before."

Aislin nodded over to the entrance. Dru stood in the doorway, wearing a crisp white shirt, black slacks, and a black leather harness that matched his glove, vials of various balms, serums, and I had no clue what else running up the leather straps. Since we'd returned the gem a week and a half ago, he never went anywhere without his gadgets. It was his own personal brand of armor now that the realm had more magic for everyone to use.

"The Queen mentioned it to Dru a few days ago," Aislin answered while Dru headed over to join us at the table.

"Why would she bring up my birthday?" I tried to contain my annoyance, releasing my hands that crossed my chest unintentionally.

Dru shrugged, kissing my forehead as he whispered, "She said she felt bad she couldn't throw you a banquet or something to celebrate since—"

"She missed a decade of them?" I finished for him.

His lips pressed into a line, and he softened his gaze. "Partially that, I'm sure, but also because we still need to...you know..."

Keep my identity a secret.

I rolled my eyes but said nothing, knowing this rowdy pub was full of untrustworthy ears.

I was still trying to process everything that'd happened since I'd arrived in Celaria about a month ago, even more so over the last ten days after returning the gem to the Evergleam. The day I found my mother after a decade. The same day I found out I'd been blessed with dragon magic.

Ever since, Aislin and I had spent our days training our elemental abilities at the fort as well as receiving hours of tutoring to understand the history of Celaria and how to draw on our inherited dragon magic. My mother believed if we mastered our transformations and honed our wielding, maybe we'd have a shot at taking down the Enchantress.

Dru was working with her to learn more about the

Enchantress. There were so many tales about her: that she wasn't from this world, she was the jilted faerie lover of Arafax's former king, she stole the souls of unborn children and turned them into her wisps. We knew the latter wasn't true, but outside of that, not much survived The Blaze in terms of texts on the subject. Dru was stuck deciphering what little information remained.

Meanwhile, dragon scales were still etched into my sides, climbing up my hips and ending just under my breasts. I checked the mirror daily, staring at the only physical reminder that I could somehow turn into a dragon. If I ever figured out how.

Aislin handed us all another set of shots, and grabbed one more, holding it out for someone coming in from the back entrance.

"Did you miss me?" a voice bellowed with enough blaring swagger to fill the large man we had come to know and love.

"Of course we did, Ox." I squeezed around as much of him as I could, inhaling the cozy smell of apple pie that wafted from the gentle giant. He lifted me up, giving me a messy kiss on the cheek.

"What have you been up to? We haven't seen you at the fort," Aislin said, appraising him.

"Queen still has me on armor shining duty." His eyes dropped to his boots, a large thumb scraping down the side of his beard.

"Still?" Dru asked.

Ox looked over at Aislin who nodded at him silently. "It's worth it."

They never talked about what happened during their meeting with the Queen when we got back from Inverno. I didn't want to pry and I wasn't sure I'd even want to know.

Dru wrapped his arm around my waist and whispered into my ear loud enough that I heard him over all the raucous music and talking in the pub. "Anyway, we talked it over and figured we could still do something for you. I know you normally have cupcakes and candles in your world, but that's not our tradition."

"What's the tradition here?"

Aislin pointed toward the back door Ox had arrived from. "Come outside and we will show you."

As the four of us walked out the exit together, people cheered and gave well wishes. My gaze collided with a few strangers huddled in the corner with raven hair and violet eyes, giving off emo-teen vibes. They looked out of place, but who was I to judge? Between my sneakers, jeans, and Otherworld slang, I got plenty of looks. Luckily, when you were surrounded by criminals, people didn't ask a lot of questions.

Seeing where my attention had snagged on the group, Dru gripped me a moment, his hushed tone grazing the shell of my ear. "Best to stay out of their way. Let's go celebrate you."

It definitely wasn't the twenty-first birthday I'd imagined back in Vermont, but it was a much better celebration than the deadly banquet with Inverno's King Redmond.

Sparks piercing flesh and armor.

Crimson sliding down the walls.

Falling into darkness.

I shook the thought from my head, realizing my friends were watching me.

Tiny lit jars had been strung from the inn, reaching across to the nearby trees. Leigh was balancing on top of a ladder, tying one end of the cord around a large trunk. The once black bark now had glowing lines running through them, sparkling like a thousand polished diamonds were ground down and painted beneath. Looking closer at the jars, small bolts danced within—Aislin's personal touch. We bathed in their luminescence, the lightning moving and flowing above us.

"It's beautiful."

"We thought you might like it." Ox beamed. "Had to make sure that Aislin kept you occupied while we got it set up."

One of the inn's whiskey-barrel tables had been carried out and held a large, clear chalice full of shimmering, swirling, peach-colored liquid.

"What's that?"

Leigh carried over some chairs and gave us a smile. "It's a wishing chalice."

"What's inside of it?"

"Sweeney used some of his breezetending to make a *Kyleigh Special* tonight," Aislin said with a smirk. The liquid continued to spiral, permanently mixing itself. Its fruity bouquet filled the air, void of any boozy undercurrent.

Dangerous.

Perfect for a twenty-first birthday celebration.

I used both hands to pick the concoction up, looking at my friends. "I don't think I can drink this whole thing and survive the night, guys."

Everyone burst out laughing.

"Don't worry, we know you're a lightweight." Aislin held her hands out to take the crystal from me.

"In the Otherworld, you make a wish on your cake and blow out candles. It's similar in Celaria, except we take turns making wishes for you and taking a sip as we pass it around," Dru explained, smiling. "Then you'll make the final wish for yourself."

"What kinds of wishes?"

"Anything you desire." Gold flecks danced in his irises burning with red-hot intent, making me blush. A shiver flitted across my skin at the memory of our time at Renovo Falls. I was still waiting for the *more* his words and touch had promised me then. Craving it even more now.

Aislin clutched the cup with her palms, staring down at the twisting cyclone within. After a few moments of closing her eyes, she lifted the glass up to the center of our circle and took a drink. She passed it to Ox, who grabbed it with a few fingers like it wasn't made of heavy glass. He looked into the cup before wagging his eyebrows, giving me a wink and sipping from it.

Next, Dru held out his hands, taking the cup. His still-ignited gaze held my attention and I wondered what he could be wishing for.

Finally making its way back to me, I stared into the shimmering drink blending and curving against the edges of the chalice. Sweeney popped his head out of The Lavender's back door and smiled, circling his wrist once before giving it a quick flick. A few pours of the Kyleigh Special rose from the chalice, spreading out to float along with the breeze.

"So that those who cannot be here may wish for you as well," he said with a gentle smile.

We watched the last specks of peach liquid ascend into the atmosphere, twinkling like stars in the evening's dusky, moonlit breeze.

Then, everyone's eyes were on me.

Dru beamed. "Now it's your turn to make a wish and finish what's left."

I tried to think of a wish, or even a handful of wishes. It

was funny how when you actually had a moment to ask for anything, nothing came to mind.

Peering into the swirling liquor, I let all the wishes spill out of my heart, one by one, until my well ran dry, emptying it of all my desires—hidden, dark, and unspoken. I brought the chalice to my lips, quenching the insatiable thirst left behind.

4

KYLEIGH

"What did you wish for earlier?" I asked, pulling Dru against me before we headed upstairs. The golden specks in his eyes shimmered in the dim light.

"You'll see," he said with a smirk, his finger tracing along my spine.

When he reached just above my tailbone, he splayed his hand, moving it in languid circles, sending a shiver of eager hope through me.

My room never felt so far away.

We strode down the narrow hallway, Flynt's men standing between the doors belonging to Aislin and I. They were *always* there. Extra protection from Flynt on behalf of the Queen. I was still getting used to it.

I sank my hand into Dru's back pocket, anchoring myself so I didn't break into a sprint. His fingers never left the valley of my spine, his touch feeling heavy despite being feather light.

Pulling out the key to my door, I fumbled in anticipation,

slipping it into the lock. Flynt's man, Roq—I think his name was—kept his head forward but looked like he was stifling a smirk. Once I heard a *click*, I turned the knob, and Dru slid his hand along the wood, pressing the door open. His presence wrapped around me, making me painfully aware of how close we were, even without touching.

My breath caught in my throat when I realized my room didn't have its usual sullen disposition. Flower petals had been scattered all over, their exquisite peach and pink tones decorating every surface of the dresser, desk, and floor. On the bed lay a wooden tray, a few utensils, and a plate holding a lopsided chocolate cupcake with white-and-peach icing swirled into a large heap—a 50:50 icing-to-cake ratio. It was the tallest cupcake I'd ever seen and leaned slightly to the right, the weight of the thick, sugary topping pulling it over.

"What's this?"

"We don't do birthday cake or cupcakes here, but I thought you might like one anyway," Dru said, shrugging. "I've never made anything like that before, and I had to create a mold for it from scratch. Your mom helped me with the recipe."

"Usually a cupcake tin holds one to two dozen." I smiled, despite still having mixed feelings about my mother's involvement.

His head shot down to his feet as he ran a hand through his hair. "I made a dozen, but...this one was the only acceptable one. You'd think I'd be better at it, considering my mom was a baker."

I laughed, pulling him in for a kiss. "I love it."

"It's a little, uh, messy, so I brought a fork and knife."

"I don't mind a little mess," I said, swiping my finger through the icing cloud and bringing it to my lips, savoring the sugary zing on my tongue. The fluffy buttercream nourished something deeply nostalgic in my soul since I hadn't enjoyed my mom's recipe in over a decade. I used to think her cupcakes were magic.

Ha.

Picking up the confection, I offered it to Dru, whose eyes were glued to my lips. "Want a bite?"

Opening his mouth, he took a tentative bite. He closed his eyes, the corner of his mouth curling up, a satisfied hum seeping from his lips.

I took a bite myself, the icing coating my nose, mouth, and chin, primness be damned. I laughed, unable to contain it, setting the rest of the cupcake on the plate.

"You've got a little something..." Dru grabbed a napkin from the tray. "Here." He held it up to wipe my face.

Before he could absorb what was happening, I tugged him toward me, kissing him fiercely. It was sensual and messy. Perfect. When we came back up for air, some frosting smeared along his bottom lip. I slowly leaned in, running my tongue over the remnants, sweeping away the evidence. With a pained groan, Dru gently pulled me away. He closed his eyes, breathing deeply, before pointing to a package sitting on my desk. "I got you something."

I sighed out my disappointment.

He went and grabbed the rectangular-shaped box, carrying it back over to me. "You didn't have to do that," I said, untying the white ribbon, pulling the lid off, and peeling back the paper inside. "It's not even my birthday."

"I know. I wanted to anyway."

Inside the box lay a pair of Chuck Taylors, their crimson shade a beautiful contrast to the white laces that ran along the top. They reminded me of a pair my mother used to wear when I was a kid—not that she'd ever be caught dead wearing them here. She was a Queen now. Low-top sneakers apparently ruined the ensemble.

"Figured you might want something to represent where you come from when we go back to your home."

Tears rimmed the edges of my eyes, but I didn't want to mess up this moment. Not when we were celebrating my do-over twenty-first. I wanted to forget the real one, to scrub that night from my mind—

"Do you like them?" Dru asked tentatively.

I reached in and took out the shoes, sitting on my bed so I could untie my worn-out pink pair. They had faded after repeated washes, trying to erase our time in Inverno. "I love them."

The last bit of cupcake summoned me, and I devoured it, leaving not a single crumb on the plate.

I let out a contented sigh.

"Was it a good belated birthday celebration?" He rubbed the back of his neck, eyes darting to the floor, seeming nervous.

"It was wonderful," I said, licking the final cupcake remnants off my lips and placing the tray on the floor, "but I have a few birthday wishes that still need granting."

I patted the bed for him to sit next to me. Using the straps of his chest harness, I swung my leg around to straddle him, and initiated a deep, unrelenting kiss. His body responded, coming to life beneath me, making me salivate more than the delicious cupcake I'd just inhaled.

"Oh, is that so?" Dru murmured in my ear, cheek grazing mine as he pulled me in for another demanding kiss. His hands skimmed over my thighs, caressing up and down a few inches. I wanted them to keep making their way up.

I unwrapped myself, gripping the bottom of my black tank and discarding it.

Dru raised an eyebrow. Keeping one hand on my knee, the other swept across my back, trailing up my spine to the lace on my black bra—the one I'd worn every time I knew I'd see him the last few weeks, hoping it would get seen. He hovered over the clasp.

Silently, I brought my hand up behind me to meet his, undoing the clasp and letting the bra drop to the floor. My breasts were heavy, pert and ready, and his eyes didn't leave them as he undid his chest strap, removing his harness before unbuttoning his crisp, white shirt. I felt him harden even more, the gold in his hazel eyes igniting.

Rocking my pelvis in his lap, my nipples pebbled, dragging against his chest. Fire coursed through me, desperate to be consumed by his kisses, his touch. His palms skimmed my sensitive buds, tweaking and teasing before his tongue flicked over one, tempting me further. Grazing his teeth along my collarbone, I shuddered a moan, building friction with each roll of my hips. My breath caught in my throat when he laddered kisses along its column, and I clutched my fingers around the buttons of his pants. His gaze lingered on the movement as I undid each one, trying not to fumble. It was as if he wanted to catalog every moment between us. He kneaded my breasts, and I arched into him, body coiling into knots, aching for release. But not like this.

"I want you ins—"

A series of powerful knocks had Dru stilling beneath me.

"Sorry to interrupt," Ox yelled through the door before clearing his throat. "Dru, you're needed at the fort immediately."

"Can it wait?" I screamed back, wilting in frustration

when Dru lifted me gently off him. He frowned, standing up and grabbing his shirt, pulling it over his shoulders.

I haphazardly threw on my tank, not giving a shit about my bra, before I opened the door for Ox. "I never expected you to be the one to cock-block."

His brow furrowed, and I knew instantly it was serious. Looking us over, he grimaced, dragging his focus to Dru. "Did I mention how sorry I am?"

"Should I come with?" I asked, seeing Aislin standing behind the giant. I scooped up my shoes, then sat on the bed to put them on.

"No," Ox frowned. "Just him."

"But Aislin is going."

"It's not safe for you."

I shoved away my annoyance. Everything had been strange since our return to Arafax, not just because of *what* but also *who* I was. I had spent years wondering what happened to my mother and I couldn't even spend time with her now that I'd found her. Meanwhile, part of me was still so angry with her and the continued distance between us only sunk the knife that'd been wedged into our relationship deeper.

"I'll see you in the morning when you come for lessons," Dru said, kissing my forehead.

"But we didn't finish celebrating my faux birthday," I pouted back at him, already knowing I'd lost.

"I know, and I hate that. I promise I'll make it up to you," he said with a smirk.

"You better." I gave him a push out the door before the urge overtook me to shoot sparks at Ox and drag Dru back to the bed.

They beelined down the long hallway, Aislin trailing

behind. She slowed her stride and glanced over her shoulder, shooting me an apologetic look.

I mouthed to her, *fill me in,* and she nodded, silently catching back up with Ox and Dru.

Heaving out a disappointed sigh, I slammed the door behind me.

5

AISLIN

"What if it's a trap?" I warned Ox and Dru, the three of us walking through the entrance of Arafax's fort-turned-castle.

We'd escaped Inverno only a few weeks ago, narrowly making it out with our lives after being imprisoned by King Redmond. Now he'd requested a secret meeting between our two territories—the same two territories that had been sworn enemies the last decade after Inverno had brought war to our doorstep, killing our royalty, decimating our homes, devastating our families, and dwindling down our population in the process.

"Can they even be trusted? After everything that happened?" I clenched and unclenched my fists, butterflies jolting erratically in my stomach.

Stealing back a precious gem, executing a dozen or so guards, not to mention Ox stabbing the King with a dragon scale... Usually those things didn't elicit a diplomatic response like calling a meeting. I'd been preparing myself for a more violent reaction from the winged tyrant.

Ox and Dru said nothing and simply followed the long, red, velvet carpet leading our way toward the throne room. Golden, recently polished dragon wings lined the walls. I hadn't seen them in years, since the last time I was at the castle with my father. Maybe they'd been put back on display because the Revered had returned?

We stopped at the edge of the dais. Arafax's Queen was seated in her throne, red stilettos poised in front of her, sipping from a fiery, golden chalice.

Before Ox could tell me to hold my tongue, I called out to our *beloved* monarch. "I don't trust any part of this. Why would he want to meet with us?"

"Well, had you followed orders, we wouldn't be in this predicament," the Queen snarked, sighing from her throne.

She had sent me off on a suicide mission that she didn't expect nor want me to return from. One where I was to do her dirty work, executing Inverno's King and retrieving the Evergleam's gem. Now I was going to have to face the man I'd failed to kill—a man I probably should have.

Years from now, would I be proud of or regret that decision?

"When did the message arrive?" Dru asked, eyes darting over to us before going back to watching the seconds tick away on his glove's clock.

"As soon as it arrived, I sent a guard to alert Sir Fergus." She looked at Dru apologetically—a foreign expression for her. "I'm sorry for interrupting your festivities."

"It's fine. We were able to have the party," Dru replied.

Just not the private one you two were trying to have in the next room.

I smirked at Dru, and he glared back at me. At least I didn't have to spend my night listening to the two of them. I was used to noisy evenings at The Lavender with all the amors and tenants *enjoying* themselves. But I didn't consider any of them friends. Being able to look Kyleigh and Dru in the eye was important to me, especially since we spent our days training together.

"Where are we meeting?" I questioned, trying to get us back to the task at hand.

"The Forum," the Queen replied, motioning to her servant who had a cushion topped with three stones. I had no idea where she was talking about. "Sir Fergus, your services are no longer needed this evening. You're dismissed."

Ox's face fell before he clenched his fist and brought it across his chest, kneeling to his queen. "Of course, Your Majesty."

Turning away without making eye contact with any of us, he lumbered out of the room.

This is all my fault.

I was grateful to be alive, but I owed him.

Dru took two of the stones from the servant, handing one to me.

"What am I supposed to do with this?" I asked, looking at the strange, coppery markings on the rock.

He held it up to the light, pointing at the numbers and symbols. "These are portal stones, enchanted for a one-way trip to a precise location."

"Very good, Dru," the Queen said, directing the servant where to place her stone on the ground. She repeated the enchantment slowly for us, letting us practice, before saying it one last time, stomping her stiletto onto the stone, and disappearing. Only specks of rubble remained.

"Ready?" Dru asked me, holding out his hand.

I stared down at the stones on the ground in front of us, lifting my boot above mine. "Ready."

Murmuring the enchantment, I shut my eyes and slammed my foot down.

WE LANDED IN AN OPEN ROOM, GLASSLESS WINDOWS EXPOSING us to the wind whipping around the stone columns, sending a shiver through me. I pulled my jacket tightly over my shoulders, walking toward the grooved windowsill to get a better view.

In the distance, uneven tips of dark towers peeked above frost-covered mountains. Rich evergreen vines climbed the tallest one, contrasting the building set against a dull-gray sky. Eyes dropping, my breath caught, taking in the steep chasm over the ledge outside the window. Just one push and someone would surely fall to their death from this height.

"Where is this place?" I asked, taking a step back from the threatening descent. The room in its entirety had been forged from uneven rock, chiseled into existence. Even the tables and chairs had uneven ridges along their surfaces, scarred by whatever hand or magic had sculpted them.

"Welcome to the Forum," the Queen said, knocking some leftover pebbles from the portal stone off her crimson heels.

A flash of blue barreled inelegantly through the corridor. White flames danced along the edges of the phoenix's wings, slowly expanding their reach as limbs stretched from the shifting form.

The Queen rolled her eyes before turning her head away from the bare King Redmond. "Forget something?"

Like clothes.

"Apologies." He chuckled darkly—not the least bit sorry. "They should be arriving any moment."

A second later, citrus and jasmine breezed through the room, knocking the wind right out of me. Commander Sloan appeared, foot stomping into the rocky floor, lurching into me with her arms wrapped around some clothes that she handed off to Redmond.

"What the—"

"Sorry about that," she said, reaching out to steady me. It was the only acknowledgment she gave me before wiping tiny pieces of gravel off the bottom of her boots. She wore no fancy armor, just a white, lacy blouse and navy trousers. It felt strange seeing her in something so...casual.

"Thank you, Sloan," King Redmond said, pulling his pants on, not bothering with a shirt. His onyx wings were tucked into his sides, one sitting slightly askew—the one Ox had managed to injure during our escape.

"Yes, thank you," the Queen agreed, shaking her head.

I stifled a laugh until my thoughts caught on part of what the King had just said. *Sloan.* "Not Commander?"

"No. Sloan has been stripped of that title," King Redmond replied, tone clipped, chilled.

Her eyes snapped to mine, icy blues bearing into me with crinkles laced around their edges, her plum-tinted lips pressed into a firm line.

I hated that she had been punished for helping me, but at least she didn't have a ruler that had wanted her dead whether she was obedient or not.

"Aren't you missing a few people for this reunion?" King Redmond scanned the room. "Sir Fergus and that timid one —Kyleigh, right? Somehow, she managed to massacre sixteen of my guards. I must admit, I didn't see that one coming." He gave a self-indulgent smirk. "She may be a more ruthless opponent than you, Aislin. Too bad you didn't send that one to finish me off, Isla."

I didn't miss this asshole. Not one bit.

The King smiled, like that idea intrigued him. Dru looked like he was going to be sick, bronzed skin a shade paler, though his gloved hand was clenched, fingers glowing. I cut him a warning look. The last thing we needed was our level-headed one losing his composure.

"Oh, Redmond," the Queen tutted. "You haven't lost your arrogance. Even after all these years."

His upper lip peeled into a full-on grin. "Some things never change, Isla. Though, some things do. Whatever happened with your marital alliance with the Grymms? Heard you ended up trading him in for a mere Otherworlder. Where's the unlucky bastard now?"

The Queen flinched but kept her hands firmly in front of her, as if moving them would unleash something she couldn't take back. "This is a good time to remind you all that while we are in the Forum, any attempt to harm another person in the room is grounds for expulsion."

"What do you mean?" *No one mentioned that.*

Dru chimed in. "The Forum was created by the people of Celaria as a central location for discourse and diplomacy. Since keeping everyone willing to listen and cooperate was a challenge, the room has been enchanted to expel anyone acting with malicious intent."

"In other words, hate me all you want, but let those bolts come anywhere near me and you'll be riding down the steep drop to the bottom of the mountain pass," Redmond said, brushing some dirt off his wings.

I shoved my hands into my pockets, shoulders tensing.

"Now that we've gone over the rules, let's get to the reason why I called you here." King Redmond moved to the table and sat down, patting it for us to join him. "Recent events have me realizing we are surprisingly on the same side."

"What caused this change of heart?" The Queen's eyes narrowed into silver slits.

"I believe we have a mutual problem on our hands," he said simply, ignoring her inflamed glare.

"Mutual problem?" the Queen sneered. "Anyone giving you a problem sounds like someone deserving of Arafax's support."

He shifted in his seat before speaking again. Even with his injury, there was no doubt he was still just as strong and dangerous as before. I would have no problem ending him right now if I needed to. Forum rules be damned. Getting my ass kicked out would be worth it.

"Oh, so you aren't having issues with the Enchantress?" King Redmond asked, raising an eyebrow.

How does he know that?

The entire room fell silent, the King and Queen glaring at each other like two venomous snakes, poised and ready to strike.

"Ah, I see. So the problem is your fiancée?" The Queen ran her nails along the jagged rock of the table, the sound grating my ears. "Maybe you should have been more careful where you stuck that dick you so enjoy showing off, Redmond."

"While I'd love to have a dick measuring contest today, Isla, I'd rather keep this brief since it would be dangerous for her to think we have any communication."

"You want to form some sort of alliance?" Dru reiterated,

trying to steer the meeting back on course. "Against the woman you're planning to marry?"

The King nodded to Dru. "I knew you were the smart one." He turned to face the Queen. "Just like I know *you* have a deal with the Enchantress."

"How would you know that?" she replied, much too quickly for the careful façade she was trying to present.

"Many reasons, though your ruby flames on display in a jar on her bookcase tells me you've visited her at least once."

The Queen's lip twitched, but she said nothing.

"The gem is back," King Redmond continued, resting his elbows on the table as he spoke. His eyes were sharp, angry—as usual—but there was something desperate glinting within them. "Gather your dragons, champions, knights, and wielders. I will bring my own power, military, and their familiars—which we know is over three times the size of your army and far superior." Sloan lifted her chin at his words. "We have protections in place at Inverno's castle should the worst happen."

"And what's the worst?" Dru asked, jotting down notes on a piece of parchment he'd summoned from his glove.

King Redmond shot out a burst of sapphire flame, igniting the paper until it was floating away in small ashen pieces. "There can be no proof of this meeting."

The Queen stood, pushing her stony chair back into the table. "I don't see why your problem needs to become Arafax's. I won't risk my people for your cause."

"It's not just *my* cause anymore."

"I'll have to agree to disagree," she said, retrieving three portal stones out of a small satchel attached to her hip and waving us over to join her. "It would be best to end this *discussion* here."

King Redmond's wings splayed wide, igniting in a wave of blue and white fire. "The Enchantress is close to freeing herself from her banishment. We can't let that happen. The few powers I've seen that she already has access to could be catastrophic against our people."

The Queen stilled, hand gripping tighter around the stones. "That's not possible..."

"She told me she's close. It's one of the reasons she'd wanted the gem. Once she's free, she intends to use it somehow. She never told me the purpose." He looked down at the empty cage hanging around his neck. "Needless to say, she's not happy with me for letting it out of my possession."

Sloan shifted uncomfortably, arms crossed.

"Aww, your first lovers' quarrel," I jabbed. "Good practice for marriage."

The Queen swirled some ruby flames with her fingertips, whipping them in small circles around her wrists. They weren't a threat, otherwise she would have been expelled from the room, tumbling over the ledge. A small part of me wished she'd get riled up.

The King strode over to us. "While the gem being removed lessened your abilities, it also lessened hers. Now that it's back, she's stronger. Still banished, but stronger. Believe me, I've seen some of what she's capable of. I'm sure there are more abilities she has access to that I don't even know about."

The ruby flames sputtered a moment between the Queen's fingers before returning to their weaving. "She doesn't have everything she needs to break the enchantments keeping her contained."

He cocked his head to the side. "Are you sure about that?"

My throat bobbed, and I found myself absentmindedly

tracing the lines of my bond mark hidden beneath my jacket. I startled, realizing what I was doing, and I scanned the room to make sure no one was watching. Sloan's icy eyes met my stare.

The King clasped his hands together, drawing back my attention. "I think you know more than you'll let on, but I understand your position. You have no reason to trust me."

"You want to prove we are on the same side? That we should trust you?" The Queen brought her fiery gaze to meet her rival's. "Continue your farce with the Enchantress and find us something of value. Something to help us stop her."

The room remained silent, the only sound coming from the whistling of the wind scraping against stone. Tension hung over the room like a thick fog.

"That's fair," he said, not elaborating further. He extended an arm, releasing a small flame of brilliant blue from his palm. "We're agreed?"

The Queen gave him a once-over. "One more thing."

"What is it?"

"That dragon you have in your dungeon. It belongs in Arafax."

"Very well," King Redmond said with a nod. Sloan's lips parted, gaping at him.

Are we truly about to go into an alliance with Inverno? Is he actually handing over the dragon he'd held prisoner for a decade without more of a fight?

Questions surged out of me, spewing at the phoenix king standing across from me, unable to be contained. "Why would you do any of this? You said you would never compromise with us last time we saw you. Now you show up here, willing to work with us?"

The Queen lifted a hand, cutting off my questions. She

handed the stones to Dru and I, placing hers on the ground in front of her. "Return our Revered first. We'll go from there."

Blue flames spiraled out from King Redmond's arm into the middle of the room. Extending her hand to him, the Queen released her own ruby fire, the flames dancing and twisting together, creating a swirl of purple hues before soaking into the stone table at the Forum's center.

"Now, I must get back to Inverno and make preparations," King Redmond said, folding his wings in before shooting out of the room, a phoenix soaring along the chilling breeze. Only small tatters of the pants Sloan had brought him lay where he'd departed from.

I still couldn't believe this was happening. The only one left in the room who didn't look distressed was the Queen, which concerned me even more.

My eyes trailed over to Sloan placing a copper-painted stone on the ground. She murmured the enchantment, her icy-blue stare drilling into me, then slammed a boot to the ground, a few fragments of rubble the only remaining proof she'd ever been there.

6

AISLIN

When it had been my turn to make a wish in the chalice for Kyleigh, all that came to mind was that I hoped we'd hone our abilities soon so that we could be rid of the Enchantress. Now, according to Inverno's King, she was becoming a bigger threat by the day.

That thought had me on edge.

I grabbed the flask Sweeney gave me last week off my night table. My original one had been confiscated along with my other belongings when I'd been imprisoned. Twisting off the cap, I sat up in bed, taking a long swig of lavender whiskey, then unclasped the back of the holster crisscrossed over my chest. Even though there was no dagger, I still wore it.

My father had given me the blade, the only physical reminder I had of my family. I should have tried to get our personal items returned when we'd discussed the terms of our alliance—not that the Queen would let anyone else have a word in the arrangement.

Removing the holster, and the rest of my clothes, I threw

on a loose sleep shirt and a pair of shorts before climbing back into bed. I was still getting used to not having Flynt's marks to follow at all hours. It made it hard to fall asleep, not shadowing prey in the dead of night. Luckily, the long and rigorous days of training at the fort helped.

Physically, I was exhausted.

Mentally, I was wide awake.

When I'd told Kyleigh about my sleep troubles, she said they counted sheep at bedtime in the Otherworld. At first, I couldn't see how that would be possible, given how much space sheep take up, but she explained that you visualized them in your mind. It seemed ridiculous, but she insisted having something to count was mundane enough to naturally get my brain to relax for bed.

While I'd normally brush off her silly Otherworld notions, tonight was different. I had no clue how I'd be able to sleep after that meeting. If Arafax and Inverno weren't adversaries, then what were we?

I wondered what Kyleigh would think about the whole thing when I told her on our walk to training in the morning. She was already angry at her mother—having to pretend that she was just another subject under her rule didn't help—and now, she'd been left out of a meeting where the Queen tentatively agreed to partner with the man who'd held her prisoner, whose guards tormented her to the point she eventually blasted them out of existence.

It would be interesting when their paths crossed again, that was certain.

I ran a hand up my arm, the one that once held the spiraling scar counting down the days until my mission to kill King Redmond needed to be complete. Even though the scar no longer grew, faint flames still stretched from my wrist, cresting over my elbow. The Queen had promised it would only need more time to fully heal. I wasn't sure I believed her, but at least the scar was barely visible instead of violet and angry.

My lids were heavy and I yawned, my body begging for the sleep I desperately needed. I released my electric power, spinning the lightning into swirls and jagged lines. It was time to see if Kyleigh was correct about this Otherworld nighttime ritual—only, why simply imagine sheep when I could make my own?

I held out my hand, the outline of a tiny, neon-purple sheep materializing in it. Tossing it into the air, I followed the illuminated zigzag pattern of the docile creature, watching it crash back into my palm before throwing another one toward the ceiling.

One.

Two.

Three.

Four...

I kept counting, tossing the sheep above me. Slowly, the fuzzy animal transformed, body elongating with pricked ears and a long, graceful tail. I counted into the thirties, my once fuzzy sheep now morphed into the glowing outline of a white fox.

Thirty-seven.

Thirty-eight.

Thirty-nine...

I watched the foxes zip back and forth, frolicking as they fell from the ceiling.

Fifty-three.

Fifty-four.

Fifty-five...

This is bullshit.

It did nothing to rest my mind.

I closed my eyes and held my hands out, tracing into the air. When I opened them, hundreds of tiny bolts twisted and coiled into a feminine rendering. Glowing strands spun around the eyes that struck my very soul. Unique armor smoothed over a curved, muscular body, a long cape flowing behind her.

I lowered my hands, watching the bolts flicker in and out. She was a woman I had no business wanting. A fixture in my dreams every night.

Sloan.

I'd wondered what happened to her after King Redmond regained consciousness. She was no longer his Commander. Was she okay? Had he punished her in other ways?

She was always so aloof—even today—making it hard to know what went on in her head.

My dreams and the electric vision in front of me kept telling me I wanted to see her again, but my brain continually reminded me that wouldn't be a good idea. We were from warring worlds. Forever pitted against each other.

We didn't even exist in the same moral realm.

She betrayed her king to better her kingdom. I had helped Arafax by retrieving its gem, but I'd also killed many of its people over the years for Flynt. It was still unclear who'd been puppeting my jobs, but the stain of those lives lost by my hands wasn't one that just washed away with a few good decisions and time.

A twinge of pain seared near the base of my neck where it joined my shoulder.

I pulled the bolts back into my fingertips and grabbed the flask off the table. Taking one more swig of whiskey to numb myself, I ignored the siren call reminding me that I belonged to someone deadlier than the Queen or Flynt.

I reached back, rubbing the irritated skin, the pads of my fingers pressing against the uneven ridges forming the heart-shaped scar.

The bond mark.

My favor is due.

7

AISLIN

"What do you think we will work on today? Enchantments, shifting, physical training, elemental magic?" Kyleigh spouted off, stirring way too much milk into her coffee, turning it light beige.

I sipped mine, enjoying the bite that came without adding all the frivolous extras. Coffee was meant to be bitter.

"Who knows? The Queen never tells us ahead of time, and I'm not sure if last night's meeting will have shifted her plans." I drank down the last few sips before hopping out of my seat and taking my cup to the sink.

Kyleigh'd banged on my door earlier than usual to wake me up and find out what she'd missed, unhappy about having been left out.

She got out of her chair, following me to rinse out her mug. As we exited the pub, I glanced over my shoulder, spotting two of Flynt's thugs, Roq and Aron, trailing about ten paces behind us. Kyleigh kept peering back as we walked.

"They are still there," I said, continuing to move through

the blackened forest that contoured the edge of Arafax's territory. The greenery was starting to poke through the ash-covered ground now that the gem had been returned. A few colorful mushroom caps in vibrant reds and purples scattered throughout the dark trees, drawing attention against their bleak backdrop. Every day, new life was growing in the kingdom, a visual arrow aimed at hope for Arafax's people.

"How are you so used to never looking back at them?" Kyleigh asked, stumbling over some dead branches rooted to the ground. "It's creepy feeling them behind us all the time."

I shrugged. "You get used to it after a decade."

She stopped a moment to fix one of her crimson shoes, tying up the laces. They must have been the birthday gift Dru was so pleased to get ahold of from the Otherworld with help from the Queen. Her last pair had been worn down, faded from all the washing she'd done to them after we returned from Inverno.

Kyleigh never talked about what happened in the dungeon and what had covered those *sneakers*, and no amount of washing could cleanse what it had done to her on the inside.

I understood her silence around the subject. As an assassin, I never wanted to talk about my kills. Kyleigh wasn't an assassin, though. She was just a girl who had more power than she knew what to do with and less control than was safe.

"I know they are here to protect us, but I'm not used to the lack of privacy," Kyleigh said, clearly deluded about the purpose of us being watched at all times. It had nothing to do with protection and everything to do with control. "Back home, it was just me and my dad in our house. Plenty of space to be alone if I wanted."

"You didn't seem to care too much about your privacy last night when Dru visited your room," I said, pursing my lips. Her cheeks flushed, despite training her face forward at the trail guiding us. "Just remember that Roq probably replayed those sounds you were making when his shift was over and he could get some of his own privacy."

She cringed, looking disgusted. "Gross!"

"I'm just telling you what to expect living in a tight space like The Lavender. Privacy doesn't exist there, especially when you're under watch. I'm sure you've heard other people fucking, and you two weren't exactly quiet last night."

"We didn't," she said, flustered. "I mean, we haven't..."

Not much surprised me these days, but for some reason, that did.

"Makes sense. Now that you're a princess, you can't let just anyone poke at your royal palace," I teased, giving my best regal strut ahead of her.

"It's not like that at all." Kyleigh took a deep breath, rolling her eyes. "I don't even think of myself as a princess."

"*Oh?* So, you're still planning to go back to the Otherworld?"

"Of course I am." Her voice was confident, but her eyes shifted at my prying. "I need to get back home to my dad and my *real* life."

"Then why haven't you left yet?"

"Dru has...unfinished business with the Enchantress. He promised to go back with me to Vermont, but I won't ask that of him until that's taken care of. Plus, I'll have the power to help once I get the dragon stuff under control and train more."

"What kind of unfinished business?"

"That's not my place to share," she said, eyes downcast. "But if there's something I can do to take her down, I'll do it."

I ran my fingers over the bond mark at my neck. It had stopped throbbing after about an hour last night, but I knew that wasn't the final time the Enchantress would be calling in her favor.

A few water wielders were outside the fort, spraying the stones. I froze, watching them work, my throat suddenly dry, as if they'd somehow absorbed all the moisture from it. That wasn't possible, but I hadn't seen a water wielder since my mother and witnessing them now brought back memories of her. Hot days when she pulled rain from the sky to cool us. Watering seedlings as she strolled through the garden with Anders. Rinsing off our scrapes when we'd tried fruitlessly to keep up with the dragons, chasing after them with the other kids from our village.

Brown water trickled from the charcoal walls, carving small rivulets along the ground in varying directions. Another man used his wind affinity to dry the stones after they had been washed. The Queen was slowly trying to rebuild Arafax, starting with its fort.

"I know that helping us with the Enchantress isn't the only reason you've stuck around, Kyleigh. You don't have to pretend with me—save that for when we're inside the fort."

She kept her eyes down, dodging some roots and various shrubbery that sprung up at random from the ground. Peeking over her shoulder, she waved to Flynt's men who nodded in return before spinning and heading back toward The Lavender.

"Look, I spent the last ten years trying to understand my mother and why she left. Now I finally can get answers. I'm not leaving without them."

I could understand that. It was probably the most honest thing she'd said about their whole relationship since she'd arrived in Arafax.

"You can get all the answers you desire, doesn't mean you'll understand," I said, placing a hand on her shoulder. "I sure fucking wouldn't."

Kyleigh's mother left her behind in the Otherworld after The Blaze to take the throne when the royal family had been executed. While she was the only one in the family's line able to rule over Arafax, that didn't negate the fact that she had disappeared from her eleven-year-old daughter and husband's lives without explanation.

"She felt like she was protecting me. That she was doing what was best for me," Kyleigh defended, though I couldn't tell if she was saying it to me or herself.

"Do you feel like she's protected and done what's best for you?"

She said nothing, slowly rubbing her palms against each other.

"You can try to sell yourself, or her, those bullshit lies, but I'm not buying it."

Her hands began to glow. Kyleigh might have more natural control over her abilities with the gem returned, but her emotions were unstable as ever.

"Fine," she replied quietly.

We walked up the stony path leading to the fort, wayward water droplets skimming our bodies. The wielder noticed us there and blanched. "So sorry," he called out, pausing his work to let us pass.

"Don't worry, it was refreshing," I called back.

He was probably just grateful to have his abilities returned and stable enough to use for his work. Now that powers were returning, it had opened jobs to them again. Seeing Arafax's people with renewed purpose did give me some measure of hope. For them.

Hope was a luxury I'd never earn with the things I'd done.

"So you and Dru, you haven't?" I whispered, still genuinely surprised. The only thing more fiery than the sparks that came from Kyleigh's fingers was the heat that emanated off the two of them when they were around each other. It usually nauseated me.

"No," she let out a resigned sigh. "I don't know why. Aside from rarely being alone, that is."

There was a part of me, a small one, that felt a twinge of jealousy watching them together. Dru adored Kyleigh. He worshiped her and her powers, even though they could be so destructive. It should have given me some measure of optimism, but it just reminded me of what I'd never have.

Someone that could love me. The *real* me—the woman who'd been stopping hearts over the last ten years.

It didn't seem possible.

Or deserved.

We passed a few royal guards, and I looked around hoping to see Ox. He had been reduced to cleaning armor for the other knights after defying the Queen's orders. Maybe she would let him back to his old post once I proved I was worth his decision to spare me? Now that I was one of Arafax's Revered, I was sure my value had increased.

"How about you?" Kyleigh asked.

"What about me?"

"Don't you ever get lonely at the inn? I mean, there are all the amors there each night, and they seem more than willing to practice their...um...skills with you," she said, a blush creeping across her cheeks.

"Ha, well yes, there may have been a time when I was younger and would entertain guests late in the evening. And I do know some amors...intimately." I combed my fingers through my hair, pulling it away from my face and tying it up. "Mainly it was a distraction from my jobs."

"Now you don't need the distraction?"

"Honestly, I probably need it more than ever." I sighed, smirking. I couldn't even remember the last time I'd taken a woman to bed.

"Then what is it?"

That was the real question.

One I knew the answer to. "I don't think a mere distraction is enough."

Kyleigh raised a brow at me, but I didn't elaborate.

WHEN THE GUARDS OPENED THE DOORS TO THE FORT'S THRONE room, Arafax's Queen was waiting on her dais, ready to greet us before our daily training and lessons. "Sorry for interrupting your celebration last night."

"I'm not," I grumbled, and Kyleigh glared at me, pink flooding her cheeks.

The Queen cleared her throat, ignoring my comment. "After practicing with your elements, you'll have a lesson with Dru to learn more about your dragon magic. Afterward, we will spend some time practicing how to access it. If we have any chance of taking down the Enchantress, we will need you both fully confident with your abilities. *All* of them." She straightened out the gold-and-ruby-vined crown atop her head.

"*All* of them? What happens if we never access our dragons?" I asked.

"I'm confident you both will master it," the Queen replied. I couldn't tell if she was truly confident or supremely deluded. Maybe a bit of both.

She descended the steps of her dais, the train of her scarlet waistcoat dragging across the marble. "Dru and I are working together to ensure you get the best education you can to make that possible."

"Well, aren't we lucky?" I made sure the sarcasm shone through my words.

The Queen ignored my tone, stopping in front of us, pops of red peeking from the bottom of her tall, black heels. The woman was always regally put together from head to toe. I couldn't believe it when Kyleigh explained how she dressed in the Otherworld.

"You also will have sparring lessons starting tomorrow," the Queen added.

"Sparring?" Kyleigh asked her mother. "How will that help us?"

"If we are to face the Enchantress, even if you have accessed your dragon forms, you will need to know how to handle yourself in combat."

"I already know how to spar. And I think it's obvious we both know how to kill," I said.

Kyleigh stilled at my bold statement.

Dru had arrived, standing silently in the corner with his hands in his pockets, not looking at Kyleigh or myself but past us.

"You may know how to kill, but how will you defend yourselves if your powers are drained or become unstable again?"

The familiar sweet-yet-steely voice charged my ears, causing my chest to tingle. I turned to find icy-blue eyes moving toward us. No armor today, she wore fitted, blue slacks with a loose, white tunic. A silver rhinestone comb pulled back one side of her silver hair. Her lithe snow fox, Mox, gave me an unimpressed glare before padding into the room.

"Sloan will be tending to your physical training from now on," the Queen said, strangely calm. "She's staying here indefinitely."

What in the blazes was this?

"What?" Kyleigh took a few steps back as sparks skittered across her fingertips.

"How?" I said through clenched teeth, eliciting a growl from Mox. "How is she even allowed to be standing here, much less *staying* here? This was not part of the arrangement."

"I don't understand," Kyleigh said, confusion etched into her forehead.

The Queen walked over to her daughter, clasping her hands around the sparks and extinguishing them. "I'm still assessing the threat King Redmond poses, but Sloan is no longer commanding Inverno's army or advising him. She is here temporarily. Just as a visitor. Not in any formal capacity for Inverno."

I refused to make eye contact with the silver-haired commander, giving the Queen a quick glare before storming toward our training room.

"Come on, Ky," I said, waving at her. Sloan shouldn't be here. I didn't trust what that meant for Arafax. For me.

"I'll let you get back to your lessons. I just came down here to remind you both to dress appropriately tomorrow."

Sloan smirked. Her relaxed tone only irritated me further. "I expect you in the sparring arena at moon's light and not a minute after. Be ready to get your asses handed to y—"

I slammed the door behind me before she finished.

64

8

KYLEIGH

I followed Aislin, discreetly slipping into the training room after she'd slammed the door behind her.

"This is bullshit," she snapped, charging over to the table across the room. She plopped down on the stool, elbows resting on her knees, letting out a frustrated growl.

"I agree," I sighed, somewhat resigned. I was used to not understanding my mother's actions at this point. As much as I wanted to build a relationship with her, to repair things between us, the fact that most of the time I had to pretend we were acquaintances made it basically impossible.

I walked over to where Aislin sat, taking the stool opposite hers.

"Hey." I flicked my finger at her, sending out a tiny spark to get her attention. She shot a small bolt to intercept it, knocking the light onto the stone floor where it sizzled before disappearing. I grinned at her.

We each brought our hands a few inches apart, creating baseball-sized spark and lightning-filled orbs.

"Ready?" Aislin threw her ball of electric power at me,

and I matched her timing, blasting out my spark one. The spheres collided, disintegrating into a mess of purple and orange specks.

"What is this?" My mother moved through the doorway, looking elegant as ever, and two guards filed in behind her.

Oh great, now we have to keep up the usual queenly pretense.

Aislin and I dropped to our knees, bowing with fists over our hearts. It was humiliating being an adult and feeling less than the woman who'd abandoned me through the years I needed her most. Having to cower before her every day for lessons made it ten times worse.

"Your Majesty," we said in unison, Aislin a bit more enthusiastic than me, but not by much.

"Go ahead and rise," she said, rolling her eyes at us as she walked into the room.

Aislin looked like she was about to lose it, her emerald eyes glinting angrily. I had gotten more adept at understanding her tells after spending most of our days at the fort training and evenings back at The Lavender.

I was nervous about staying at the inn at first since Aislin made Flynt and his crew out to be complete monsters. Honestly, they hadn't been anything but polite to me since I'd arrived. Even Flynt. He stayed in a room across from ours, making sure his men were always around to keep us safe. Aislin viewed their protection differently, but I was trying to not let her bias influence me.

They couldn't be worse than Kaeghan and the other sadistic guards that had terrorized us in Inverno.

"How are we supposed to trust them?" Aislin boomed, glaring at my mother.

I didn't understand it either. How would Sloan handle working with me after what I'd done to her guards? Wasn't it dangerous to keep the King's former commander housed under the roof where we were training and Dru was researching? What if she reported to Redmond, who then reported to the Enchantress? They were engaged, after all. "She could be a spy for King Redmond."

Aislin nodded in agreement.

"Sloan could be using this as an opportunity for herself; however, I don't think she is," my mother said, sitting at her stone-slab throne in our training room. "Regardless, you both will benefit from her expertise. She's one of the fiercest warriors alive. And one of the most honorable."

"How well do you know her?" I asked.

"Inverno and Arafax weren't always enemies," she said as a servant brought her a tray of fruit. She plucked a ripe berry that matched her lipstick and popped it into her mouth. We waited in silence for her to finish her thought. "Our families go back decades."

"But truly, how do we know she isn't here spying to get back in King Redmond's good graces?" Aislin shot some bolts at the targets lining the wall. She hit her mark each time, even managing to split one in half, spearing a hole into the charcoal stone behind it. Aislin broke targets regularly, usually when she was pissed off—which was also pretty regular for her.

"We don't," my mother replied, waving over the guards to clean up the broken target. They hurried, disposing of it while replacing it with a new one that had been sitting in the corner. "However, she and the King are useful to our cause right now."

"What's that supposed to mean?" My shoulders tensed.

"It means as long as the alliance suits Arafax, they live."

How was this the same woman that tucked me into bed at

night and told me stories about knights and dragons and magical princesses?

Fuck.

Those probably weren't *just* stories.

"Anyway," she said, simply. "No need to worry about that yet. Lessons first, and then we can go see the dragon after. Dru is tending to her now."

"Is it—she—okay?" I hated how vague she was being. I'd waited a decade for clarity and understanding and everything with her was secrets and veiled riddles.

"Why do we have to wait?" I dug the balls of my sneakers into the ground.

"After," she repeated, voice clipped enough to let me know it wasn't up for discussion.

My shoulders dropped. I couldn't fight her openly, it would be inappropriate behavior between a Queen and her subject, but for a mother and daughter, this was a normal exchange. It felt weird to feel like I missed out on something that my friends assured me I was *so lucky* to have avoided. *Mother-daughter fights.*

What I would have given to be fighting with a mom instead of spending my teenage years wondering what I could have done to be worthy of her return. Now that I knew she had been sitting on the throne in Arafax, I had the answer.

Nothing.

"Why don't you two show me more of what you were doing before I got here?" She pointed to one side of the room. "Aislin, go there."

Then she gestured for me to stand across from her. "Now face each other and create those orbs again."

"Yes, Your Majesty," I said through gritted teeth, glaring at her. I wished she'd send the guards away so I didn't have to keep up this stupid charade.

Even though we had already done this, messing around for fun, something about the way my mother had us pitted against each other made my stomach twist in knots.

Aislin nodded at me, forming her lightning sphere. I followed, molding my sparks into a tightly woven ball of light.

"Good job, ladies." My mother clapped her hands together. "Now make them larger."

We pulled our hands apart, the balls growing until they were about the size of a beach ball.

"Larger," she said as she continued picking at the fruit on her tray.

I exaggeratedly threw my arms open as far as they would go, the sphere becoming larger than my body.

"Set it on the ground and step into it," my mother said, calm despite my obvious attempt to goad her.

I placed the ball on the ground, letting it teeter a moment before it balanced on its curved edge.

My body tensed. I had built a circle of sparks around me before when we had escaped Inverno—when I was under the influence of dragon dust—but I hadn't done anything like it since. I also had never walked through my own fiery power. Considering I'd burned myself when my sparks emerged, I didn't have any desire to.

Aislin finished growing her lightning ball and was reaching a hand toward the center. As it passed through the electric barrier, her shoulders relaxed, and she stepped the rest of the way in. Her bright-green eyes darted around, taking in what she had created, releasing a deep breath once she realized she was safe within.

"Your powers are not built to hurt you," my mother said, turning to me. Sweat dripped down my forehead in concentration, and I tried to not let my apprehension get the best of me.

"If that's so, how come Aislin has those lightning scars still and I've burned myself before?" I called out, incensed but not tearing my eyes away from my task.

"That was before the gem was returned to the Evergleam. Now that it is where it belongs and the realm's power source is back, the old rules should apply." She walked over, standing between us. Our two giant orbs only a few feet from her on either side.

"What are the old rules?" My chest started to warm, the power beginning to drain my energy. Part of me wanted to leave—to walk out and tell my mother off.

"What I'm teaching you in your training. That is, if you're willing to actually listen," she said, glaring at me.

Now I *really* wanted to tell her to fuck right off, but I couldn't talk to her that way as her subject. Us lesser folk needed to kneel and bow and do as we were told by our queen or risk punishment. The guards stood there, uncomfortably shifting at how much I had already questioned their beloved monarch's instructions.

The embers swirled in front of me, and I held out my hand, following what Aislin had done. Pressing my fingers through the barrier, the heat pushed back against me, but it didn't burn. I wiggled my hand from inside the orb, turning it over to make sure I didn't have any marks. Once it felt safe, I closed my eyes and stepped through.

Beads of reds, oranges, and golds spun so fast I almost couldn't tell they were moving within the curving edges of the orb. I sighed, proud of my bravery, and stretched out my hand, letting the incandescent specks pass through my fingertips.

Energy was pouring out of me rapidly, the tiny flares swarming faster, and I tried to focus on them to stop the dizziness that was overtaking me.

"Take back control, Kyleigh," my mother called from outside my raging cocoon. "Pull your sparks in."

They seemed to freeze, but now the room was spinning around me.

"Help her!" Aislin shouted, her bolts crashing to the ground. Disappearing.

Looking at my mother through the fiery wall that divided us felt like the first time I was *truly* seeing her. She lifted her hands above her crown, releasing swirling ruby flames that curled around the giant orb, herding my sparks back in and giving my energy a small reprieve. It was enough help to allow me to pull my power back into me before collapsing onto the stone. My chest heaved in quick, shallow breaths as I tried to gather my thoughts.

I hated her. Hated how easily she managed her powers and how minuscule she made me feel when I used mine. She wielded her fire like it was an elegant extension of her. My sparks were more like a pack of wild beasts that needed taming.

I had felt so strong when I'd used them to escape Inverno. Now I just felt like the scared little girl who'd come through the portal, sparks shooting everywhere. With the gem back, I should have been more stable, more secure, more powerful. And the fact was, I was. *Most* of the time. But *never* during the lessons with my mother, and I fucking hated feeling weak in front of her. I knew I was failing at controlling my emotions, like Aislin had called me out on when she taught me about my ability, but how was I supposed to do that around my mother after everything?

On one hand, I wanted her to know how much pain she'd caused me. On the other, I didn't want to give her the satisfaction of knowing the true impact her leaving had. Meanwhile, I couldn't safely act either way because the last thing we could have was someone breathing word to the Enchantress that the other half of my mother's deal was in Celaria.

Within her reach.

Once she knew my mother was trying to work around their bargain, she would come for me.

There was no other option than to be ready for her.

9

KYLEIGH

"Where are we going?" I asked when we veered off down the corridor instead of toward the exit leading to the arena, the only area I imagined was big enough to house a dragon.

Frost framed the doors, stretching its glacial claws along the walls. A chilly breeze carrying the scent of pine skated over the threshold of the room we'd been taken to when we'd partially shifted that first night in Arafax.

Shivering in the doorway, I peered into the frigid bedroom. Sheer, white curtains skirted the snow-kissed balcony, long icicles dripping slowly from its railing, melting into small pools that reflected the day's radiant moon.

My eyes trailed back toward the bed. Hidden under the fluffy down comforter was a woman with a mop of sable curls and deep-umber skin. Frosted flecks floated from her lips, ascending midair, hovering over everything. Tiny snowflakes lightly dusted all the surfaces in the room. It was like peering into a shaken snow globe.

I glanced back at my mother. "Who is that?"

"You've met before, just under different circumstances," she replied, not taking her softened gaze off the slumbering figure.

The woman's eyes fluttered open. Golden orbs with long slits eyed me momentarily before closing again with a labored huff. I couldn't breathe. The regret over not freeing the dragon had haunted me ever since we'd escaped.

My throat went dry.

I rasped out in surprise, "The dragon...it was her?"

My mother waved her guards away and waited a few moments before speaking. "That's Neve. The one your middle name honors. My childhood best friend and your godmother."

My godmother? I didn't even know I had a godmother.

Aislin stood behind us, shifting foot-to-foot with her hands in her pockets. "So, she's like us?"

"Yes. Until Kyleigh told us about the dragon, we'd thought they'd all been killed the night of The Blaze. It turns out Neve was very much alive, just stuck in her dragon form after the gem had been stolen. She couldn't shift back. If you'd never found her, I don't know if we would have learned what really happened to her." My mother's expression was sullen. "She arrived late last night with Sloan and one of King Redmond's personal healers. A show of good faith for our alliance."

"I still don't understand why Sloan is here," Aislin said to my mother, brows knit.

"She asked to come," she replied. "They were close, before."

"King Redmond was convinced the dragon had killed his

fiancée and father." Aislin strode over to the bed, inspecting the woman. "You're saying he was wrong?"

"She may have killed his father, King Reynard, but Neve is very much alive." My mother looked down at her friend with an expression akin to tenderness. Nothing like the chilling, impassive one I'd become accustomed to pretending there was no prior relationship between us. "I'm having Dru help coordinate her care. She's not doing well and needs a lot of rest from being stuck in her other form for so long."

It was strange to think that I'd been petting a person hidden beneath the beautiful, blue-scaled dragon in the dungeon.

"Is she going to be okay?" I hoped more than anything she would be.

But being trapped by her fiancé for a decade, compounded with the abuse from the guards—I didn't know if she would ever be. Trauma wasn't something you just rinsed away. It lingered like a heavy fog, clouding your beliefs, tainting your thoughts. I would know. I wrestled with it daily.

"She hasn't been awake long enough to give us a clue about her mental state," my mother continued, placing her hands on my shoulders. I flinched, shaking off her unexpected gentleness.

"I'm hoping she will be able to teach you more about your shifting abilities once she's well enough. For now, she needs rest."

She would be the best to teach us. I had no clue how to summon my dragon, and I'd rather fail in front of Neve, whom I barely knew, versus continuing to fail in front of my mother.

Aislin pulled up a seat next to me. "So, is this why we are supposed to suddenly trust King Redmond? Because he returned Neve and hasn't exposed that she can shift?"

"I'm not saying that we should trust them, but there's a bridge being extended. We need to build every one we can before we take on the Enchantress. Every alliance could prove useful."

Dru walked in, giving me a small smile before lifting Neve's hand to check her pulse and jotting down something on his chart. Next, he pulled part of the blanket off, exposing her side. Small patches of scars pocked the curved markings on her skin. Blue scales rippled out from them, riding along her torso before disappearing again.

The scars on her skin were obviously leftover from the guards' abuse and looked awful. For her sake, I hoped they'd be gone one day.

"She's still not fully stable in this form," Dru said, putting some balm over her scars while Sloan stood watch from the doorway. "Once she is, hopefully it will answer some questions for you and Aislin."

My eyes shot up between him and Sloan, breath catching in my chest. Did he really say that in front of our enemy?

"It's okay," my mother said. "I spoke with her when they arrived. She knows you both can shift, and she's promised not to share that with Redmond without our go ahead in order to stay here."

Aislin's mouth opened before quickly snapping shut, probably not wanting to say something snarky that would get her in trouble.

I had so many questions, but I decided to stick with the one that repeatedly nagged at me. "Shouldn't we be powerful enough to take the Enchantress on once we got the hang of our dragon magic?"

"We don't know how many deals she's made. Or with whom." The Queen rested her hand on her shoulder. "She's been collecting abilities from those she's drained of powers over the years. If she finds a way out of her exile in the Silent Woods like Redmond claims she's getting close to, we wouldn't stand a chance. She could easily devastate our kingdoms. That's why your training is so important. Along with this alliance."

A servant walked in with a tray of food. Aislin grabbed a plate from it, stacking it to the brim with fruit, cheeses, and various green veggies I was still trying to remember the names of. She popped a cube of cheese in her mouth and let out a satisfied groan. "Any idea what her deal with King Redmond includes?"

"No, but I intend to find out," Sloan interjected as she straightened up, eyes locked on Aislin. The former assassin just continued to gorge herself on her post training meal.

"Will we be seeing King Redmond here?"

Would I have to face him again?

I still didn't know if there would be any repercussions over the explosion I'd caused. Sloan hadn't made mention of her guards yet, but the King was terrifying. I grabbed a handful of strawberries, some cheeses, and an unknown green vegetable that reminded me of a baby carrot and shoved some in my mouth to avoid thinking more about the intimidating-as-fuck phoenix king.

"That will certainly be unavoidable at some point, considering our alliance," my mother said before sipping from a golden chalice. She nodded to the figure hidden beneath the covers. "But since he needs to keep it a secret from the Enchantress, I don't think it will be much. Though I'm sure he'll want to check on Neve."

Sloan nodded in agreement then slipped out of the room.

I knew my mother was right, though I wouldn't admit it. I remembered the extra chair, the throne, and the rings that hung from the chain around his neck. The King did horrible things, but he was driven by revenge over losing the woman he'd loved. He and my dad had that grief in common.

Now both of the women they loved were alive and well. While King Redmond had been the cause of so much pain for Neve, and I'm sure held some guilt over that, my dad still had no clue what happened to my mother.

Just another reason I was prolonging leaving here. I missed him so much, but I knew I would have to come up with something to tell him when I saw him again.

What would I even say? The truth? He would probably think I was crazy. Some days, I still wondered if I was. I couldn't lie to him, but there was no way to make the truth any less painful. I didn't want to reopen that wound.

Aislin interrupted my thoughts with another question. "What does this mean for his engagement to the Enchantress?"

"There's no way he would choose to marry her," my mother said.

"That's true, but if he has a deal with her, it might not be simple for him to break his alliance." Aislin scratched the back of her neck.

My mother held a beat before responding. "We will stay wary of being overly trusting of Redmond and his people...but I don't want to shut that door if we need it open."

"How can you say that when he burned down your kingdom? Your people. Your family," I asked. How could we move past the destruction he'd caused and how horribly he'd treated us?

"Haven't you learned anything?" My mother leaned in next to me, taking a strawberry off my plate and eating it. "There's always more to the story."

10

DRU

Hanging the white cloth from the ceiling, I peered over at the black illumibox sitting on a small table at the back of the room. I felt along my shoulder strap, detaching a pair of illumilenses from next to the row of healing balms and burn repair elixirs I'd concocted.

Running my hands over the last two vials, the ones containing contraceptive tonic, I sighed, the memory of Kyleigh's bare skin under my palms, across my lips, against my chest, consuming me. Between the interruption and the fact that I'd left to go to a meeting she'd been excluded from, it wasn't a great combination for winning her affections.

I'd need to find a way to make it up to her.

I placed the lenses over my eyes, attaching the frames to my temples. I'd swiped the glasses from Halston, saving them, along with a slew of other fascinating Otherworld objects, to integrate with Celaria's magic when I returned.

Aislin and Ky walked into the small room I'd turned into a makeshift lecture space. Aislin eyed the vials I wore, spotting the two peridot-tinged ones. She gave me a wink, cooing just above a whisper, "I see you like to always be prepared."

Her attention to the contents of the vials made my cheeks heat, and my eyes snapped to Kyleigh. She smiled at us, clueless to Aislin poking fun at me.

Phew.

She probably assumed they were another set of healing elixirs, especially since I wore them daily. Not that I expected something would happen...but I didn't want anything holding us back when the time arrived.

I swallowed the lump settled at the back of my throat, trying to focus on objectively tutoring the women in front of me.

"Would you do the honors, Aislin?" I asked, nodding at the illumibox.

She moved over to the corner of the room, tucking her chocolate and violet braid behind her ear. Placing her hand on the onyx cube, she fed her lightning into the source point, then she flipped the power switch on its corner.

Light spilled from the box, filling the expanse of the room. I walked over to the magical projector, pricking my finger on the end of the needle hovering above the source point. Once the blood dripped and absorbed onto it, the light began to spin until the picture on the sheet matched the one in my mind. A beautiful, glowing, green dragon beat its wings, suspended above us all.

"Wow," Kyleigh said, her dazzling silver eyes full of wonder. It was easy to forget she wasn't from here. She'd never seen a dragon fly, something Aislin and I took for granted in our childhood. The only one Kyleigh had ever seen had been Neve, though we didn't know her real identity at the time.

Watching the dragon above us made me wonder, after being trapped hundreds of feet below ground for over a decade, would she be able to soar again? Would she even want to?

I'd need to check on her after today's lesson, so I twisted a gear on my glove, setting the time so my alarm would remind me. Neve's healing was one of my top priorities. She held so many answers that would help Kyleigh and Aislin with their transition, and I was hopeful she would prove to be a treasure trove of information.

Realizing I'd been staring in Kyleigh's direction too long, I cleared my throat. Aislin grinned roguishly at me. "I wanted to open things up today to see what questions you have about your newer abilities."

Aislin pointed to the sky and released a tiny bolt, letting it float above her finger, getting my attention. "Can you explain champions?"

"Champions? What are those?" Kyleigh asked.

Of course she opened with a topic that would lead to questions that were uncomfortable to answer both as their tutor and as Kyleigh's...*boyfriend*. The term seemed insignificant compared to the things we'd faced in the time we'd spent together. "Why do you want to know about dragon champions?"

Aislin reclined in her chair, putting her boots up on the table and wrapping her hands behind her head, maintaining her façade of confidence. I understood it because I recognized it in myself—the need to come off put together despite the things desperately warring within your mind. She nodded up at the dragon floating above us. "My father was a champion. My mother had dragon magic and they were bonded somehow. King Redmond also mentioned them at last night's meeting."

Kyleigh released an annoyed sigh, still probably angry about being left behind.

"How does it work?" Aislin's eyes met mine with a twinkle of curiosity. I shifted in my seat, and she chuckled, seemingly amused that the topic made me squirm. "Who are they? How do we get them?"

"Champions are those who are bonded to the Revered and have the ability to ride their dragon as well as mingle with and wield their abilities."

Aislin's eyes narrowed, then she threw her arms up in the air. "How did I not know that my mother could do this?"

Blazes.

I had been so focused on Kyleigh that I hadn't even fathomed how this impacted Aislin. The dragon she had seen growing up was her mother and now that ability had been passed to her. It had to have opened some wounds.

I realized that *both* women in front of me were healing just as much as their dragon sister who lay sleeping down the hall.

"How are champions created?" Aislin asked again, pointing up to the floating pictures made of light. I took a moment to collect myself, knowing that whatever I thought next would be illustrated for all to see.

"The bonds are solidified at the Evergleam in an intimate ritual that involves a specific enchantment using blood magic." I cleared my throat. "Their convergence is the catalyst that initiates the bond that is then cultivated between the dragon and their champion."

Tapping the lenses at my temple, the dragon in front of us morphed into the grove, the Evergleam lit at its center. Two people, signifying the dragon and their champion, walked side by side toward the tree, one placing their hand on it.

"And by intimate ritual, you mean?" Kyleigh asked, her focus pinned to the image projected above her, throat bobbing as her silvery eyes bulged.

I cringed, already knowing the error I'd made before bringing my eyes up. The dragon had shifted into a woman, the profiles of the two figures moving together in a carnal embrace.

Aislin smiled up at the moving pictures, basking in my distress. "Convergence was his polite way of saying fucking."

"*Oh,*" was all Kyleigh managed to get out, her eyes transfixed on the explicitly illustrated scene. Her silver irises dragged down to mine, momentarily molten before shooting to her lap.

Did the temperature in the room spike?

I pulled at my shirt, sweat beginning to soak through the neckline. Scurrying over to the illumibox, I flicked the power button, heaving a sigh of relief once the box shut off. Sitting back down, I grabbed my glass of water and took a sip to buy time before I had to answer more questions or explain my wandering mind that had created the image above.

"So is the pairing chosen for us or do we decide who we're fornicating in the forest with?" Aislin asked.

Kyleigh looked like she was mortified, but also trying to stifle a laugh.

"They are chosen—at least they are supposed to be—by the person who carries dragon magic." I still needed to pick Neve's brain since some details couldn't be found in any of our texts. "Then the dragon within has to accept the bond."

Aislin leaned forward, wringing her hands together as she stared off, deep in thought. "And once this...*convergence* takes place, the champion can wield the dragon's elemental magic?"

"Yes. And the dragon is powered by the strengths of their champion as well, magical and not. How it works is really dependent on the coupling and how they choose to nurture the bond."

"Do we have to have champions?" Kyleigh asked quietly.

Oh.

"No, it's not a necessity. Not every dragon has had a champion and there may have been a few cases where a dragon bonded more than one champion at their ceremony."

"More than one?" Kyleigh whispered to herself, eyes wide.

"But if we need to face the Enchantress, we should consider finding champions sooner rather than later?" Aislin released a strand of lightning, twisting it along her fingers. "At least that's what it sounded like when King Redmond brought it up, though I'm sure he doesn't know how champions are...forged."

"It does strengthen both individuals in terms of battle," I said, letting out a sigh. I didn't want to color too much of today's lesson with my personal feelings. "Which would be helpful, of course, but not necessary. The Queen and I are working to find what the best routes are for taking on the Enchantress when the time comes."

Kyleigh rolled her eyes. I knew she didn't enjoy the amount of time I spent with her mother at the fort, but every piece of information we uncovered was vital in formulating a plan to take down the Enchantress, protect Arafax's people, and keep Kyleigh safe.

Aislin finally let her lightning spool back into her hands as she ran her thumb over her chin. "Is there a way to break the bond once it's made?"

"What do you mean?" Kyleigh asked.

Aislin shrugged. "If it's helpful, couldn't we just find someone short term to beat the Enchantress and then break the bond down the road?"

I kept my gaze away from Kyleigh, too afraid she'd read between the lines of my instruction, uncovering the man that desperately wanted to let his heart leap before thinking through every aspect. "It doesn't work like that. These bonds are nurtured over time, meant to last forever. I've never seen anything saying that's possible to sever. Something like that could be detrimental to both the dragon and their champion."

Aislin cocked her head. I could almost read her mind saying *you're just advocating for this so you can bond with Kyleigh and her magic.* It was the one thing I worried about most of all —Kyleigh thinking I wanted to be her champion in order to access her powers. That couldn't be further from the truth.

"So, you'll probably be Kyleigh's champion?" she asked.

My throat constricted.

"No!" I blurted, fumbling over my words.

Kyleigh glared at me, maintaining her silence. My eyes dropped to my lap, figuring out what to say next. "I-I—"

The scrape of her chair against the floor told me I was too late in formulating an appropriate response. Kyleigh shot out of the room before I could try to salvage the situation.

11

DRU

Tick—tick

Tick—tick

Tick—tick

I held the miniature scale by the blood-smeared tip, watching its golden body swing back and forth like a well-timed pendulum. Gliding it across the map, I followed its beat, slowing my arm when its rhythm began to stutter.

Tick...tick

Tick...tick

Inching it further down, hovering over the center of the map, I closed my eyes as I continued to listen. Listen and hope.

Tick.

Tick.

I took a deep breath, shifting it lower a smidge.

Silence.

Opening one eye, I found the balanced tool suspended by a patch of blackened trees that split through Celaria's topography.

Fuck.

My heart plummeted into my ribs, and I sucked my finger into my mouth, the coppery tang of the needle-kissed spot somehow soothing me amid the realization that I was right.

My sisters were in the Silent Woods.

I'd always wondered if the Enchantress had taken them. If she'd added them to her swarm of wisps. My new contraption, while brilliantly designed, had just confirmed my worst fear.

She had.

And that knowledge complicated things.

I'd retreated to the fort's study after checking Neve's vitals, working on the finishing touches of my locator. Repurposing a scale—an item I'd discovered in the Otherworld—I could take someone's blood and use it to find them or their closest family members.

It was the first time I regretted being right.

I thumbed through the tome in front of me, jotting down some notes. So many texts had been destroyed during The Blaze, it made this research nearly impossible. I envied my father, who'd been a scholar in Arafax's royal library. What knowledge he held in his palms each day. I couldn't imagine how incredible it must have been.

The Queen said there was a sacred text with more information about dragons and their champions, but neither of us had been able to locate it among the archive's small leftover collection.

A pounding came at the door before it swung open, a guard holding it for the Queen to enter. I wiped my hands on my trousers before kneeling and bringing my fist across my chest. "Your Majesty."

"Dru," she said with a nod, lips pressed in a thin line and

hands clasped in front of her. "I heard from my guards that your lesson ended rather abruptly."

I stood, sliding my hands into my pockets. Swaying back and forth, I kept my eyes from making contact, then walked over to the tome I'd been browsing. "It did."

Rubbing the nape of my neck, I tried to appear engrossed, studying the text in front of me, writing down a few more key details about the layout of the Silent Woods, praying she'd stop the topic there.

She came next to me, placing her hand on top of the book. "What did you tutor them about today?"

I guess the topic isn't over.

"They asked about dragons. Aislin wanted to know about champions and the bond. How it works."

"Ah," she said, picking her hand back up and bringing it across her body to rest on the top of her shoulder, stroking it lazily. "And that made you uncomfortable as an instructor or because you are romantically entangled with my daughter?"

The last words were a whisper but sent my gaze around the room, ensuring we were truly alone. I knew how important it was for their secret to remain that way. If the Enchantress knew Kyleigh was the Queen's daughter, she'd find a way to get to her. I wouldn't let that happen. She'd already taken too many people I loved from me.

The Queen had made a deal decades prior. In order to avoid freeing the Enchantress from her banishment, she had recklessly agreed to give up her firstborn's power. At the time, she never believed her firstborn would see Celaria, remaining safe from the deal. Unfortunately, I foolishly brought Kyleigh through the portal to save her from the members of Halston's secret society, Vindicatio Vis.

I had no idea the Queen had a daughter, much less that it

was Kyleigh, but my actions had landed us all in more danger. Now, according to King Redmond, the Enchantress was close to figuring it out.

"Erm...both?" I said, shrugging. "I wasn't prepared for the questions that would come up. But once Neve is awake, I'm confident she will be an invaluable resource."

"I see." Her face was unreadable.

As intelligent as I was, being around Kyleigh made me feel like a bumbling idiot. In an attempt to not pressure her about considering me as a prospective champion, I ended up sounding like a careless jerk. I'd have to prove to her how much I wanted this, to stand tall at her side and be with her.

However, I still wasn't sure how the Queen felt about it.

I shut the book in front of me and pushed it to the side, ready to change the subject. "Have you been able to find that missing sacred text on the champions?"

"I haven't. We will have to keep moving forward without the information. Ideally, Neve will be able to fill the gaps."

Hopefully she would be awake long enough to give us answers soon. Every day felt like the unsettling calm before a tempest. Knowing that now I would have to find a way to get rid of the Enchantress without further harming my sisters only made it more brutal.

If it came down to it, I'd have to choose to save Arafax over them. That's what the Queen would demand of me. Would I be able to obey?

The Queen pulled over a chair, surveying the notes I'd put together. Her eyes darted to the scale, but she didn't ask about it, probably assuming I'd tell her if it did anything useful. We'd always had a good relationship, especially since I'd found ways to manipulate the small, unstable amount of magic left in Arafax after The Blaze.

She looked over the plans I'd been developing to rebuild Arafax's grand suspended staircase that used to lead up to the castle. Even if we couldn't find another earth wielder to accomplish it, we could build a makeshift elevator—as they called them in the Otherworld—and utilize a few air wielders until we had more options. No one had been in that castle in over a decade, its presence like a personal taunt every time I passed under its towering shadow.

"These are looking good. Any new developments in researching the Enchantress?" she asked, voice somewhat strained, eyes a bit more dull than their usual glow.

"Are you okay?" I asked, using the distraction to avoid having to talk about my sisters with her until I'd had more time to formulate a plan.

"I'm fine," she snapped. "Let's stay focused on your update. The research—how is it going?"

"It's...going. I am still trying to figure out who the Enchantress was prior to tethering herself to the magic she now wields and what she would have done in order to amass said power."

"Maybe there's something Redmond will find for us during his...reconnaissance?"

Pausing my note taking, I turned to the Queen. "If he has a deal with the Enchantress and is engaged to her, will he actually give us any information to help us bring her down?"

She pointed at my paper. "If he wants this alliance, he will. You should interview him. Besides, he sent Neve here. That tells me he thinks this is where she's safest."

I added King Redmond to the paper. "What makes you think we can trust him? That he will be inclined to come to our aid?"

"Not everything is dependent on trust, Dru. These are desperate times."

"But—"

"I don't have to trust Redmond to know he still cares for Neve. He loved her enough to destroy a kingdom, didn't he?"

"Is that truly love?"

"A love worth burning down the world for." She directed her eyes at me, letting ruby flames collect in her palm and billow into the shape of a heart. "Wouldn't you do the same?"

It was hard to rationalize the actions of the man who was responsible for my parents' death and the loss of my sisters. All I could manage in response was, "I suppose love can defy the laws of logic."

The Queen paused a moment, tapping her ruby nails against the space just above her mouth. "Speaking of...I know you care deeply about Ky."

My eyes shot up to hers. "I do."

What is she getting at?

"We both know she'd be safer out of reach of the Enchantress."

"What are you thinking, Your Majesty?"

"If you care about her, you'll find a way to convince her to go back with you now to the Otherworld until it's safe." She grasped my hands, forcing my eyes to meet hers. "It's the best thing for her, but if it comes from me, she won't listen. It has to come from you."

Was it for the best? I understood keeping her out of the Enchantress's reach, but once we had all three dragons—even without champions—we would stand a much better chance against her evil. "What about defeating the Enchantress? The work we've been doing to find a way to be rid of her—"

"Leave that for the rest of us to worry about."

"I see."

Maybe I'm not as useful as I thought.

Had she sent me off to Halston because she had no use for me in Arafax? Now that magic had returned to our kingdom, maybe she didn't need me anymore.

"If she agrees, I can get you safe passage back to Halston first thing in the morning."

"*If* she agrees." That was a huge *if*. Things weren't exactly great between us after the lesson earlier. "Don't you want more time with her? She's your—"

"She's in danger," the Queen snapped. "Who she is, both to the kingdom and myself, is all the more reason she needs to go. She was kept away for a reason."

"What if you can't figure out a way to vanquish the Enchantress?"

"Whatever you can't get done before you convince Kyleigh to leave Celaria, I will handle personally." She placed a hand on my shoulder, tilting her head to the side and my gaze dropped to the floor, feeling uneasy about her orders. "Believe me, Dru. I have a vested interest in getting her back here."

Staring at my shoes, I tried to figure out how I was going to approach this with Kyleigh tonight.

A gentle hand lifted my chin. "You mean a great deal to Ky. Do whatever is necessary to get through to her. I can send word once you both can return to Celaria."

"And what if she doesn't want to come back?" This plan would no doubt hurt her.

"Anything worth having comes with sacrifice." The Queen extinguished her flames. "If she doesn't wish to return when the time is right, then that's the price I'll pay to keep her safe."

12

KYLEIGH

few leftover drops of whiskey skimmed the edge of the shot glass before making a ring around where I'd slammed it on the counter.

"Keep 'em coming, Sweeney," I said, pointing to the ceiling and circling my finger, embers hovering above us.

"Of course." He gave a cautious smile, grabbing The Lavender's signature blend and refilling my drink just over halfway. I glowered at him until he brought the handle back up to make the pour level with the rim.

"Why don't you take one with me?" I asked the handsome breezetender.

"I probably shouldn't."

Flynt's deep voice drawled over the noise of the pub. "It's okay, Sweeney. The boss doesn't mind, as long as you pour one for him too."

Sweeney's eyes dropped as he pulled out two more glasses, setting them on the bar and pouring the thick, amber liquid into them.

"What's got you throwing back whiskey quicker than my lot tonight?" Flynt asked, striding up next to me.

"Ever think things are finally starting to work out for you and then—BAM!—not so much?"

"Aw, is peaches down on her luck tonight?" He tucked a strand of hair behind my ear before patting me on the back.

"You could say that." Luck had nothing to do with it. Dru had acted so strangely during our lesson today. It was infuriating.

"What should we toast to?" I held my glass up, some liquor splashing on my hand.

"To luckier days ahead," Flynt said, eyes fixed on me as we clinked shot glasses.

Sweeney gave me a gentle cheer and I tried not to spill out more whiskey before I got a chance to drink it. I tapped the glass on the counter, then brought it to my lips, chugging it down. My whole mouth felt numb, the whiskey tasting no different than water at this point. Probably not a great sign. I'd had about three-ish shots already, and I was nearing my threshold of hurling all my regrets into the toilet.

"Another?" Sweeney asked tentatively. I could tell he was ready to cut me off but was too much of a pushover to say no if I asked.

"Last one."

He poured it to the brim.

Good man.

Too many thoughts swirled through my mind—annoyance that I hadn't summoned my dragon magic since I came into it, the weight of what having a champion would mean, and then the way Dru had responded about it. If that's really how he felt, then fine.

Fuck him.

Not literally, unfortunately. That hadn't happened yet, which brought its own level of frustration.

I knocked back the last shot. "Thanks, Sweeney. Put it all on my tab," I scoffed.

My tab. *Ha.* I hoped my mother—excuse me, my queen—enjoyed getting tonight's bill when it made its way to her.

I hopped off the barstool, thinking I was much more graceful than I was. Flynt managed to catch me under my arm just in time so I didn't faceplant on the floor, gripping me firmly but surprisingly gentle for the leader of his own criminal network. "Woah there, peaches. Where are you trying to get to?"

"I need some fresh air."

"I gotcha. Hold on tight." He steered me toward the exit, and I instantly thought back to my first night at Halston, trying to get Anna to leave the library. The very same night I met Dru. Little did I know where we would be now—in a whole other realm. Literally.

Flynt kept up his swagger, waving at patrons and chatting briefly with his crew while he escorted me away. Tobacco wafted from his mouth, and I stared at the flex of his jaw making steely circles. I'd always thought guys who chewed were gross. Flynt was no dreamboat, but he somehow made the disgusting pastime look cool.

"Think I could try some?" I asked, giving him my best puppy-dog eyes.

"Maybe another time when you're not so close to puking on my good boots," he scoffed.

I kept my eyes forward, the room and its patrons blurring past us. He brought me to the back of The Lavender where my friends had celebrated my faux birthday with me, sitting me in a chair. Sweeney walked out a moment later, carting a whiskey-barrel table, Leigh following behind with another seat.

"Leave us," Flynt said, reclining across from me.

I didn't see them go, too busy holding my head with my hands, folded forward between my legs, hoping the spinning sensation would stop. I'd been feeling dizzy since tutoring this afternoon. Now it was just for a different reason.

Flynt stood, his boots stepping in front of me. "May I?"

I gave a single slow nod, worried that if I did it too fast or too many times that I might hurl.

Don't puke on his good boots, Ky.

A calloused hand brushed my neck, Flynt pulling my hair back, securing it with I don't know what. I honestly didn't care.

I'm never drinking again.

"Take some deep breaths," he said between chews of his tobacco. He walked a few paces away, and spat it out with a wet *thwap* before returning to his chair.

Sweeney came out with a glass of something clear and a copper mug with bubbling red liquid.

"Water for you," he said, placing the glass in front of me before handing Flynt the mug. "And your usual Roderick."

He shuffled off before I could say thanks.

Flynt took a long swig of his crimson brew. "Why all the whiskey tonight? You didn't strike me as the type."

"And what type do I strike you as, Flynt?"

"The kind of woman who doesn't wash their woes down with whiskey." He took a long sip from his mug before clanking it down on the table.

"Well, I am tonight."

"I see that," he said, brow furrowed. "Drink some water."

After a few extra-deep breaths, I reached to the side, grabbing the glass and bringing it in front of me. Taking a few small sips, I cocked my head. "Why are you out here, Flynt?"

"Look, I'm a salty asshole, but I'm also a businessman. I promised the Queen my crew and I would keep you safe while you're under my roof. Letting you drink yourself into oblivion is bad for business."

"You really have a way with words," I huffed out, taking another few sips.

"I don't, but fortunately that's not necessary in my line of work." He winked before standing and walking toward The Lavender. "I better get back inside. Lay off the whiskey for a while, peaches."

Alone in the quiet outside, only the faint sound of revelry coming from the pub, the questions started swirling into my head.

Why can't I summon my dragon magic?
Why was Dru so quick to say no to being my champion?
Do I even want a champion?
Why am I still here?

Ever since I'd learned the truth about my mother, I felt at odds with myself. I wanted to take advantage of being with her, but we spent almost every day hiding who I was, constantly in fear that someone would report back to the Enchantress about my existence. It made it impossible to build any sort of real relationship with her.

Beyond that, there was part of me that loved my powers now that I was getting more control over them. The prospect of turning into a dragon freaked me out, but I still wanted to do it. Being here, in Celaria, it felt *right*—like finally having enough puzzle pieces fit into place to see what you were creating...like I weirdly belonged in this puzzling fairy tale world.

"What's on your mind?"

Aislin was sitting in the chair across from me. I had no clue when she'd gotten there or how long she'd watch me wading through my sloshed mind.

"Flynt said you were out here. Figured you might want some company." She gave a low chuckle. "Heard you may have enjoyed a few shots."

"A few too many."

Her voice was quiet, laced with a tenderness I wasn't used to seeing from her. "Dru didn't mean what he said. You know you make that poor sap nervous."

"I honestly don't know anything right now, Aislin." Giving myself a moment to make sure I wouldn't be sick, I inhaled slowly before releasing the breath. "I thought we—I thought we were in this together when Dru agreed to go back with me. Now, I'm not so sure."

"You need to talk to him."

"I don't know how to do that without throttling him."

She smirked. "Well, you better figure it out."

"Why's that?"

"He's waiting for you over there." She nodded to the doorway.

Dru's eyes were pinned to the floor, his hazel irises peeling up to greet me. I let out a long sigh, slowly standing, worried any quick movements would have me too dizzy to walk. Aislin caught me under my arm, giving me extra stability as she escorted me toward him. "Why don't we both help you back to your room?"

Dru shifted my weight, getting under my other shoulder. They assisted me up the stairs and down the hall. Everything felt like a blur. Before I knew it, Aislin was helping me out of my shoes and propping me up on my bed. Roq was outside my room, as usual. The perfect little guard dog.

Dru had disappeared, causing my heart to race, but reappeared a few minutes later with a bin and another glass of water.

"Here." He placed the cup on my bedside table, then slid the bin on the floor by the bed, just in case. I didn't even want to think about it.

"I'll be downstairs seeing Sweeney if you need me," Aislin said, then pulled the door closed behind her.

"Why does being my champion scare you so much?"

Welp, I guess I'll just come out and say it.

"You're intoxicated," he said, stating the obvious.

"Fucking duh! I live above a bar, Dru." I gestured wildly around me. "It's the best place to be intoxicated!"

He frowned, his voice softening. "That may be true, but you're unusually drunk."

"Well, if you came to talk, then talk." I tried to use my huffiest voice while also fighting the urge to grab the bin.

Dru's mouth opened for a split second before shutting again, lost for words, like he'd never seen a wild twenty-one-year-old in her naturally drunken state. "Why don't I let you get some rest? I can pop back later once you've sobered up."

"I just need you to be honest with me. Tell me what's going on."

His throat bobbed. "We need to get you back to Vermont."

My body stilled, and I swore I could feel my chest crack right down the middle, heart thumping rapidly against my rib cage. "What?"

We still had so much left to do. We couldn't go back yet.

What if Vis is waiting to bleed me out all over again?

Dru rubbed the back of his neck, plopping down at the bottom of my bed. "The Queen and I still haven't found a guaranteed way to keep you safe from the Enchantress. If King Redmond is telling the truth, she's getting stronger and is closer to freedom than ever before."

"I know I haven't been able to summon my dragon yet, but we can keep working. And we have Neve now!" Once she was well, we could find out more about our magic. We just needed more time to let her get better.

Placing a hand on my leg, Dru stroked lazily. It was distracting, and I wished he'd scoot a little closer...

"Even if we can keep your identity a secret long enough for you to access it, we still don't have any firm information pointing to that being able to get rid of her threat," he said.

"What if our dragons had their bonded champions?"

Okay, the whiskey had officially incinerated my filter.

"It's not something you should rush into, even if it would get rid of the Enchantress."

He was lucky I was in control of my sparks. I'm pretty sure they would've shot out of my ears if not. "You're sending me away because it's easier? You said you would go with me."

Was he seriously going back on his promise?

"I will. The Queen has helped me secure safe passage for both of us."

Oh? Was this his idea or hers?

"You'd just abandon your work for the Queen? How will they figure out how to stop the Enchantress? I know this is personal for you, Dru." I looked into his eyes, my drunken state making the flecks of gold seemingly spin within the hazel. "Don't you want to find a way to help your sisters?"

His voice dropped to a whisper. "Of course I do."

"Then why would we leave now?" I leaned into him, our lips a breath away from touching.

"Please, consider this. I don't want to put you at risk." It came out as a rasp, a plea. "I can't lose you too."

"You won't." I crushed my lips to his, gripping his shirt for dear life, the world reeling around us.

"I'm not leaving." I pulled back from the kiss, my voice firm—well, firm-ish, considering I was still drunk off my ass. "*We're* not leaving."

A streak of blue passed across the sky, snagging our attention. Dru dashed to the window, and I stumbled over in seemingly slow motion. A fiery blue and white phoenix soared above the tree line, casting an eerie glow below. "Is that—"

"It is," Dru replied, keeping his eyes on the flaming bird.

The first time it flared against Celaria's midnight backdrop, I thought I'd seen a shooting star. Nope. Just your average phoenix-shifting tyrant passing through.

Maybe we needed the King's assistance, but I didn't see how a true alliance with Inverno would be possible. Sloan wasn't my issue—I knew she had been directed to keep us locked away on her king's behalf. At the end of the day, she had given us the gem.

King Redmond, on the other hand, I didn't trust. I probably never would. My mother believing him so readily just showed me how truly desperate she was when it came to the Enchantress's threat, and her obvious attempt to get Dru to wear me down about leaving only confirmed it.

Dru's fingers rested on my back, tracing circles that sent a shiver through me. I looked up at him, taking in the gold flecks in his eyes that had captivated me since we'd met.

"I should head back to the fort to get some more research

done before I get to bed," he said, concern etched into his brow. He moved toward the door.

"Wait," I croaked, clutching his hand while it was within reach. "Stay here tonight instead?"

"Of course." He grinned. Unbuckling his leather chest strap, he held it in one hand while he unbuttoned his shirt with the other. I might have drooled a bit at the sight of his bronze, muscled chest, but I'd totally blame it on the booze if he asked.

He put his clothes in a pile on the chair before coming back to the bed. Climbing under the covers, he held them up for me while I got settled in. My hand trailed down the hollow of his stomach, and he shifted at my touch, giving me a gentle kiss.

He patted his chest. "Lay down and rest, Ky."

I guess this was strictly going to be a slumber party. But when I nuzzled into the crook of his neck, I realized it was for the best. A moment later, the spinning room sent me over the edge of the bed and facedown in the bin.

Fucking whiskey.

13

NEVE

A blue halo pooled over my face, waking me.

I squeezed my eyes shut, fighting the light spilling into my darkness.

All the oxygen had been sucked from the room, its refreshing and comforting chill replaced by a suffocating blanket of smoky chestnuts and whiskey. A hushed breeze wafted toward me, breaking up its density, accompanied by the graceful flap of wings.

Is this real?

I gripped the sheet, thumbing along the soft linen, grounding myself, half expecting them to shred beneath my touch. They didn't.

Because I had *fingers.*

Not claws.

I was back in Arafax.

Home.

A knock cleaved the silence, and I stilled at the sound, knowing once they realized I was awake, the questions would come.

Then the pitying looks. The wonder at what happened while I was locked away.

I wasn't ready to answer any of it. To deal with any of it.

Until I was, I'd keep on *sleeping*.

Boots smacked against the floor, then a familiar calloused hand gently looped through mine. I'd recognize the warm working hands any day.

Sloan.

Part of me wanted to reach up—to hug her and confide everything I could recall. She was one of my closest friends once upon a time. But what seemed like just yesterday was over a decade ago. A decade I'd spent right under her nose, but never truly seen.

What were we to each other now?

"Come back to us, Neve," she sighed, sounding lost. "We need to know you're okay."

I still didn't understand how she had ended up in Arafax with me. Shouldn't she be with *him* in Inverno?

Her boot tapped the ground, fingers fidgeting nervously against my own.

"Please," she croaked, squeezing my hand. "I can't tell what Red's doing. He's suddenly pushing for an alliance with Arafax. They don't fully trust me here—not that things would be better back home. My own men view me as a traitor. Red too."

No. That couldn't be possible.

I wanted to return the squeeze. Reassure her that everything would be okay.

But it'd be a lie. I didn't know anything.

Not anymore.

I'd spent my life rooted in my convictions, self-assured, believing in Celaria's peace. Now memories of the last ten years slipped through my mind, haunting me. Any comfort I felt flitted away too quickly to tether me in place, leaving me caught—adrift between the islands of what I'd previously believed and the reality of all that'd happened since.

"Hopefully you'll wake up soon and we can face this together, old friend." She released a rich exhale before her weight shifted off the bed and she padded away.

When I heard the faint click of the door shut, I blinked my eyes open, stretching the lids from a day of forcing them closed. I half expected to find myself back in my cell, iron bars skewing my view, trapped in my dragon form.

I tilted my head down, lifting the comforter for confirmation. No scales in sight, other than the markings disjointed by scars that lined my sides.

Footsteps pounded along the corridor outside my room.

Snapping my head back to the pillow, I stilled at the shadow clogging the small shaft of light spilling under the door. I held my breath, unmoving, waiting for them to pass.

Once they did, the tears I'd held back seeped on the white pillowcase, making small puddles on the linen, illuminated by a pair of golden rings. My eyes burned, and I knew they were shifted into their slitted form. Wiping the tears away, I quietly sifted through Sloan's words.

Was it possible for our two kingdoms to truly align and work together?

Not likely.

14

REDMOND

Chilling exhales from the dragon's bloodied maw.

Daggers of ice spiraling toward my father.

The blue creature crashing to the ground in Inverno's dungeon.

Neve's trembling body beneath frigid shards of ice.

I replayed the moments over and over, trying to understand where I'd been so blind.

How did I not know the woman I was marrying was also one of Arafax's most powerful dragons? I never thought their beasts could be shifters. The fact that I shifted in and out of phoenix form only made me feel like more of an idiot.

I still wasn't sure how Isla would feel about me soaring so close to her fort, even with our alliance, so I kept the flyover quick, diving and sweeping past the windows. Just a momentary glimpse to know she was okay.

Neve slept in her bed, surrounded only by the empty room coated in frost. I flew in between the white curtains, hovering above the bed, watching her chest rise and fall beneath the snow-covered comforter. Her breath came out in white puffs, chilling the air.

She was alive. *Safe.*

I needed to keep it that way.

When she shifted to her side, gripping the white sheets with her hands, it brought back that familiar ache for her. The feel of her silky skin against mine, slinky curls slipping between my fists, lips and tongues a blizzard of mint and pine. If only I could rewind the threads of time to when we were young and idealistic.

In love.

Fate had other plans for us.

A gentle knock at the door had me out of the room in a flash, peeling across the onyx sky, headed back toward Inverno. I still had a kingdom to rule and an alliance to foster. People depended on me.

I couldn't fail them. Not at this.

Not ever again.

Soaring between the midnight clouds, I stalled over the dead thicket of trees. The air filtering into my nostrils was off, earthy and wilted. Wisps didn't smell like rot doused in soil. Oxygen ripped away from my lungs, spotting dark shapes rising past the canopy.

Coming straight toward me.

I dipped lower, trying to see what they were. Squinting, I shifted my gaze. A chill spread through my eyes as they ignited from their usual midnight into bright cobalt, illuminating the area ahead. Contorted, ashen figures jolted into the sky, hurtling toward me—a sea of humanoid bodies with tusks, claws, and pointy teeth.

On pure instinct, I beat my wings, lifting away from

them. Their dark maws pulled into snarls and their limbs reached for me, ready for attack.

My heart stammered, eyes searching for a safe escape. I barrel-rolled to my left, and the creatures smacked into an invisible barrier, snarling and scraping at it.

I held my breath, hovering midair to watch them, ready to bolt if they broke through the veil.

A pulse beat through the air, and their heads snapped up in an unnatural angle, facing the sky. The hundreds of mangled bodies were ripped backward, sucked into the blackened canopy.

What the fuck was that?

The magic the Enchantress had access to exceeded far beyond what I'd imagined. I'd need to find something soon to give us an advantage because if those things ever made it past their boundary, we wouldn't stand a chance.

15

KYLEIGH

I grabbed the bottom of my shirt and wiped my mouth, clearing my throat and standing as Aislin dropped my hair back in place, the coral waves flying in all directions. I hadn't bothered brushing it, still too hungover from my brief love affair with whiskey the night prior.

Sparring lessons were this morning and I already looked like I'd gotten my ass kicked. As someone with zero fighting experience, other than a few kickboxing classes at the local gym, I was dreading today's training. Sloan had no clue what she'd gotten herself into, agreeing to train someone as uncoordinated as me.

"You gonna make it the rest of the way okay?" Aislin asked, snatching a tie off her wrist and handing it to me.

I pulled my hair back, sweeping the strands into place, still not used to their drastic coral color.

Is my dragon this vibrant?

The idea of finding out excited me, but I was scared it would be just as painful as it was when my dragon magic had manifested, shredding at my insides, my bones popping out of their sockets. I expected the full shift to be much worse.

The thought made me shudder.

"I'm sorry I'm making us late. It's definitely been light out for a few hours at least."

"It's fine. I promised Dru I'd help you get to lessons since he had to go do some research this morning. Besides, I don't mind pissing off the Commander," she said, smirking.

"Former commander," I reiterated, trying to remember she was supposedly on our side. "What is your deal with her anyway?"

"What deal?" Aislin turned her gaze forward, tugging at the bottom of her leather jacket.

"I get not trusting her—I don't either—but it still must have taken a lot for her to come here and work with us, especially after what happened to her job and the guards..." Keeping my eyes locked on my crimson sneakers, I stopped the thought there.

Aislin was quiet when she spoke, her tone gentler than usual. "You know you can talk to me about it, Kyleigh."

"There's nothing to say."

There really wasn't.

"They were horrible to us. No one blames you for—"

"They weren't *all* guilty of being horrible," I said, eyes cast to my feet as I shuffled over the root-covered dirt. Dru's words from our time at the falls had stuck with me. Heat radiated through my chest. While I was learning to embrace my powers and how they could help us get rid of the Enchantress, the guilt over knowing I'd hurt innocents twisted my insides into vicious knots.

Aislin should understand not wanting to talk about it.

"I've killed way more people," she stated, as if attempting to placate me.

I halted. "Is that supposed to be comforting?"

"No. Maybe." She shrugged. "I don't know what it's supposed to be."

"It is what it is. Can't go back and change it now." I picked up the pace. Streaks of mauve painted the sky above, and Arafax's castle eclipsed the ground ahead of us.

We bypassed the fort's entrance, weaving through its stony labyrinth leading to the arena.

"Now, are you going to tell me what your deal with Sloan is? You avoided my question about her earlier and I still don't know what happened the night we escaped Inverno."

"It is what it is," was all she said, throwing my words back at me, but I noticed a few small bolts tumble to the ground, kicking up puffs of dirt.

I smirked to myself but let it go, knowing better than to push her further.

A whistle pierced the air from above, and we scanned the sky for its source. The silver-haired knight was wrapped around a tall support beam, climbing up using only her arms and legs. Sweaty and slightly covered in dirt, she had apparently begun training in our absence.

For the last few hours...

"I hope that's not what she has planned for us today," I whispered to Aislin who was preternaturally still, staring up at the intimidating ascent Sloan had scaled seemingly for the hell of it.

"I see you two finally decided to show up," Sloan called, scuttling her way down the beam and springing off to land delicately next to it. She was athletic with a strange warrior-like grace that was mesmerizing for someone as uncoordinated as myself.

Aislin murmured, too low for me to hear—probably something snarky. She glared at Sloan, the lines of her face tightening.

"I'm sorry," I chimed in. "It was my fault."

"Dru warned me that you were a bit...out of sorts last night. Doesn't give you an excuse, or *you*," she said lifting a brow at Aislin whose fingers were threading with lightning. "Were you hungover too or just being lazy?"

The brunette's eyes flared before shrinking to slits, shoulders tensing.

Is she about to shift?

I blinked, ready for her to blow up—to explode—but instead her neon streaks retracted into her fingertips. We both released a deep exhale, most likely for completely different reasons.

It was just us in the arena, my mother's royal presence absent. Dru was nowhere to be found either. Maybe he was off delivering the news to his queen that I refused to be her good little peasant, cowering away in the Otherworld.

"Hold out your arms," Sloan directed, hands on her hips.

I extended them out in front of me. Aislin looked skeptical but followed my lead. Sloan walked to the edge of the arena before picking up and carrying over a large rock. She dropped the slab into Aislin's arms, and I watched her tremble from its weight.

She kept her head high, avoiding eye contact with our instructor.

A few moments later, a twin rock dropped into my arms, heavy enough to already cause discomfort.

"Now what?" Aislin asked, gaze still pinned straight ahead. "I thought we were supposed to be sparring."

"You *were* sparring for today's lesson, but combat starts with arriving prepared," Sloan said, her tone unnervingly smooth despite the vitriol fueling her words, "which neither of you were today."

My arms were already starting to feel unsteady in their outstretched position.

"You will hold these slabs for the amount of time you were late. 126 minutes. If your arms become too tired, you can take a short break, no longer than five minutes."

She checked the watch on her wrist, pressing some buttons on it. "Thanks to Dru, I have a timer on here we can use."

I groaned. "I'll have to thank him later."

Sloan smirked, pleased with my reaction to today's torture tactic. "Time starts now."

⸻

THE CHARCOAL SLAB POUNDED INTO THE GROUND, AND DUST billowed up into my face, sending me into a fit of dry coughs. My arms throbbed, numb, but somehow still aching.

I refuse to lift them again today. Maybe tomorrow too.

Sloan passed on the message that the Queen had requested my presence at lunch during one of my many five-minute rest breaks.

It had taken me over three and a half hours to complete my required penance for being late. Each time my arms slunk below my waist, Sloan would demand that I get them "up!" She claimed it would help me get used to holding my arms up in my basic fighting stance.

I was pretty sure that was bullshit.

Aislin sat quietly, watching me from the arena's outer ring—in solidarity, I supposed. She never dropped her slab or let it waver. Not once. Instead, she just glared daggers at our silver-haired sadist of an instructor. It was like she had something to prove. Some unspoken challenge. Every so often, Sloan would stand a few inches from Aislin, staring right back with a grin, seeming to find Aislin's attitude amusing.

"Alright, you both are dismissed," Sloan said, grabbing a stone under each arm and carting them off to the side with ease. "I expect you to show up tomorrow. *On time*. That's when the *real* work begins."

I groaned, snapping her attention to me. "Other than those unruly sparks you have, how do you plan to defend yourself? Just let your emotions be the source of your strength?" She strode over, cradling my chin between her fingers. "True strength has nothing to do with power."

"I think the Enchantress would disagree," I said, flicking my fingers and releasing small sparks at her. She slid out of the way, accidentally bumping into Aislin who looked like she'd been the one struck by my outburst.

"My sparks seem to help me just fine," I said, exiting the arena without looking back at either of them. Aislin probably agreed with Sloan, always complaining about the burden of her abilities.

But she didn't understand.

Power was everything when you'd spent your life wielding none.

ONE OF THE SERVANTS ESCORTED ME TO MY MOTHER'S chambers, and I stood a moment, taking in the space she'd called her own for the last decade. Sitting against the opposite wall was a massive bed covered in scarlet satin and veiled by sheer, golden curtains. Past it, was a modest balcony, set with a small table and two chairs.

My mother sat cross-legged in one, barefoot, wearing a simple white blouse and red pants, chestnut hair pulled over to one side. It was unsettlingly casual for the Celarian version of my mother. This was much more the image of the woman who'd raised me. For some reason, that immediately set me on edge. My molars ground together, jaw pulled taut.

What is she playing at?

"If you called me here to get me to change my mind, it won't work."

"What are you talking about?" Waving her hand in the air, she beckoned me toward her, continuing to stare out at the kingdom partially shrouded by the looming, inaccessible castle suspended above us.

She dismissed her staff, waiting until it was only us in the room. Once the door clicked shut and footsteps were distant, I spoke. "I know it wasn't Dru's idea to leave Celaria and go back to Vermont."

"It's my job as your mother to protect you." She let out a sigh. "One day when you have children of your own, you'll understand."

"When I have children of my own, I won't *lie* to them. I won't *use* them as a bargaining chip before they're even born." I pulled the chair out, scraping it against the ground, causing my mother to flinch as I sat across from her. "Don't be mad that I won't let you play puppet master when *your* choices landed us in this mess."

She said nothing.

"We are staying," I continued, trying to keep my face impassive, controlled. "I'm not leaving until the Enchantress no longer poses a threat."

I wouldn't let anyone use me as a pawn.

"What about the kingdom?" she asked, gaze slightly pained.

I ignored her expression. "What about it?"

"You're next in line to rule."

"I don't want it. Enough of my life has revolved around you." I'd spent the last decade trying to become what I stupidly imagined she wanted. I refused to continue wasting my energy living for someone else.

"What is that supposed to mean?" Her jaw was clenched, tension drawing it into sharp angles as she spoke.

"It doesn't matter. Once we've helped here, I'm going *home* to Vermont. With Dru."

"I see," she said, letting some flames swirl between her fingers, weaving them effortlessly.

"I hate being away from Dad, not knowing how he is doing, if he's out there worried about me, or hurt. Especially after what *you* did to him." My nails dug crescents into my palms. I shook my hands out, dropping them to my sides, willing myself to not let any powers come through—especially not in response to hers. "He doesn't deserve to go through someone disappearing on him all over again."

"Your father is a very capable man." She gave a soft smile as she stared out at the lavender fields ahead of us.

"I thought if I ever saw you again that I'd actually have my mom back. Not *this*."

Not more lies.

"I have to apologize," she interjected.

Was this the moment where she finally admitted she'd messed up leaving my dad and I behind?

She crossed her arm over her chest, squeezing her shoulder with a shudder. "I'm going to have to take a rain check on lunch. Something's come up."

I guess that's a no.

"Well, that's perfect because I wasn't hungry anyway." Before she could say anything else, I strode out of her chambers, dashing out the fort's doors.

"Let's go," I called to Roq, not bothering to stop as I headed toward The Lavender.

16

AISLIN

A copper claw gripped my throat. Tightening. Breaking skin. Blood dribbled down my neck, and she peered up at me, onyx eyes shimmering. Swiping up the blood, she trailed her finger over our bond mark.

Scraping along my ribs with her free hand, her shadowy tendrils caressed their way around my thighs, parting them as I fought to clamp them shut.

"We both know you can only deny me so long, Aislin. We made a deal."

She squeezed my airway, and I rasped for air, grasping for purchase.

For anything to free me from her clutches—

I woke up gasping, rolling to the edge of my bed, hand clasped around my neck. Trembling, gaze darting around my room, I slowed my breaths despite the cadence throbbing in my temples.

It wasn't real.

The heart-shaped mark stung, the Enchantress's summoning angry.

What the blazes was that?

I gasped out shallow pants, fumbling for the flask of lavender whiskey on my bedside table, only to find it empty of all hope to numb my affliction.

Not real.

After splashing some water on my face and getting dressed, I trudged down the narrow hallway, patting at my thigh holster, feeling naked when I was reminded once again that my dagger was gone. I didn't need it, but its absence stripped away a sense of comforting security.

Leigh stopped me at the top of the stairs. "Heading out for training?"

I descended a few steps before peering back up at her. "Yes."

"Here. I packed you some snacks to keep up your strength." She brought over a small fabric satchel and handed it to me. I savored the feel of its warmth against my fingertips.

A lump caught in my throat when I peeled open the pouch, spotting bread laced with streaks of red and purple. Berry bake. My favorite. It was an Arafax specialty that my mom and I used to make together when I was little.

Leigh and I had recreated her recipe in The Lavender's kitchen during my first few years living there. The memory of being covered in flour floated into view before disappearing at the sound of Flynt chuckling. I twisted to find him blowing me a kiss from the bottom of the staircase.

"They have food at the fort," I said turning back and holding the sack out to her, blinking away a few tears.

"Oh," her shoulders slumped, "of course they do."

I wanted my relationship with Leigh to be better, but I didn't know how to let go of the past. Every day that I endured Flynt and his men just reinforced my anger at her. Even though I wasn't used as an assassin anymore, I didn't feel free. I was still under the watch of Flynt, the Queen, and now the Enchantress, who even managed to find her way into my dreams.

I had seen some kindness from Flynt toward Kyleigh, but I didn't trust that his generosity wasn't threaded with malintent. Some alternative wicked agenda.

With Leigh, it was too hard to separate her from Flynt when it came to my feelings, but deep down, I knew they were completely different individuals. I spun back to face her. "Actually, your berry bake sounds wonderful. Thank you, Leigh."

A smile beamed across her face, her eyes shimmering as if they could release tears at any moment. She watched intently while I broke off a piece and popped it into my mouth. It was the perfect blend of sweetness, the berry mixture hitting my taste buds in a delicious wave. I let out a contented sigh, and Leigh's smile widened.

"Thanks," I said quickly, descending the staircase and bolting out of the inn before either of us could say anything more.

WHEN I SHOWED UP ABOUT TWENTY MINUTES LATE FOR OUR sparring lesson, I watched as Kyleigh bounced harshly against the arena floor, adding to the grime already coating her shorts. Coral-streaked hair stuck to her face, and her cheeks were flushed, gray shirt patched with dark, damp spots, sticking to her curves. A pair of gloves covered her hands, painted with copper swirls of faerie blood.

She and Sloan were running through boxing drills, Kyleigh alternating jabs with dipping low, attempting to evade Sloan's counterstrikes. It was easy to see that hand-to-hand combat was not Kyleigh's strong suit. She tripped over her own feet, falling and letting out a string of curses.

"Ugh. I suck!" she fumed, brushing herself off but mostly just smearing dirt across her shorts. She remained hunched over, grabbing her arms and wincing from what I assumed were leftover aches from yesterday's *lesson*.

"Your reaction time is sloppy, but you've got moxie," Sloan said, flashing her a silky smirk. Holding out a hand, the silver-haired taskmaster helped Kyleigh stand. "This time, I want you to think like you're an ash grizzle."

"An ash grizzle?" Kyleigh raised a brow. "We don't have those..."

She trailed off, obviously unsure how much Sloan knew about her origins.

"In the Otherworld," Sloan interjected. "The Queen filled Redmond and myself in on the big mystery about where you are from. I have to say it explains a lot about your *eccentricities*."

Bet she didn't tell you Kyleigh's her daughter, though.

Sloan moved behind Kyleigh and lifted her elbows into a defensive stance. My core pinched, a twinge of an unfamiliar emotion threatening to breach my carefully constructed walls. Shifting her knee forward so that Kyleigh's knees were flush with hers, Sloan began to raise her boot, tapping Kyleigh's thigh to indicate she wanted them to move as one. "Ash grizzles are huge and covered in gray fur with silver tips. They use their formidable claws to slice at fellow predators. They also can release smoke when they huff aggressively."

She flattened her palm against the back of Kyleigh's gloved hand, then lunged forward swiping their arms across an invisible target. "Make sure you're leaning into the movement. You can't be afraid to use the force of your body to take out your opponent."

Sloan guided Kyleigh, moving forward with slashes and jabs, knocking her off balance a few times when she was too tentative.

"What are you wearing?" I asked Kyleigh when she stopped for a break, my eyes darting to the copper-stained gloves.

She rasped. "Dru created them as a way to keep our powers in when we work on combat so we don't have to worry about hurting Sloan."

"Well isn't that ingenious of him," I said flatly.

"Here's your pair." Kyleigh pointed out another set sitting at the edge of the arena. I held them in my hands, running my thumb over the swirls. A tiny arc of electricity left my fingers, absorbing into the circular lines of copper.

"No thanks." I shook my head, looking over at Sloan. "Unless you're too scared to fight me without them?"

I tossed the gloves onto the ground at the frosty former commander's feet. Kyleigh looked alarmed but said nothing.

"It'll take more than a few little bolts to scare me off," Sloan chirped, beckoning me forward.

I gulped back the lump in my throat, rolling my shoulders before bringing my arm across my body to stretch it out.

Remember, she's the enemy.

"Ready?" I asked, cracking my knuckles.

"Always. Hand-to-hand combat only today." Her blue eyes glinted, then dropped to my hands. "If it gets to be too much and you need the gloves, just say the word and we'll stop."

I pretended to yawn. "Are we going to fight? I'm bored."

I didn't want to be around Sloan more than necessary. It was hard enough seeing her all the time in my mind these last few weeks, wondering what had happened to her after we'd left Inverno. Now she was embedded at the fort and I was supposed to trust her—

"Hit me," she instructed, tucking silver strands behind her ears. "I can tell you don't want to be here, so get in one shot without using magic and the lesson will be over."

She brought her hands up in front of her face defensively, the muscles in her arms tensing in preparation for my attack, revealing awe-inducing definition in her shoulders and biceps.

"You going to make a move or keep staring?" she taunted. A vision passed through my mind, glowing strands of lightning painting a picture over my bed, only instead of the illuminated outline, she was there—

Stop daydreaming, you idiot. Focus.

I shuffled forward, swinging my arm across my body, full effort behind my attack. More agile than I'd anticipated, Sloan dove, grabbing around my thigh and sweeping my legs out from under me, toppling me on my ass.

Kyleigh's grimace caught my attention from the edge of the arena. Sloan was ready to go again, shuffling her weight between her legs.

Okay, so *this* was how we would be fighting.

Getting back up to my feet, I took my time wiping the dirt off my pants, trying to buy myself a moment to think of the best strategy to lead with. Sloan didn't hesitate to charge at me, though, arms slashing like she'd showed Kyleigh earlier. I wove under her elbow, grabbing around her waist and tackling her to the ground.

Her eyes widened in surprise.

Yes, I've been trained to fight, you arrogant ass.

"You probably shouldn't have underestimated me," I huffed, straddling her hips to pin her in place. A glint danced in her eye, and I pulled back my elbow, ready to punch that look right off her face.

As I unleashed my right hook, she thrust her knee into my ass, knocking me off balance. Startled, I tumbled out of her reach.

When I stood up, she was waiting for me, pressed back onto her haunches. A feral smile lit her face, making her look more like a wild animal than a pristine, formally trained knight. "I expected more from Arafax's esteemed assassin."

"I expected more pomp from Inverno's prestigious commander." My eyes narrowed to slits, and I surged at her with a balled fist.

Sloan's vision snagged on something, icy stare glazed over. My knuckles met her jaw with a loud *crack*, and she stumbled back, blinking rapidly, cupping her face. Blood slipped through her fingers.

Shaking off the dirt from my knuckles, I wiped my hand on my pants. "Guess I'm dismissed."

Sloan's brow furrowed, but she nodded, despite refusing to make eye contact with me.

Kyleigh held out a glass of water to me, wide-eyed. "Remind me never to get on your bad side."

"Don't you forget it," I replied with a wink, lifting a hand to turn down her offering.

Striding toward the exit, the whirring of a knife breezed past my ear.

"Blazes!"

The blade wedged into the edge of the arena's enclosure caught my eye, an amethyst hilt poking out from it.

My dagger.

I pulled it from the barrier, turning to find Sloan gone, Kyleigh staring off to wherever she'd headed. I sprinted off in that direction, weaving through the fort's maze, but once I stepped onto the crimson carpet leading to the entrance, I came to a halt.

Why was I even following her? So what if she'd returned my dagger?

So what if I'd stormed off after landing a stellar punch that may have bloodied her up a bit?

I'd played by her rules today and I was free to leave.

Citrus and jasmine swept away my brooding, and I found Sloan leaning against the stone wall outside the labyrinth.

"Fuck," she growled, the sound guttural, like it was ripped from her chest. She was distracted enough to not even notice me. As I stalked closer, she broke out in a sprint, glacial eyes pinned to their purpose.

"Sloan!" I called out, trying to catch up to her, boots pounding against the ground, picking up pace.

She turned her head a moment, nodding in the direction of where she was heading. "It's Sir Fergus."

"Ox? What happened?" I shouted, closing the distance between us. She was faster than me, but my legs were longer, helping me stay with her strides.

She barely looked at me, blinking uncomfortably slow.

"What's wrong with you?"

Shaking her head, she pivoted toward the Silent Woods.

Toward the Enchantress.

I gripped the tingling spot on the nape of my neck.

Fuck.

The blackened trees came into view, and I hesitated at their edge. Sloan broke her run, turning to look at me. "He's hurt."

"How do you know?"

"Mox," she huffed out. "I have him keeping an eye on Redmond—when he visits the Enchantress."

Did she not trust him either?

I didn't move, too scared that if I got too close to the woods I'd be at the mercy of the Enchantress and her wisps. But if Ox was in trouble... He was the closest thing I had to a friend. And I owed him my life. "Let's go."

My feet hit the root-covered ground of the Silent Woods. Nothing seemed different from when I'd wandered into this forest months ago, like something had stopped magic's vibrance from seeping in. Being here, now, only made it more apparent how much Arafax had changed since the gem's return to the Evergleam.

The ground crunched beneath my boots, and I patted my amethyst dagger strapped to my hip. It felt good to have it back, even though I knew it would be a child's toy against the Enchantress. But now I also had a new arsenal of electric weapons at my disposal that I didn't have the last time I'd seen her at her cabin.

The further we got into the woods, the less pain I could feel stinging from the bond mark, replaced now with a magnetic pull from the Enchantress that became stronger.

A low hum began thrumming against the trees we passed.

Sloan's second-sight through Mox gave her a clear path to Ox, so I continued to follow her, ignoring the tether coaxing me toward the cabin.

A deep scream rang out through the tree line, haunting like a wounded animal.

Ox.

Mox's white body stood out against the trees, and he growled, jumping and ripping into the darkness surrounding him. As we got closer, translucent forms buzzed around us. A swarm of shadow wisps encircled Ox, almost completely blocking him from view, their contorted bodies blade thin, slashing into him.

What is he even doing here?

Ignoring the surge coming from my bond mark, I lifted my arms, sending lightning slithering around the surrounding trees, over their jet-black branches.

Sloan's eyes widened.

"Don't go near any of it," I warned. "I am trying to bait the wisps. I don't know how long it will take for them to realize I'm the source."

From the way the Enchantress summoned repeatedly, she wouldn't be able to resist getting her claws on me.

The wisps spread out, whipping their heads back and forth, sniffing out the signature of my magic, much too powerful to ignore now that the gem had amplified my abilities. Watching them under the spell of their ethereal mistress, there was no recognizable humanity. Not a trace. Only dusky shells carrying out cruel orders.

Obeying.

Once enough of the wisps had cleared the way, we saw Ox lying motionless on the ground. His clothes were ripped, and deep gashes marred his body. His rugged face was nearly beyond recognition, coated in blood and dirt. Maeve and Maisie lay next to him, smeared with crimson ichor.

17

AISLIN

"Help me with him," Sloan called out, attempting to lift Ox from the ground and lay him across Mox's back.

I rushed over, shooting iridescent spears through the blackened forest, causing the wisps to frantically bump into each other in confusion.

Ox groaned, body slumped over Mox's white fur, staining it with blood. Without Sloan speaking another word to her familiar, he plodded off.

She drew her sword, gripping it in both hands, swinging at the shadows whirring around her. Meanwhile, the wisps' hums grew stronger, tracing the lightning back to its source. They swarmed around me, licking up my spine, tugging at my hair. Rooted in place, my body refused to retreat from their lure.

Sloan's blade rang out, slicing through the wisps circling me, their shadowy silhouettes scattering in pieces. Their divided forms froze in place, then slowly stitched themselves back together.

They pulled back a moment before diving toward me, Sloan continuing to fight off dozens of them. I couldn't peel my eyes away, the biting song of the sterling defender's blade the only thing breaking up the hypnotic vibration ensnaring me. Her body was a weapon honed over years of training, perfectly blended with subtle, yet deadly curves.

The closer the translucent sirens came, the more mesmerized I became by their swelling pitch swirling around me, blotting out everything else. Lightning seeped out of my fingertips, crawling over the trees and underbrush, painting the Silent Woods in swaths of shadow.

"What's going on, Aislin?" Sloan yelled over the humming.

"Go," I said, entranced.

Citrus and jasmine invaded the breeze of spectral figures beckoning me to their master. "No fucking way am I just leaving you here."

"J-just go," I stuttered, urging her to leave.

To flee.

Before she ended up like the bloodied heap that Mox carried. Barely breathing. Barely clinging to life.

Her calloused hand gripped my shoulder, shaking me, but I didn't move. Couldn't move. The wisps' pulsing energy flowed through me, making my eyes roll back in my head. Heat flared through my vision, and I knew from the sensation that they had shifted into their slitted dragon form.

"Don't. You. Fucking. Dare." Sloan's firm, yet syrupy voice filtered through the buzzing that filled my skull, pushing out everything else around me.

I gasped when a strong arm clamped around my waist. Blinking away the burning feeling in my eyes, I watched the shadows prickle my skin, slipping between us.

Before I could tell what was happening, the ground began to move beneath me.

WHEN I OPENED MY EYES, I WAS UPSIDE DOWN, FACE LEVEL with Sloan's tailbone as she sprinted toward the edge of the Silent Woods.

I tapped her leg. "You can put me down now. I'm not an invalid."

"I know that," she huffed, hurling us past the boundary so the sorceress could no longer snap me back into her clutches. Once Sloan was able to slow her momentum she stopped, bending down and unloading me gently onto the ground, both of us panting.

Excruciating pain ripped through my mark, the Enchantress summoning me *again*. I grasped the base of my neck, wincing, white spots peppering my vision.

Did she sense how close I was?

Sloan staggered over to me, hands braced on her knees while she focused on slowing her breathing. "What happened back there?"

"The wisps," I heaved with a relieved sigh. "They usually hunt those with power. I knew mine would be too hard to resist."

Plus, I had a deal with their mistress. But Sloan didn't need to know that.

"Are you okay?" Her voice was brittle, laced with concern. Her fingers traced along my arm, ascending toward the mark hidden under my jacket. I quickly placed my hand on hers.

"I'm okay," I said, not sure how convincing it was.

I was anything but.

She crossed her arms, grabbing the bottom of her sweat-and-blood-soaked tank and pulling it over her head, stripping down to her delicate, pale-blue bralette.

"What are you—" My heart sank into my rib cage.

The blood on her tank hadn't been from Ox.

She'd been hurt.

Rippling abs that would normally have me awestruck were slashed through with a series of shallow cuts, crimson dripping from the wounds. She balled up her tank, pressing it against her skin, stifling the bleed.

"Blazes," I whispered, taking a step toward her. "Are those from the wisps?"

She just nodded.

This was my fault.

"You should have left me there. They wouldn't hurt me. My powers are too tempting."

Icy-blue eyes sliced up to mine, twin daggers piercing straight through me. "I couldn't just leave you there."

"No need to get heroic on my account," I chided, quickly trying to ward up my defenses.

"I didn't *need* to," she said, a smirk playing on her plum lips. She tucked the soiled tank into the top of her trousers and began walking in the direction of the fort. "I wanted to."

This could all be a game. It would be easier to believe it was.

But I knew better.

Here she was, trudging on despite the bleeding, despite the fact that she'd carted my ass miles through the woods. She'd put herself in harm's way for Ox and I, two people she'd locked away in a dungeon when she'd stumbled across us in the woods. She shivered a moment, crossing her arms over herself and squeezing tightly, as if that could provide some kind of warmth.

I removed my jacket, resting it over her shoulders. "Here."

"Thanks." Her fingers grazed mine, sending a chill through me, as she slipped her arms through the leather while we walked on, the fort growing larger with every step.

"Sloan?" Her name slipped past my lips before I could stop myself.

She froze in place before pivoting to face me. "Yes?"

"Next time I need rescuing, don't."

"Don't?" She lifted a brow, tilting her head.

Peeks of pale skin stole my attention, her swelling crests illuminated by the moon above. She looked good in my jacket. *Too good.* I swallowed, my throat suddenly dry.

"I'm not worth it," I rasped out.

Her silver tresses blocked half of her face, hanging in thin strands. My fingers reached out and tucked them behind her ear, wafting the scent of jasmine and citrus toward me. She sucked in a breath, pupils widening like saucers, and her teeth grazed her bottom lip. "I'm very capable of assessing the situation, Aislin."

"I know you are. That's why I would be pissed if you went and got yourself hurt again on my account." This woman who held my thoughts, my dreams—a woman who, for some unknown reason, saw me beyond just the useful weapon that I had been for years...

Like a woman possessed, I slid my hand tentatively to hers.

She opened her palm to meet mine, and when my fingers skimmed it they tingled, lightning skittering through my veins. I glanced down, making sure my hand wasn't glowing in response to the electricity charging through me.

"You have a kingdom that needs you to fight for it," I reminded her.

She firmly twined our fingers together, pulling my palm to her heart and letting it rest there. "So do you."

Bu-bump.

Bu-bump.

Bu-bump.

I stared down at my hand on her glistening, milky skin, chest rising and falling, defenseless beneath my touch. Fisting the jacket, I tugged her to me, crushing my lips to hers. For a moment, she held still, possibly from shock, before she gripped my neck and surged into me. Her kiss was brutal, commanding, smooth—just like I'd imagined. She had her own addictive nectar, a citrusy sweetness I couldn't get enough of.

Our tongues dueled for purchase, tangling us up in a reckless moment of insanity.

Because that's what this was.

Insanity.

The moment I let my walls crumble down, let her breach that carefully constructed barrier, I knew it was wrong.

I jolted away from her. Leaving her with her mouth opened slightly, dumbstruck.

Even if we were on the same side of this war, even if she wasn't using me to garner her position with King Redmond, Sloan existed on a moral high ground I'd never ascend to.

Her eyes dropped, following her finger that ghosted along her lips, like she was etching the memory of our kiss into them.

"I-I'm sorry. I don't know what came over me," I sputtered, stepping backward toward the fort. Knowing about my jobs and what I'd been made to do was not the same as talking about it or seeing it. I hated that she knew who I was. And a knight like her, a beacon to her people, deserved better than an assassin who'd spent the last decade of her life surviving in the shadows.

"Ais—"

"I shouldn't have done that," I blurted out. "I need to go see Ox."

And with that, I turned on my heels and darted toward the fort.

18

AISLIN

Peeling open his eyes, Ox's face scrunched in pain, inspecting his battered body. Dru finished cleaning up his wounds and wrapping his leg with bandages.

"I've looked better," the knight croaked out, giving a labored chuckle.

"Blazes, Ox!" I gave his shoulder a gentle nudge. "What were you doing in the Silent Woods *alone*?"

"I found Maeve and Maisie left by my house today and wanted to put my girls to use."

Apparently, Sloan was a busy woman.

"You're an idiot," I sighed. "Are you trying to make me regret not stopping your heart?"

He pressed up to his elbows, coughing a few times from the effort. "Probably would have hurt less, to be honest," he said, voice barely above a whisper.

Probably.

If he was still going to have such a sense of humor about everything, even after being seriously injured, I wasn't going to shy away from interrogating his ass. "What happened?"

His face drained of color. "I might have borrowed Dru's glove."

Dru's eyes snapped to him, his gloved-hand pulling the bandage tightly around Ox's shredded calf muscle, making him hiss. "Borrowed? You mean stole without my knowledge."

"How could he steal it?" I asked Dru. "You're never without your glove."

"He doesn't wear it in the shower," Ox said, coughing out a laugh. "By the way, Kyleigh's a lucky lady."

He winked at Dru, who just groaned.

"Stop making light of this, Ox. It's not funny," I seethed. Leave it to him to laugh his way through a near-death experience. He might be acting like everything was fine, but his body was covered in bandages blooming with red.

"Well, you have to admit it's kind of funny. Damn glove barely fit over four of my fingers!" Dru offered him a glass of water, and he took greedy sips, dribbling some down his beard. "I mean, I just got my ass handed to me by a bunch of sexy shadow things. Didn't see that coming." He wiped his chin with his forearm bandage.

Neither did I. When the wisps ensnared us last time, nothing about them seemed malicious. The change in their demeanor left me uneasy. King Redmond's words rang through me.

Still banished, but stronger.

"What was your plan?" I asked Ox, wondering what had preempted this bold move.

"I was thinking I'd get their attention and move things along with ridding us of the Enchantress. If I got a few swings in, maybe *entertain* her for a bit"—I rolled my eyes—

"then we wouldn't have to rely on an alliance with King Redmond. With Inverno."

I didn't trust King Redmond or the alliance between our territories either, but his warnings seemed more accurate than I'd given him credit for.

And Sloan? Could I trust her? After that kiss, I still felt discombobulated—at war with myself about what to think of her.

As if on cue, the silver-haired warrior slowed to a halt in the doorway, catching her breath. "Mind explaining why you ran off like that?"

"I wanted to check on Ox," I said, keeping my eyes trained on the scuffed-up giant.

He beamed at me, and I gave him a quick kiss on the forehead before ruffling his auburn locks.

The bond mark stung, and I brought my hand across the top of my shoulder, rubbing it. All the more reason for me to stay away from Sloan.

Dru eyed me suspiciously, pulling a few vials from his shoulder strap. "Why don't we get you cleaned up a bit?"

My lips parted, but Sloan cut me off before I could decline. "Yes. Tend to her first. I'll stay with Ox."

"Of course." He led me out of the room and down the corridor. White puffs burst from his lips, both of us shivering as we neared the entryway. "Neve's resting, most likely asleep, but I have more supplies in her room. Come on."

We entered the frozen room and, as he had predicted, Neve was asleep, her brown skin less pallid than before.

"How is she doing?"

"Slowly recovering. She still isn't talking, sleeps most of the day, but that's to be expected. I can't imagine what she's been through." He stared down at his feet, running a hand through his dark brunette waves. "I should have listened to Kyleigh about helping her. If we had figured out a way—"

"Stop that, Dru. There's nothing you could have done." I moved in front of him and lifted his chin so he couldn't avert his eyes from mine. He needed to hear this. "You were right. There wasn't enough time. If you had spent any more of it in the dungeon trying to get the dragon out, you'd have been captured or killed. Kyleigh would have still needed to blast them to escape. Either way, the outcome's the same."

His lips flattened into a line. "You're right."

Well, that was probably painful for him to admit.

"You're the numbers man," I said, a small smile lifting the corners of my mouth. "What are the odds everyone would have made it out safely without harm?"

He didn't respond, instead pouring healing balm from his vials on a cloth and cleaning up my dirt-filled scrapes. I tried my best not to flinch as he swiped the medicine over my opened skin.

"Does she ever talk about what happened down there? With the guards?" I asked, voice softening.

He shook his head.

I placed a hand on his shoulder, patting it a few times, even though the sting in mine was almost unbearable.

Dru dabbed the cloth, getting more healing balm on it from the vial.

Using her newfound abilities to kill a few dozen guards was no small thing, and Kyleigh's silence about it had me concerned. It wasn't affecting her like it should, or she was suppressing it—either was a dangerous thought. "You should really talk to her about it. Aren't you worried?"

"Of course I am. How can you even ask me that?"

He lifted the cloth to the heart-shaped mark, and I snatched his wrist back, stopping him. "Don't."

"But it's obviously bothering you," he said, pushing my hand aside and placing the cloth on the mark again. "I know you prefer to do things on your own but let me do this."

Shaking my head, I nudged his arm. "There's nothing you can do for that one."

"What is it?" He squinted at it, moving his face closer to inspect the scar. "May I?" he asked, holding up his finger to touch it.

I nodded. I hadn't told anyone about the bond mark or the details of my deal with the Enchantress. Only Ox knew about it, and I only ever saw him the evenings he briefly visited us at the inn. I couldn't tell if the Queen was keeping him away on purpose or if he was avoiding us because he was ashamed of his demotion.

I'd never be able to repay him enough for sparing me and braving the consequences—not to mention the fact that he'd almost gotten himself killed today trying to stupidly save us.

Dru ran a finger over the mark. "Does it hurt when I touch it?"

"Not any more than it normally does when..."

"When what?"

I wasn't sure if I should tell him—mostly because I didn't want the Queen knowing about it. But Dru had never done anything to break my trust in him. If there was someone who could offer a solution to any problem, it was him.

"When the Enchantress summons me."

"What?" His eyes narrowed. "Explain. Now."

I told him everything about the Enchantress letting us go when we'd been trapped by her on our way to Inverno and that I now owed her a favor. A nameless favor, for the time being.

"She gave me this," I pointed to the bond mark. "And she's been making it hurt, I think to get me to return to the woods. It only seems to be getting worse."

"And you're saying everyone she has a deal with would have this mark?"

"Have you seen the Queen's bond mark?"

"I haven't."

"Sounds like I'm not the only one who's left out details. If they have a deal, she has to have a mark."

Dru mulled over my words a moment, hand gripping his chin. "You're right. I need to find out more. Is there anything else you've noticed?"

I didn't want him to think I was crazy, but if I wanted his help, he needed to know all of it—even if it didn't make sense. "I think she's been popping into my dreams."

"What do you mean?"

"Last night, I saw her in my dreams and..."

"And what?" Dru asked, placing a hand on my shoulder.

"She threatened me. Hurt me."

"And you're sure it wasn't a nightmare?"

"I'm sure."

"I need to know everything you can remember about your time with the Enchantress." Dru pressed a stud on his glove, and a paper and pencil emerged from his palm. "As well as anything you can recall about her cabin—any items she had—and the wisps."

DRU HAD A FULL PAGE OF SCRIBBLES JOTTED DOWN, A GARBLED mess of information I'd spewed at him over the last fifteen minutes. I wasn't used to confiding in someone, but I felt a small sense of relief having shared a bit of my burden with him.

"Is there something about the wisps you think can help us?" I asked him, noticing his follow-up questions focused on certain subjects more than others.

"I'm not sure, but anything we can learn is a solid lead toward eliminating the Enchantress."

"I know you want to help the Queen and Arafax, and of course protect Kyleigh, but this interest—the focus you've had with hours of being away and researching—there has to be more to it than that."

He stared down at his notes. "The night of The Blaze, my parents got my sisters and I to the edge of the woods before going back to help at the castle. My sisters were taken by the wisps—by the Enchantress. I still don't know exactly what happened to them."

I rested my hand on his. Having lost my family that same night, I would hate the thought that my brother was somehow in the Enchantress's clutches.

Dru continued. "All I know is that she has the answers in that cabin. More than what I'm currently working with at least. The Enchantress is too big of a threat to leave alone, but if my sisters are somehow still there, still able to be saved... I don't want to do anything reckless that would make it impossible to help them."

"Does Kyleigh know what you're working on?"

"She knows about my sisters, but I don't talk about too many specifics when it comes to my work for the Queen. Her mother's a touchy subject for her."

He picked up the vials, attaching them back to the row on his strap. "Promise you won't go back there without alerting me first?"

"I will"—*think about telling you.*

Dru scanned the bond mark one last time, then gently patted my shoulder. "Thank you for putting your trust in me."

Trust. Was this what that was?

"Don't thank me. Break this tether."

19

NEVE

I wiggled my toes, missing Mox's mass of fluff warming the bottom of my bed. He'd been one of the few sources of comfort for me over the last decade when I was held in Inverno's dungeon. Sloan had sent him off to keep tabs on Redmond's visits with the Enchantress. Apparently, the evil bitch's collection of shadow wisps had attacked Sir Fergus, who was being kept in a nearby room while they monitored his healing.

I'd spent the last week feigning sleep, privy to everyone's secrets.

It was shocking how much people divulged when they believed no one was listening. I guess it was easier to be vulnerable when you were alone, even if that aloneness was next to a comatose stranger.

Sloan came by about once a day, squeezing my hand, telling me repeatedly how sorry she was. She didn't know I was being held captive in the dungeon or about what the guards had been doing—as if those things weren't obvious to me. I was there, after all.

"What do I do, Neve?" she'd asked, voice more strained than usual. "Red wants me to stay here, to earn my spot back as commander, but I don't know what I want. He's not the man he once was."

One morning, she let something slip that shot fire through my veins. "Red's engaged to the Enchantress."

I'd had to school my face to keep from gritting my teeth, willing my ice to quell the fire coursing through me. She'd stilled a moment, watching, waiting...almost catching onto my awareness.

Almost.

In some ways, being in my dragon form would have been easier. Safer. All those years locked away in Inverno's dungeon, it felt like I was on the outside, watching every-thing, suspended above the scene as the guards tore into my flesh. I told myself that it wasn't me, pretended the abuse didn't take its toll, while they took and took from my dragon. From *me*.

They'd ripped away what they believed to be the most valuable part of me.

Ha.

My scales would grow back. My body would heal, one day wiping away all traces of their cruelty. But there was something even my scales, one of the strongest things in Celaria, couldn't protect. My most precious possession.

Something I'd never again let someone claim.

My heart.

I might be free from my cage, but I would lock that eter-nally damaged part of me away.

My love for Redmond had blinded me to what his father had been up to, costing me the last decade of my life. Costing Arafax

—the very people I'd sworn to protect as their Revered. Even if it had been unintentional, even if he had done it *for me*, it didn't negate the outcome. He'd decimated my kingdom, killing my friends and family, then held me captive the last ten years.

It was unforgivable.

Dru popped in, quickly checking my vitals and chatting on and on about Kyleigh.

The moment I saw her, I knew she was Isla's daughter. We had spoken about her so many times over the years. They had the same silver eyes, same fiery disposition when provoked. She reminded me so much of her mother at that age—before she'd been sold to the Halston elite as part of an alliance.

Then Isla told me yesterday that those same bastards tried to use her own daughter to come here. The last thing Celaria needed was those zealots finding a way in.

While it broke me to send Kyleigh away in those final moments in Inverno, she wouldn't have made it out alive otherwise.

I owed her for what she did to those guards.

I should have been around to help protect and nurture her. She was Isla's biggest secret. One I never even told Redmond about.

One of the many veiled lies between us over the years we were together.

"I'm in love with her," Dru admitted in a whisper, making me guess he hadn't shared that information with Kyleigh yet. I remembered being that way once. Young and foolishly full of hope.

Unfortunately, a heart like that never lasted in a world as harsh as this one.

There were always people who would take and take for themselves.

Like the Enchantress.

Everyone seemed to have a different score to settle with the evil, wing-wielding bitch. I'd do whatever it took to repay what she did to the people I loved. To me.

Some things just couldn't go unanswered.

My heart beat wildly in my chest, purpose driving me out from hiding within my psychological cocoon.

My eyes fluttered open.

This time for good.

20

KYLEIGH

I groaned, rolling out of bed and hobbling toward the door in the dim moonlight, still sore from the last few days of Sloan's training. I cursed under my breath at whoever had chosen to ruin a perfectly good night's sleep.

Turning the knob, I yawned. "What is so i—"

Gold-spun eyes peered at me through the cracked doorway. I smiled, gripping Dru's suspenders, greeting him with my lips, and savoring the rich coffee on his tongue. He pulled me closer, edging kisses along my neck, then stepped back, leaving my lips buzzing.

He adjusted himself before clearing his throat. "I'm sorry to wake you."

"Um, don't be sorry if you're gonna come here and kiss me like that." I moved into the frame of his arms, pressing my hips into his.

He groaned, looking pained, and gently kissed my forehead, combing back the wild strands of hair that clung to my face. "I came as soon as I could—"

"Is Ox doing worse? Did something happen?" I ushered

him into my room, grabbing clothes from my dresser. Sitting on the bed, I fed one foot through my black leggings.

The iron-rich stench that filled his room the first few days after his attack had kept me away, reminding me too much of the crimson-soaked walls of Inverno's dungeon. My stomach lurched at the thought.

"No, it's not that." Dru's voice was gravelly, eyes pinned to me, watching the material slide up my legs. His throat bobbed, encouraging me to take my time.

"Neve's awake," he said, a smile teasing the corners of his lips.

I sighed, relieved and thankful for some good news, and tugged on a cream-colored sweater before lacing up my crimson shoes. "How is she?"

"Aware." He grinned wider, running a hand through his brown waves. "I've spent the last few hours asking her questions. Learning about your dragon magic."

The knots in my chest unraveled. Maybe now that Neve was awake, I'd be able to understand my new abilities. The sooner I mastered them, the sooner I wouldn't need to be hidden away from the Enchantress and the rest of Celaria. Then, maybe I'd actually get some real time with my mother before returning to my dad in Vermont.

Each day felt like such a wasted opportunity with her. Would she feel like less of a stranger to me when this was all over with?

"That's amazing, Dru," I said, clasping my hands behind his back, resting them at the valley of his spine. Peering up at him, I bit my lip. "Did you come all the way here just to share that news or was there something else you wanted from me?"

"I always want when it comes to you." He squeezed me

tightly against him, kissing me deeply. "But that's not why I'm here."

I held him by his straps in protest, and he grumbled to himself, too low for me to hear. Gently taking my hands, he lifted them to his lips before brushing back more of my bedhead. "I came because she asked for you."

<hr>

I WAS EXCITED AND NERVOUS TO FINALLY TALK TO NEVE—THE woman behind the scaled friend I'd made during some of my darkest days in Inverno's frigid dungeon.

"Dru mentioned you wanted to see me?"

I shivered as I padded into the dimly lit room. The night breeze beat against the sheer, white curtains, the scent of pine clinging to everything. I drank in the rich velvet sky, the icicles along the balustrade slowly dripping into small puddles on the balcony.

"I did." Her tone was hoarse, like it'd been scraped raw. It was so strange to hear her voice for the first time.

Her hand grazed her throat, and she gave a small cough. "Still getting my voice back. Come sit."

I moved to the side of the bed, brushing off a few snowflakes scattered on the comforter before scooting next to her and grasping her outstretched hands. Running my thumbs over her deep brown skin, I noted how soft and pliable it was—nothing like the sapphire scales she wore in her other form. Tight brunette curls nestled close to her head, and rich, illuminated caramel irises stared back at me. She was absolutely stunning.

"Thank you for everything you did to try to save me when we were in Inverno." The amber pools of her eyes pulled me, every word she rasped drenched with sincerity. Despite looking completely different in her human form, the feelings I had being around her were the same.

"But I wasn't able to." My voice sounded brittle, hollow, my mind recalling the night I'd been trying to forget. Blasting the guards was my last attempt to get her out and I couldn't even make it count. The effort took too much out of me to save her.

I failed her.

I failed myself.

Now people were dead because of my decision. Some of them, I didn't lose a wink of sleep over. Others, ones I'd never know, haunted my dreams.

"Look at me, Kyleigh." Neve hooked a gentle finger under my chin, aiming my attention at her. "I'm *here*. Back in my human form after living over a decade without it. Something I never hoped for before you and your friends found yourselves locked away in the dungeon. I thought I'd die there, no one ever knowing who I truly was. I probably would have without your help."

She had a point, but pretty words and breathing belief into a thought were two very different things. I didn't want to regret what I'd done. I wanted to believe it was necessary. Necessary to save the dragon that was trapped. Necessary for Dru and I to escape. But even if it was, there were people grieving because of my actions.

My intentions had been good, but the road to good intentions led—

"Stop."

Can she read my mind?

"I spent the last ten years locked away in that cell, only having my regrets for company. I won't let them define my future and neither should you. Besides, you're my goddaughter. My first act as your godmother is to repay the favor by helping you with your dragon."

I scanned the room quickly, making sure we were alone, since she'd just laid claim to her relation to me. "Did the Queen—" I lowered my voice, "My mother, did she tell you?"

"Oh, Kyleigh, as soon as I saw your eyes I knew." Neve laughed. Her smile was contagious, and I found my lips parting into one of my own. "You've only just discovered me, but I've known you your whole life."

"How is that possible?" I asked, in shock at her admission.

"Your mother, of course. We communicated for years through the corium portal stones. We had a regular time to chat each month, so we could update each other. I was her link to what went on in Celaria, and she told me all about her life in the Otherworld."

"You're the contact that stopped talking to her after The Blaze? The one that made her decide to come back."

"I am. Though I would have never told her to leave you behind to come back here," she said, eyes pleading. "Please know that."

She braced herself using the headboard to pull up to a seated position in the bed. "So, I'm sure you're curious as to why I called you here tonight."

I propped the pillow behind her back, grabbing a glass of water from the nightstand and handing it to her. "I am."

The once raspy tone to her voice was now threaded with a low, firm element. "I know from speaking with Dru earlier that everyone here is working toward getting rid of the Enchantress. I can help."

"You literally just woke up." She needed to rest. We'd only seen a few weeks of what had taken place the last ten years.

There was a lot of healing ahead of her. "Besides, we aren't ready."

I still couldn't summon my dragon, and while my elemental powers had gotten stronger, they were no match for going up against the evil sorceress.

Neve swung her legs over the side of the bed, tentatively putting weight on her feet. I grabbed her arm and brought it around me to give her some extra support as she stood. She rolled her ankles before prompting me to walk with her around the room, dragging her feet with each step. "I can help you stop pushing away your dragon."

"Pushing it away?" Neve gestured toward the built-in balcony, and I walked her over there slowly. "I have been trying to think of how to summon it. What am I doing wrong?"

"Our dragons come forth when we are truly ready for them. There's no special skill needed to summon dragon magic, it's as much a part of us as blood and bone once you receive the gift."

"What was it like when you got yours?"

"Shocking. My grandfather was a dragon. I had no idea at the time, of course. It was a deeply held secret that only he and my grandmother, his champion, knew about. When I became of magic age at fifteen, I got my ice and water abilities along with my dragon. Luckily, your aunt understood what was happening since she was one. She was able to help me along with Aislin's mother. Having those who had been through it to guide me was everything."

"I'm glad you're here." I truly was. While I didn't know Neve that well—I'd only just met her *technically*—I felt like I could trust her.

"Me too," she said, placing her hand on top of mine.

"What do I need to do?"

"There's a reason why your dragon refuses to reveal itself to you." She looked out at the mountains in the distance. "And the one responsible for that is you."

"Well, if I knew how to get my dragon to reveal itself, I would do it. Wouldn't I?"

She cocked her head. "I don't know, you tell me."

I silently watched the moon illuminate, pinks and purples streaking the sky. "When can we start?"

"I requested the Queen let me train you and Aislin after your lessons today," Neve said. "Have a good session with Sloan first. She'll make a warrior out of you in no time."

"Ha! We'll see about that." I chuckled. "Looking forward to our lesson later."

It was a lie.

At least a partial one.

While I was glad to have Neve here, safe and back in her human form, now I had no reason not to be able to summon my dragon. Honestly, deep down, I'd already known the truth before Neve spoke it.

It *was* my fault I hadn't been able to shift yet.

21

AISLIN

I searched for Kyleigh all around The Lavender, only finding Flynt skulking down the hallway, a few new splatters of blood decorating his coat. He smiled, a glimpse of chewing tobacco peeking from his gums. "Miss me around here last night?"

"What were you up to?"

"Wouldn't you like to know." He pulled out the key to his room. "Just because you've got some in with the Queen now doesn't mean the *work* stops."

The kills.

The thought made my chest go tight, heart hammering against my ribs.

"Must be nice not needing to earn your keep anymore," he sneered, pushing open the door to his room and stepping in.

I wanted to tell him to fuck himself, but I just shrugged and padded down the staircase. I made my way into the empty pub, spotting Sweeney sitting at the window seat, reading a book. Steam rose from the cup on the small table next to him, the bitter, glorious scent of coffee filling the space.

"Whatcha reading?" I asked, giving him a kiss on the forehead.

He smiled up at me. "A book about pirates, gods, and magic."

"Sounds interesting."

"You know I'm a sucker for a good love story."

He was. Since I'd known him, Sweeney had blown through hundreds of stories where love won against all odds. I made fun of him often for it. Love seemed like such a luxury for someone who spent her days following marks, ending them with one voltaic touch.

Besides, I'd seen the pain and suffering that came along with it. Love meant building a connection with someone that was too precious, too valuable, to lose. For me, the eventual trip wasn't worth the short-term buzz. But Sweeney, he always believed in it, romanticizing true love and destiny—probably from all the books he read.

He smirked, cocking his head to the side, like he'd already spotted the question begging to leap off my tongue. "What's on your mind?"

"In all my years here, I've never seen you with someone long term."

Sure, a few travelers, men from town, and occasionally one of the handsome amors who lived upstairs, but nothing romantic. For someone seemingly infatuated with the concept of love, it was strange.

"And?"

"You're such a romantic," I teased, before bringing my voice lower, "but...have you ever been in love?"

He sat there a moment, looking stunned. Probably

because it wasn't a subject I ever brought up without something snarky to say.

"It's a bit early in the morning to ask that question without providing some liquid mettle." He laughed.

Carrying his mug to the bar, he grabbed a handle of whiskey from behind the counter and poured some into his coffee. He took a few long sips before setting the bottle down. "Why do you ask?"

"No reason." I didn't even really know why, but ever since Sloan had closed that gap between us, breaching the wall I'd so carefully constructed, I couldn't stop thinking about her.

The way her eyes captured me, luring my attention away from the wisps. The press of her curves bending with mine. The taste of her lips.

I needed to stop thinking about that damn kiss.

"Um...I just realized I never asked."

"I was in love once."

"Who was he?"

"His name was Pierce. He was a royal guard working at the castle. An earth wielder." Sweeney took a deep breath, then smiled with his eyes shut, like he could somehow inhale the memory of him. "I haven't spoken his name in a very long time."

"I've never met an earth wielder." There weren't a ton of wielders left in Arafax, and earth manipulation was a rarity, like my lightning.

"There haven't been any since The Blaze, but they were coveted for their ability to manipulate rock, trees, the ground. A group of them held enough force to move a mountain. Many helped build the realm."

"What happened to Pierce?"

His smile faltered.

"I never saw him again after The Blaze. He had taken some kids through the woods to try to get them to safety." Tears welled in his eyes, and I grabbed a napkin from the counter, handing it to him. He dabbed his lids, then put the napkin down, placing a hand on mine. "I was actually out looking for him when I found you."

A knot sank deep into the pit of my stomach. "I'm so sorry, Sweeney." If he hadn't been looking for Pierce, what would have happened to me after The Blaze?

"I am too. But when I saw you there, hiding in the woods, all alone, it felt like a sign."

I popped up enough to give him another peck on the forehead. As much as I resented the things I'd had to do for Flynt over the years, Sweeney had given me another chance at a family after I'd lost mine.

"We were together for six beautiful years. It broke me to lose him during The Blaze, but it taught me an important lesson."

"Which was?" It was hard to think of The Blaze cultivating anything positive. It had devastated Arafax and its people—most of our population wiped away, homes and businesses gone, families ripped apart. With the gem stolen, the few people left didn't have enough manpower to rebuild. We were only starting to see the beginnings of that now since its return.

"It taught me to be grateful for every memory. Even the tiniest fragments. Waking up early to read in bed or walking to the market together. The small moments are the ones that stick with you. The ones you end up missing most." His voice was hushed, cracked like how I imagined he felt on the inside. "I wouldn't trade them for anything."

Regret swept through me at bringing up a topic that had

dampened the mood. The last thing I had wanted to do was make Sweeney relive something painful. "Would you fall in love again if the right person came around? Even after all the hurt?"

"Of course. Nothing is guaranteed in this world or the next." He walked to the windowsill, placing his whiskied coffee on the table and sitting back down on the window seat, propping his feet up on a nearby chair. "I don't know if I'll ever have that kind of opportunity for a great love again. Pierce was my heart. But if the world is willing to place love in your path, it's always worth the sacrifice."

"Did you know right away?" I asked, unable to stop myself. "With Pierce?"

"I don't think that's possible. You can have that initial spark of attraction, but that's usually just passion and lust pushing you." He smirked, waggling his eyebrows. "Love is more like a steady breeze that forces you to collide, lifting you both up."

I raised a brow, unsure if I believed anything he was saying but still too intrigued to stop myself. "What if it doesn't lift you *both* up? What if it drags one of you down?"

"Then, my dear, it's not real love," Sweeney replied, shaking his head.

That's all I needed to hear. "I'm going to go make myself some grub before another long day."

He shook his head at my change of subject before nodding toward the kitchen. "Help yourself."

C*RACK.*

Yellow slid down the side of the metal pan, the gooey egg

pooling in the middle. The scent of buttery goodness wafted through the kitchen, and my stomach rumbled, ready to inhale my breakfast. I added some salt and pepper, whipping the mushrooms, yolks, and egg whites before tossing around the scramble.

"Cooking me breakfast already? How quickly things have escalated." Sloan's silky voice trailed through the kitchen, startling me, and I dropped the spatula into the hot pan.

Without thinking, I scooped it up, burning the tips of my fingers in the process. "Fuck!"

I shook out their sting, scrambling over to the sink and running them under the water. Sloan followed, grabbing my hands to inspect them herself before I shot out some small bolts to get her to back off.

"What are you doing here?" I grumbled.

She crossed her arms, pinching her pale brows together. "You're supposed to be in the arena for sparring lessons in five minutes. So, I think the real question is what are *you* doing here?"

I wiped my hands on my pants, inspecting the pink of where they had hit against the pan. It didn't look like it would leave any lasting marks, thankfully. I spooned the eggs on a plate, leaning back against one of the prep tables as I began eating. "What does it look like I'm doing?"

"It looks like you're about to sit down for a leisurely breakfast."

"Well, technically, I'm standing," I said, nodding toward the exit. "Head on back to the fort and I'll get there when I get there."

She headed over to the kitchen door and opened it, holding it until I re-entered the pub. "You know what I think?"

Lifting the piece of toast to my mouth, I took my time devouring my breakfast, ignoring her. She continued, undeterred. "I think you were trying to skip sparring lessons."

"Why would I do that?" I asked, giving my most innocent tone and acting appalled between mouthfuls.

Sloan ripped the now empty plate from the counter before I grabbed it and used dish washing as another distraction. "Because you're freaked out about what happened the other day?"

"I am not freaked out," I said, letting my smugness coat every word. "In case you forgot, I was right next to you, rescuing Ox from the wisps. Don't I get some extra days off for my stellar display?"

"You'll get some extra days off when the Enchantress is no longer a threat," she replied, pointing toward The Lavender's doorway, frost coating her words.

Sweeney was pretending to be distracted by his book.

Nosey jerk.

I followed her, looping under her arm with my arms crossed to avoid accidentally bumping into her when she held the door exiting The Lavender. Sweeney gave me a silent wave goodbye, and I shot him a glare.

"Look, Sloan, I understand that we are mixed up in this strange alliance between our kingdoms, but at the end of the day we are enemies. Beyond enemies. Your king is responsible for ruining my life. My family is dead because of him. Because of the territory you serve."

Her gaze lingered over me a long moment before drawing back up to meet mine. "I know what the history is between our kingdoms, but we don't have to be enemies." She firmly brushed silver strands behind the shell of her ear. "I'd like to at least be friends."

"At least?"

"Maybe I got it wrong, but I thought there was something between us," she said softly, voice just above a whisper. "I'd hoped maybe while I was here—"

"Nothing to be hopeful about," I snapped. "We'll never be on the same side, Sloan. Even if *your* king and *my* queen want to play pretend. I don't want anything more than to just get through this farce and get the Enchantress out of our lives permanently."

"Some of that may be true, but I don't believe you mean all of it."

I hated that she was right. That I wanted things I had no right to want. I needed to keep my walls up. To make those barriers endure. Because if I let them crumble, if I crossed those delicate boundaries again, I didn't think I'd be able to draw them back up.

"You don't know the first thing about me, Sloan."

The fort came into view, and we maneuvered around the workers repairing the outside. As the path narrowed, Sloan held out an arm, gesturing for me to go first. "You forget that it's been my job to know everything, Aislin. Especially the things my *opponent* thinks they can keep hidden away."

"At least you're finally admitting we are opponents." I walked past, refusing to glance at the striking woman beside me. "You think you've got me all figured out, Sloan? Let's hear it."

"I know you've lived here since after The Blaze and losing your family. You spent years working for Flynt, dealing out death for him. You were sent by the Queen to get the gem and assassinate Redmond—"

"*Wow*, you've got it *all* figured out," I scoffed, turning to her to give a slow applause. "People are more than just facts. You know that, right?"

She pushed me into the stone wall lining the outside of the arena, her hands clutching the sides of my leather jacket. "I'm not finished."

My eyes darted around, wondering if anyone was watching. Meanwhile, Kyleigh was probably already in the arena pissed that we were late for lessons this morning. I moved to turn my head, but Sloan gripped my chin, dragging my attention back to her icy stare.

She leaned toward me, her face mere inches from mine, her voice a silvery whisper in my ear. "You made sure your friends could escape safely when you held back my men. You were willing to face the Queen's wrath after deciding to spare Redmond. You traded yourself for Ox's safety in the Silent Woods. Despite all the killing you've had to do, Aislin, you're not a killer. Deep down, under that brash exterior, you care."

I didn't respond, trying not to pay attention to the feel of her breath on my neck.

She pulled her face away and let go of me, stepping a few feet back. I stayed pressed against the stone, too afraid of my traitorous heart to move. "When we met, you had the ability to kill me in an instant. We both know that you could have electrified me. You *chose* not to, even against someone dressed as your enemy."

I shot lightning into the ground, exploding dirt all over the bottom half of her white tank. "What happened—the kiss —it can't happen again. Drink some booze. Enjoy an amor on me. Whatever you need to do to erase it from your memory. It'll be better for the both of us."

"You don't mean that," Sloan said, brushing the brown

flecks away. Using her boot, she filled the holes I'd made in the ground. "If I thought what was going on between us was simply erasable, I would."

She reached out, stepping closer before she trailed a palm over my hip, up toward the cup of my breast, following the curve of my dragon marks, freezing me in place. My vision sharpened, a tingling behind my eyes, and my breath caught, her touch sending electrified chills along my skin that coiled deep in my core.

Her pale eyes were wide, reflecting my shifted ones back to me.

I wanted to lean into her. To give in to this incessant thrum between us.

Instead, I gripped her wrist, blinking away the magic amplifying my vision, pulling her hand off me.

"You think I'm a kind person, Sloan? Think you know me so well? Then please realize I'm trying to do you a kindness."

I stuck my hand up, letting lightning crawl along it before she could come closer.

A warning.

"Nothing more can come of this."

Sloan began to walk away, arms tight at her sides.

Maybe she did realize.

"This isn't the end of this conversation," she called over her shoulder.

Maybe not.

"Get your ass to the arena in the next five minutes. I'm going to grab Kyleigh," she commanded, eyes on the fort. "Sparring lessons have nothing to do with whatever's going on between us."

"There is no *us*," I said, striking every syllable with calm precision.

She chuckled to herself, turning to me as she walked backward with no less confidence. "Some things are inevitable, Aislin."

Didn't I know it.

What she didn't realize was that I had something else that was more inevitable than my attraction to her. The best thing she could do was stay away.

I slipped my flask out of my pocket, taking a few long sips to help numb the sear pulsing from my mark—more painful and persistent than ever.

22

KYLEIGH

The more I practiced, the more my dragon eluded me.

After over a month of training with Neve, I was still no closer to summoning my dragon magic. I worked with her every day, even on the days we didn't have scheduled lessons. The most I had been able to do was get my wing buds to pop out. That didn't seem like it would be too useful against the Enchantress.

Dru sat in on our sessions, taking notes, absorbing as much as he could about our magic. He hoped to recreate some texts for future generations to have.

I sat, legs crossed, in the middle of the arena, looking like a yogi, trying another one of Neve's visualization techniques. This time, I was supposed to find the creature in my mind. Considering how all the other attempts had gone, I didn't have much hope it would work.

The problem with trying to envision my dragon was that I had no idea what it looked like. Did it have pointy scales? A rough snout? Massive claws? The only dragon I had ever seen was Neve's, and she was beautiful, somehow lithe, even in her beastly form. I doubted mine would have that much finesse.

"You should be able to see your dragon in your mind."

I huffed, scrunching my lids tight. "Still nothing."

"Take some deep breaths," Neve guided, always way more patient than I could ever be. Her voice was now becoming silvery, its former raspiness disappearing more with each passing day.

I inhaled, counting to four before I held for another four and then released for eight—repeating over and over until my face felt like it would tingle right off.

My shoulders bunched, hunching forward, and I rolled them back a few times in an effort to shake off my frustration. "It's not happening."

"Let's try something different," Neve said, sitting down in front of me.

Aislin stood at the edge of the arena, majestic, violet wings streaked with thick, black veins dragging on the ground behind her while she tried flexing and arching her back to get them to lift. Envy flared in my chest, only slightly sated by the fact that she struggled.

"I've almost got these bitches under control," Aislin heaved, squinting and taking a few steps forward. The wings brushed against the dirt, coating the bottoms of them. Squeezing her arms and back, every muscle up through her jaw tensed as she hoisted them off the arena floor, making it a handful of paces before crumpling to her knees. Her wings hung limp over her shoulders, chest surging with each gasp.

"Fuckers," she muttered, wincing, folding them back before they disappeared completely. "One day I'm going to figure this out."

Neve gave her an encouraging smile. "You are so close, Aislin. It's much easier when you are in your dragon form. Your body isn't truly built to accommodate them." She waved over the wing-wielding brunette. "Come here a minute. I think we can work together to help you both with your dragon magic."

Yes, please come help Kyleigh who's made zero progress despite working with me every day.

I tried not to be jealous. I was happy for Aislin, really. Seeing her wings at least gave me hope that I'd be able to do more someday.

Aislin padded over, stretching out her neck, then settled in the space between Neve and I so that we made a small circle. I peered up at Dru chatting with my mother who'd decided to make an appearance. They looked to be glancing over some of his notes. She hadn't been attending our sessions lately, and the times I had asked to visit her chambers, her guards claimed she wasn't seeing anyone. I was still nothing more than her special guest—an elevated peasant—so I kept my distance.

Maybe I'd misread the situation, but I thought she'd wanted to repair things between us.

Cowering in her fort seemed like an uncharacteristic choice for her. But what did I know about the person who'd raised me over a decade ago? It would probably be better to let go of the memory of someone that didn't exist, at least not anymore. It only clouded my perception of the woman that seemed to be abandoning me all over again.

"Hold hands," Neve said, reaching out to Aislin and I. "Since our dragons are connected, I'm wondering if envisioning mine will help summon yours."

"At this point I'll try anything."

I grabbed their hands and closed my eyes, taking a few deep breaths. My vision blurred, becoming opaque, as I pushed any external thoughts from my mind.

After a few minutes, a blue figure appeared in the distance. Neve's dragon. It was too far to see clearly, but my mind just knew, the sapphire creature now a permanent fixture in my memory.

"Aislin, since you've already summoned your wings, picture those for now. Let's try to get the rest of your dragon into view."

I couldn't see what was happening, but the blue, blurry shape was moving around. Aislin's hand squeeze mine, breath catching. "I can see your dragon, Neve. It's found mine."

"What does your dragon look like?" I asked.

"Purple and black with a pearlescent belly," Aislin replied, tone cocky enough that I was certain she was smirking. "Badass."

Trying to focus on my happiness for her and not the fact that I was a failure once again, I kept my attention on the sapphire dragon who'd now started moving with a purple pal tagging along.

Neve's voice pulsed through my ears, "Time to find yours, Kyleigh."

"Okay," I wavered.

Please let this work.

If I could just see it, then I would know what to picture in my mind as I tried to make the shift. That was better than the big nothing I was currently working with.

A peach egg shape sat in the distance behind the pair of dragons, and I squinted, trying to figure out what I was looking at. It didn't make sense, but I felt a connection to the orb.

Neve and Aislin's dragons disappeared from view, the once opaque backdrop morphing into something stony and familiar. Red painted the walls, chunks of flesh slowly sliding down them, plopping into bloody puddles on the floor.

The dungeon.

Dizziness swept through me, chased by the urge to throw up. I tried to let go of Aislin's and Neve's hands to cover my mouth, but they both gripped harder.

"No," Neve urged. "You must face what is holding you back."

"I don't want to." My hands quivered, and I clenched them tight, accidently punching crescents into their flesh, trying to suppress my rising panic. "I want to get out of here."

Neve and Aislin gripped my hands before I could pull them away, tethering me to the vision. To the memory.

"We've got you," Aislin said, offering me a morsel of reassurance.

So much blood.

The smeared walls were closing in. Pressing down on my chest. Burning behind my eyes.

Focus, Ky.

I brought my attention back to the egg shape I'd seen before, realizing it wasn't an egg at all.

A pair of coral-and-pink watercolor wings with red veiny branches bursting from their buds had curled around the rest of my dragon's body, cocooning it from view. Protecting it. I sensed its fear, trapped in the memory I'd fought so hard to keep hidden away where I didn't have to acknowledge its desire to replay over and over, sawing at my shredded sanity.

And suddenly I understood the reason I couldn't summon the beast within.

I'd spent so much of my time in fear, defending myself when I arrived in Celaria—but that night, I'd become something others feared. What if that was only the beginning? If I had been able to do all that without stable power, what if my dragon gave me even more power? If I unleashed it, who would be in control? Me, or the beast within?

I let a few sparks fly from my hands, causing Neve and Aislin to release them. Curling into a ball, I sobbed and sobbed until tears refused to come. A hand ran gently down my spine, the comforting scent of leather and coffee grounding me.

I knew what I needed to do, but could I accept what I'd done?

I'd killed those people.

How could I forgive myself for the blood on my hands?

What if this dragon made me a monster—a bigger danger to those around me?

Was I willing to risk myself, and possibly those I cared about, to access its magic?

23

KYLEIGH

"So, you wanted to talk with me?" Neve asked, pouring us faerie wine in a set of gold chalices on her bedside table.

The ice and snow that once coated her room were nearly gone, only a slight chill from the breeze making me shiver. Sheer, white curtains swayed out into the open balcony like a pair of wandering ghosts. In the distance, the Grymm Mountains stood in their rocky, gray glory, snow covering their tips, kissed by the last bit of iridescent light rippling from the day's moon before it shifted into dusk.

Neve braced herself on the end table, and she winced, arms wobbling.

"Do you need to lay down?" I asked, nodding toward the bed. She still wasn't fully recovered, but each day I saw her she stood longer, grew stronger.

"No, I'm okay. Trying to give my two legs some extra work. I may go out flying later." She took a few ginger steps, crossing over to the other side of the room.

"You go out flying?"

Smiling, she walked back toward me before taking a sip of her wine. "Yes. Sometimes I go out to an old favorite spot of mine. I wait until dark, though, so I don't draw too much attention. We still aren't sure who can be trusted."

I swirled the crimson liquid in my chalice before bringing it to my lips, savoring the scent of dark cherries and pomegranate with a gravelly undercurrent—the taste sweet and equally gritty. "Why would anyone help the Enchantress?"

Neve sighed. "People don't *want* to help her, but she can be incredibly persuasive. She finds ways to manipulate them to do her bidding. Her deals give her power, and power is what she craves most."

"Have you met her before?"

Her jaw clenched. Taking a hand to her cheek, she massaged her face. "Promise me something."

"What?" I held my breath.

She moved her hand to mine, pausing there, tone firm. "Promise you'll never make a deal with her."

"I promise," I agreed. Like it was even a question. I wouldn't be that stupid after everything my mother's deal had done to both myself and my dad. "Would having a champion better our chances against her?"

She took a long swig of wine then grabbed the bottle, refilling her chalice. "It would."

Bringing my cup up to my lips, I drained its contents, then shoved it out for Neve to refill, but quickly changed my mind, setting the cup down. This topic was not the kind meant for polite cupfuls. I extended my open hand, grasped the bottle of liquid courage, then took an indelicate swig. "Dru's been avoiding the subject."

"Is there something you'd like to know?" she asked, raising an eyebrow.

"Yes." I sat on the bed, gulping down more wine before kicking off my sneakers and laying back. The peppery aftertaste was becoming more pronounced with each sip from the bottle. Neve made her way to the other side, setting her chalice on the night table and climbing next to me. "Why didn't you tell Redmond what you were? Why didn't you make him your champion all those years ago if it would have made you stronger?"

"That's...complicated. He was the prince to our rival kingdom. Though they weren't enemies then, relations were still...tense." She stared up at the ceiling, legs crossed and hands wringing together. "I had to keep my identity a secret. Not even our own people knew who the dragon shifters truly were, and that information in the wrong hands would have been crippling to Arafax."

"But how did you keep a secret like that from him?" I asked, realizing the bottle of wine was almost empty and I felt nowhere near the end of my questions.

"I hated lying." She heaved a long sigh, reaching for her wine. "I was in love with Redmond, but I had a duty to Arafax as one of its Revered."

I still didn't understand. If she loved him, how could she keep such a big secret from him? If my duty to Arafax meant lying to those I loved, I didn't want it. Not that I was planning to stay anyway. "You were a few days from marrying him, though. Wouldn't the truth have come out eventually when you were his queen?"

"His father, King Reynard, wasn't trustworthy. Our king, your grandfather, had decided that I could tell Redmond, and Redmond alone, after we wed. I'd planned to tell him on our wedding night and ask him to be my champion."

"You would have made our enemy your champion?"

"Redmond wasn't our enemy," Neve said, turning on her side to face me. "We believed in a united Celaria. Our marriage would've been a symbol of that by uniting the land's two largest territories, if it had ever come to pass."

I sat the bottle of faerie wine on the night table next to me, its contents sloshing around the emerald glass. "Would you have still made him your champion if he had no power of his own to wield?"

"Are you asking because of Dru?"

"I am." I trusted Dru. Trusted him with my power and my heart. But the way he held back from me... I couldn't tell if that trust was returned. Maybe he still saw me as a monster? Maybe my powers scared him too much to be tied to them, and me, forever.

I wanted him to be my champion, but the fear of rejection terrified me. Pressure built behind my eyes, but I held back the tears demanding release. What if he saw the real me—messy and raw—and didn't want me back?

"It wouldn't have mattered to me. It's not about the power that the champion brings, it's more the combined force they create. There must be a level of trust between a dragon and their champion. That's what matters most—that you trust and make each other stronger through the bond."

Neve sighed. "Honestly, it would have never worked with Redmond as my champion. Too many things between us were coated in lies. That's no way to forge a bond."

"Do you think you'll ever choose a champion? Once you heal, that is."

"I'm not sure. It would probably be smart in terms of taking on the Enchantress, but the idea of tying myself to someone after everything that's happened..."

She shrugged, running a hand along my cheek and

tucking some strands of hair behind my ear. It felt strange to be nurtured like this, in this maternal way, while my real mother hid away, cold and isolated. "Are you concerned about making Dru your champion?"

"No. But he's been weird about it, and I'm not sure why. I think it's because he's seen what my powers can do." I let the tears fall, landing in scattered drops on the pillow. Neve covered her thumb with the sleeve of her shirt, wiping away the tracks still clinging to my cheeks. I hated crying in front of people but coming to Celaria had opened the floodgates and I couldn't seem to keep the dam from breaking. "I'm afraid he doesn't want to be bonded to me because of it. When the subject came up, he was cagey."

"Do you want me to talk to him?" Neve asked.

It was a genuine offer, but I needed to stop hiding from the truth. "No, I think this is one conversation I need to have with him on my own."

We could keep avoiding this discussion, veil it with pretty words and kind gestures, but under the surface, a harsh truth would always exist. I didn't even know what Dru's truth was because I had been too afraid to find out. But never asking him wouldn't change things, it only prolonged this awkward dance we were doing around it.

Luckily, the wine was working its magic, and I felt braver than I had in ages. "Actually, there is something else you can help me with."

Neve didn't miss a beat. "Anything."

"Can I hitch a ride?"

24

DRU

Leaning back in my chair, I closed my eyes and yawned, stretching my arms out wide. When I opened them, I found a large golden orb staring at me. I fell out of my chair, stumbling to get back up, watching the dragon hover outside the window. The flap of its iridescent-sapphire wings sent papers flying from my desk, littering the floor.

As she flew closer, the light of the room cast a spotlight on Kyleigh gripping just above Neve's wings, beaming at me. "I'm breaking you out of here!" She laughed, looking lighter than I'd seen her in weeks, her blonde and coral hair flying wildly behind her. "Neve is going out tonight, and I figured it'd be fun to catch a ride."

A ride on an actual dragon? I had grown up seeing people on the backs of dragons, most notably the champions, but I'd never had the opportunity to do it myself. My pulse raced, and I sprang off the floor, curiosity brimming.

I took a deep breath, glancing around at the scattered papers strewn on the floor. "Just give me a second." I scrambled around, collecting them up and stacking them haphazardly, then scribbled out a note on my desk in case the Queen came by.

Neve maneuvered closer to the window, making shallower strokes with her wings, and I threaded one foot over the windowsill, avoiding looking down as I swung my other leg out. I grabbed Kyleigh's outstretched hand, and she pulled me on behind her.

Once I settled in, hugging Kyleigh's waist, I ran a hand along the dragon's glossy, iridescent-sapphire scales. The ridges were surprisingly rough, making it easier to grip. She took off, leaving me awestruck. It was fascinating the way her scales oscillated, the small crevices between them expanding and retreating as her wings pushed against the wind.

She seemed so strong, soaring comfortably against the night sky. I was still wrapping my head around the fact that this dragon was also the woman I had come to know—one I'd helped nurture back to health. Down by my foot I could see the patch where scales had been removed, new scales beginning to grow in their place.

"Where are we going?" I asked.

Looking over her shoulder, Kyleigh responded with a shrug. "I'm not sure."

The sky was nearly black, only a hint of purple tinging its hue, the moon a waning crescent surrounded by blinking stars. I couldn't see too well ahead of us. I didn't think Neve would take us to Inverno, but we were headed in that direction, according to the compass on my glove.

As we drew closer to the rocky tops of the Grymm Mountains, Neve tipped her snout forward, taking a steep dive, plummeting toward the ground.

Kyleigh let out a surprised shriek, and I swore I heard the sapphire dragon huff out what sounded like a chuckle before stalling midair. We hovered over a small cliff leading to a darkened cave. Fluorescent plants covered its mouth, illuminating a ledge for us to land on. Neve halted before stepping onto the cliff, then lowered herself to let us off her back.

Glowing fauna sprouted from the cave's rocky walls, the various shades of bioluminescent greens and blues calling to us like a beacon. Odd neon flowers burst to life, opening against their pitch backdrop, a distant hum coming from within the expanse.

What section of the mountains are we in?

Tiny whispers echoed from the cave, and Neve sauntered over, laying down, blocking its dark opening as if in warning, watching us.

Kyleigh grasped my hands, her silver eyes staring into mine, their glow stark against the darkness surrounding us.

"What are we doing here?" I asked her, brows bent in confusion between the strange scenery and late-night flight.

"I wanted to talk to you about something important, away from the fort and everyone there."

I took her in my arms, inhaling the sweet scent of cinnamon. "What is it?"

She kissed my cheek before tracing her lips up to the shell of my ear. "First, I need you to close your eyes."

I shuddered, my breath catching at her tone, and I obeyed, drawing my lids closed.

Kyleigh took a few steps away from me and then I heard clothes rustling.

What's going on?

I peeled open one eye to discover she was naked, stunning me with her beauty—I hadn't seen her disrobed since our time at Renovo Falls, not that I could ever forget it. Every facet of her was etched into the recesses of my mind.

"No peeking!" she blurted out, half laughing.

"Okay." I squeezed my eyes tight, hands clenched at my sides. It took all my willpower not to open them, knowing I was missing moments of her being alluringly bare before me. All I heard was the wind whipping around us and her feet plodding away from me, followed by a long exhale.

"Whatever you hear next, promise me you'll keep your eyes shut." Her voice sounded small, strained, but with a hint of determination I couldn't help but admire.

However, I didn't love what her warning implied.

She cleared her throat, reminding me that she was waiting for an answer.

"I promise."

I focused on my breaths, squeezing my eyes tighter, resisting the urge to open them. Silence hung like a heavy blanket in the air. Everything felt still.

Too still.

A scream ripped through the breeze, and my eyes snapped open.

25

KYLEIGH

Prickling heat barreled through my limbs, shooting out from my core.

Blood seeped down the stone walls, pooling at my feet, dripping down the staircase.

Blue chiffon clung to my body. Chunks of flesh, rust-colored smears, and bits of armor stained the skirt of my dress.

I was back in Inverno's dungeon.

Ahead of me, where the guards once stood, was a water-color oval—my coral-and-peach dragon in its perfectly constructed cocoon.

My eyes stung, watering as I unclenched them to check on Dru.

His eyes were shut, his hands gripping his sides, muscles bunched, like he was forcing himself to be still.

I shut my eyes again.

Only I could move myself forward.

It is time.

Looking down at the crimson-smeared steps, I slowly

descended the staircase toward my dragon. As the distance between us lessened, I heaved deep breaths, a painful inferno rushing through my body. My mind was completely quiet, fixated on the vision in front of me. I just had to close the gap.

One step forward.

Then another.

And another.

Until I was standing inches away from the shivering creature, its wings wrapped tightly around itself. Lifting a hand, I trailed my fingers along the scarlet veins lining the edge of its translucent wings splashed with peaches, corals, and white.

The creature stilled.

I inched my hand along the wing, tentatively nudging one to unfold. Wrapped within its shelter, my breathing slowed, the violent image around us disappearing.

Waves of peach and rose washed over the pearly scales covering its body. Silver orbs stared into my own.

My dragon wasn't terrifying, she was terrified.

I'm sorry. I ran my palm over its textured scales. *I was afraid.*

Afraid of my own power.

Afraid of what it meant.

But being afraid wouldn't rid me of my fears. It would only allow them to consume me. And while I couldn't take back the things I'd done—things that made me both proud and ashamed—I would never move forward if I couldn't accept it all.

Dru's words from my first days in Celaria stirred in my mind.

You are still just as beautiful as before, but now you stand out a little differently.

Even if Dru didn't still feel that way, I now believed his words, and that had to be enough.

The dragon nodded in understanding.

Sparks released in a small flurry from its snout, swirling around me, igniting me from the outside before burrowing into my skin. A guttural scream tore through me, the smell of smoke and cinnamon piercing the cocoon of my dragon's protection before I let the pain and the fire swallow me whole.

I loved Dru, and while I believed he loved me too, we'd never have anything real between us if I refused to show him all of me, even the jagged bits.

My eyes opened to find him gaping me at me, stunned.

UNFOLDING MY WINGS, I SPLAYED THEM WIDE, PATCHES OF corals and pinks and opalescent whites swirling across them. I blinked a few times, taking in the pointy snout that jutted from my face, radiant scales trailing up it.

Shifting my weight, I kicked some dirt with my clawed feet, testing the feel of them.

Dru stepped forward, reaching up, and I bent down into it. He ran his ungloved fingers over my snout before lifting his hand to compare it to the size of my eye. "Kyleigh, you're magnificent."

He pressed his lips to the corner of one of my scales, and I let out a satisfied hum.

Then his smile faltered, turning to Neve. "Is she going to have trouble returning to her other form?"

She looked over at me shaking her head.

Silly boy.

Cocooning within her wings, my sapphire sister shrank down to her human form. Dru averted his gaze, pink staining his cheeks before he pressed a stud on his glove. An oversized blanket emerged from its center, activated by the faerie blood's expanding enchantment. Handing the bundle to Neve, she wrapped it around her with a smile in thanks.

"Alright, Kyleigh, it sounds like your man misses your human form." Neve chuckled. "Fold your wings around yourself, then picture it."

I followed her instructions, pulling in the watercolor wings until they cocooned me. Unlike shifting into my dragon form, this felt like an icy wind gripping and twisting my body, bones cracking like broken twigs as I transformed. Once everything snapped into place, I shook out my neck and rolled my shoulders.

Dru's eyes locked onto me, roving over my skin, warming everywhere his gaze lingered.

"I'll give you two some privacy," Neve said, walking off. "Call out when you're ready to fly back, unless you want to take your chances testing out your flying skills. I wouldn't advise it, though."

Dru and I stood there a few moments, silently staring at each other.

"It's time we talked," I said, eager to get this conversation started.

Dru picked up my clothes and held them out, probably not wanting to be rude, even though he couldn't stop staring, which I didn't mind one bit. Seeing how much he wanted me still, it was everything. But I needed to know where he stood. I needed to hear it.

I took my time getting dressed, trying to formulate where to begin.

"What do you think?" I asked, voice low and unsure.

He rubbed the back of his neck, adjusting the collar of his shirt. I couldn't breathe, couldn't think about anything else, waiting for his response. "You'd take my breath away no matter your form."

I finished tying up my laces, warmth staining my cheeks. Heading to the ledge, I sat down and dangled my feet over the edge. I patted the space next to me, and he knelt, kissing my forehead then sat by my side.

Adrift in his hazel pools flecked with gold, I pulled him in by his collar, diving in for a deep, lingering kiss. I needed him to know how much I wanted him.

His chest heaved when I dragged my lips away, needing to finally get out what I came here to say. "I want you to be my champion, Dru."

He stilled, brows shooting up. "What?"

"I want you to be my champion."

"Look, Kyleigh..." he began, eyes trailing over to the ledge, legs kicking back and forth. He held my hands, thumbs caressing my clenched knuckles. "You should take more time to think about this. You shouldn't rush into this decision out of any sort of obligation to—"

"I don't need more time. I've made up my mind." My tone was fully serious. I wanted nothing more. Hands shaking, I bit my lip to stop its quiver. The cage around my heart rattled, like it might fracture into a million pieces, but I chose to press on and be brave. "This is what I want."

Dru's breath hitched, and I leaned in, pressing my lips to his, desperately needing connection in this moment where I felt more vulnerable than I ever have.

"I'm in love with you, Dru," I murmured against his lips.

"I'm in love with you too." He scooped me into his lap, and my pulse quickened as he held me close. "But it feels selfish wanting you for myself when I don't have any powers to offer in return. It isn't logical for you to choose me."

I gripped the collar of his shirt, stealing him back from his burning thoughts. "Fuck logic. You of all people should know that strength comes in many forms. And you make me stronger, Dru. You give me strength."

A few of my salty tears mingled on our lips as they collided. "I don't need a warrior, or wielder, or someone with influence. I just need you."

It was the truth. My truth. And I needed him to know.

"If you're worried about being bonded to me with every-thing that happened...I'll understand. But if you want to be with me, if you still want to take down the Enchantress and return to the Otherworld together, I want you to be my champion."

"Of course I want to be with you, Ky. You've captivated me from the moment I met you, before I knew who you were or what you were capable of."

"Does that scare you?" I needed to know. "Do my powers scare you?"

He paused, seemingly trying to find the words. My palms became clammy and began to glow, but I rubbed them on my jeans, smothering the light out.

Dru grabbed them in his, running his thumbs in soothing circles on their backs. "Your power is part of you. It's beauti-ful, fierce, passionate. I've seen it do incredibly wonderful things. I've also seen it do some terribly violent things."

As much as I wanted to avoid his rejection, deluding myself by not asking the questions that scared me wouldn't change that. So I snapped my tear-rimmed eyes up to his. If he was going to break me, it would be to my face.

"But I am in love with you, Kyleigh. *Every* part of you." He gripped me closer, peppering kisses along my cheek and throat while he whispered, "Nothing you could ever do will change that. I have been scared, but not of your powers. More so that I'm not worthy of them. At least not yet. It's why I've been working so hard. I need to prove myself."

I thought my heart would rip straight out of my chest from how heavy and forceful its beat had become. He had been just as afraid of being rejected as I was. "You have nothing to prove when it comes to me."

I hated that anyone had ever made him feel inferior, anything less than brilliant. And now, the most vulnerable parts of ourselves had been put on display for each other to judge, to run away from if we wanted.

But here we were, only wanting each other. Just as we were.

I stroked his cheek with my palm before whispering, "So, you'll be my champion?"

"Yes," he beamed. "I'll need about a week to make sure I understand everything involved, though."

I nodded eagerly in agreement, pulling his lips back to mine.

26

AISLIN

Every morning before sparring, Sloan came to The Lavender to have breakfast and coffee with Sweeney, Kyleigh, and me—if I wasn't in my room trying to hide my pain, that is. When I didn't make it down for breakfast, I normally blamed being hungover, waving my flask around.

Sloan had insisted on taking over walking us to the fort each morning—a much welcome reprieve. The three of us would talk the whole way—Kyleigh often answering our questions about the Otherworld and its people, Sloan talking about Inverno and its familiars. I'd always been curious about their people, how they bonded their animals and how their magic worked.

Sloan pulled back a few silver wisps of hair, pinning them in place with a rhinestone comb depicting tiny glittering snowflakes. While she didn't wear her armor anymore and the colors in her wardrobe had expanded from Inverno's sapphire shade, I'm sure she missed her home.

"I assumed I'd have a snowy owl or a sweet doe. Something wise or gentle to balance my—"

"Intensity," I slipped in, teasing her.

She pursed her lips, lifting a brow at me. "You haven't seen *intense* when it comes to me."

Warmth streaked through my chest under her gaze. I still found myself thinking back to our kiss more than I'd ever admit to her—or anyone, for that matter. Spending these morning walks together wasn't making it any easier. Regardless, I had to admit I enjoyed her company, even if this alliance was only temporary. I'd miss these mornings after she inevitably returned to Inverno.

Kyleigh cleared her throat. "So how did you know Mox was your familiar?"

"He sought me out when I was about fifteen, as just a tiny kit. After a month of him following me around, refusing to let me out of his sight, I accepted the bond." Her gaze shifted in the direction of the Silent Woods, and I sensed she missed her companion. "I honestly wasn't sure if he'd be the best animal to have as my familiar, but he's proven himself invaluable."

The idea of familiars seemed beneficial, especially after seeing how helpful he'd been to Arafax since he'd arrived with Sloan. I could see how they had aided Inverno in thriving, especially in comparison to Arafax after The Blaze.

Every day, Arafax felt warmer and more alive—more like it once was. The day's moon shone brighter, glistening against the pink-and-purple glazed sky. The ash-covered ground in the village began sprouting vibrant-green vines, short grass, and tiny white and red flowers. Barren trees stirred to life, copper buds bursting from their branches, their blackened bark now lined with shimmering sap.

Everyone seemed to be enjoying the power boost. Kyleigh had finally been able to shift as of last week and practiced daily with Neve. Some days it worked, other days her mental blocks took root, unwilling to budge. Progress didn't always ascend in a straight line. Sometimes it was necessary for the path to scale or descend along the way.

My lightning had become much easier to wield; however, I hadn't made the full shift to my dragon yet, only summoning my wings. Unlike my coral-haired counterpart, I didn't need Neve doing some mystical guru bullshit to get my magic to work. It was an intentional choice.

I'd always hated my powers. I'd spent years wishing them away. Now I had *more*. Even though I wasn't used for them like I had been, I didn't know if I wanted this. More power meant more ways to be exploited.

I could also use my power to free myself, like the Enchantress reminded me when I'd met her en route to Inverno. But I also knew claiming freedom in that manner would come with a cost. What was I willing to do to be on the other side of power?

I'd finally started to feel like more than a weapon to be wielded by someone else. I had friends, people who'd willingly risked themselves for me. Ones who cared seemingly without conditions.

Maybe that's what scared me most of all.

As a dragon, would I be a new iteration of what I once was? Or would I be able to soar above the agendas of those around me?

Unfortunately, the Enchantress's agenda was interrupting my waking hours with pain and my sleeping ones with nightmares.

Dru had concocted a numbing balm to put on my bond

mark, lessening the effects of the summoning, but since I never knew when she would call, I ended up debilitated for a handful of minutes until I got my wits about me enough to apply the balm. Its aid only lasted about an hour once applied, so when I wasn't in my lessons, I made sure I was in my room, hiding away so no one would see me suffering.

The pain had gotten to the point of blinding, happening a few times a day and rendering me nearly unable to function. My mind and body couldn't keep this routine up any longer. I couldn't put off visiting the Enchantress.

She'd won this battle.

Tonight, I'd head to the Silent Woods.

27

AISLIN

Glowhoppers pranced over the dead shrubbery, the only company I had in the Silent Woods.

That was, until I heard the *whir* of something in the air, followed by a *thud*.

I scurried behind an oversized stump, peering out to see where the sounds were coming from.

A frantic mumble carried through the trees along with more whirs. I crawled across the root-covered floor, getting close enough to make out the shapes of four men. Two of them held one against a tree, six knives sticking out from his partially slumped body.

"Ten points!" one of them cheered, keeping the man upright with one arm while twisting the dagger deeper with the other. The captive groaned, eyes clamped shut, chest heaving shallow breaths.

My body froze.

"Shh," the too-familiar voice hushed, a knife gripped tightly in his hand while the other extended out, measuring his trajectory. His men snickered, watching Flynt prep another dagger before sending it into the captive's eye. Blood trickled down his cheek, his untouched eye glazed over.

Flynt strolled up to his victim, pressing two fingers to his wrist. He paused, then beamed at the others. "Dead. That's fifty points."

"One hundred ten, boss. Well done!" said one of the men. The other pulled out the knives, wiping them off on his pant leg.

Flynt bowed. "Next time you'll get a shot at beating me, Lap."

I couldn't move. Couldn't think. Pressure pooled behind my eyes, and I willed my hands not to glow.

Don't do anything reckless, Aislin.

The man was already dead, his fate sealed the moment he'd been taken by the thugs.

Lap dragged the body to Flynt. "Looking forward to it, boss."

"Head back to the inn," he told them, pulling a satchel from the dead man's pocket and tossing it over, "go get your knobs wet, on the house."

The men whooped, dividing the coins up while they walked off.

Flynt gripped around the man's ankles and hauled his body through the woods.

Why didn't he have the others doing this kind of stuff?

It seemed strange for the boss to be handling grunt work. I followed, staying farther out, a shadow trailing behind him.

Was this how he handled jobs now that I wasn't dangling from his strings?

Guilt gnawed at me with each step. I was glad to be done with killing, but I knew if I'd been tasked with ending this man's life, it would have been kind in comparison. Merciful, even.

The Enchantress's cabin came into view, and I hid behind a tree, waiting to see what Flynt did. Making his way to its entrance, he was greeted by four wisps who took the body from him and carried it inside.

I crouched low, silently nearing the cabin. When the wisps flew out through the back window and dropped the body into the heap, I paused, holding my breath. As I got closer to the rear of the cabin, I spotted a large hole dug in the yard.

Hundreds of gray and black husks were piled on top of each other, limbs and bodies interwoven.

A lump caught in my throat as I realized what I was staring at.

A mass grave.

So this is where the wisps had thrown the husk I had seen on the dais when I was here last.

They were people Flynt killed.

People *I* killed.

Wood scraped against the floor of the cabin, and I crawled closer, trying to glimpse inside. I had spent so many years following marks, I was used to watching, waiting patiently for the best opportunity to strike. This was nothing new—the only difference now was that I was the one deciding my prey.

Lifting myself up so my eyes came just above the windowsill, I very quickly saw what was causing the sound.

Flynt pulled the tree-trunk table closer to the black velvet chaise, sitting at the base of its cushion. Sprawled along the lounge was the Enchantress, head thrown back in ecstasy. I grimaced, eyes following Flynt's hand running up her leg.

On the table was a small pile of blue powder, half already segmented into thin rows. I would have recognized that powder anywhere after my dance with it back in Inverno. How had it landed here? Had Flynt brought it with him or had the Enchantress somehow gotten it from the fucking Inverno guards?

Flynt bent over the legs in his lap, snorting a row of the dragon dust, then laid back, continuing to stroke the Enchantress's thighs, one hand disappearing up the lace of her skirt. She let out a satisfied hum, making me cringe.

A few minutes later Flynt's eyes darted to the leftover dust and he tapped the Enchantress's ankle. "Don't want to be wasteful. Especially since there isn't a steady supply anymore."

There better not fucking be.

She moved her legs a moment while he stood and swept up the remnants before taking the jar to the bookcase covered with assorted treasures. He placed it on the top corner shelf, my lightning only a few jars away, bolts still weaving within.

"This is why I never put my trust in idiots." She peeled herself off the chaise, striding toward him. Her copper talons glinted in the light, and I flinched, reminded of how easily they could drain my powers. "And neither should you."

What was she doing with Flynt, though? He had no powers.

She used her pointer finger to adjust the top of his tunic then pushed it into his skin enough to draw a bloody line as she trailed down his chest. Taking her finger away, she licked the metallic tip clean, eliciting a grunt from Flynt. When she gripped the bulge of his pants, it took every ounce of strength for me not to get sick.

"Remember, Flynt, you continue to supply me with everything I require, and when I'm free from this cage, you'll be rewarded." He was still as a statue while she clutched him through his pants.

"You don't even know what I'd want."

"Oh, Flynt, you may be the big boss now, but don't forget that I knew you before all that. I remember what you truly desire."

Bile rose in my throat at the confirmation that they were working together.

All this time, he'd been pulling my strings for *her*?

I thought the Queen puppeted Flynt, and in turn, he puppeted me. Heat streaked through my veins, tiny bolts shooting from my fingertips onto the ground. It was no secret I wasn't fond of Arafax's ruler, but now, knowing Flynt was working with the Enchantress...that was even more harrowing. That I had any part in her plans, even unintentionally, made me nauseous.

"Unfortunately, while I'd love to keep chatting...among other things...I have another visitor that requires my attention." She let go of him, pointing a sharp finger at the door, and he let out a frustrated huff before grabbing his coat. "Thanks again for the visit. And the deliveries."

He frowned a moment, adjusting the tent in his trousers before closing the door behind him.

Flynt was under her influence. I had never felt safe at The Lavender since he'd taken over with his criminal network, but that feeling had now amplified. I needed to keep Kyleigh far away from him, but what would I say without divulging how I knew about them meeting like this. Without admitting I'd been here myself.

The Enchantress clapped twice, directing her wisps into

another room. When they returned, a few of them were carrying what looked like a lump of black fabric. She reached her arms overhead, and her minions fluttered around her, shielding her from view. "Why don't you come in, Aislin?"

I went wholly still.

Fuck.

How long had she known I was there?

"I was starting to run out of ideas for summoning you, but I do have ways of extending my reach if necessary. Been sleeping well? How's that silver-haired warrior you seem to be so infatuated with?"

I stood, climbing over the windowsill. "How—"

"Dream weaver, darling," she said, stepping away from the crowd of wisps. She'd changed out of her dress, opting for a sheer number that had black material strategically streaked across it. "They don't travel much, so when Flynt found one, it was quite a rarity. Mind magic takes things to another level, don't you agree?"

"I wouldn't know," I replied, keeping my eyes trained on her face.

"Shame," she said, circling me. She removed my leather jacket, running her copper claw along my neck to where our bond mark was rooted. Scraping its outline, she let out a sigh. "You're certainly proving to be a disappointment. I expected more."

"Is that so?"

Her wisps hovered above us, huddled together in small groups, watching us intently. The Enchantress licked her crimson lips and moved behind me, taking my hand. She pressed her body into me, the fabric so thin I could feel her nipples drag across my back. "You'll find I can be very giving as long as my purposes are being served."

Electricity released from my clenched fists, the bolts dancing over her copper-tipped claws. Gripping my wrist, she moved in front of me, bringing my knuckles to her mouth, sucking in my power between her lips. I tried to pull away, but she clutched my wrist tighter, her claws digging into my flesh.

My chest began to surge with light as bolts painfully wriggled and fought for escape. Every second she drained my power my body wobbled more, the effort to remain standing becoming almost too taxing to continue.

"I apologize, I almost got carried away," the Enchantress said, stopping herself and taking a step back. She traced a copper-tip over her lips. "There's just something so alluring about your abilities. I can't put my finger on it. Your powers even taste different than before. Richer, more indulgent...*smoky*. I wonder why that is?"

"No clue." I could feel the buds of my wings aching to display the full span of my new powers as she beckoned them, but I squeezed my chest, willing them back down. "What is this favor you've been so desperate to collect on?"

"Nothing huge. Just bring me something," the Enchantress said with a smirk.

I crossed my arms, shrugging. "Just anything or do you want to clarify?"

I kept my face unreadable, not wanting to let any knowledge of what she suspected cross my expression.

"Being banished to this small patch of land doesn't mean I am not well versed in what goes on in the realms." She hummed to herself, her hands tracing lazy circles along her abdomen and breasts. As if just noticing I was still there, she turned her gaze to me, tone returning to a sensual command. "I've heard from your associate, Flynt, that you've been going to the fort every day to work with the Queen. I believe she is keeping a secret from me."

Fuck.

"I believe she's withholding *someone* from me, to be exact. An heir."

"Wouldn't the kingdom know if there was an heir to the throne?"

"I can sense power, you know. Power like that...it calls to me."

A wisp flitted over, handing me a sheer copper siphon. I held it out in front of me, inspecting the object that was about the size of my fist. "What if there is no heir?"

"I'm rarely wrong when it comes to sensing power," she said, clasping her hands. "Whoever the heir is, the Queen would be keeping them close. Learn their identity and bring me their blood."

"And if I don't?"

"I'm being very generous here. I could ask you to bring me the heir. All I want is a measly vial of their blood." She placed a hand on the center of my chest, and my lightning pulsed beneath her talons, heart fluttering against my ribs. Streaks fed out from me, and her onyx eyes glittered, head tossed back while she consumed more of my power.

There was no question that she was stronger now. I could feel it in the way she depleted my energy, the intensity and ease of it.

"You can choose to refuse me my small favor, but you'll be joining my wisps in exchange. I would enjoy playing more with your powers... But I believe in the fairness of choice."

My chest heaved, arms becoming heavy.

A moment later a bright-blue phoenix flew through the window, shifting into the very naked King Redmond.

"Getting started without me?" he asked the Enchantress, eyebrow lifted at me.

She let go of me in an instant, and I doubled over, trying to catch my breath.

"I wouldn't dream of it," she crooned, strutting toward him in her barely-there ensemble and running her tongue along the seam of his lips.

He accepted her seductive invitation, pulling her flush against him in a lingering kiss that made my stomach churn. I had to admit, he was pretty convincing.

This was my cue to leave. I needed to figure out what to do with the wicked bitch's request.

Turning her attention to me, she trailed her hand along his back. "I believe you two have met."

"Yes. We must stop meeting under these circumstances," I deadpanned, my eyes staying glued to the wall behind him, wondering when he would find some fucking pants. His arrogance was vexing as ever.

"Last time I saw you, you were too cowardly to kill me," he said, bringing his arms around the Enchantress. His midnight eyes locked with mine, as if reminding me to play along.

"Last time I saw you, you were passed out in a pool of your own blood. I'd happily do a reenactment for your bride-to-be, if you'd like." I beckoned him toward me. "After you put some clothes on, of course."

Just then, a few wisps flew in carrying a black robe that they slipped over his arms.

Thank fuck.

"Well, as much as I've enjoyed the pleasant surprise of your visit, you'd better be going. Unless you want to join us?" She devoured me with her stare while I glared daggers into

Redmond's skull. His throat bobbed, but he held still, trying to disguise the discomfort that idea gave both of us.

"I'm not much in the mood for sharing you tonight, darling," he said, scanning her seductively.

"Very well," she sighed, tracing the edge of the King's robe with a copper-tipped finger. "I'll expect you back within two weeks' time."

King Redmond waved me off, and I nodded in silent thanks, grabbing my jacket and shutting the door quickly behind me.

28

I stumbled my way over the root-covered forest floor, not slowing until I saw moonlight beyond the tree line.

King Redmond might think he had the seductive siren of the woods under his thrall, but I knew better. If he truly was working against her in secret, it was only a matter of time until she found out, and we would all be at risk.

Then there was the matter of the dragon dust.

Did the King know that Flynt had been bringing a supply to the Enchantress? And how did the Enchantress and Flynt know each other?

My mind was a storm of facts and theories crashing into each other. Maybe Dru could make sense of it all—he always seemed to be the one to wade through these tempests.

A low, menacing growl rippled through the darkness.

Coming to a halt, I let a few strands of lightning dance out from my palm and grabbed my dagger with my other hand. Bared teeth accompanied a lithe body covered in plush, white fur. Mox stalked out from behind a bramble with his hackles raised, pushing his massive snout into my side.

"Ouch! What the fuck, Mox?"

He nudged me through the trees, growling any time I paused or tried to make a snarky remark. I tripped, fumbling over the roots and dead tree trunks that littered the uneven terrain. Mox didn't stop herding me out of the Enchantress's territory until there was a hauntingly familiar silhouette in the darkness. One that sent a shiver through me.

"Let's go," Sloan said in a clipped tone, eyes flaring when Mox pushed me against her white, satin blouse lined with peeks of lace. I cleared my throat and took a step back, taking her in. Her hair was disheveled, clinging to her face, and her longsword was fastened to her back. The streetlamps of the small town en route to The Lavender highlighted the bags under her eyes. She looked exhausted.

"Why are you here?" I asked, avoiding the pointed glare she was giving me. "Trouble sleeping?"

"You could say that." She sighed, pursing her lips.

Mox still had his snout pressed into my back. "Is he going to stop this anytime soon?"

"This is how tonight is going to go." Sloan stopped a moment, placing a hand on my shoulder to turn me toward her. The lines of her face were hard, etched in seriousness. She remained calm as she spoke, her words piercing me with the intensity behind them. "First, we are going to escort you directly to your room. Then, you're going to tell us what you were doing visiting the Enchantress."

"How did you know where I was?"

"Two sets of eyes, remember?" she said, patting Mox on the head. "He's been keeping an eye on Redmond for me."

My gaze narrowed on her before whipping to her snow

fox companion. He snapped at me, glaring with his big, onyx eyes. "I thought *friends* were supposed to trust one another."

"We both know there's more than friendship here."

I scoffed at her in response.

"Besides, I *do* trust you." She cocked her head, glancing over at me as we started walking again. "But seeing you coming out of her cabin? That has me concerned."

"Why don't you let me worry about myself." I really didn't know what else to say. If I'd seen her coming out of the Enchantress's cabin, I wouldn't trust her, yet here she was, saying she still trusted me. That she was worried about me.

Would telling her the truth gain me another ally or put her in unnecessary danger? Would she report back anything I said to King Redmond? I felt like I could trust her, even if I didn't trust her ruler. But until I could talk to Dru—could wrap my head around the Enchantress's request—I didn't want anyone else to know.

The Lavender's pub and about half the rooms above it were still lit, the inn's buttery glow stretching along the ground in front of us. The red-haired amor, Roxie, grasped the window ledge, her breasts spilling out of her nightgown as she leaned forward. Flynt pounded into her, his skin drenched with sweat.

That's one way to work off the dragon dust.

He grunted, thrusting into her and winking at us. I looked away, trying not to throw up after seeing him all over the Enchantress earlier. When I grimaced, Sloan snorted, shaking her head, and we made our way to The Lavender's back entrance. "Nothing I haven't seen before."

"Oh, really?" I mused.

She must've thought I was grossed out by the display, but that had nothing to do with it. I was used to Flynt's debauchery. This was a usual occurrence around here. I was more disturbed by the knowledge that my marks were now husks that served some purpose for the Enchantress.

A revelation I wanted to strike from my mind.

"You forget I was raised in Inverno's army. Fucking with little to no privacy is nothing new to me."

Is she talking from personal experience?

I gulped, heat prickling along my neck and gliding across my chest at the image. Her stare lowered. "What are you thinking about?"

"Nothing," I blurted out, tethering my gaze to the floorboards. I pulled the neckline of my jacket tighter around me, stepping into The Lavender's rear entryway. "Um, you can just leave me here."

Sloan lifted my chin up, and my eyes met her clouded, pale-blue irises, striking me speechless. A slight smirk peeled at the corner of her lips. "Wouldn't dream of it."

"Fine."

Mox looked especially ridiculous following us up the narrow staircase. The sound of my heart banging against my ribcage drowned out the revelry downstairs and the groans escaping from various rooms down the hall. Roq was standing guard in the hallway. Kyleigh must already be in bed.

Stopping in front of my door, I fumbled for the key in my pocket a moment before slipping it into the lock and twisting until I heard it click. I opened the door, and Sloan leaned against its frame as I walked into the room. "Aren't you going to invite me in?"

Blazes.

The last place I wanted Sloan was in my bedroom. Alone, she'd question me more about the Enchantress before I had time to sort out my favor or the other things I'd seen. Alone, I might let those walls crumble down again. "You'd like that, wouldn't you?"

"I think that answer is obvious." She raised an eyebrow, looking around the room, taking in its sparse details. If she was trying to learn more about me from my bedroom, she'd be disappointed. When her eyes landed on the bed, I felt my throat constrict.

"Do you still think about our kiss?" she asked, leaning toward me with one arm braced on the doorframe, making me wonder if I had the discipline to not kiss her.

Why did I keep pushing her away? I could simply give in to this attraction between us. She was beautiful, strong, and obviously experienced from her prior comments and confidence. Fucking didn't have to mean anything. I could treat her like any of the others—a night of distraction, nothing more.

It would be so easy to give in. To finally know what her skin would feel like against mine, the sounds she'd make, how she'd look when she relinquished the control she commanded so effortlessly.

No matter how hard I tried fortifying myself against my feelings for her, she had somehow found a way to slip through the mortar. But I knew if I went there with her, it wouldn't be just that.

"Sloan," I croaked, like all the moisture had been sucked out of my mouth. I didn't need this right now. Not when I had to think about the Enchantress's request and how I was going to handle it.

I pulled her inside the room, shutting the door behind her and leaving Mox outside. She smirked, pleased with herself.

I gestured for her to sit in the sole chair in my room,

taking deep steadying breaths as she sauntered over to it. She sank back in the chair, looking up at me, a glimmer of hope set in her eyes despite the exhaustion beneath them.

"Look, of course I think about the kiss. How could I not? But—"

She let out a groan, and a huff from Mox sounded on the other side of the door, as if he were just as frustrated as his master. Sloan leaned forward, hands clasped with her elbows resting on her knees.

"Sloan..." I began, backing up until my thighs hit the bed. Gripping the blanket, I searched for the best way to say what I needed to. "The thing is, wanting this with you is wrong. You're a knight. One serving our rival territory. Maybe if The Blaze had never happened... Maybe if I hadn't become what Flynt wanted me to be... There's no way this ends well for us."

"But you don't work for Flynt anymore." The neckline of her blouse sat slightly askew, subtly exposing the top of her lace bralette. She caught my gaze, smirking as she adjusted herself, rousing me out of the momentary lapse in my mission to turn her away. While her confidence unnerved me, it also drew me in.

It was maddening.

"I don't work for myself either," I said, tightening my grip on the blanket. "Neither do you. You may have been relieved from King Redmond's service temporarily, but you still obviously care about him enough to send Mox away to follow him."

"You're right," she said, clasping her hands in her lap. "I do still care about him and Inverno. He's my friend. Inverno is my home."

Maybe it was finally sinking in.

"But I also care about you and a better world for *all* our people." *Maybe not.* "Don't you want that too?"

She reached out and, like a woman possessed, I went to her. She ran her thumb along the faint scars left from the Queen—one of the many reminders that I still didn't have a life that was my own. Something that would always remain out of reach for someone like me.

"Of course," I said, pulling my hand away from her despite the desire to remain under her possessive touch. "Of course I want that for our people. But why should I put trust in this alliance?"

"I'm not saying you have to trust our alliance, but what have I done to garner your distrust?"

Nothing.

I dropped my eyes to my boots.

"You know you can trust me," she said, standing and stepping toward me. She gripped my chin with one hand and the top of my thigh holster with the other. "You might be willing to pretend and deny there's something between us, but I'm not afraid to fight for it."

"That's the difference between us, Sloan." I didn't move, not wanting to be away from the woman who captivated me but too scared to allow her any closer. "I am."

She leaned closer, her mouth a breath away from mine as she whispered, "Are you at least going to tell me what you were doing with the Enchantress tonight?"

"It's none of your concern." I suddenly became much more aware of my heartbeat quickening. My neck heating.

Her brows furrowed, watching me, but she didn't move. "I am definitely concerned. She has sunk her claws into the people I care about. What does she want with you?" She released my chin, grazing my throat before her hand splayed between my collarbones, its heel resting at the crest of my cleavage. "I know she can be very persuasive and alluring—I have seen her effect on Redmond—but she's fucking dangerous, Aislin. You don't want to entangle yourself with her."

Entangle? What does she think I was doing at the cabin?

It was amusing to feel a bit of power. I moved my mouth to her ear, brushing it along her cheek as I whispered, "You sound jealous."

Sloan's body went preternaturally still. She stepped away from me, and I stumbled forward a step before catching myself. "I'm woman enough to admit that if you were fucking the Enchantress, it would tear me to shreds. But the last thing I'd be is jealous."

"Is that so? You know, some say she's quite alluring..." I smirked, throwing her own words back at her, trying to ignore her declaration and the way it made me covet things I had no business wanting.

"She may be, but the only pleasure she wants is what serves her. I suspect," her eyes drew up my body, and I bristled, not wanting to encourage her appraisal, "you want more than that."

"That doesn't sound all that terrible." I shrugged off the tingle that surged through me at the way the words dripped from her tongue. "I mean, it seems to work for your king so much he's willing to marry her."

"Redmond is a fool."

I smirked in response. "Finally some common ground for us to lay on."

She raised a brow, making me instantly regret the accidental innuendo. "You can deflect as much as you want, Aislin"—I huffed out my annoyance—"but at the end of the day, I know that kiss between us wasn't a mistake. I'll be here when you're ready to admit that to yourself."

"Won't be happening." I gulped back the part of me that wanted to beg her to stay.

"Is that so?" She smirked, tucking silver strands behind her ear and taking a few steps toward the door. "We both know who you'll be thinking about when you reach between those thighs tonight."

I shifted my feet, zipping my legs together, resisting the need pulsing through me. The last thing I could do was give in.

"I'll be here before training tomorrow morning." She opened the door to Mox waiting outside for her. Glancing over her shoulder, she grinned, giving me a parting nod. "When I see your skin flush, I'll know I was right."

29

REDMOND

My tongue trailed its way up the blue icing lining my betrothed's thigh. She moaned her approval, dusky tendrils reaching out from her wings, tethering my wrists and ankles in place.

She slid her hands through my hair, their glittering-onyx hue climbing up her arms, higher than the last time I'd visited.

She plucked a piece of spongy, white cake from the small plate and shoved it into my mouth, her finger lingering over my lips. I sucked the leftover crumbs from their pads, pushing down the urge to gag, resisting any facial reaction that was less than bliss.

It's all a game.

I had to play devoted fiancé or risk the future of my people, of Celaria's people. If that meant putting myself at risk every time I had to come to this cabin until I found something useful to help eliminate the evil woman in front of me, I'd do it. There had to be something here that would lessen the guilt weighing me down since I'd discovered the truth about Neve. About the dragons.

"What do you think?" The Enchantress's voice spread thick against my ear, smothering out my thoughts. "White cake with mixed berry icing?"

It was gross. Too sweet. My pulse raced as the sugar thrummed through my veins like a hit of smoking stems.

"Maybe," I said, plastering a charming grin over gritted teeth.

"I know you've done all this before, but regular wedding planning just seems so *dull*. I thought we might revamp it. Make it fun."

I nodded before I could flinch at her words, trying not to let them affect me. She wanted that. A reaction. She loved feasting on my pain as much as my power.

I had done all this before, only I had been marrying a woman I actually loved. Someone I wanted as my queen. One who would have helped me unite the realm. There was none of that here, just a forced alliance caked in blood and lies.

"Next?"

She pointed to the coppery line of icing that started just above her knee and traveled high enough that shadows barely covered the glistening lips beneath. She never wore anything under her lace—something that used to turn me on, but now just made me want to throw up all the cake I'd sampled tonight.

Clenching my eyes shut, I ran my tongue along her thigh, stopping at the edge of her skirt. The metallic tang mixed with sugar concocted a strange, savory flavor. She popped a black piece of sponge cake in my mouth, and I chewed slowly, willing down the bile rising in my throat. "What is this?"

"Faerie-blood icing and ashen cake," she smirked, and I tried to swallow the contents that mixed in my mouth. Spitting it out wasn't an option. "To represent us both."

Bitch.

I swallowed a few extra times. "How thoughtful."

She pushed a pointy heel into my chest, her tendrils twisting around my flesh until it stung. I schooled my face, maintaining its pleasant façade. "How thoughtful...what? Do I need to retrieve the talisman again?"

"How thoughtful of you, my dark queen," I replied, the threat of the trinket making the ashen cake catch in the back of my throat.

Before she found another creative punishment, I lifted her hips, sliding them to me, then used my tongue to shut her up.

THE ENCHANTRESS SPRAWLED ON HER BARREN TREE-TRUNK throne, sated, onyx eyes rolled back in her head. The shadowy tendrils that had restrained me with violent fervor retracted, swaying gently. She'd finally fallen asleep.

She seemed different tonight. Hungrier. Insatiable. More unhinged, if that were possible.

Bruises bloomed on my wrists and ankles, and I ran my fingers along them, unsurprised. The Enchantress enjoyed leaving her mark. I staggered over to the handle of whiskey sitting on the tree-trunk table, sloshing it around my mouth to burn away the last few hours of my life.

Wandering toward her shelves, I watched my feathers swirling in a jar. A few new ones had been added tonight. What purpose did she have holding them captive?

I peered over my shoulder to make sure she was still sleeping.

Scanning the shelves, I noticed ruby flames contained on a lower shelf. I lifted the lid in curiosity, watching the fire stir. Relaxing my wings, I ignited them before curling one in to touch the contents in the jar. It seared, but instead of burning me, it climbed along my own phoenix fire until the top of my wing glowed purple. It was fascinating how the two seemingly opposite entities sparked into something brilliant and new.

The movement of wisps flying in through the walls had me snuffing out the flames, pulling my feathers in against me.

I hated the spectral creatures that came off as nothing more than aimless, dead, and blindly obedient to whatever the Enchantress wished. However, there was also something curiously aware about them.

As if they could sense my discomfort, the wisps flurried into a back room, shutting the door behind them. *Good.* Last thing I needed was those creepy fuckers watching me. The Enchantress loved making them watch, commanding them to participate. She got off on it—probably because I hated it.

I didn't have much more choice than they did in the matter, imprisoned in a cage of my own construction—bars welded from my ignorance and rage.

I'd wasted my time weakening Arafax over the last decade when I should've used that energy to fortify us against the Enchantress. Maybe we wouldn't be in this mess if I had.

How many others would suffer by her hand if she got free?

Everything she'd said told me she was close, and my gut told me she wasn't lying.

A small jar caught my eye, tucked into the top corner of the shelves, only made visible by the lightning that bounced around in another one nearby. It was filled halfway with pale-blue powder. I slid it toward me, lifting the lid and then running my finger through it. Out of the corner of my eye, I noticed small, matching specks sprinkled over the top of the table, little flecks stuck within its crevices.

An inferno punched through my chest, threatening to spill out as I clenched my fists, willing the sensation away.

Dragon dust.

I'd recognize that shade anywhere…

Neve.

How did it end up here?

Sloan had found a bag of dragon scales in the dungeon after our prisoners escaped. While we utilized shed scales to fortify our armor, I had never directed them to be taken from the dragon. From *her*.

When I learned later from Sloan what had been happening, what had caused the scars that ran along Neve's side, I was furious.

They'd used her for dragon dust. I'd assumed for themselves. Now, seeing this here, I wasn't so sure. I never told the Enchantress about the dragon held in my dungeon. If she'd been getting dragon dust from my guards, what else was she keeping from me?

Did she know Arafax's secret? The one I'd discovered weeks ago—that its dragons were really its people.

My chest flared with heat thinking about the slumbering bitch I'd just tongued into oblivion. How easy it would be to kill her in a moment like this... If only I fucking knew how. She'd taken my power enough times for me to know that wouldn't do anything to her.

I placed the jar back on the shelf, taking inventory of everything else I saw there. Among the many tomes and leather texts, one stood out. Its worn, black leather was embossed in faerie blood with symbols I'd never seen before. I flipped through it, making sure not to damage the ancient pages. None of it made sense to me, but if I got it to the fort, maybe Dru could find a way to decipher it.

I had to get it out of here.

The wisps were still out of sight while their mistress slept. It would be easy enough to leave now, she was used to me slipping out in the night. I was a king with people to serve, after all.

Giving a final glance to ensure it was safe, I grabbed the tome and rearranged the nearby books. There must have been a hundred texts on these shelves.

She wouldn't notice one missing.

Slicing my palm, I whispered an enchantment, making the book shrink down. I opened the empty cage around my neck, sticking it inside before clasping it shut and walking out the door.

30

DRU

"Queen isn't taking visitors," one of the guards called gruffly, sticking out a hefty arm to block me from the doorway.

"Good thing I'm not visiting," I said, pushing past them. I knew they wouldn't do anything—even if the Queen didn't want to admit it, she needed me. Arafax needed me. After King Redmond had dropped off a tome he'd found in the Enchantress's cabin, I went ahead and did some research on my own before heading to her chambers to let her know about it. Every piece of intel I gathered was an integral piece in the Enchantress puzzle. I only had to figure out how they fit together.

The room was dark, only a few candles lit, giving it a dusky glow. Huddled against the wall was the Queen, one hand covering her head. Blood seeped from under the hand placed over her shoulder. She peered up at me, eyes full of tears. "I told them not to let anyone in here," she seethed.

"What can I say, I obviously charmed them. Plus, King

Redmond finally gave us something that might be useful. A tome. But I have to figure out how to translate it."

"Well that's good news," she sighed, looking pleased but pained.

I lowered myself down to her level. "Let me see," I said, turning on the light. Pulling over a few chairs, I helped her on one and then sat next to her. Tentatively reaching for her shoulder, I lifted her hand.

A chunk of skin had been flayed off, edges jagged around the wound. A bloodied dagger sat on the night table.

It looked like an act of desperation.

I squinted at the lacerations, trying to see the root of the Queen's issue. "Is that—"

"It hurts so bad," she said, eyes sunken in, dark circles framing them. It was the most vulnerable I'd seen her in the years I'd known her. "I had to make it stop."

The patch of missing flesh was about the same size as Aislin's bond mark.

"How often has the Enchantress been contacting you?"

The Queen flinched at the name, silver eyes snapping to mine.

"I don't know," she heaved. Pointing at a golden chalice on the table, I grabbed it for her, glancing at the crimson liquid within. I waited while she took a few sips of wine, wondering if her answer would be similar to what Aislin had told me. "It has gotten more persistent. It all blurs together. I haven't been able to sleep because I'm afraid she'll reach out to me in my dreams again. That she'll find out about Kyleigh through them..."

"You can't stop sleeping."

"I know," she conceded, placing her hand on my forearm. "There's a dream weaver from Alucinor staying at the inn.

Ox has been bringing him here to help so I can sleep. I can't put Kyleigh at risk. Not after everything I've sacrificed."

My chest clenched. If the Enchantress learned about Kyleigh and found out she was in Celaria, then she wasn't safe. None of us were.

Not waiting for my response, the Queen continued, "She must know something. I don't know why else she would want to see me. It's been years since she's summoned me."

"Maybe it's because she is more powerful with the gem returned?" I grabbed the healing and numbing elixirs from my shoulder strap and poured them on the wound. Poking my head out of her chambers, I asked her guards to grab some medical supplies from my room. Then, I collected a towel from her washroom and held it against the Queen's shoulder to stop the bleeding.

"Why didn't you tell me about this?" I asked, pinching the bridge of my nose with one hand while I held the towel in place. Crimson bloomed through the fabric, and I added more pressure on it. "We could have figured it out together."

The Queen looked down at her mess. "You should have taken Kyleigh when I asked."

I stilled. Part of me agreed. The other knew better.

"You could have made her," she seethed.

Trying to stay the voice of reason, I placed my other hand on her shoulder. "Look, you may have left her all those years ago, but I know you didn't teach your daughter to run from her problems. She told me so."

The Queen huffed, brushing my hands away to hold the towel in place herself, but her gaze softened. "According to her, I did run from my problems."

"Once we are championed, we will be that much stronger against the Enchantress. I'm close to figuring out how we can be rid of her for good. I can feel it. We just need a bit more time."

"Time is the one thing slipping away from us," she replied, eyes fluttering closed before popping open again. She released a heavy sigh.

A knock sounded at the door, and a raven-haired man stepped into the room, lilac eyes with blue coiling in their depths.

The dream weaver.

I recognized him from The Lavender. The small group he'd been with had all stuck out among the crowd. Now I realized why. They were weavers.

This was my first time meeting one, but I'd read a lot about their magic. They had various specialties, all having to do with the mind. Could this dream weaver really combat the Enchantress's use of similar magic?

"Thank you for coming, Reve," the Queen said, ushering him over to the chair by her bed.

"Of course, Your Majesty." He bowed before taking a seat with his legs crossed, back poised. Removing an onyx talisman from his neck, he handed it to her. She dipped her head, slipping it on, then climbed into her bed, legs crossed, nodding at me to leave.

"Goodnight, Your Majesty," I said, bowing my head.

"You won't tell anyone about this," she ordered before I left her chambers.

The Queen hated looking weak, always having to keep up her regal façade. She was an enigma—her two sides constantly at war between isolated, cold steel and a radiant inferno.

Despite the tension that overtook the interactions between her and Kyleigh, I could tell she loved her fiercely.

However, it was almost as if she didn't know how to anymore. Maybe that's what happened when everything you loved was stripped away from you for too long.

It was apparent the Queen was getting desperate, and she was right. We were running out of time. We'd already seen what the wisps were capable of with Ox's attack.

If they were unleashed—if the Enchantress was—there'd be no telling what she could do. We still had no clue what she was after.

Whatever it was, I would stop at nothing to figure out how to defeat her and free my sisters.

KICKING MY SHOES OFF, I COLLAPSED INTO BED. HUNDREDS OF thoughts and snippets of information swirled above me, and I tried to pick through them all amid the cloudy haze. The problem was, for every fact I had, there was rumor, hearsay, and fable obstructing the answers. The tome was helpful, but without knowing what it said, it wouldn't tell me much. I'd poured over the royal library and come up empty handed. Maybe King Redmond would have more luck using Inverno's.

Getting back up a moment to grab supplies from the cabinet, I sat down on my bed, cleaning the needle and vial. I searched for a pronounced vein, tapping the skin above it. A purplish-blue streak came into view and I sank the needle into the skin, numb to the quick sting. Clenching and unclenching my fist, I drew a few vials of blood.

I had been stockpiling it since we'd returned. It would take a larger offering of my null blood for any stronger enchantments to be successful.

Anyone could perform magic with their life force as payment. Faerie blood was rare to come by for most. Theirs was the most powerful, followed by those blessed with abilities. Then there were nulls. While it took more blood for me to do the same enchantment, it was still possible.

Basic spells did small things like giving light, summoning objects, shrinking items, and more, but you had to know the enchantment to do it. The higher-level incantations were reserved for those who had access to the knowledge in certain books, which after The Blaze had nearly disappeared.

Base-level spells were learned in school, though not many children were in Arafax. There weren't many born over the last decade here—not that people couldn't bear children, but many survivors of The Blaze were afraid to bring young ones into a world they'd come to fear.

One day, Arafax would have a future. I'd see to it. It was one of the reasons I'd spent those years learning in the Otherworld, adopting ideas from their technology to improve our kingdom and enhance the magic we had access to.

I went to place the vials into the small refrigerator in my closet, pausing when I heard the *click* of my door opening. I came out into my bedchambers to find Aislin, lips pressed in a thin line. "We need to talk."

I LISTENED, TAKING MENTAL NOTES AS AISLIN TOLD ME ABOUT her visit with the Enchantress.

We finally knew her request: the blood of Arafax's heir.

Kyleigh's blood.

The Queen was right. The Enchantress knew.

Aislin sat on the edge of the bed, hands clasped in her lap. "I mean, it seemed like a simple request at the time, so I knew there had to be more to it with how blood enchantments work."

"You're right." Once an enchantment was cast, it was very hard to break. Blood left a magical signature. Only the person who had cast the charm or someone in their direct lineage could undo it. It was why Kyleigh had been able to open the portal. Her ancestor had forged the portals between our worlds. Everwood Grove was veiled by former dragons, therefore only Kyleigh, Aislin, and Neve's blood-lines could access it with the right incantation. "It could free her from her banishment. It could give her access to the Evergleam, the portal to the Otherworld, and who knows what else."

"Fuck." Aislin stood, pacing back and forth as she ran her hand over the mark at the nape of her neck. "There's no way I can give her what she wants."

"We will figure this out. You did the right thing telling me." Her hands were shaking, and I pulled her in for a hug.

"I don't know what to do, Dru," she croaked out against my chest.

"In order to help you, I need to know everything. What happens if you refuse?"

She stepped back, wiping away a few stray tears that I knew better than to address, brushing off her jacket. "If I refuse, she'll turn me into a wisp."

Like my sisters.

When she turned them, did they die? Did she absorb their powers or simply collect them? If the Enchantress was destroyed, would the wisps be destroyed alongside her? There were so many answers I desperately needed. If there was a way to save my sisters, I had to find it. I couldn't lose them again. Not when I finally had proof they were still alive.

"We won't let her do that to you, Aislin." I needed to come up with a plan but there were too many other things weighing on me. It was hard to see clearly through it all. "The champion ceremony is tomorrow night. After that, we will figure this out. Just give me a day or two to think it all over."

She nodded before getting up and leaving.

Laying back and staring at my ceiling, a whole new set of troubles began circling above me. But the fact was, they would still be there tomorrow, and the day after that, and the day after that. There was no use trying to fix it now, as much as my mind desired to. I needed to focus on tomorrow's ceremony.

In less than twenty-four hours, I'd become champion to one of Arafax's Revered. More importantly, I'd be tied to the woman I loved for eternity.

31

KYLEIGH

I stood in front of the mirror looking unrecognizable.

My usually unruly coral and blonde waves had been pulled into two braids, secured together by a rhinestone comb—one that Sloan let me borrow. The corseted bodice of a pale-peach dress hugged my curves, leaving nothing to the imagination. Hundreds of shimmering stones glittered like tiny stars reflecting the light, perfectly matching the comb in my hair. I ran my hand across my stomach, watching the dress twinkle when I twisted my body, scrutinizing myself from different angles.

"It's very...attention grabbing." I tried not to let my insecurity show about wearing something so tight.

"Well, this isn't a public ceremony," Sloan said, giving me a playful wink.

Thank fuck for that.

"Dru won't be able to take his eyes off you."

Heat flushed across my cheeks, and my eyes lowered to the ground.

We still hadn't been together, not in the way I wanted. Dru had been so busy with research and prepping for our ceremony, I'd barely seen him the last week. Part of me found it super romantic, the other was wildly frustrated. It felt like extra pressure having our first time during the ceremony. Only twelve more hours—not that I was counting or anything—until Dru would be mine and I'd be his, officially tied to each other for eternity.

I knew I was young, at least for people in my world, but having a champion wasn't the same thing as having a spouse. It was *more*. An unbreakable bond. Even the past dragons and their champions lived on in their own beautiful way through the Evergleam, forever powering all of Celaria with the bond they'd created.

I wanted that permanence with Dru. Never apart. Never *left*.

Sloan tapped my shoulder, snapping me out of my daydream. She stood behind me holding out a sheer, glitzy robe, and I slipped my arms through the loose sleeves that fastened at the wrists. Swirls of rhinestones billowed up the material, matching the designs on the Evergleam.

"Neve was nice enough to show me the grove so I could recreate it," Sloan said, picking at the skirt. She wrapped a pale-peach belt around my waist, pulling the two sides of the robe together and clasping it in the center. The sheer gown fell around my feet with a long train lingering behind me, stunning and ethereal.

Perfect.

"I love it." Trailing my fingers along the tiny gems, I watched them catch the light, illuminating the walls with a thousand magnificent rainbows.

The silver-haired warrior squatted at my feet, fussing with the train. It was so strange to see the same woman who kicked my ass at sparring practice work so meticulously with delicate beading and chiffon.

When I had asked Sloan if she would make my dress for our champion ceremony, she had enthusiastically accepted. Nothing existed to tell us what the attire looked like before, and my mother was too young to remember when her sister had done hers. This Sloan original would be the first ceremonial gown in over three decades.

Sloan grabbed her measuring tape, placing it on my hip and bringing it down to where the train ended, jotting a few notes on a scrap of paper.

"It's almost where it needs to be," she said, tucking the pencil behind her ear and circling me again. She grabbed a pair of scissors and sliced through the excess fabric with the same finesse she wielded her sword. "Go ahead and get changed. I'll make sure the finishing touches are ready for tonight."

I looked in the mirror one last time, staring at my outfit that was far flashier than anything I'd normally wear. It would take Dru's breath away.

I wished my dad were here, the thought of him making tears rim my eyes. I always envisioned him seeing me in my gown on my wedding day. Not that today was a wedding day, but it felt just as significant. While this gown wasn't meant for widespread viewing, and the ceremony was private for obvious reasons, it felt strange to do something so big without his blessing.

Dru promised we'd have a traditional wedding once we went back through the portal and got settled. We would just tell my dad we were engaged in the meantime. He would love Dru, his blessing wouldn't be hard to get.

A few knocks sounded at the door, then a pause before it groaned opened, exposing two royal guards who parted, making room for my mother to glide in. She was stiff, as per usual when she was in queen-mode, and had her hands clasped together. "Sloan, may we have a moment?"

"Of course, Your Majesty," she said, bowing swiftly before leaving the room.

She better not be here to talk me out of this.

"You look beautiful." Her heels clicked against the floor while she surveyed my gown from every angle. "Sloan's craftsmanship is outstanding. I should ask her if she'll do a few gowns for me while she's here."

"She did an amazing job."

"I never expected to see this day," she said quietly, running a hand through the sheer layers.

"Whose fault is that?" I mumbled to myself, annoyed but trying to remain calm. The last thing I wanted to do was have a meltdown and mess up my beautiful dress.

My mother's lips pressed into a thin line and her eyes narrowed, deep crescents lining the bottoms of them.

Guess I didn't say that as quietly as I thought.

She stood behind me, placing her hands on my shoulders, not acknowledging my last remark. "Dru is a good man."

"The best."

She stopped in front of me, clasping my hands. "I love you, Kyleigh."

I held my breath. It was the first moment I'd seen my mother not hidden behind her royal presence. The one that seemed to swallow me up anytime she was around. "I know you'll probably never forgive me, but always remember that."

Stunned at her words, I clutched the crystal gown between my fingers. Before I could summon a response, she stepped away from me and quietly slipped out the door.

Back to playing pretend.

Crumpling to the ground, I let the tears fall. I was so tired of pretending.

After all these years separated, I finally had my mother within reach, but I still didn't understand anything about her. I was really no closer to her than I was prior to plummeting through the portal.

I barely knew who I was anymore.

A Celarian.

A magic wielder.

A dragon.

A princess.

A bargaining chip.

The world spun around me, and I clung to my dress, thinking hard about what I could control to bring my surroundings back into focus. The one constant in my life here was Dru, always steadying me with his calming intellect and kindness.

Another knock came at the door, Sloan whispering through the wood, "Is it safe to come in?"

"Yes," I called to her. She opened the door and I peered up at her. The beautiful dress was smooshed around me, my torso the only thing sticking out of the heaping pile of chiffon. She helped me up, straightening out the material.

"I'm sorry."

"Never be sorry for having a heart," Sloan said, wiping my checks with some fabric scraps. "How we feel—what we do about it—that's what makes us who we are."

She hung the sheer outer shell of the gown near her

sewing station. Shimmying out of the bodice, I handed it to her, throwing on a blouse and leggings for my last few errands before tonight.

I wanted everything to be perfect.

Dru deserved nothing less.

32

KYLEIGH

I placed the last few jars of my sparks along the path of Everwood Grove, tiny orange and coral flecks floating within them. It had taken me a solid hour to fill each jar without breaking them, and I was so freaking proud of myself. It was also a great way to ensure I released some power before things got...intimate. From the preview I'd had, I wouldn't be feeling too in control of my powers when I finally got to take this step with Dru.

Hundreds of peach and beige flower petals blanketed the ground leading to the Evergleam. Ox and Neve had offered to help me, most likely to escape the fort and their healers for a bit, and had carted bushels of blankets and pillows into the grove, arranging them into a cozy spread nestled beneath the majestic tree.

Seeing it now conjured visions of Dru and I, bodies intertwined, lit only by the Evergleam's glow. Desire shot through my core, bursting into a million butterflies, thinking about the moment when our bodies would fuse together. Then we'd spend hours stoking the connection of our bond.

Walking barefoot toward the gigantic tree that powered Celaria, my gown fluttered gently against the petals sprinkled across the underbrush. There was something so calming about my feet pressed to the dirt with nothing in between. Being in the grove with my magic felt right.

Dru will be here any minute.

The thought sent a thrill through me. Dru had extracted a few vials of my blood so he'd be able to access the grove when it was time. Ox had planned a get-together in his honor, a bachelor party of sorts to keep him occupied while I finished getting ready. He'd done so much research and work leading up to tonight, it was only fair I take on the final details and let him relax a bit.

Dropping to the cloud of blankets and pillows, I arranged them around me, then I stood, trying to come up with the best seductive pose to accentuate the stunning dress Sloan had constructed for me. I slid one arm up the tree, leaning into it. The bark pressed into my side, scratching my skin. Turning, I arched my back so my ass and shoulder blades were the only things touching the trunk. My hands skimmed along the etchings, and I rested my head against the Evergleam.

Perfect.

Popping a strawberry into my mouth, I stared out into the illuminated Everwood Grove.

Dru was taking forever.

After standing seductively pressed against the tree for an eternity, I had made my way down to the nest of blankets. I draped my gown over me, picking at the fruit plate I'd brought for us.

Did he lose track of time?

Shooting crazy ass sparks from my fingers was my superpower. Patience wasn't.

He'll be here soon, Ky. I took a deep breath, suppressing the part of me that was beginning to get pissed.

I rolled onto my back, bringing a hand behind my head, staring up at the tree. Thousands of glowing teardrops hung above, swaying in the breeze, their light flitting across my skin. The bark's carved flames billowed from the roots beside me, reaching up into the branches.

Maybe I should just go get him?

Collecting a handful of berries from the tray, I stood from my fluffy cloud of blankets. Flattening the skirt of my robe, I strode down the petal-covered path of Everwood Grove, popping the fruit into my mouth. Wispy hairs unraveled themselves from my braids, and I tried to tuck them back behind my ears. I definitely didn't look as pristine as I had when I entered the grove hours ago.

I'm probably just being dramatic.

It only seemed like more time had passed because I'd been anticipating tonight for so long. Dru was due to arrive around moonset. As soon as I made it out of the grove, I would see the day's moon glowing in the sky and realize this was all an overreaction.

Grabbing the small blade I'd tossed to the side near the entrance, I pierced the skin of my fingertip and let a few drops of blood hit the ground. My heart pounded, muddling the sounds of my murmured incantation. Pulling my hands apart, I unlocked Everwood Grove's enchantment, opening to find Arafax's dilapidated village in front of me.

A few more houses were being renovated, leaving the towering fireplaces of the former buildings as memorials for those lost to The Blaze. In the background, the glow of the moon had already receded, a dark-plum sky casting a shadow over Arafax.

Dru was definitely late.

I STRODE TOWARD THE INN, BARE FEET SCRAPING AGAINST THE small rocks and jagged fauna littering the ground.

"Ouch!" My dress snagged on some wayward roots, thorny vines curling around them. *Fuck.* I knelt, gently removing the thorns from the fabric and rubbing out the small imperfections scattered along the skirt's train.

As I came up to The Lavender, its patrons' eyes widened, taking me in. I hadn't thought about how inappropriate I must look in a tiny, skin-tight dress and shimmering overlay, walking up to a very public place. They probably thought I was an overdressed amor. Ignoring their stares, I spotted Ox's head hovering above the crowd. I stayed outside, poking my head in the doorway. Whispering to Aron, one of Flynt's men, I pointed at my friend. "Can you grab Sir Fergus for me?"

Aron chuckled, gaze lingering a little too long before waving to Ox. He staggered over, towering above everyone else. A big smile spanned his bearded jaw. Wrapping his arm around my shoulder, he gave me a squeeze, smelling like apple pie drenched with stale beer.

"What are you doing here?" he slurred, eyeing me quizzically.

"I came to collect Dru," I said, stepping back and fixing

the shimmering train of my dress. There were numerous tears on the bottom, and I prayed Sloan never saw what happened to her masterpiece. "Did he lose track of time? Party a little too hard?"

Ox's eyes narrowed. "He's not with you?"

"No. I came here to get him. I've been waiting for him at the Evergleam."

That had him looking no less concerned, which upped my own concern about twenty notches. "What is it?"

"He left before moonset to meet you." Ox ran a thumb over his auburn beard, eyes darting around. "A few hours ago."

What?

My pulse clamored, acid pooling in my chest. I released a few intentional exhales, making sure I was still breathing.

This is fine.

"Oh." I adjusted my dress, suddenly very aware of its tightness. "Maybe he had to go check on something at the fort?"

"Prolly!" Ox beamed, swaying a bit while he waggled his brows. "He was excited for tonight."

"I'll go find him. Looks like you need to sleep it off." I spun him to face The Lavender. "You okay to get to your room tonight?"

Walking in a lazy zigzag back toward the pub, he called to me, "Come get me if you don't find him there."

I trudged in the direction of Arafax's fort, wiping away the stray tears running down my cheeks. Roots caught at the bottom of my dress, but I kept moving, letting them shred the material. My heart pounded, bile clawing at my throat. My feet were covered in small cuts, but I didn't stop to even acknowledge their sting.

Sloan came into view, the rocky fort looming in the distance behind her. "What are you doing out here?" She scanned me up and down, taking in the tattered dress, and frowned. "Everything okay?"

"Yeah. I will be. I'm sure." I tried to take a deep breath.

I'm just overreacting. We will laugh about this later when we tell our children the story of tonight.

"What are you doing out here?"

"Just finished decorating Dru's room for you guys for after the ceremony," Sloan replied, giving my shoulder a squeeze as she passed. "He was so excited when he split off from me to head to the grove earlier. Can't wait for you to see the room."

"Oh," I said quietly. "That's really nice. Thank you."

"Don't mention it." Her brows knit together, and she stopped walking. "You sure you're okay?"

My chest tightened, skin heating. My body felt like an inferno that needed to be released. The markings on my sides began to itch.

I just nodded, ignoring the tears welling in my eyes, and waved her off. I had to stay calm until I figured out what was going on. "Ox is stumbling around the pub and might need some help getting to his rooms for the night."

"Okay," she said hesitantly. I waved her off one more time, giving a small smile so she'd walk away.

Don't freak out.

I tried to focus on my breathing, but it was too late. The freak out was already happening.

Here I was again, the girl in the chiffon dress. Left without a reason.

Why did everyone leave?

Unfastening the belt at my waist with trembling hands, I

clawed off the sheer overdress. A glow prickled under my skin and my pulse picked up speed. A fiery tingle radiated from my chest.

Is this what a heart attack feels like?

Twisting pain stabbed beneath my shoulder blades, like I was being ripped from the inside out. I shot my head skyward, a scream ripping from my throat. Floating orange, coral, and pink circled around me in slow motion before increasing their pace, encasing my body in an ardent cocoon.

Sparks. *My* sparks.

Nails pushed up from their beds, fingers elongating and transforming into claws. Wings sprung from the buds notched into my back, splaying wide with the crimson veins etched across them.

My claws shredded the peach material covering my body, eyes flaring with heat. As the sparks closed in on me, vicious and beautiful, I pulled my wings in to shield my skin.

There was nothing I could do to stop this.

I closed my eyes, letting the pain consume me.

A blinding light burst in all directions, and in a single heartbeat, my dragon magic exploded forth in its scaled entirety.

33

AISLIN

"Still enjoy a classic Lavender Fizz or is it only the signature over ice for you these days?" Leigh asked from behind the bar.

Sweeney had the night off to celebrate Dru with us earlier. Now he was tucked away in bed, dead asleep. Ox was off gallivanting somewhere. I didn't know how he was still on his feet after drinking nearly a full keg's worth of honey ale.

"I've been known to dabble with a Fizz every so often," I said, a smile begging to cross my lips before I hoarded it away.

Leigh seemed stunned that I was speaking to her. I understood why. I usually kept my communication with her to one-word answers and snappy phrases. It was just too hard for me to be around her. When I looked at Leigh, I thought of Earl. And when I thought of him, I was reminded of my hands stealing his final breaths. Even if he would have died soon after, I'd never forget that first kill against my fingertips, ending the person who had given me shelter when I'd lost everything.

"One Lavender Fizz coming right up," she said, pouring clear, bubbling liquid into a mug, before adding a squeeze of lemon and a sprig of lavender. Then she threw in a copper straw, just like she used to when I'd first moved in.

I was so quiet back then. Unsure what to even say. Sweeney could talk to a rock and be content. He'd sit there, teaching me and talking for hours without a care that I didn't reciprocate.

Meanwhile, Earl was always busy handling the books and guests. Every so often he would bribe me with hard candies he kept in the top drawer of the inn's office desk. I savored those candies and those moments when he told me all about the inn and how he ran it.

Leigh rarely left The Lavender, but she didn't have the numerous duties back then that she did now that Earl was gone. She'd won me over quietly, never one for big gestures or bold statements. Since I spent so much time in the pub, she'd worked with Sweeney to create a non-alcoholic drink for me to enjoy—The Lavender Fizz. It was the one drink she would pop in to make just for me.

The first night she'd served it to me was the first time I'd spoken since I'd started living at the inn, shocking all of them. Honestly, talking had never been the most important thing between Leigh and me. Our bond had formed over the quiet moments. The space that didn't need to be filled with words.

I took a sip of the Fizz, bubbles bursting against the roof of my mouth.

"Thank you," I said. It was probably the most pleasant thing I'd said to her in years.

Her mouth spread into a grin, and she looked toward the entrance of the pub. I peeked over my shoulder to see what had snagged her attention.

Icy-blue eyes skated around the room until they locked on mine. Sloan strode over with a smirk and sat on the stool next to me. "I'll have what she's having," she said to Leigh, dropping a few coins on the bar, then spinning around to lean back on her elbows as she faced the pub and its patrons, taking in the scene.

I was about to say something, to stop her from ordering my childish beverage, but Leigh swooped in before I could, shooting me a gentle but stern look. She pulled out another mug, setting it on the counter and filling it with bubbles. Sloan peered over her shoulder, watching her squeeze in the lemon and throw in a sprig of lavender, raising an eyebrow at me while Leigh worked.

"I have some guests to check in," Leigh said once she was finished, pushing the drink toward Sloan. She scurried out from behind the bar, heading toward the front.

Spinning to face the bar and sweeping back some of her silver strands, Sloan pursed her plum lips, parting them slightly and placing the copper straw on her tongue. I shifted in my seat, squeezing my legs together, gaze pinned to her mouth.

"I see you squirming over there." Sloan smirked, taking another casual sip of her Fizz before licking some excess liquid off her bottom lip. "And I have to say, I enjoy it."

Her eyes streaked down to the floor before raking all the way back up, stopping at my lips. I desperately wanted to grab her by the shirt and pick up where we'd left off with that damn kiss. Instead, I took another sip of my drink, attempting to ignore the chill that shot through me, causing my thighs to clench tight.

She set her Fizz down before leaning close and tucking an errant strand of hair behind my ear. The graze of her nail skimming my neck pulled my focus. "Before you distract me further, I need to talk to you about something. I ran into Kyleigh on my way back from setting up their room for tonight—"

Shouts sounded around the pub, and patrons flooded out of its entrance. Sloan's eyes widened, face etched with concern as she took my hand. We ran out to see what was causing the commotion.

That's when I saw it.

Saw *her*.

A dragon with coral-and-pink scales soared above, partially translucent wings blanketing the sky overhead. They beat with graceful precision, and I watched Kyleigh, entranced. I hadn't seen her shifted into her dragon form, and she'd never flown before that I was aware of. Standing on the balls of my boots, I tried to spot Dru on her back when she dipped lower, letting out some strained huffs.

"Where's Dru?"

"That's what I wanted to bring up," Sloan whispered. "She seemed upset and was looking for him."

"Wasn't he supposed to be at the grove with her?" I asked, spotting Flynt's face locked on the dragon, mouth twisted into a sadistic grin.

"He was. We both left together, and he headed in that direction," she replied. I listened to every word, but I didn't take my gaze off Flynt.

What is that fucker smiling about?

He nodded to Roq who headed back into the pub.

Kyleigh lowered herself to the ground, crouching when she landed. Silver orbs darted around all the people standing there, watching. She twisted her neck down low, peering into the tavern, eliciting a series of shrieks and awe-induced cheers. Lifting her head back up, she started poking her snout into each of the inn's windows on the second and third floors.

She was looking for someone. Dru maybe?

The coral dragon roared then cocked her head away from the inn and stared back at me, a flare of recognition igniting in her eyes. She roved over, hunching her shoulders and dropped her scaled face to rest on the ground next to me. I patted her snout, stroking the scales. They were rougher than Neve's but had an opalescent sheen of white mixed in with her coloring.

It was so strange to think Kyleigh was underneath there. Even stranger that I had a dragon form hidden within me as well.

Shimmering liquid rimmed her silver orbs, pooling at the bottom, forming a droplet. It fell to the ground, sloshing over my boots.

"Dragon tears!" a slender woman shouted, running forward with a copper mug. She caught the next droplet, so large that it spilled over the sides. Kyleigh snarled at her, sending the crowd back a few paces.

I stepped between her and the crowd, holding my arms out with my lightning weaving its warning to stay back.

"Why don't we get out of here?" I asked her, hoping to get her away from an audience until we could figure out what was going on.

She dipped her snout, nodding. Bowing her shoulder down at an angle, I used her neck to assist me, gripping it to climb onto her back. It took a few tries until I could figure out how to stabilize my boots on her scales enough to swing my leg over. I hugged around the dragon's neck, praying I didn't fall off and plummet to my death.

"Can she come too?" I pointed to Sloan.

Kyleigh stayed bowed and extended out her wing, using it to pull Sloan over. The silver-haired warrior climbed up with minimal effort.

Of course.

She sat casually behind me, one knee bent, the other leg resting alongside mine. She brought one arm around, splaying a hand across my waist, her thumb skimming just under my ribs. Her soft chuckle breezed against my neck.

"Let's go," I said to Kyleigh, reaching forward and patting the top of her head.

The crowd stood there, gaping up at us.

The coral dragon stalked off, increasing her pace until she began to lift off the ground. I grasped the scales along her neck, squeezing my legs for extra grip, Sloan held tighter to me.

And we flew.

34

AISLIN

Circling over Arafax and the surrounding woods, Kyleigh's snout snapped frantically around, searching for Dru. Every time I felt comfortable flying near the clouds, she'd dive low, peering into houses or wooded areas. I gripped her scales tightly, using them and Sloan's body to steady me, praying to the stars above that I wouldn't fall.

"Don't get too close," I said, leaning forward against the wind, wanting her to avoid the Silent Woods for both our sakes. I could feel the Enchantress's pull when we edged the border, coaxing me through the thrum of our bond mark.

Kyleigh's pace slowed as heavy blankets of wind hit us.

"Why don't we take a break? You need to rest your magic," I reminded her, hoping she would see reason before we ended up crash-landing somewhere we didn't want to.

Sloan patted the dragon's side, rubbing her scales in encouragement before pointing toward the ground. "Land near the stream. That way we can walk back to the inn without drawing attention."

I huffed a laugh to myself, peering over my shoulder at her.

Her eyes flared to mine. "What?"

"You may have the commander stripped from your title, but it's still in your nature."

She smiled, wrapping her other arm around my waist and clenching me so close a coin wouldn't even fit between us.

Kyleigh slowed her wings, heading toward land as gracefully as she could. Wings faltering and hitting the ground, her body shuddered, tilting forward suddenly and sending us flying through the air. Sloan kept herself clutched to me, spinning us slightly in our descent. She slammed against the ground, absorbing the brunt of the impact, bounding across the dirt with me curled within her arms.

Sloan didn't move.

I scrambled quickly around her, grabbing a shoulder and rolling her over to face me. Her entire body was limp.

No, no, no.

Tilting my head, I brought it level with her chest, squinting to make out its rise and fall. If there was movement, it wasn't enough for me to see. Scooting closer, I rested my cheek over her heart, listening for its beat, my fingers fumbling along her arm trying to find a pulse. Was she—

"You can't get rid of me that easily," she huffed out weakly with a smirk.

My chest unclenched, releasing a sigh as she pushed up on her hands, rolling out her shoulders.

Standing up, I brushed the dirt off along with the fears that had gripped me by the throat moments ago. The chilly touch of a gentle finger brushed over my bond mark.

I flinched.

"What is that?" Sloan asked, eyes scanning the scar.

I slapped her hand away. "It's nothing."

"Whatever you say." She unknit her brows, walking over to Kyleigh who was slumped naked on the ground, blanketed in dirt. Small gashes covered her feet.

What the hell happened to her before she came to the inn?

Sloan picked her up, hoisting her over her shoulder, and I removed my jacket, positioning it to cover her as modestly as possible before we headed back to The Lavender.

SLIPPING IN THROUGH THE BACK, WE TRIED NOT TO DRAW ANY attention from the pub's raucous crowd. We found Roq skulking up and down the narrow hallway. Sloan had me peek in Ox's room, making sure he'd made it there to pass out for the night. He was fully clothed, drooling on the comforter.

"He's out."

She sighed in relief. At least we knew where he was.

"What's this?" Roq asked, raising an eyebrow at Kyleigh slung over Sloan's back. "Someone have a little too much fun?"

"Fuck off," she scoffed, using an arm to push him away. He stepped aside, moving to the other end of the hallway.

"Bitch," he muttered under his breath as he walked past.

Eyes still trailing Roq, Sloan whispered, "One of us needs to stay with her at all times until she wakes up."

I nodded.

We stepped in front of Kyleigh's door. "Fuck."

"What?"

"I need to get the key from Leigh. She obviously doesn't have hers," I said, indicating Kyleigh's state of undress.

Turning and descending the staircase, I walked into the office, rummaging through the drawer of extra keys until I found the one I needed.

A velvet sneer came from the doorway, "Where are you going with that?"

I threaded the key into my back pocket. "Just helping a guest into their room, Flynt."

"Where'd that dragon go?" He stepped closer, grabbing my wrist. "The one that so graciously let you ride on it. Curious..."

"It flew off," I replied too quickly.

He cocked his head. "Why *you*?"

"Just liked me, I guess. I can be quite endearing." I smirked. "You'd know that if you weren't always trying to control me."

Shaking his head, he leaned against the doorframe, blocking my exit. "I don't have to try. I am in control, Aislin. Think you can go off and be free of me? Have a happily ever after with that silver-haired slut and your faux *family* with Leigh and Sweeney? It won't ever happen. I own you. Them. The Lavender. And so much more than you could even imagine. There isn't a corner of this world you could hide in that would change that."

His words stung like poisoned-tipped arrows, sinking deep, injecting venom into my resolve.

"I want that dragon, and since it seems to like you so much, you will help me get it," he said simply, as if it were as easy as catching a rabbit in the woods.

Too much would be at stake if Flynt or his men knew that Kyleigh and I were dragons. Neither of us would be safe. We already weren't just by being at The Lavender with them.

"I didn't realize you were so desperate for a wingman," I

replied coolly. "Sad your dragon dust supply ran out for your dates with the Enchantress. Didn't realize you had so much trouble getting—"

Thwack!

The sound of the back of his hand striking my face echoed in the tight space. It fucking stung, and I paused, trying to collect my thoughts, knowing my cheek was a dark, angry shade of reddish-purple. I swiped my thumb across my split lip.

"Don't toy with my ability to give you mercy. There will come a point where I won't."

"Mercy? From you?" I spat at his feet, blood mixed with the saliva. He'd never struck me before—he hadn't needed to —but now that his favorite pet wasn't being pulled by his leash, the master was angry.

I started to laugh. Not in a heard-a-good-joke way like with Ox. No, this was primal, guttural. Psychotic.

Leigh walked into the office, stopping when she saw us, brows drawn in confusion. I crouched down, continuing my cackling.

"What happened?" She knelt, trying to look at my face.

"What I always knew would, Leigh. What you should have thought about before you allowed him here, ruining our home. Our lives."

Is she really so oblivious?

I held my hands out, lightning flickering before it coiled around my arms and chest as I stood. "They're here because of you. Earl's dead because of you! Both of you!" I stood there, seething at Flynt and Leigh. They stared at my bolts weaving in and around my body, as if seeing it for the first time. They'd only ever seen it contained to my fingertips. My chest heaved, adrenaline coursing through me.

A flash of coral pulled our attention outside.

"I'll deal with you later," Flynt ground out, running into the pub to alert his crew. I turned away from Leigh, the lightning still pouring over my skin, heading to find Kyleigh's dragon outside. Lifting my eyes up, I found Sloan's head poking out a window, looking flustered.

"What are you doing?" she yelled at the dragon. The creature beat its wings, whipping her in the face with the windy current.

People filed out of the pub's doors to see the mythical creature, and those who noticed me, despite the dragon flying, froze in shock. Many of the regulars had seen me in here for years with no clue of the deadly threat that lay within The Lavender's decade-long charity case. I reeled my electricity back in, walking toward the coral dragon.

An arrow whizzed past my shoulder, piercing Kyleigh's wing. Taking a step forward, calloused hands grasped me before I could get to her. Thrashing back against Roq and Lap who'd pinned my elbows back on either side, I watched three more arrows slice into her wings. She screeched, crashing to the ground, flapping them erratically.

The pub's patrons let out horrified gasps. Arafax's dragons were Revered. No one would ever think to harm them.

But Flynt wasn't everyone.

A dragon was just something else for him to control.

Kyleigh's orbs squeezed shut as she whimpered, a few errant sparks bursting from her nostrils.

A silver knife flew past Lap's cheek, its cry the only warning as it headed toward its intended target. Lifting a hand, Flynt caught it by the handle before it could sink into his chest.

My eyes whipped around to the window where Sloan had been, but no one was there.

"Everyone back inside. Nothing to see here." Flynt tucked the knife into his holster before pulling out a satchel stuffed full of coins. He tossed it to Leigh, smiling at the gawking patrons. "Enjoy a round on the house."

The crowd retreated into the pub, Leigh ushering them inside, looking distressed.

Flynt stalked toward the crumpled dragon.

Kyleigh clamped her eyes shut, chest heaving slowly up and down. "Well, aren't you magnificent, peaches?"

Peaches...

He knows.

How could he know?

Fuck.

Did that mean he knew about me?

"Oh, Aislin," he said, tone full of condescension. "You didn't think I became this powerful by being an idiot, did you? I grew up hearing all about our dragons and the power of their champions. When the Queen had asked me to protect Kyleigh, I knew she must be special. Then I heard a rumor about a dragon flying at night a few weeks back. What could be more special than protecting one of Arafax's Revered?"

Protecting its heir.

"Plus, I may have *borrowed* a few texts from the royal library the last time I met with the Queen. Very enlightening material." Kneeling down, he stroked Kyleigh's neck, and she peeled up her lips in a growl, exposing rows of razor-sharp teeth. "Look how beautiful you are."

He nodded to his men, continuing to stroke her. "Don't move, sweetheart. We'll get these arrows out of you."

Kyleigh snapped her maw at him a few times before she attempted to lift her snout off the ground, eyes fluttering. Flynt simply laughed, as if her failed attempts to bite him were playful. "Not the most romantic way to go about this, and I know I'm not your intended, but I promise to make it enjoyable for you. I heard you can also be a bit bloodthirsty, according to my associates in Inverno."

His men ripped the arrows out, inciting desperate whines from the coral dragon. Once they were all removed, she began to writhe and roar in the dirt as her body contorted and rearranged itself. All that remained were the buds from her wings and the scaled marks traveling up her side. Blood pooled around her filthy, scrape-covered body.

I struggled against the men holding me back. "You're a monster, Flynt."

"Of course I am," he said, shrugging. "Who better to wrangle a dangerous monster than an even more dangerous one?"

"Let me through, fuckers," Sloan grunted, elbowing one of Flynt's men in the face before punching another in the groin.

Fight, dammit!

Streaks crawled along my skin, making Roq and Lap jolt off me. By the time Sloan got close to me, stomping on Aron's foot before twisting him to the ground, I'd gotten myself free. I ran and knocked Flynt away from Kyleigh, planting myself between them, trying to shield her from view of the crowd.

"She already has a champion!" Lightning returned to my hands, glaring at him. "You're too late."

"Is that so?" He laughed. "Then where is her *champion?*"

"What did you do?"

My mind instantly flitted to the heap of bodies littering the Enchantress's yard.

No.

I refused to give the thought another moment's hold over me. I had to believe Dru was alive.

"Unfortunately, Dru had other plans this evening," he replied.

My chest clenched as lightning crackled across it. I repeated the question. "What did you do with him?"

"I did what I had to." He spun to face two of his men. "Get her out of here. You know where to take her."

They walked over and picked Kyleigh up, a scream ripping from her throat. I lifted my hands, my lightning forming into spears. Sloan sent a knife whirring into the leg of a captor, and he staggered to the ground, bringing Kyleigh with him.

Her eyes snapped open, glaring at the men who'd been hauling her away, and she unleashed a deafening screech. The two men exploded, a sea of sparks bursting from their chests. Her head dropped, laying in their leftovers, blood pooling on the ground around her.

I took a step toward her—

A series of loud pops rang out from behind me, and I turned to find more bodies erupting, detonating from their chests in a bloody ripple of flesh and bone. Spark-made shrapnel flew in all directions and I ducked to avoid the blast.

When I stood, only two bodies were distinguishable where Flynt's crew had crowded around us. Sloan and Ox were standing next to each other, chests heaving as they caught their breath.

All of Flynt's men.

Gone.

Just messy particles of floating gore and ash hurtling into piles on the ground.

"Blazes," Flynt's voice echoed from behind me, sounding surprised. I pivoted, finding Leigh clutched in front of his chest, limp, covered in blood and debris. Completely unscathed behind his human shield, he stared at the massacre, then drew his gaze back to Kyleigh, ignited. He shrugged Leigh's body off of him, sending her crumpling to the ground.

"Leigh!" I shouted, bolting toward her, icy fear streaking through my limbs.

A loud crack snapped my attention back to Flynt...and the massive crossbow in his hands.

The loud whoosh of an arrow flew past me.

"No!" I screamed, following its trajectory as it hit Kyleigh in her side, her scaled marking his perfect bull's-eye. Her body contracted upon impact, and she yelped, curling into the dirt. Blood wept from the wound, covering her dragon marks, and she lay there.

Motionless.

A flash of white bounded in front of the crowd gathered in The Lavender's entryway, Mox growling at them. Sloan moved toward Ox and Leigh.

"I've got them," she called over her shoulder. "Help her."

I ran over to Kyleigh and placed a hand on her wrist. Blood was everywhere, tingeing the air with its metallic scent. Her pulse's haggard beat dragged through her depleted veins.

"You *are* a bloodthirsty little thing," Flynt mused, feeding another arrow into his crossbow. There was no hint of grief in his tone as he looked around at the piles of his dead crew before aiming the weapon at her. "I can't wait to see what kind of mayhem we make together."

I scrambled over Kyleigh, rooting myself in front of her. Pushing up from the ground, I summoned my bolts, even though they were starting to drain me. I had to keep Flynt away from her.

"You want a monster like you?" I threw out ropes of electricity. They wrangled Flynt's body, dragging him, his boots leaving two deep grooves in the dirt until he stood in front of me. "Don't forget about the monster you already created."

I gripped the lapels of his jacket, tugging him close so he could hear every word that slipped between my gritted teeth. "I'd give you mercy, but I seem to be all tapped out."

Streaks of lightning sank under his skin, and he shrieked, my bolts slowly pouring through his veins, down his arms, his legs, all the way to his toes, bypassing his vital organs. That would be too swift of a death. Too merciful.

He didn't deserve my mercy.

His entire body convulsed, engulfed in their glow, and I held him there, never unlocking my eyes from his, watching as the bolts trailed back up the length of him, weaving around his heart and lungs, igniting his eyes from within.

I wanted to ensure he felt every streak of pain charging through him, every bolt. Two hundred forty-three deaths' worth.

Eventually, his body stopped moving, his mouth hanging open in a permanent, silent scream, and I released my lightning, letting him fall to the ground in a stiff heap.

Pale-gray smoke billowed off him, filtering the scent of burning death into my lungs.

Ox crawled over to Kyleigh, holding her limp body close to him, sobbing.

I turned back to the patrons huddled in The Lavender's doorway, some crying, others trembling, their eyes darting around the scene in front of them.

My attention circled to Sloan standing just a few feet away, cradling Leigh in her arms. Her eyes were wide, lips parted but saying nothing.

She'd seen what I'd done. A side of myself I'd tried to keep hidden from her.

There was no hiding now.

35

NEVE

uted blue seeped through the iron bars. Grasping the metal, I screamed, hating its icy bite against my skin. Frost rose from my fingertips, coating my cage. The blue shone brighter, stinging my eyes. I snapped my chin down, hiding from the light source.

Cerulean light pierced the corners of my eyes, pulling me from my slumber. It was the fourth night in a row I'd had this dream. Trapped in the darkness, only the hazy shade emblazoning my view, its warmth fighting against the cold rushing through me.

I usually woke every few hours, my mind needing reassurance that I was no longer imprisoned beneath Inverno's castle.

Heat permeated the air, my eyes opening to find an ignited form in the corner of my room. Its blue and white wings flapped against the chilled breeze.

Please tell me I'm still asleep.

I groaned. "Redmond?"

Shifting against the moonlight, the flames extinguished in

a ripple until all that remained was my former lover, the man I'd waited a decade to see *me*—what was hidden beneath the scaled beast he'd come to loathe.

He rarely visited the dungeon in my years there. The first few times, I'd tried to do anything to show him that he held the key to my freedom dangling around his neck—the Evergleam's gem. That it was me, the one he'd been mourning, right in front of him. His vengeance blinded him in those moments, and I was certain it'd tainted so many I hadn't been present for.

I'd seen Kyleigh's desperation when she tried to rescue me the night she escaped. Whatever had happened with Redmond at that dinner had shaken her.

While this man looked familiar, he was wholly unfamiliar —no longer the Redmond I knew. The man he'd become had done things his younger self, the one I'd loved, would be appalled by.

Now he finally knew the truth, but I wasn't the same woman either. There were too many fractured pieces to even begin contemplating how to put myself together.

We were two different people now.

Redmond stepped out of the darkness, and the soft glow of the night's moon caressed his powerful silhouette. I scooted back against my headboard, grabbing my extra pillow and throwing it at him with more force than necessary.

"Cover yourself," I demanded, keeping my gaze purposefully locked at eye level.

"You never had any complaints before," he said with a smirk, strategically pinning the pillow in front of him.

"Well, I think we'd agree that a lot has happened since then." I pulled the blanket up over me, bringing my knees into my chest. I thought back to the blue glow that'd permeated my dreams. "Have you been coming into my room?"

"I have," he said, voice just above a murmur. He strode toward the bed, keeping the pillow in place. "I needed to talk to you. I needed to say—"

"What can you possibly say in this situation?" There was nothing, nothing he could say to right the wrongs that had been done to me. The cruelty that had started with his father, King Reynard, and had continued with his indifference and his guards' abuse. "Sorry you locked me away? Sorry you let your guards shred me for years? Sorry you aligned yourself with *her*?"

He flinched at the mention of his new queen-to-be. I tried to keep my tone cavalier, unaffected—I refused to show him anything else. "There's absolutely nothing you can say, Redmond."

He knelt by the side of my bed, resting the pillow in his lap, reaching for my hands. I tucked myself into a tight ball, cowering away from his touch. His eyes dropped, and he clasped his fingers together. "*I am* sorry. For all of it. I know it will never be enough, but I'm trying here, Neve. I'm fucking trying to make things right. Can't you see that?"

"Is this alliance between Inverno and Arafax real? Because if you hurt any of them, so help me, Redmond, I will use every ounce of strength I regain to ruin you."

"I'd expect nothing less." His midnight gaze locked with mine. "But it is real. Our kingdoms *must* unite to do this. I don't expect forgiveness, but we have to give our people a chance. Inverno can't take her on alone. Neither can Arafax."

"You don't even know the full impact of your actions," I seethed before exhaling the blizzard of emotions whipping through me.

"Seems there was a lot I didn't know," he mumbled to himself.

My shoulders raised, tension rolling through them, buds erupting from my back, wings threatening to shoot from them. I still hadn't gotten my shift fully under control—part of the healing process I was still working through. "What's that supposed to mean?"

"How about you being a fucking dragon, for starters?" He jolted to his feet, forgetting about the pillow. "Didn't think that was something to share with someone you were about to spend your life with?"

I kept my eyes from lingering down the deep *V* that once sent shivers through me. He paced back and forth, then he stopped in place, gripping his dark hair as if he were about to rip it out. "You knew of my phoenix form even though it was a secret from your kingdom. You didn't trust me enough to reciprocate?"

"I planned to tell you after we wed," I said, anger stinging my chest. "Not that I owe you an explanation."

His hands clenched around my icy words. "What about my father, Neve?"

"You know what I did."

I killed him.

I'd do it again, too.

"I do. But I still don't know why. Why would—"

"Some explanations are better left alone, Redmond."

My mind tossed me overboard, back to that night.

The lies.

The rage.

A flurry of icicles piercing flesh. Redmond crouched over his bleeding father, screaming into the wind. Then everything around me becoming a blue-and-white inferno.

Arrows punctured my scales, hurling me into a blackened void.

Waking up to iron bars obstructing my view.

He'd believed he lost two loved ones that night—his father and me—but it had only been one who perished by the claws of the other.

"You aren't going to get any good answers here. Now get out," I demanded, pointing at the door. "I have a healing session soon, and the last thing I need is to see...someone who hinders that."

"Just let me—"

"Apologies won't solve anything—for either of us. You want to build an alliance with Arafax? Build one. But leave me out of it."

His shoulders slumped, wings splaying out in a wave of blue flames. Then he flew out the window and into the night.

I let the tears I'd frozen behind my eyes melt freely down my cheeks and scrunched back under my covers.

"Didn't expect to see you down here so early," a deep rumble echoed through the infirmary. I peered up from my mat to find Sir Fergus smirking at me from the doorway across the room.

He was sitting on the cot and Brighid, our petite, platinum-blonde healer, stood a few feet away, scowling up at the giant warrior. She tapped his shoulder, getting his attention and gesturing at him in frustration. Groaning loudly, he crossed his arms and pulled off his shirt. She frowned, scrutinizing his bandages. A few had yellowing smears on them, making the healer's frown deepen.

He smiled tentatively at her, and she rolled her eyes. Throwing her hands in the air, she stomped over to grab medical supplies from the cabinet.

"Overdoing it again, Sir Fergus?" I called out, shaking my head. He was supposed to be resting, but any time I saw him around the fort's grounds, he was carting around big items or tending to various chores that he had no business doing while healing. "You're going to give Brighid a heart attack if she has to keep dealing with soiled bandages every time you're due here for a visit."

"Aw, Brighid loves taking care of me," he said, puffing his chiseled torso and clasping her hands in his. "Don't you, beautiful?"

She gave him a gentle smack before pouring some healing elixir on his chest. The massive warrior hissed in pain at the tiny healer who just laughed. "Serves you right, cheeky bastard."

"I'll be with you as soon as I'm done, Neve," Brighid said, lifting Sir Fergus's arm with a grunt. She wrapped fresh gauze around his midsection to cover the healing wounds—some had reopened or worsened after everything happened at The Lavender.

I refocused on my stretches, retracting and expanding my wings, controlling the partial-shift between my dragon and human form.

Sir Fergus's eyes were glued to me. Hopping off the cot, he grabbed a glass of water from the countertop and walked over. "That's fucking mind-boggling to watch, you know that?"

I tightened the straps of my camisole, making sure every-thing was tucked in and away from his viewing. The last thing I needed was my breasts popping out in front of

Arafax's most notorious rake. Of course, fixing myself dragged his attention exactly where I was trying to aim it away from.

Pink bloomed on his cheeks. "Um. I'm sorry, I wasn't meaning anything by it. I've never really seen someone shift before. Into a dragon that is. I'm still wrapping my head around Kyleigh being able to do it."

Kyleigh had retreated into her dragon form when she woke up after Sloan and Sir Fergus had rushed her to the fort. She was in bad shape, refusing help from anyone and shooting sparks from her snout when we tried to go near her.

"You're fine," I replied, trying to clear the awkwardness in the air. "You're welcome to stay while I work with Brighid."

"What are you working on?"

"I get a little anxiety about shifting back and forth now. It doesn't come as natural as it did before..."

His eyes softened. "Before you were stuck?"

"Yes." I rolled my shoulders back, trying to loosen up. I knew I'd be sore after our session. "I'm working on controlling different parts of my shift at a time. Strengthening my wings so I can hold a partially transitioned form again."

"What does that look like?" he asked, childish curiosity shaping his words. He cleared his throat. "If you don't mind me asking, that is."

Standing up, I shook out my shoulders, the sound of my wing buds popping breaking up the silence. I sucked in a breath, pushing my wings out from my back, expanding the width of the infirmary. Holding them up a moment, my shoulders tensed before the weight became overwhelming and they collapsed to the ground. "I used to be able to hold them up for hours, to fly with them not fully in my dragon form, but I've lost that strength."

Brighid came behind me, kneeling, trying to lift one of my wings.

"Can I help?" Sir Fergus asked.

"You don't have to."

"I know that, but it's not like I am off saving the realm right now." His gaze dropped to the floor a moment before coming back up to meet mine. "I'd like to help."

I nodded, and he smiled, placing his water on the counter before shifting his attention to the healer, waiting for instructions.

He moved to the other wing, mimicking Brighid so both were supported. She wiggled my wing, and I pulsed them slightly, working against the resistance of their weight. After a minute, I was panting, hunched over and fighting to catch my breath. "I can't fucking do this."

"I know it's hard," Sir Fergus said, heaving an exasperated sigh. "My strength was one of my biggest advantages, especially with my size. Now I feel like a weakling in comparison to where I was a few months ago. Even getting Kyleigh back here, something that used to be nothing at all, reinjured my leg a bit."

"Maybe if you actually let yourself heal..." Brighid grumbled to herself.

He frowned, not validating her argument with a response. Sir Fergus was a knight, one of the highest ranking in Arafax. At least he had been. Being reduced to shining armor—and resting—was not his forte.

I'd watched Sloan struggle with her role after being removed as Inverno's Commander, how it shook her, even when she didn't want to let it show. Training Kyleigh and Aislin had given her purpose, a focus to tether herself.

"How about we make a deal, Sir Fergus?"

He was enjoyable company, always making the others laugh in the dungeon, no matter how bleak things got. How different my days down there would have been if I had his persistent good nature.

"Call me Ox. My friends do." He chuckled, bracing his eyes to the ceiling before bringing them back down and raising a bushy, auburn brow. "What did you have in mind?"

"You take the rest Brighid prescribed and help me." Confusion etched the lines of his face, and he stroked the reddish stubble along his jaw. "I want to get strong again. You can help me get into fighting shape so we can kick some Enchantress ass."

He beamed, excitement billowing through eyes the color of rich cocoa. "I can do that."

"Good," I replied, returning the smile. "I don't want to have to freeze your ass since you haven't been resting up like you should."

Brighid massaged my shoulder blades, and I retracted my wings. "Makes my life easier if you can keep him out of trouble for a few days."

The healer continued kneading out knots of tension stored in my upper back from the daily work I'd been putting in. "Very well. Rest up today, Sir—Ox. I'll be ready for a lesson tomorrow."

"Sounds great." He started to walk away, grabbing the glass of water from the counter before hesitating and mumbling something to himself. He turned back to face me. "I promised Aislin I would do a sweep of Arafax tomorrow for Dru since Kyleigh's..."

"Still in her dragon form."

He nodded.

"We can go together before our lesson," I said, glad there was something I could help with. "Having a dragon fly you around should make it much easier, not to mention faster."

Ox choked on the water he was sipping. "Um"—cough—"fly"—cough—"on you?"

"Don't tell me you're afraid." I snorted, tilting my head. It was amusing to see such a giant man, a warrior, so disarmed.

"I'm not." He wiped his arm across the wet stubble on his face. "But I'm a bit larger than you."

"Is that so?" I put my hands on my hips, pursing my lips. "It's obviously been too long since you've seen my dragon form."

His eyes bulged a moment. "True," he croaked.

"So I'll see you tomorrow at moon shine?"

"Moon shine it is."

36

REDMOND

"I've been ordered to keep an eye on you," Sloan said, handing me a pair of charcoal pants, eyes averted from me until I'd slid them on.

Her tone was stiff, which in her defense was warranted. Things were tense between us. I had been so furious at her for betraying me, letting it cloud the bigger picture of why she'd done it in the first place. It was just another way my rage had fucked with my life. She'd been my friend since childhood. One of the few genuine ones—the life of a prince always fraught with those who called themselves *friends* in exchange for favors.

"That's fair," I replied, nodding curtly.

She gestured to the labyrinth of dark stone that curled around the outside of the fort.

I'd poured through Inverno's texts to see if there were any clues as to what the book contained and came up empty-handed. I still wasn't fully sure what language the runes were in the tome.

"This way, Your Majesty."

Fuck.

Things were bad. Sloan never gave a shit about my royal status, only using formalities when we were in public.

Commander Syler, her father, had been appointed as the one to train me. Meanwhile, she'd sat in on our sessions, usually smirking while her father kicked my scrawny, unco-ordinated ass. One day I snapped at her, inviting her into the ring to spar with me.

She didn't even hesitate.

I realized a few things that day. One, her father had been going way too easy on me. I had a lot to learn. Two, his daughter would be the best warrior in the land one day. What she lacked in physical mass, she made up for with agility and tenacious strategy. She bested me, over and over, my pride challenging her round after round.

Sloan never held back her attacks, not even for her prince. When I finally conceded, I'd never been more sore in my life. She brought me healing balm and water, then sat next to me, giving me shit as if I were any one of her fellow squires.

We'd been friends ever since.

I witnessed her rise up Inverno's ranks over the years, serving under her father until his passing about five years ago. I knew right away she would be taking his place. There was no one else I trusted more.

My father always believed a good king needed discipline and to hone as many skills as possible to protect his kingdom —something I carried with me to this day. I still trained as part of my routine, often with Sloan...until everything happened the night of the banquet. The bitterness I felt without my friend and confidante vanquished my motivation.

"I have to ask, was Dru able to glean anything from the tome I'd left with him?"

"No. Not yet."

"Are you really going to talk to me like we are acquaintances?"

"I'll act like I know you when you act like the man I knew." Sloan peered over her shoulder, ensuring we were alone. "I swear if this alliance is a farce, I will jam my sword so far—"

Bursts of vibrant rose and crimson twirled along the breeze. Lifting my hand to capture a few, they sizzled against my palm. Hints of toasted cinnamon and cardamom tinted the air, accompanied by an inhuman whine.

I cocked my head, moving toward the sound, tracing the path of the fort's maze.

Sloan looked hesitant, hand readied on the scabbard of her longsword. Not that I would try anything, but it was a little worrisome to wonder who Sloan would side with if it came down to it. Would she serve her legacy and our lifetime together in Inverno? Or would our fractured friendship and my removal of her stature—not to mention her interest in the assassin tasked with taking my life—be enough to flip her blade against me?

Another whimper echoed against the stone, drawing me out to the arena.

My breath caught, awed at the dragon in front of me. "Who is that?"

Sloan sighed, looking around before bringing her voice to a whisper. "Kyleigh."

Gold, orange, and pink spread across the wings curled around her, blocking the rest of her from view. I knew from the way she was hunched over and the puncture wounds breaking up her smooth, opalescent wings that she must be in a lot of pain.

She was beautiful to behold. Breathtaking despite her gruesome injuries.

But if it was anything like it was for me in my phoenix form, holding the shift took immense energy and taxed the mind along with the body, making it nearly impossible for her to heal from those injuries.

Sparks rose up from within her shelter, riding the wind in an array of pinks and reds and oranges. I had seen her unleash those same sparks in my banquet hall the night she escaped, before using them to take out my guards.

"How long has she been able to shift?" I asked Sloan, spotting an additional wound on the dragon's abdomen. It was large and oozing. "Who did this to her?"

Sloan cleared her throat, keeping her voice clipped. "She's only been able to shift a week or so. Hasn't shifted back since she was attacked at the inn by Flynt and his men. They took Dru, and we can't find him."

Shit. There goes our best shot at translating the tome.

Piping hot anger burst through my veins. I never trusted Flynt, always avoided utilizing his services if I could. I was suspicious he'd been working with my guards, with the Enchantress, all along. Here was another dragon, one that'd been hurt, that could be connected to him. And *her*. "And where is Flynt? I have questions I need to ask him."

Sloan lowered her voice. "Dead. Along with the rest of his crew," she said, impatience swathing her tone. "I can brief you on the rest if you'll just come with me." She turned, taking a few steps back toward the fort, but she stopped when she realized I wasn't following her.

The dragon in front of me hardly seemed like the woman

who blasted my guards and then went on to slaughter a band of criminals a few days ago. Hiding within her wings, trembling, she looked weak. Scared.

After the night I'd lost everything, I'd retreated into my phoenix form for a month. Sloan had been able to coax me out of my grief enough to get me to shift and take my place as the new ruler of our kingdom. If she hadn't, I'm not sure how long I would have remained hidden away in the mountains.

My humanity had left me in those moments after I'd lost Neve and my father. Honestly, reflecting on the things I'd done, I wasn't sure I'd ever gotten it back. Rage and vengeance had consumed me for the last decade. All I wanted to do was cocoon myself away from my shame like the coral dragon in front of me.

I didn't begrudge her desire to shield herself from reality.

But hiding away didn't change the reality of the situation.

Staring up at the fantastic dragon, I reminded myself that the young woman who escaped my castle months ago lay within the creature that was now about ten times my size. I stepped closer, and her wing lifted, giving me a clear view of a scaled snout before it shot a line of fiery sparks toward my feet. I jumped out of the way, cursing loudly.

A low rumble erupted from her chest along with more flaming specks. She might be trying to scare me off, but the last thing I would do was act afraid. I sent out a few rays of blue phoenix fire, twirling it around her threat and herding it to me. I plucked up a rosy flare, smirking as it nipped at my fingertips.

The dragon tilted her head, silver orbs pinned to me, huffing a few times, as if trying to make up her mind about me handling her power.

"I know we didn't meet under the best circumstances," I said, holding my hands up by my shoulders in surrender and letting her spark drift away. "But you really need to shift back, Kyleigh. You won't be able to heal otherwise."

"Let's go," Sloan gripped my arm with one hand, nodding back toward the maze.

I held fast, digging my heels in the ground. "Wait."

"If the Queen sees you here with her, I can't guarantee you'll keep that alliance you're claiming to be so committed to."

"Why?" I asked, attention steadily on Kyleigh, who kicked her claws up behind her, ready to charge.

"Because you don't have a good track record with our dragons," drawled a familiar voice from behind me. Despite the apparent ease with which Queen Isla spoke, there was fury laced through her tone.

She was right, and there was no reason for Kyleigh to trust me. I'd captured her—trapped her in my dungeon. My guards had tormented her enough to make her lash out with the only power she had. I understood how deadly new abilities could be without the stability of the Evergleam's gem. Their deaths marred my hands as well as hers.

"She's hurt and needs to see a healer," I said, turning to find the Queen's silvery gaze glaring at me, her hand stroking her hair over her shoulder. "Her recovery will be significantly hindered otherwise."

The dragon paused a moment, as if weighing her thoughts, before opening her wings and expanding their reach as far as they would go. She roared at me loud enough to be heard from the nearby village, flinching against the pain of her injuries.

"You should leave."

"Stop hiding, Kyleigh," I said, ignoring Isla, trying to recall what Sloan had said to me all those years ago. "You can't fix what you refuse to face."

Her dragon was formidable, possibly larger than Neve's sapphire form, and the silver orbs of her eyes burned bright in their intensity. She glared, if I could guess the expression, huffing at me as she slouched back down.

"Dru needs you. Don't you want to heal so you can get to him?"

The Queen strolled forward, the satin train of her scarlet gown flowing behind her. "Don't make the mistake of believing I won't happily sever that handsome face from the rest of you if you harm those I love or my people ever again. For Neve's sake and the future of my kingdom, I'm willing to work with you. Temporarily. But you need to go. Stay away from her."

I couldn't blame her. Though I didn't personally kill her family or choose to attack Arafax, my father had been the one to go after them and the gem. He never told me why, though. When Commander Syler had brought the opalescent stone to me, I locked it away in a cage so I could always carry it with me. It was the last thing my father had done for our kingdom. I knew it was important to him.

It wasn't until Inverno saw the effects that I realized how much the gem had been worth.

Now we would have to work together to protect both our kingdoms and the rest of Celaria.

Stepping closer to the dragon, I ignored the warning growl coming from her. I reached an arm out, and she bared her teeth at me but stayed still, the silver pools of her orbs so bright, so familiar... My eyes went wide. "She's your—"

"Dragon," Isla finished, gaze darting to her guards, a subtle demand to not say more if I wanted to keep my balls.

Kyleigh was her daughter. The heir to Arafax's throne.

Isla hadn't flayed me alive for keeping her own child imprisoned in my dungeon, which meant she needed this alliance just as much as I did.

"What the fuck is *he* doing here?" an angry voice growled out as the sound of footsteps approached. Two guards walked alongside Aislin, and it was as if on cue that my shoulder blade began to throb, like her giant companion was impaling me with one of Neve's scales all over again.

Somehow, she'd decided to spare my life that night. Part of me wished she hadn't. I could have died clutching my anger at Arafax for all I'd lost. Now I had to deal with the harsh reality: I'd been the root cause of my own misery.

Aislin stomped over in her boots, lightning crawling up her arms. "I don't know why you think we can trust him," she seethed, eyes going wide a moment later as she knelt, suddenly remembering she was talking to the Queen, "Your Majesty."

Bolts crackled against the ground, but she remained on her knees. The Queen looked pleased with her prostration—something I was certain wasn't easy to get.

"I need to speak with *her*," Aislin replied, anger wafting off her. Lightning spooled back into her fingertips. "She's had enough time to wallow."

Kyleigh lifted her coral head, scales rippling, and she swiveled her neck to the side a moment before ducking back down and bringing her wings around her.

I narrowed my eyes at the angry brunette. "She's hurt and won't get better unless she shifts back."

"Why do you even care? Guilty conscience?" Aislin

crossed her arms, making no move to extend the bridge I was offering. "Fuck off before I change my mind about letting you live."

"Feel free to try," I said in challenge.

A screech ripped through the air. The sight of opalescent wings beating against the watercolor sky was enough to interrupt our pissing match.

37

"If she keeps flying, she could crash. Her wings haven't properly healed." King Redmond almost sounded concerned. It was probably just a show for the Queen to keep up their alliance, or some strange, warped version of guilt over his misdeeds. Either way, there was no way I'd ever trust the feathered fucker.

Exhaustion swept through me from the last few days of staying by Leigh's bedside when I wasn't out trying to find leads where Dru could have been taken. Her burns were slowly healing, but she still hadn't regained consciousness from the blast. She hadn't even moved a pinky. I'd watched every finger, toe, and eyelash, praying to the stars above that she would be okay. I didn't deserve their blessings, but I begged for them anyway.

The rational side of me knew Kyleigh didn't intentionally hurt Leigh, that she was fighting to save herself. The other side, the one that kept watch over Leigh in that infirmary bed, was pissed beyond measure.

My body pulsed, my rage over what had happened at the

inn flickering under the surface. Meanwhile, Kyleigh had decided to be a coward, hiding away in her dragon form. She should be out searching for Dru, leaving me to pick up the other pieces of her mess.

Instead, I was handling it all.

I ripped off my leather jacket, throwing it on the ground next to me. "If she's going to be like this, then let's see how she does hiding from one of her own."

Shucking off my pants and shirt, I pictured my dragon, buds popping between my shoulder blades. Purple and black wings expanded from my back.

King Redmond retreated a step, Sloan moving defensively in front of him gripping her scabbard. I couldn't forget the look on her face after I'd murdered Flynt. I'd unleashed a new, terrifying facet of my electric wielding. One that had her now protective of that asshole.

I don't know why I expected anything less.

Well, she'd already seen the monster within when I'd slain Flynt. What was a mere scaled beast at this point?

Heat surged through my eyes. They snapped their attention to Sloan, my vision clearing to the point where I could see every strand of silver on her head, and I knew they had slits driving through the middle of my emerald orbs.

I hadn't summoned my dragon yet. I'd been afraid of what would happen if I was seen.

What if they feared me?

But another question terrified me more.

What if they saw it as another way to use me?

To own me.

Sloan was the only one here I considered trustworthy, and I didn't even understand why. She was the enemy.

Her brows were stitched together, and she looked worried. "Aislin, what are y—"

The sound of bones cracking and reforming filled the arena. The shaded markings climbing along the sides of my abdomen sprouted pointy iridescent-purple buds. I screamed as they pierced through my skin, covering the planes of my body. A scaled snout extended from my nose and chin. Ashes clogged my throat, a foreign sensation crackling through it.

Sputtering out coughs to clear my airway, jet-black smoke spread in front of me, tiny purple bolts peppering the smog like electric confetti.

I padded forward, hurling myself into the sky, eyes locked on a coral-twisted tail. Beating my wings haphazardly against the wind, I pushed on, as finessed as I could for my first time flying, barreling toward Kyleigh, roaring into the open air. She was losing altitude, struggling against the breeze.

Getting closer, I shot violet bolts at her from my nostrils. Would she understand me in this form? I had to try.

You need to stop this, Kyleigh.

Her head cocked awkwardly, as if trying to shake my presence away. Arafax's castle sat ahead of us, hovering above the ground. I hadn't seen it this close since I was a child. Its golden splendor was still awe-inspiring, shaped like curved flames billowing into the purple watercolor sky. Kyleigh paused a moment, taking notice of the structure. I took her hesitation as an opening, knocking into her and sending us tumbling onto the abandoned castle grounds.

Our bodies crashed into the copper walls, the unstable structure beneath us shaking. Pinning the coral dragon beneath me, I opened my maw, placing my teeth around her neck, threatening to clamp down.

Running away won't help us find Dru. He needs you.

Snarling into her ear, I released her as I felt her body contort, shrinking into a tiny naked heap on the floor.

Kyleigh clutched her knees, sobbing. I pictured my body, wincing through the pain of my bones cracking. Shifting back was uncomfortable, but I was relieved that I'd been able to do it.

"Stop crying," I seethed. "You don't get to play the victim here. Not right now. Too many other things are at stake."

"Fuck you, Aislin," Kyleigh grumbled, stumbling a bit as she stood, obviously still adjusting to her human form after days of isolating herself in her dragon magic. "You have no clue what I've been through since I was *forced* here."

She stalked toward me, wobbling every few steps, eyes filled with teary rage. "I've been stabbed, burned, captured, imprisoned, harassed, and shot at. Mul-ti-ple times," she shouted, waving her arms wildly. "Months ago, I didn't even know magic was real. Now it's everywhere, running through me, and it seems the only way I can control anything happening to me is to use it. I'm so fucking sorry about Leigh, I just..."

She sank to the ground, her body shaking from the force of her sobs. "I didn't mean to hurt her. You must know that. I was just trying to protect myself."

Releasing a sigh, she continued sniffling as she wiped her eyes with her arm. Ooze dribbled from her wing buds and the large wound on her abdomen, blotting out the markings that trailed up her side. "I saw Ox there and knew I could focus the blast away from him...I didn't know she was out there. I would never hurt Leigh. Not on purpose."

"What happened that night, Kyleigh?" I asked, sinking down next to her.

"Dru never showed to our ceremony. I waited for hours. When I went to go find him at the inn, Ox said he'd left for the grove already. I figured he'd gone to the fort, that something important had come up in his research, but on my way, I ran into Sloan who said she'd walked with Dru toward the grove. That she'd just come from decorating our room. Dru's room," she corrected. "All I remember after that is feeling like my soul was burning, splitting in two. The transition was so fast, I couldn't hold it in."

"Do you have any idea where he is?"

"No. I've gone out every day, flying around all the nearby territories, and I don't sense him anywhere. Maybe if we had been able to complete our bond, I could. Of course I managed to screw things up. Even if I do find him, he probably won't want to be my champion anymore."

"Why do you think that?"

"Dru didn't look at me the same after what happened in the dungeon." Kyleigh peered up at me with tear-rimmed eyes. "When he finds out what happened at The Lavender, about Leigh, he won't want to be tied to this." She attempted to sweep her arms over herself but was unable to lift them past a certain point.

"We will find him, Kyleigh."

"What if he's dead? Or injured?" she said, glancing down quickly, grimacing at her abdomen. A hysterical sob ripped through her. "The only people who could have told me where he is are dead now. I failed him."

Killing Flynt and his men definitely made things more difficult, but I wasn't going to tell her she was right. "Dru is stronger than you give him credit for. We both know he's resourceful. He's probably figuring out a way to get back here as we speak."

"Maybe," she whispered, the slump of her shoulders telling me she wasn't too confident about that. Sighing loudly, she looked up at the castle next to us.

Thick coppery-gold towers stretched into the clouds, curving at varying angles to create a torch's flame, the symbol of Arafax. Debris littered the empty castle grounds surrounding us. I nodded my head at the entrance, and Kyleigh followed me, slightly hunched on her injured side.

"We're still naked," she laughed, shaking her head and bringing her clasped hands in front of her as modestly as possible.

"I have a feeling we will need to get used to that if we'll be shifting so often," I said. "Maybe there's something left inside that we can throw around us, like a curtain or a discarded gown."

White-marble columns, splintered with gold and crimson accents, lined the Great Hall as we entered the castle. It was dark, the only light coming from the doorway, casting a dusky glow into the open space. Everything donned a thick coat of dust.

In the middle of the hall stood a massive charcoal slab of rock, gold melded through its center, spilling over the edges and feeding into a series of dragon statues that circled around it.

A shriek pulled my attention away from the artistic display, and I spun to find Kyleigh staring at a pile of decayed remains. I'll admit, I'd never thought about those who died up here after the floating stone staircase leading to the castle had fallen. No one had been able to return since—

"Oh my God, how long have they been up here?" Kyleigh asked, hands shaking at her sides, tiny sparks sinking to the ground from her palms.

"No one has been here since The Blaze," a gruff voice echoed through the hall, instantly raising my hackles.

"What are you doing here?" I spat out, spinning around with bolts flickering across my fingers, venom poised for our unwelcome visitor. "Get out."

King Redmond stood under the arches of the castle's entryway, wings splayed wide.

38

KYLEIGH

ing Redmond took one step forward, more into the light, his naked body still preternaturally perfect. Muscles rippled over his frame, his outstretched wings extinguishing into their sable hue. He lifted his arms, and I drew my eyes level with his, but it was a moment too fucking late. Once again, I'd caught a completely accidental glimpse of his dick. I blinked a few times, trying not to think about the fact that it looked like it could split someone in two.

Yikes.

He smirked at me, eyes blazing cobalt before returning to their usual midnight. Did he know I hadn't avoided seeing? Either way, it made the skin across my cheeks heat.

"For the love of Celaria, please put on some clothes," Aislin groaned, emerald eyes flicking to the ceiling. "You have five seconds to cover up before I shoot my bolts at your precious appendage."

"You do realize you're also naked, and you don't see me

gawking at either of you," he said smoothly, keeping respectful eye contact with us.

I instinctively crossed my legs and arms. Aislin wrapped herself in some lightning, strategically covering up. I did the same with my sparks.

"What are you doing here?" I asked him.

He glanced over his shoulder, blue flames rippling out across his wings. Curling them inward, he let the fire circle around him, covering him enough so his junk wasn't on display. "Thank you for the idea."

My eyes flared, stinging with heat and amplifying my vision. I blinked away the sensation until they felt normal again.

The King arched a brow at me.

"Answer the question, King. What are you doing here?" Aislin's tone was full of venom, and she crossed her arms in front of her. "Come to see your handy work?"

His jaw ticked. "I know you don't believe or trust me, but I had nothing to do with this. The Blaze, yes. Not *this*."

"Shifting blame...how *kingly* of you," Aislin snarked, pointing at the pile of bodies I'd discovered moments ago.

He stilled.

"We don't have time for petty arguments. We need to move them and give them proper burials. Then I need to find Dru," I said, wanting to focus on what truly mattered right now.

"That could take hours," Aislin sighed, shaking her head. "Besides, we don't bury our people."

"Then we'll do whatever you normally do, but they deserve better than to be left here, discarded."

"Look, continue to hate me, I don't fucking care, but let me help with this." King Redmond walked over, pushing some remains into a pile on top of a rug. His eyes shot to my side, and he frowned. "Besides, Kyleigh shouldn't be doing this while she's injured."

Aislin glared at him but grimaced when her attention snagged on my back. My wing buds stung and cool liquid dribbled down my shoulder blades. I didn't even want to see my abdomen. I knew it was bad, but I also knew that some of these people were my family. Dru's family. If I found him, I wouldn't be able to look him in the eye knowing I'd just left them like this. "After we finish here I'll get them looked at."

King Redmond's gaze narrowed, obviously not believing me.

"I promise..." *I'd think about it at least, once this was done.*

"Don't you have kingly duties to attend to in your ice castle?" Aislin asked him.

"Yes, but this is more important." He continued piling up the remains, then folding the edges of the rug in the center before dragging it all toward the entrance.

"I'm sure you don't know this, as shifting is new to you, but you heal much slower when you are in your other form. You shouldn't have waited so long. It looks like your wings and your side are infected."

I glanced at the green pus seeping down over the scaled markings. Snapping my attention back to King Redmond, I glared, annoyed that he was trying to be helpful. I'd prefer to keep hating him. "I don't take orders from you."

"Of course not, Your Highness." He bowed his head.

I stilled, breath snagging in my lungs. He knew who I was. *Fuck.*

"I'm not going to tell anyone," he whispered, midnight eyes peering into mine. "But I need to do this. Let me, and your secret is safe."

"Are you really trying to blackmail me into letting you help clean up your own damn mess?"

"Whatever it takes."

I let out a frustrated groan.

"Need me to zap his ass, Kyleigh?" Aislin asked, looking up from her work and noticing my discomfort.

"It's tempting. But just let him help, Aislin. We'll finish faster and get on with our lives."

"Thank you," he nodded, grabbing a massive rug that was covered in dust and dragging it over.

I turned to Aislin. "If you shift, we can load them onto you to fly down. I'd do it myself but, if what he's saying is true, I'm not sure I should be shifting too much until I heal."

"It is," he muttered.

"Very well." Aislin crouched down a moment, black and purple wings springing from her shoulders. Her green eyes began to round out, slits striking through their centers, and scales rippled over her skin. The cracking of bones echoed through the barren Great Hall.

Ignoring the pain as best I could, I walked over to the rug and helped the King fold it up. He gave me a small bow of his head, reminding me that he knew my real identity—Arafax's princess.

I'd spent so much energy hiding who I was, suffocated by the fear someone would find out. Getting this small reprieve to do something for the victims of this tragedy without any formalities and pretense was invigorating. Whether or not I was ready to acknowledge it openly, they were my people.

Hours later, we had moved most of the bodies below Arafax's towering castle. We'd braved the blood-splattered throne room, finding muted jewels, and rusted tiaras sitting atop piles of decomposed remains of Arafax's royal family.

My family.

Being here was like meeting the ghost of something I'd never known. I couldn't help but wonder if I had a right to mourn a life I'd never been a part of, people who didn't even know I existed.

Maybe I did. Maybe I didn't. But it stung, nonetheless.

For the first time since I'd arrived, I felt bad for my mother. She hadn't seen her family since leaving Celaria decades ago, all of them killed by the time she'd returned. They had been decaying out of reach, a spectral shadow hanging above the fort she'd taken residence in.

Did their deaths haunt her?

"How do you honor the dead?" I asked Aislin. Another reminder that I barely knew anything about this world. I could never be Arafax's Queen. I'd always be a less than suitable ruler. Plus, most of its people were terrified of me after everything that transpired at The Lavender.

My mother would have to find another solution for the throne when I returned with Dru to the Otherworld. Even the name of where I was from reminded me that I was an outsider here. That I didn't belong.

"We burn them. Let their souls fly northbound, where they're destined to rest," Aislin said, eyes downcast.

"Well, let's get the Queen and get it done." I still didn't want to call her my mother in front of King Redmond, despite knowing he was aware of the secret.

He bowed, eyes shifting to Aislin's. "Make sure she's seen

by the healers." He turned to me, "You'll be no use to Dru if you continue to let those wounds fester."

I didn't know if he meant the ones currently oozing or the ones that were unspoken.

Unseen.

It was hard to believe this was the same tyrant that murdered two of Flynt's men at a banquet a few months ago, but then again, I didn't have much room to talk.

Aislin just rolled her eyes at him. "Thanks for your concern, but Arafax can handle its own."

"That's fair," he said, walking away with his head down. Blue flames licked the base of his spine. "Just don't forget, we are on the same side now."

"It'll take more than Inverno trying to clean up its mess a decade too late for me to believe that," she replied.

"You're not going to come to the send-off?" I asked. Isn't that why he'd done this? To alleviate his conscience. To feel less like the monster he was.

Did it work?

"That's not my place," he said simply, before igniting his wings. In a ripple of blue and white flames his phoenix took to the sky.

"Ugh, I fucking hate him," Aislin scoffed.

I couldn't blame her. I hadn't forgiven him for my time in Inverno's dungeon, and he had done way more to Arafax and Aislin personally than he had to me. But even monsters weren't only comprised of vicious talons, scales, and claws. Even one like him.

It took me a few extra minutes to shift due to the extent of my injuries in my human form. Once I did, I flew back to the fort, Aislin's purple dragon trailing behind me.

Redmond had already jetted away from the castle, but I noticed he didn't fly off toward Inverno.

After we'd cleaned ourselves of the dirt, blood, and unnamed muck that covered our bodies, I sent word through the guards to notify the Queen. Today had taken too much out of me, and I was not ready to deal with her myself. Thankfully, she quickly made pyre preparations for later in the evening.

Aislin escorted me to the infirmary, and the healer winced when she saw the state of my wounds. I bit down on a leather strap in my partially shifted form, Aislin holding my wing out while the healer cleansed the wounds before spreading a balm over them and wrapping them up. Then she cleaned and properly stitched my side. The arced markings would probably heal ragged. Perhaps a visit to Renovo Falls with Dru once he was back could fix them.

But maybe some scars weren't meant to simply disappear.

I DIDN'T HAVE THE STRENGTH TO KEEP MY WINGS OFF THE ground in my half shift, so Ox met me at the infirmary with a change of clothes sent by my mother. He and Aislin steadied me, Neve joining us next to the stones of the castle's fallen staircase for the funeral ceremony at dusk.

In simple charcoal frocks, Celaria's color of mourning, we watched my mother walk out to the front of the crowd. "I've often wondered what had happened that day. If I had been here, would I be in this pile alongside my brothers, my sisters, my parents," she sank down, running a hand along the dirt, "my nephews?"

Tears streamed down her cheeks. For a moment she looked like the mom I remembered.

"A thank you to those who retrieved them today." Her eyes met mine, lingering as more tears flowed.

Clearing her throat, she tore her gaze away. A wall had come down for a moment, shooting right back up where it would probably remain.

"Let them finally find their way," she said, holding out her hands. Ruby flames ignited the pyre, circling around the mass grave in an array of oranges, reds, and whites.

The embers collided into each other, lighting the darkening purple sky. What was left of Arafax's lost scaled the breeze, climbing up into the clouds and trailing north toward eternal peace.

39

REDMOND

Hours later, I scaled the fort's rocky labyrinth, smoky remnants billowing overhead.

I couldn't stop thinking about the decayed remains we'd discovered in the castle. The remains of my father's last order. Some of them so tiny...

It made me hate him all the more.

Seeing the damage only reminded me how important it was to fix things between our kingdoms. But despite my desperate need for our alliance to work, I couldn't fault Arafax for how they felt. His decision inherited me Arafax's hate, but it wasn't like I hadn't earned their wrath for my own misdeeds.

I had.

I deserved worse, considering what I'd unveiled in my dungeon mere months ago.

I didn't deserve Neve's forgiveness. I didn't expect it. But that didn't mean it wasn't something I craved. Something I'd spend my days atoning for.

The extent of Neve's physical injuries was something I'd

305

always regret. Glimpsing Kyleigh's injuries today had those horrible memories of Neve's fresh wounds flooding back— no clockwork talisman necessary.

Being new to shifting, Kyleigh wouldn't know how much staying in her other form would harm her recovery. It was, unfortunately, why Neve still struggled, needing to go to regular healing sessions. At least Kyleigh'd gone to see a healer.

Ash scraped at the back of my throat. Pressing myself against the base of the craggy rock walls, I reached into my holster. Approaching bootsteps echoed off the surrounding walls, and I lifted my arm, holding out the flask.

Sloan grabbed it out of my hand, twisted off the cap, and took a swig of Inverno's smoky whiskey. She tucked the flask into her own holster before extending out a hand. When I reached out to her she gripped my shoulders and rammed her knee into my balls.

I doubled over in pain, coughing from the much-deserved hit. A moment later a pair of trousers landed in my lap.

I guess she's still pissed.

"What are you doing here? We're still trying to hunt down Dru. Hopefully once he's found he can make some sense of the tome."

"I want"—wheeze—"you back as my"—cough—"military advisor," I spat out. I held up a hand in case she was planning to land another blow while I caught my breath, quickly threading my legs through the pants. "Once you return to Inverno, reclaim your post as commander."

Sloan stepped back, leaning against the moss-covered rock behind her, crossing her arms. "So I can serve you and Mistress Evil once you marry her?"

"That's not happening, Sloan. At least I hope not. I just

need to figure out how to keep everyone safe and get us out of this," I said, heading over to the spot next to her, sitting down on a large rock that jutted up from the ground. I shifted, trying to get comfortable, the pointy edges pressing awkwardly into my still-tender balls. "That tome has got to have something. I know it."

Sloan pulled the flask back out, guzzling it down and handing me the empty vessel. "I didn't realize how desperate you were getting by offering up your kingdom and your hand to the Enchantress."

"She has dragon dust, Sloan. *Blue* dragon dust," I ground out. "I saw it the last time I was there."

"If she has blue dragon dust, does that mean she could have been working with our guards?" Sloan asked, concern dripping through her words.

"She'd have to use someone else. Like Flynt or his crew. Someone on the outside who could procure things. But really, would it surprise you if she had something to do with it?"

I really wished Flynt hadn't already been killed so I could have done the honors. I'd been so blinded by my own miasma of grief, I hadn't seen anything around me clearly. "Do you think she knew about the dragon? About Neve?"

Sloan sank to the ground, resting her back against the stone. She pulled out a small satchel and popped some bread into her mouth, talking between chews. "There's little I think the Enchantress doesn't know. So if you're to keep her off your trail, you better be a very convincing fiancé until we figure out a way to get rid of her."

Dread pooled in my stomach. I wasn't looking forward to visiting her again. Hopefully the book I'd found would give us some answers. Tomorrow I would enlist a small contingent of my army to search for Dru—not that I believed he would be found in Inverno, but it never hurt to check. I could send a few up to Cicatrix too…somewhere I'd avoided for years, but it would be worth it.

"What is your deal with her, Red?" Sloan asked, cocking her head to the side.

"It would be better for you not to know." I walked along the path to try to think, a moment later I turned, finding myself greeted by the point of her longsword—the one that I'd gifted her when she became a knight.

"Are you going to use my own gift against me?" I nodded toward the blade, inching forward enough for it to prick my skin.

"Are you going to keep playing games?" she retorted, tapping my chin with her sword. "You want my allegiance and help in this, you don't get it blindly."

She was right. Respect and allegiance shouldn't be given freely. They were earned. I'd earned it from her years ago, and I'd need to earn it again. Sloan had always been my greatest ally. My partner. Something I'd lost sight of for far too long. "What does she want from you?"

"She's promised me Celaria. Rather, she promised my father. His deal was transferred to me when he died."

Her skin paled, but her eyes remained fixed on me, trying to process what I'd said. "I'm to marry the Enchantress, and we are to rule over the entire realm side by side."

She placed her sword back into her scabbard, crossing her arms once again. "So, your father was planning to marry her?"

"I guess. She never outlined their arrangement, just explained to me the deal I was thrust into when the mark appeared. She's been calling on me ever since." I had been stupidly naïve enough to be distracted by her sensual promises and punishments. "At first, I thought it was all in my head, the searing sensation, but then I saw it. The mark."

"What mark?"

I began undoing the buttons of my trousers.

She threw her hands in front of her eyes. "Woah, I don't need to be seeing any of that, Red. I have seen enough when you shift back and forth—an eyeful of no thanks that I avoid like the plague."

"You want proof of my mark?" I asked, shaking my head. I pulled the waistband low enough to expose the heart-shaped scar at the bottom of my pelvis. "I'm giving you proof."

"Shit," she said, uncovering her eyes and bending down to see it clearer. She stood back up and grimaced. "Pretty intimate spot to have a mark like that. Must feel splendid when you are summoned."

"You have no idea." I howled. Leave it to Sloan to find a way to make me laugh about being tethered to evil incarnate.

She chuckled—a sound I'd missed these last few months. A moment later, her eyes shifted intensity, as if recognition flared through her mind. "It causes pain when you're called on?"

"Yes. Excruciating pain. The longer you try to ignore her summoning, the worse it gets. Relief only comes intermittently between her calls. The pain doesn't recede completely until you step foot in her cabin."

Sloan ran her hand through her hair, then balled her fist, punching the stone next to her. "Fuck."

"What is it?" Her sudden change concerned me. I'd never seen her like this. I reached for her bloody hand to inspect the damage.

Ripping her hand away, she pulled out her own flask and

poured some whiskey on it before twisting the cap back on. Tearing off the rim of her tunic, she wrapped the fabric around her knuckles.

"I need to go." She turned and sprinted away, not even giving me a second glance.

What the infernal realms was that?

40

NEVE

"Blazes!" Ox bellowed, gripping my scales tightly in his palms. I craned my neck to find him with his eyes snapped shut, head tilted away, mouth pulled into a tight grimace.

I huffed out a laugh, watching him slide off my back and collapse to the ground. When he stood, he clutched his knees, heaving out his breakfast in the foliage.

"Nope—I'm not—built for flying—Neve."

"We didn't even get in the air."

"Same thing," he replied, wiping his mouth with the back of his hand. He turned away, still hunched over, catching his breath.

Closing my eyes, I summoned my dragon magic to me. Bones cracked, popping into place. I felt along my body, making sure all the scales had disappeared, leaving only the fragmented markings emblazoning my side.

"You going to be okay, Ox?"

I'd forgotten that not everyone enjoyed riding. Dru and

Kyleigh had been my first riders in over a decade, and neither of them seemed to mind.

Meanwhile, the giant man in front of me couldn't even make it off the ground without getting sick.

He adjusted his shirt, running a hand across the nape of his neck, tossing his head back. "I'm fine."

Bringing his shoulders back, he zipped up his spine, the warrior within him emerging as he turned around to face me. "Just need some more practice is a—"

The words died on his tongue as he took in my nudity. I peered down, seeing the deep ridges of scars notched into my sides. Luckily most of my wounds were invisible. But the ones on the surface, they had a story to tell. My story.

Ox's eyes were wide, cheeks under the stubble of his beard kissed bright pink, hands stiff at his sides.

"It's a naked body, Ox. Nothing to be afraid of."

He cleared his throat, unbuttoning his shirt without a word and tossing it to me. A series of intricate tattoos embellished his chest, blending into a dragon's tail that trailed down the corded muscles of his arms. My throat went dry, and I clamped my mouth shut, willing myself to swallow. Clarity drifted through my vision, eyes shifting to slits a moment, and I blinked the sensation away, my eyes dropping to the ground.

I need to get this shift under control.

"Don't play modest on my account." I shrugged into the shirt, the material drowning me, buttoning it before rolling up the sleeves. "We both know you've seen hundreds of them."

"I mean, maybe not *hundreds*..." He thumbed over his beard, cheeks still flushed. "Not that I've counted," he added with a wink.

"Got something to eat?" I asked, trying to change the subject when his gaze narrowed on the lingering proof of my abuse. I refused to give those memories power over me. To be ashamed of what had happened.

The shame belonged to my abusers.

"Is that a real question?" He raised his eyebrows, reaching into the pouch attached to his belt and snatching out a few cubes of berry bake. My mouth watered at the sight.

"You want some?"

"Is that a real question?" I scurried over, a shiver of excitement trilling through me. I couldn't remember the last time I'd had the delicious treat.

He pinched a cube of bread between his big fingers, lifting it up to my parted lips. My eyes zeroed in on the sweet, delectable treat, the smell of strawberries and black-berries mixed with butter and sugar pulling me in as Ox drew it closer to my lips.

He smirked, tossing the cube backward and catching it in his mouth. "Think I'm gonna feed you by hand like some sort of peasant?"

"I honestly don't care how you feed me, as long as I get some of that berry bake in my mouth. Come on, Ox. Don't tease a girl."

"I would never," he replied in mock offense. He grabbed a few more cubes, then unclasped the pouch and handed it to me. "You're welcome to the rest."

Taking the bread, I gave him a nod in gratitude, then popped a piece between my lips. The citrusy berries burst on my tongue, mixing with the light buttery bread.

"Mmm. So good," I groaned, shoving a few more cubes into my mouth.

Ox stared at me, transfixed, pink staining his cheeks before he dipped his gaze to the ground.

I beamed, collecting up some berry bake crumbs from his shirt I was wearing, making sure I didn't miss a single bite. "So, I guess no flying for our search today?"

Ox sighed. "Yeah. I probably should get going since it will take me awhile."

"Want some company?" Finding Dru was important. He'd been at my bedside, helping me heal every day since I'd come here. Plus, I wanted to learn more about the man that'd been locked away with me in the dungeons not too long ago. I'd met Ox a few times before The Blaze, when he was only known as Sir Fergus. He served the crown dutifully, and always knew how to have a good time, spinning captivating tales.

But that was over a decade ago. So much had happened since then. So much had changed.

People had changed.

Including me.

Including him.

"Didn't know if it'd be too much for you," he said, perking up a bit. Maybe he was also grateful not to be alone.

A dazzling grin spanned his auburn jaw. There was an odd sort of comfort being around him. A familiarity despite not being much more than acquaintances in the past. While his beard and hair had the silver kiss of age woven through them, his face a tad more hardened—when he smiled, with all his boyish charm, it reminded me that some parts of us were too imprinted on our soul to shift.

No matter how weak I'd felt in the dungeon.

No matter how helpless.

Some things could never be taken away, no matter how much they'd robbed from me.

Deep down, there were pieces of myself that remained untouched.

Unbreakable.

"I can handle it. But I'd like to grab my own clothes first." I pointed to his oversized shirt hanging off my frame, swallowing me up. "And a pair of shoes would be nice."

"Sounds like a plan," Ox said. He held out his arm, and I threaded mine through it, walking with him toward the fort as he discussed the morning's itinerary.

The sooner we found Dru, the better off we'd be facing the Enchantress. I wanted to be at my strongest when that time arrived.

Until then, I'd take my unbreakable pieces and build myself anew.

41

TRAVIS

I ran my fingers through her golden curls, gripping a fistful of them. Gorgeous, on her knees in front of me, her baby blues were hooded with desire while her hands grabbed my ass, yanking me deeper into her warm, wet mouth.

"Holy shit, you're perfect," I hissed through gritted teeth, the crown of my cock hitting the back of her throat. Her freckled cheeks hollowed as she peered up at me, humming along my shaft—my complete undoing. Swirling her tongue up and down my length, she lapped up every last drop.

My chin collapsed against my chest, and the edges of her mouth peeled into a grin, gaze bolted to mine. I wrapped her locks around my fist, pulling her to my lips, tasting the remnants of my claim on her tongue.

"Ready to give me what I asked for?" She walked backward, a smile playing on her lips. She trailed a hand from her collarbone down to the center of her breasts, descending past her belly button.

I cocked my head to the side, amused. "Think you've been a good girl?"

She nodded eagerly, eyes glinting in the dim light. Turning away from me, her ass swayed seductively, strolling over to the circular table usually reserved for our feasts. Everyone had left after tonight's celebration and now she'd be my dessert. Pressing her palms onto the table, she inched forward, cheek sliding against the wood, legs spread wide, just how I liked. I swiped my hand up her center, feeling how drenched she was.

"I suppose you've earned it."

Gripping her hips, I sheathed myself inside her in one deliciously slow thrust.

"Fuck me," she cried out.

I happily obliged, picking up the pace, pistoning in and out of her. She thrust her hips back, arching into me, using the table for support.

As she bucked against me, I wrapped my arm around her to pinch and play with her clit, making her swell around my cock, the crown of it hammering deep into her.

"Travis! Fuck!" Her screams reverberated off the chamber walls as she came, making me feel like the god I was, tipping me over the edge. She collapsed onto the table, heaving a satisfied sigh. Pressing my hand into the small of her back, I pulled out, admiring the way my cum painted streaks along her thighs.

Smirking to myself, I wandered over to our pile of discarded clothing, sorting through the heap.

"Hungry?" I asked, throwing on my boxers before slipping on my jeans.

Grabbing her clothes, I brought them to her, sweeping

the curls away from her face and placing a kiss on her forehead.

She slapped my ass, replying with a smirk, "Famished."

I chuckled. "I'll go see what's in the fridge."

Her eyes darted to the ceremonial chamber door. *Tsk, tsk, tsk.* A curious mind ticked beneath that just-asking-to-be-fucked exterior. She'd been desperate to know what's behind that door, but she hadn't asked.

Yet.

She would, though. That girl was fearless. It drove both me and my dick fucking wild.

I walked out of the room and into the underground tunnels beneath Halston University. She wasn't a member of the order, so she couldn't join in the revelry of our Founders' Day celebration but sneaking her into the room afterward was fun...for both of us.

Like so many other kids at this school, she's thirsty for an invitation, seeing the parties, the exclusivity, the influence. *The power.* They all wanted it—wanted to be a part of our secret society. If they only knew that behind the spectacle that sparked the university's rumor mill, we were just a bunch of misfits, never where we belonged.

You'll never amount to what you could be, Travis.

Words I'd heard regurgitated over the years by my father and his friends. All self-indulgent losers that wouldn't know real power if it fisted them in the ass.

I padded down the dim hallway toward the kitchen, in search of the leftovers from tonight's celebration. Turning the corner, my heart stuttered at the looming figure hidden in the shadows at the end of the corridor. "Fuck! Lurking much?"

Slipping into the dim light, hands in his pockets, I came

face-to-face with my father. He cleared his throat. "Sorry to interrupt. I waited until you were...finished."

"How considerate," I grumbled, running my hands through my hair, a half-assed attempt to conceal my annoyance. I continued toward the kitchen. "What do you want?"

His lips were pressed in a thin line, the creases of his brows pulled tight, but his voice remained impassive. "How did the rest of the Founders' Day celebration go?"

The question made me skeptical. He didn't give a fuck about our celebrations. As long as the school looked good and our society's aims remained a secret, that's all that mattered to my old man. Everything was about appearances and, of course, securing funding for the college.

"Good. Everyone is excited for it to be the last holidays *here*," I said, reaching into the fridge and grabbing some small leftover sandwiches and a few water bottles.

"You think you'll somehow magically be the one to pull it off after decades of our people trying?" His lack of belief in me garnished each word. He shut the fridge door and stared down at me.

"I do."

Turning away from him, I started back toward the chamber. The last thing I needed right now was my hookup wondering why it took so long to get some post-fucking snacks.

"And how about the last time you were so confident you'd be successful, Travis?" my father asked, his condescending tone outweighing his need to look at me. "You failed. Spectacularly."

My hands clenched around the plate, the vein in my temple throbbing, but I kept moving, trying to think of a calm response.

I'm twenty-one. Too damn old to let him get to me.

"Well, considering you dated her mom and had no clue she could open the portal, who is the bigger failure here? Maybe if you hadn't sucked so much, she wouldn't have run off with Craig Roberts."

That could've been calmer.

He scowled, hands opening and closing repeatedly at his sides.

"You'll show me respect," he seethed, slipping them into his pockets to stifle his rage. Not that I hadn't seen it in action before. "You have no idea how spoiled you are. How entitled. I've given you everything you could ever want."

How have you given me everything I ever wanted? You've never asked.

I didn't feel like getting into it with him. Not here. Not now. Probably not ever. If things worked according to plan, I'd never have to see the bastard again.

"I'm sorry. I know I'm lucky," I said, taking a bite of my sandwich before I said something I'd regret—like the truth. Nothing I ever did was good enough for him, but he'd see. And when he did, he'd regret ever underestimating me.

"Are you sure you're not too distracted? I see you've taken up with that Devreaux girl."

"Anna and I are just having fun," I replied coolly, unscrewing the cap of my water and taking a sip.

"Bringing an outsider into our tunnels and chambers?" he asked, disapproval laced through every word. "You can fuck anywhere on campus, Travis, but how would your Vis brethren feel knowing you're desecrating their sacred space with someone who isn't one of us?"

"You should be thanking me," I said simply, refusing to let him get the best of me.

"Thanking you?"

"Yeah, when she used that map of the tunnels you so carelessly misplaced in the archives, she showed up at our chambers. I was able to do damage control."

The day after recruitment, we had cleaned up the chambers, making sure to leave no trace of Kyleigh being there. Years of rituals under our belts, our order had become very adept at quick clean up. Everyone else had left, but I stuck around thinking about how we could find another way through the portal since Kyleigh had closed it somehow—I guessed that library loser had helped her.

Hearing a sound on the door, I went to open it, finding Anna trying to pick the lock on the chamber entrance. I couldn't pretend I wasn't part of Vis, I was hanging around their chambers, so I told her I was in the organization. My father was the school president, so it's not like that was a shock.

She sucked me off *twice* that night. For intel? For fun? I didn't give a fuck. Our *arrangement* kept her close enough to make sure she didn't learn the truth about Vis. Plus, she was a sorceress in the sack.

"Funny what you consider damage control," my father said, shaking his head.

"She's harmless. Besides, it lets her think that she'll be recruited next year without bugging me too much about what we are up to right now. And I've been able to make sure she didn't look too much into her roommate suddenly disappearing."

"What happens when she doesn't get an invitation next year?"

"Won't be a problem. Won't be here."

"You better fucking hope so. Her parents are huge donors to Halston. We can't lose their support."

I had a plan. One that I was certain would work. I'd prepared my whole life for Celaria. Now I knew how to get us there. I'd make it happen. My father was just jealous that he had missed the opportunity.

A thrill shot through me, thinking about finally making it to our rightful home. Our powers. I had only heard stories about the realm, but abilities of all kinds existed there. Whatever lay dormant inside of me would be great, I just knew it.

This was what I was born for, after all.

"I have it figured out," I said, heading to the chamber door and waving him off. "You worry about your donors and students. Let me handle this."

Leaving him outside the door, I shut it behind me. Anna was already waiting for me in the heated pool. I put the plate on the ledge and stripped off my jeans to join her.

"You really think I'll get an invite next recruitment?" Anna asked as we walked back toward her dorm a few hours later.

"Anna, you're an incredible woman." She smiled at my compliment. "Any organization would be lucky to have you."

I didn't like lying to her, so I avoided it, sticking to the truths I could share. It wasn't hard. She had the whole package. Any other prestigious secret society would be begging to recruit her. She couldn't help she wasn't born into this.

Honestly, she had no idea how lucky she was. It was a burden growing up being told your whole life you weren't where you should be. That you'd always be less than you could be.

Maybe if things were different, I'd have been able to make her mine. Her family had the kind of clout that would bring Halston even more prestige if I were planning to take over after my father retired.

If.

She was a fuck fit for a king, but fate had different plans for who'd be my queen.

Anna grinned, giving me a swift kiss on the cheek before swiping her key at the entrance to the dorm. "Have a great day, Travis."

"Oh, I will," I said, winking at her.

Her eyes lingered, the door shutting, and I waited for her to head inside.

Then I whizzed across the Quad, the center of campus still asleep, too early for most students to be out and about, wading through their hangovers. I rolled up the sleeves of my green flannel shirt, heading toward the building nestled in the Quad's corner.

Not many knew Halston's secrets, but I did. I knew them *all.* Being the son of the president of the university, I grew up exploring every inch of campus. All the hidden pockets, even ones hidden from my father, were etched into my mind.

I walked to the rear of the building, pulling out my switchblade from the back pocket of my jeans. Running it along the center of my palm, I waited until blood bubbled up from the slit.

My father thought we didn't have any access to magic over here, so he'd never tried.

Idiot.

Little did he know, any enchantments Richard Halston put into place worked if activated by his ancestors.

Taking my bloodied hand, I traced along the outline of the door. The only thing covering the corium was the ivy vines sculpted into Vis's scripted symbol. I waited for the stone to absorb and accept my offering, then pressed my palms into it. As if falling into a wall of quicksand, I stepped through the entrance.

Using my cell's flashlight to see where the fuck I was, I wove through the corridors, ones I'd memorized as a child, until I found the door I'd been seeking.

My father thought he'd handed everything to me, but I'd sweat and bled for this my whole life. He'd been grooming me to be Halston's president. I'd been grooming myself to be Vis's savior. Its king.

When the enchanted lock reunited with the key residing in my blood, I opened the door.

Don't worry about me, Father, I've got my plan.

And it's sitting right in front of me.

42

AISLIN

"How long do you think she'll be like this?" Sweeney asked, sitting next to me with a grim look on his face.

"Well, it's been almost four days. The healers aren't sure about the full extent of the blast."

"I should have been there, not passed out."

I placed a hand on his shoulder. "There's no way you could have known this would happen. What Flynt would do. How Kyleigh would react."

"Or the fact that she's a dragon?" He shook his head in disbelief. "I never had a clue it was our own wielders."

"Yeah." My eyes speared my boots. "Quite a shock."

Part of me was relieved that Flynt and his crew were gone. No more criminals taking residence at the inn. However, now we'd lost significant income that had kept the place running. Without people staying there more permanently, and visitors deterred by recent events, there was a good chance The Lavender would go under.

I'd spent the night retrieving my hidden stash of money.

Hopefully it would keep the inn afloat while Leigh recovered and we figured things out. Parting with my built-up safety net, I handed the satchels over to Sweeney. "Take these back to the inn. The best thing you can do is keep things running. Can't leave the thirsty patrons waiting."

"Are you su—"

"Yes. Take it."

He needed the distraction that being back at The Lavender would provide, and the last thing I wanted was for Leigh to wake up having lost the inn.

If she woke up.

Sweeney hesitated, looking torn at the prospect of leaving Leigh here to get back to The Lavender.

"The healers have been coming in a few times a day to work with her." I shrugged. "If her condition changes, I'll make sure you know."

I needed her condition to change.

I needed her to wake up.

I was angry at her for lying there, helpless.

I was angry for the words I'd left unspoken; the heavy fog that hung between us the last nine years.

I'd blamed Leigh for Flynt. For her naïvety leading to Earl's death. For the criminals and fuckery that took place on a daily basis at the once quaint inn at the edge of Arafax's village.

It was her choice to let them in, to convince Earl to invite them to live and thrive there. Her decision. Standing by and watching as Flynt's rot spread, his criminal dealings only growing—that was also her choice. And while I still held her responsible for those things, I'd never even allowed her a chance to explain herself. To hear her out.

Now I didn't know if I ever would.

Wake the fuck up, Leigh.

I'd withheld forgiveness for so long that I'd replaced it with a wall. One I'd forbidden her to slip through. Anytime a small crack allowed for some light to shine in, I'd scoop up the mortar of past transgressions and spread it thickly over the offending weakness, blotting out any illumination.

"Go. I'll keep an eye on Leigh."

"You've been here almost nonstop." Sweeney squeezed my hand between his. "You need your rest."

"I will get some soon." I shifted in my chair, giving him a hug.

"Any news on Dru?" he asked.

"We still can't find him." Kyleigh was waiting for the healers to clear her to fly again. Neve and Ox had returned empty-handed. There was one area I knew hadn't been checked, and I hoped beyond hope Dru wasn't there.

The Silent Woods.

What would I do about the Enchantress's deal? I was a few days from needing to decide, and Dru wasn't here to help me find a solution.

Guess I'm on my own.

"I'll be back," I said to one of the healers, and then I headed out of the infirmary and up the stairs, weaving the narrow halls until I came to Dru's room.

I opened the door slowly, peeking my head through to make sure no one else saw me slip in. Moving toward the back of the room, I headed into the closet, opening the door of the cooling box. I'd seen the vials of blood he'd been stockpiling. If he stored anyone else's in here, perhaps I would have options.

I didn't want to do it, but I didn't see another choice. This would have to suffice. A last resort. I was running out of time.

It was the story of my life: puppeted by one shitty master after another.

Sifting through the vials, I checked their labels, listening for any movement outside the room. After thumbing through about ten, one marked with a script *K* caught my eye.

Shutting the cooling box door, I stalked out of the room—

"I think if he'd been hidden away in his room we would have found him by now," an annoyingly familiar voice echoed from the other end of the corridor. The Queen was dressed in a red robe that trailed along the carpet behind her. Deep circles hung beneath her silver eyes.

"How's your sleep been?" I mocked, stomping toward her. "You look like you could use a royal nap."

She tensed, then a moment later relaxed her shoulders, drawing out her ruby flames.

Caught ya.

They wove and danced among themselves, climbing along her arms. Taking a deep sigh and checking to ensure we were alone, she pursed her lips before narrowing her eyes on me, ignoring my comment. "Find anything in there that would help us locate Dru?"

"No. But it doesn't seem like you've been trying too hard to find him," I said, glaring at her. "No one good enough for your precious princess?"

"I've only ever wanted the best for Kyleigh."

"So you're finally admitting to yourself that you're her mother?" I whispered.

"I've been her mother from the moment she took her first

breath, and I'll be her mother long after I take my last." She clenched her fists tightly, extinguishing her flames before sliding her hands into the pockets of her gown.

"You're not denying that you weren't happy with them being in love. With him being her champion."

"It's naïve to think that love alone is enough." She gestured for me to follow her as she headed out toward the throne room. "When it comes to survival, sacrifice compensates where love falls short."

I shook my head. "When will you realize that all your sacrifice did was lose you the very thing you sacrificed for?"

She refused to reply but flinched, telling me she hadn't missed a syllable. Turning on her heel, she glided down the red strip of carpet toward her plush, golden perch.

Patting the copper vial in my pocket, I exited the fort, running straight into a very tense-looking Sloan. "You've been avoiding me."

"Not sure if you realized this, but I've been a little preoccupied since the inn."

And yes, I've been avoiding you since you watched me shock the life out of Flynt.

She combed her fingers through her silver hair, tucking back some strands. "I tried to give you time. Tried to let you come to me first and give you space, but we are past that now."

Her blue eyes pierced mine, an icy expression paired with her sharp tone. "Where is it?"

"Where is what?" I asked, taking a step back.

Sloan matched me step for step until my shoulders slammed into a rocky wall, the chill of it a shock to my system.

"Your mark, Aislin," she said, her honey-smooth voice cracking. "The one *she* gave you."

43

KYLEIGH

I pressed my wings against the wind, finally cleared by the healers. Not that I would have waited any longer for their approval—I needed to find Dru. It had already been four days since his disappearance and so far, all our search parties hadn't even found a lead. I headed south, soaring above The Lavender and the stream that ran behind it, unsure of where this world ended in any direction. Maybe one day I'd explore it all.

"Blazes," Ox heaved from behind me, and I craned my neck to spot him around my flapping wings. He gripped Neve's sapphire scales with one arm, a semi-filled bag clutched in the other. He gagged, stuffing his face into the sack's opening and hurled. The blue dragon's head shook, golden orbs rolling at her struggling passenger.

I'd run into Ox and Neve on my way out this morning just as they were heading to search for Dru. They were concerned about me flying alone while my wings finished healing, so I agreed to go with them.

I slowed my pace to help Ox out, passing over a strip of

land plush with greenery that covered any life that may exist beneath. Four tall stone pillars reached skyward, making a rectangle, the only things peering above the darkened canopy. There were markings on the spires, but nothing I recognized, and threads of what looked like iridescent yarn, crisscrossed over each other, attaching to tips of the pillars like a spiderweb awaiting prey.

Do people live there?

The trees ended with a steep cliff, dropping down to an ocean unlike anything I'd seen before. The water, if that's even what it was, rippled in a pearlescent white, reflecting the vibrant purple, pink, and sunflower-colored sky. Waves crashed against the rocky wall, and I dove parallel to it, wanting to get a closer look at the substance below.

A shriek rang out from behind me, and I huffed out a laugh, knowing Ox would probably yell at me later about this. I skimmed the surface of the foamy, white liquid, realizing the water was blanketed in tiny bubbles. What lay beneath?

A long mane of iridescent purples and blues jolted out of the water. The mermaid bobbed up and down, a thin layer of bubbles covering her breasts from view. She waved at us, milky eyes glinting and rows of sharp teeth exposed in a vicious smile. I nodded my head, accidentally collecting some bubbles on my scaled chin, forgetting how close I was to the water below. Last time I'd seen her was when I'd first arrived in Celaria, and she didn't seem too pleasant then.

"Hey, Opal!" Ox bellowed, voice slightly wavering as he attempted to resuscitate his charm in the mermaid's presence. She blew him a kiss before diving into the fizzy ocean, tail whipping rapidly, propelling her toward a cluster of six small islands.

It was doubtful Dru was all the way out here considering Flynt's men would have had to get him to those islands in the span of a few hours. They didn't have a dragon to get them quickly from one place to another. I let out a huff, smoke billowing from my snout, before I turned, heading in the direction of the fort.

Landing next to the stream, I shifted into my human form, my bones contorting and snapping back into place. Ox tumbled off Neve, grunting in frustration and brushing the dirt off his slacks.

He stripped off his tunic and folded me into it. Half his chest and one arm were decorated in a series of tattoos, wrapping their way down to the flame at his wrist. His shirt reached my knees, and he put his arm around me giving a quick squeeze.

Neve shifted back into her human form, too, much more gracefully than I did, and Ox threw her a slip from the compartment attached to his belt, keeping his gaze pinned to the ground.

"Enjoy your first flight?" I asked him as he hunched over the stream, rinsing out his mouth.

"First and last." He gargled between gulps of water.

We walked toward the inn, and I hesitated when we got to the pub's entrance. I'd tried to steer clear of the people at The Lavender ever since the night I'd blown up Flynt's crew. "Why don't you guys go in and have a drink? I'm going to slip in the back so I can wash up and get dressed."

"Don't fret, Kyleigh," Ox whispered. "They're just getting used to the idea of everything. Many are grateful for what you did—giving our people that had been trapped in the castle a proper send-off."

A small consolation considering what they'd seen me do a

few nights prior. They knew I was a dragon. Knew I was dangerous. Now they either stared, frightened, or cowered away when I was around.

"I wouldn't hold it against them if they hated me forever. I fear myself as much as they do. Maybe more," I said, brushing some unruly coral strands behind my ear.

"They'll come around." He smiled. "And one day you'll be their—"

"Nope." I cut him a sharp glare before he said more.

My eyes darted around. Until we were rid of the Enchantress, no one could be trusted knowing I was Arafax's heir. I still wasn't thrilled King Redmond had figured it out, but he promised he wouldn't say anything. As long as he kept that promise, it was fine. If not, I wouldn't have a problem removing him as a threat.

I wasn't the same girl he'd met back in Inverno.

A pair of silver-haired amors whispered to each other, staring at me. I'd recognized them as the set Flynt had enjoyed many evenings just down the hall.

"Don't worry about them," Neve said, wrapping an arm around me reassuringly. "They're probably concerned about still having a place to stay now that Flynt is gone and not bringing business to The Lavender."

I turned to Ox. "Tell me more about Flynt's business."

"He was the man who got you anything you needed within Celaria and outside of it." Ox raised his eyebrows before looking around to make sure no one was eaves-dropping.

"Flynt used to bring us dragon dust," he said, shooting Neve an apologetic look.

"Just keep talking," she said, urging him on.

"Then his crew smuggled other forbidden elixirs, drugs,

items from anywhere—you wanted it, he got it for you. For the right price, that is."

"Wait. So you're saying he knew a way to get things in and out of my world?" I asked.

"Well, yes," Ox replied, looking down at my bare feet. "I'm pretty sure that's how you were able to get those weird lace-up shoes for your birthday. The Queen has used him for years to procure things for her. He even procured Aislin so she could send her to retrieve the gem and off King Redmond."

I sat there stunned, never having thought about my mother's connection to Flynt. If he had a way to get things to and from the Otherworld, could Dru be there?

I already knew there was a portal to the Otherworld within the cavern on the other side of the Silent Woods, but Dru had sealed that up after we'd crossed through it and going that close to the Enchantress was too dangerous right now. There had to be other portals, I just didn't know where they were. But I knew someone who did.

"Ox, I need you to meet me here tonight."

He sat upright, ready for my next command—ever the eager soldier. "I think I know where Dru is, but I'm going to need backup."

Ox beamed. "You don't even have to ask. Let's go find that little bugger."

I WALTZED PAST THE GUARDS OUTSIDE MY MOTHER'S CHAMBERS, releasing sparks from my fingertips as they tried to stop me.

The Queen was in bed, shoulder bandaged up, with a strange gem hanging around her neck. She flipped through a massive textbook that had to be centuries old. Golden symbols traced the spine, written in a language I'd never seen. Letting out a frustrated sigh, she slammed the book shut.

"Doing some research," she said, her usually even tone cracked and brittle. Her eyes had deep circles etched under them.

"You know who would be helpful with that text?" I cocked my head to the side.

She pursed her lips, ignoring the question. "How is your healing? You know, you really shouldn't be out flying alone."

"Neve flew with me today. And Ox."

She laughed. "I'm sad I missed that."

I found myself smiling with her for a moment. She got out of bed, grabbing a red robe draped on a chair in the corner, pulling it over her simple white nightgown.

"Mom?" Her eyes shot up to mine. It was the first time I'd called her that out loud since I'd seen her again. Since she'd determined it was safest no one knew who I was. "I need your help, and I think after everything you put me through—put Dad through—you owe me."

"Everything was done to keep you safe."

"Yes, that's what you've said," I replied, willing myself to stay composed to get the answers I sought. "I know you were arranging safe passage for Dru and I to go back to the Other-world. Was that through Flynt?"

"It was." Her eyes dropped to the ground, her hands wringing together.

"I want to know what routes he used to get things to and from the Otherworld."

Small flames ignited in her palms, but she clenched her fists, hiding them from view.

Maybe she isn't always as in control as she seems?

I followed her out to the balcony. She rested her elbow on the banister and turned to me, bringing her voice to a low whisper. "If I tell you how, will you promise me you won't do anything dangerous?"

I shook my head. "I won't make a promise I can't follow through on."

She sucked in a breath, the crinkles around her silver eyes hardening. "Very well."

44

AISLIN

Sloan's words surged through me.

The mark.

She knows.

I cleared my throat, shutting off the electricity I felt every time I found myself pinned by the silver-haired warrior in front of me. One of her hands was bandaged, digging into the stone next to my head, the other pressed into the space between my collarbones.

I trailed a finger over the bandage, inspecting the small patches of crimson that had bled through along her knuckles. "What happ—"

"Why were you in the woods that night I saw you at the Enchantress's cabin?" Sloan clasped my hand tightly with her injured one.

I raised my eyebrows at her, cocking my head to the side. "You mean the night you had Mox spying for you?"

"Don't change the subject," she said, glaring. "You know I had him there to spy on Red. It had nothing to do with you."

I hated how she called him Red, like he was more

endearing than the murderous asshole he truly was. "Likely story."

"It's the truth." She removed her hand from the wall to trail it up my shoulder. As it passed over my bond mark, I flinched, and her eyes snagged on the spot. She didn't say anything more, didn't ask. Just continued trailing her hand up to grip the bottom of my chin, forcefully coaxing my eyes up to hers. I scowled at her, but I didn't move away.

She was so close. My eyes went to her lips, their plum hue against the paleness of her skin beckoning me to taste them again. My chest rose and fell, the rapid beat of my heart mere inches beneath our entwined hands. But once I crossed that line, one that I'd teetered on before, there was no going back.

"You should stay away from me," I whispered.

Her brow furrowed. "Why would you say that?"

"Because, Sloan. I'm dangerous. And so are you. This won't end well." I stepped out of her reach before I felt the urge to kiss her again.

Walking away from the fort, Sloan stomped like an angry shadow behind me. I didn't look back, though, just listened to her boots crunching into the ground in sync with mine. "If the other night at the inn wasn't warning enough, I don't know what will get the message across to you."

"You mean killing Flynt? The Queen should give you a medal for that."

"Of course you'd think that, Sloan. That's been your life. Medals and parties for your valiant deeds." I continued to walk ahead of her. "At some point you'll have to go back to Inverno where you belong."

"What is this really about?" she asked, an arm winding tightly around me, pulling me backward until I was flush against her. "The real reason you keep me at arm's length."

I couldn't tell if this was some sparring hold I wasn't aware of or her version of foreplay. Either way, it was working for me.

But I needed it not to.

"I don't know if I can trust you."

"This again?" she groaned. "What have I done to make you think you can't?"

"Let me go, Sloan." My voice was hoarse. "Before I do something we both will regret."

"I'll consider it," she said, her breath sweeping through the strands of my hair, causing me to shiver, "if you tell me why."

Sighing, I took a moment before I garbled out the truth. "I've spent the last decade being used. The Queen used me to get to Redmond. Flynt used me too, for his hits. Now I know the Enchantress was using Flynt who used me to deal out those deaths..." Her grip around me softened, breath catching at the admission. "Meanwhile, you're a knight—working for Inverno. I've spent my life hating everything you've spent yours honoring. What happens when he asks you back there? How do I know anything I confide won't be repeated to him, repeated to the Enchantress?"

She sighed, letting out an exasperated growl that shook through me. "You can trust me, Aislin. Whether I return to Inverno or not. We are on the same side. *We*, as in *you* and *me*."

Releasing me from her grasp, she stepped back, and I wrapped my arms around myself, exponentially colder than I had been moments before. "That's a nice sentiment. And I want to trust you—"

"You should."

I strode to a mossed-over everwood tree and slid down,

bringing one knee to my chest and letting the other leg relax on the ground. "Look, Sloan. Even if I wanted more between us, to be on the same side, my life has never been my own. It still isn't."

Sloan knelt in front of me. "Does this have something to do with your visit with the Enchantress? The mark you have?"

"Yes," I said, running my hands through my hair, tucking it behind my ears. "But it's better if you don't know. Dru was one of the few who knew, and no one knows where in the realms he is."

"All the more reason to talk to me about it." Sloan rested her hands gently on my knee, looking at me with all the reverence I didn't deserve. "I get that we are different. I'm used to having an army behind me, backing me up. You've handled things on your own for the most part. But I can't help if I don't know what's going on. Let me help you."

"I made a deal with her. She'd captured Ox and I when we were heading to Inverno..."

Sloan kept calm, nodding for me to continue. After one truth had escaped, the rest came pouring out.

I told her about how the Enchantress had been summoning me since I'd returned and about the dreams. How they had gotten more and more threatening, more painful, until I couldn't take it anymore and finally went to learn what she wanted from me.

Sloan reached forward, tentatively placed a hand where I'd flinched before, and grabbed the neckline of my tunic, pulling it down enough to expose the heart-shaped bond mark. I may have been the one who had electricity running through my veins, but when she touched me, all I felt was hers.

"So now you know. It's better to stay far away from me, Sloan. And Redmond too." I placed my hand on top of hers, trying to quell the current I felt crackling beneath my skin. "I know he's your friend, but he's engaged to the Enchantress. You saw what her wisps did to Ox. Imagine what will happen if she gets even more power, or if she finds a way to leave the woods."

I swallowed, every ounce of saliva in my mouth evaporating. "Whatever she has planned, you can't be on the other side of it. I don't want to drag you into my mess."

"That's where you're wrong. Because I'm already on the other side of it. I'm on the side that keeps you safe. The one that also keeps the realm safe," she said, sliding her palms up the sides of my face.

I couldn't resist leaning into her touch despite everything in my head telling me this would end up with one or both of us devastated.

Maybe she was right.

Maybe we were on the same side.

Leaning in, she combed her fingers through my hair, wrapping it around her wrist and tugging it so my face snapped up to hers. The motion zinged my scalp for a moment before turning into waves of something deeper that pulsed through me.

"I know you're worried we're too different." The fingers of her free hand traced up and down the faded etching on my arms, and I held still while she stripped me bare with her gaze. "But our differences don't change how I feel about you."

My breath stuttered, heart beating wildly in the confines of my chest. "But you're a knight. Inverno's Commander."

"You should know better than most that a title doesn't define a person. Commander, assassin, knight, dragon—they are just parts of us. Right now, we are *you* and *me*. We can choose who we'll become."

I shook my head. "I wish it were that simple."

Looking up into her pale-blue eyes, I placed my hands on the waist of her pants, trailing nervously along their edge. "We are the choices we make, Sloan. I'll never be able to make up for the things I've done. The lives I've taken."

"I won't say to forget the past. That would be naïve. Our past makes us who we are." She brushed her lips against my forehead. "But if you don't believe you have a choice in how it defines you, you're wrong."

Tears welled in my eyes, and I lifted my hands from her to wipe them away before she tried to. Even if we could be together, that didn't change that I had a deal I would need to follow through on. "What about the Enchantress?"

"Fuck her. We'll be stronger than her, together," Sloan said, peppering kisses down my cheek and neck, stopping where the mark branded my skin. "I need to know something."

I raised my eyebrows, waiting.

"Do you want this?"

Her steely gaze sent a chill through me, making my toes curl in my boots at the thought of how badly I really did *want* this.

But I couldn't say it. Couldn't verbalize it in fear that saying it aloud would give her false hope if I couldn't find a way out of the Enchantress's deal.

"Do you trust me, Aislin?" She hugged around me, my own layer of armor, lending me her bravery.

"I do." My pulse raced as lightning climbed through my veins, adrenaline surging. I'd finally admitted something I'd denied for so long. A knowledge I was too afraid to trust even myself with.

She shifted back on her knees, bringing her fist across to her heart in a bow. She wore no armor, but the position was no less regal. No less reverent.

Her eyes lifted to mine.

"Make me your champion."

45

AISLIN

Her words pelted through me, stronger than the rain that began to fall. Tiny droplets pricked my lashes, descending onto Sloan. The white of her tunic clung to her, hundreds of raindrops kissing her exposed skin. Seeming to not even notice, she remained kneeling, awaiting my answer.

This woman. This warrior. Born into a kingdom I'd spent years hating. A kingdom that had caused so much destruction to my very own. Sloan was duty-bound to it. Despite wanting to be with me, her feelings couldn't be stronger than the post she'd tied herself to, following in her father's footsteps.

Could they?

"What about Inverno and returning to your duty as commander? There's no way you could do that as my champion. You'd be tying yourself to Arafax. Your rival kingdom. The enemy."

She shook her head, looking down as she rested her arm on her knee which now sat in a pool of murky rainwater.

"How many times do I have to remind you that I'm not your enemy?"

"Honestly?" I huffed, the rain's pressure increasing. "Probably daily, considering I met you at sword point."

"That's fair." She grinned, blinking through the droplets as they hit her face. "I'll happily remind you daily—as your champion."

This woman. She truly believed we increased our value *together*. So much so, she was willing to bet eternity on it.

"I'm not brave like you." Taking her hand, I lifted her up with me, getting to my feet. I bit my lip, trying to find the courage. "I think I'm in love with you. And that scares the shit out of me."

I'd never said the words before. Hadn't heard them since I was a child. But I loved her. As maddening, inconvenient, and impossible as it was, I did. Somehow, she'd not only captured me back in the woods, she'd managed to ensnare my heart. I'd told myself I'd never let someone possess me in such a way. But with Sloan, it felt like—if I were truly ever free—we could possess each other in equal measure.

"Then I'll be brave for both of us," she said, shaking out her mop of saturated silver.

We stood there, staring at each other through the falling water. Her clothes were soaked against her, muddy knees contrasting her once-amethyst trousers. The sheer, white tunic exposed the subtle curves of her breasts, her nipples pressing through the outline of a simple nude bra. She didn't seem to be affected by her own situation, too busy raking her icy gaze over me, giving me chills.

I grabbed the neckline of her tunic, crushing my lips to hers.

There was nothing tentative when it came to Sloan. Her

fingers laced through my hair, gripping it tightly in her hand, the other wrapping around the small of my back. I grasped her top, kissing her feverishly until she opened to me, our tongues colliding in a sensual rhythm.

"I love you too, Aislin," she murmured against my lips. Then she pulled back, shaking her head, amusement lighting her features.

"What is it?"

"You still haven't given me your decision."

"I thought that was obvious," I said, ghosting her lips with my own. Taking her hand, I led her forward, feeling more courageous than I ever remembered. When was the last time I'd made a decision that was truly my own?

Walking with her in the direction of Everwood Grove, I pulled her arm, pinning it to the base of my spine.

"I choose you, Sloan. I choose *us*."

EMPTY JARS LINED THE PATH OF EVERWOOD GROVE, THE dimmed sparks floating within leaving an eerie glow. I had been so focused on Sloan's proclamation and my own decision that I'd forgotten Kyleigh had waited for Dru here just days ago.

Beige and peach petals crunched beneath our feet, the rims of them browned.

Lit by the Evergleam ahead was a pile of blankets and pillows, obviously left before everything else that night crescendoed into its explosive finale.

There was a sadness about the grove, seeing it like this. But there was also a beauty in it. The glowing teardrop crystals hung from the branches, their colors reflecting onto us and the rest of the trees.

I looked back at Sloan, making sure she hadn't changed her mind.

"Tonight is about no one but us," she said confidently, hope threading the words. She reached around me, splaying one hand across my waist. The other gripped my shoulder.

Us.

The word reverberated through me, thrumming deep in my core. Sloan's thumb stroked the base of my neck, and I spun around, unbuttoning her soaked tunic that clung to her delicious curves. I palmed her breast over her bra before slipping my fingers under the strap, undoing the clasp with the other. Stripping it the rest of the way off, she let the tunic sink to the ground.

I freed myself of my own shirt, watching Sloan shimmy out of her now-darkened amethyst trousers. Naked, aside from a handful of straps that somehow managed to leave something to the imagination, my eyes greedily drank their fill of the fiercely stunning woman in front of me. She stepped forward, unbuckling my holster.

Tonight, our bodies would fuse together. So would our magics. Our lives. Champions were meant to balance and strengthen us as dragons, and nothing about how Sloan treated me made me feel that we would be anything less than empowered in every way, nurturing our growing bond in the years to come.

Unbuttoning my leather pants, I struggled to pull them off, Sloan assisting as we laughed at our ridiculously soaked state. Once the amusement subsided, recognition sank in: we were both in our undergarments and there was nothing stopping this from happening anymore. To be more accurate, *I* wasn't stopping this from happening anymore.

Sloan prowled toward me. Before she could back me into the Evergleam's bark, I grasped her hand, twisting her around so she landed against it. My palm slid to her waist, and I knelt, picking my dagger up from the ground with my other hand. "How does it feel being the one backed up against a tree?"

"I'd normally hate it. But I'm okay with it in this instance." She smirked. "What's next?"

I kissed her deeply, then stepped back arching a brow. "Now we seal our bond."

The whoosh of a blanket flying in the air startled me, and I jolted back, watching Sloan grip the trunk of the tree and one of its sturdier limbs, using it to climb up.

"Throw me some pillows," she called down.

I grabbed three, tossing them up one at a time along with another blanket. She caught them, spreading them out and creating a makeshift nest for us. Then I handed over my dagger. Once she'd perfected the spot, she climbed toward me, offering me a hand. I wasn't as spry as Sloan, but I'd had plenty of climbing experience scaling rooftops when I'd trailed marks over the years.

I ignored the sting of the bark, crashing into the pile of fluffy pillows and blankets next to her. She lifted her palm to mine, and I swept my blade across it, then did the same thing to my own. We joined hands, mouths colliding in a tempest of lips and tongues.

I heaved a breath, stopping the kiss so I didn't forget what Dru had taught us about the ceremony. "Now we press our hands into the bark."

Sloan did as I directed, both of our chests rising and falling, ready to continue where we left off. Murmuring the incantation, I initiated the ceremony. *"Dilían cró derkomai bitháiach caur."* I repeated the words a few times in case I mispronounced anything. Looking up at all the glowing crystals, the ones that remained untinged, I wondered which would come to life tonight for us.

"You ready?" She reached around my neck, bringing me closer to her before trailing kisses along my jaw, descending until she reached the edge of my shoulder.

My face surged with heat. "Well, there's no turning back now."

"Regretting it already?" She chuckled, cocking her head to the side.

"Not at all." Running a hand over her cheek, I brushed back some strands of her hair, still glistening despite their dampened state.

"Let me look at you," Sloan said, pressing up to her knees and skating her icy gaze along my body. I shivered. She'd seen me naked before, but I'd never felt so on display. I frowned down at the scars that adorned my chest and arms. As faded as they were, they still made me feel *other.*

"Your scars are no less beautiful than the rest of you," she said, clicking her tongue at me. "Now let's make sure that magic takes hold."

She circled my wrists, directing them to a large tree branch in front of me. I stood, leaned forward against it. Beginning at the edge of the faint flame scar, Sloan brushed her lips, tracing their pattern up my arm.

"Keep them there," she whispered, commanding me in place. I glued my palms to the Evergleam, focusing on the swirling beige carvings, willing away the nerves jolting through me. Sloan climbed in front of me, pressing her lips to my collarbone.

Moving downward, her palms circled my breasts. Then she flicked her tongue over my nipples.

My lids shut, relaxing into the sensation, a satisfied moan escaping my lips. When my eyes opened, I found Sloan kneeling before me for the second time tonight.

"Remember what I said," she coaxed, her gaze darting to my hands flattened against the bark. I held my breath, her palms skimming the inside of my thighs, parting me gently. Tracing her fingertips across the waistband of my underwear, she peeled them down slowly, icy blues staring up at me. Stroking up my inner thigh, she kissed along the other, inching torturously toward my center. I reached to grab her hair, to aim her where I desired most, desperate for friction.

"Ah-ah-ah," she said, sitting back on her heels. I growled in frustration. "Hands up."

I wiggled my hips, trying to shake out the tingling sensation that threatened to consume me if she didn't touch me again, and soon.

Palms pressed to the tree, I jolted as her warm tongue slid up my thigh, fingers widening my stance. I grasped the branch, trying to hold my balance. Her tongue explored me, and I moaned, leaning into the tree. She licked clear up my slit, striking me deliciously, testing and teasing to gauge my reactions. As she increased pressure, lightning skittered beneath my skin. My legs trembled, and she wrapped one hand around my thigh, holding me in place, the other tweaked at the sensitive bud of my nipple.

"Blazes!" I gasped out, throwing my head back. My eyes opened. The Evergleam began to radiate purple light through the oscillating designs, glistening like a million facets lined the bark, cascading from where my hands lay and expanding out until the entire tree had transformed.

Sloan focused on my writhing body with singular purpose, not even noticing the tree's transformation.

"Look," I whispered, barely able to make out the word.

"*Whoa,*" she said, eyes widening, awestruck. "Guess it's working."

It only seemed to encourage her. She gripped my ass, lifting my leg to wrap it over her shoulder, pulling me to her mouth so she could continue to devour me, commanding my body's pleasure. Every so often I would stare down at her, watching the strategic finesse she had staking her claim over me.

I curled my back, hips trying to shift against Sloan, who held them in place. My nails scraped at the bark, small pieces breaking off between my fingers. She speared into me with her tongue, nose grazing my clit, and I trembled, clutching her shoulder and the branch as I came.

My chest warmed, light pulsating from me. Electricity crackled from my body, weaving itself around the tree.

Waves of release poured out of me, one after another, sending me into aftershocks. I stared at my bolts diving toward Sloan, my eyes going wide.

"No!" I screamed, trying to reel my powers back in. Fear and confusion ripped through me.

And then time stopped.

I watched in horror as my bolts crashed into Sloan, wrapping around her until she was glowing, illuminated by my power.

She looked down, her entire body blanketed by my electricity. She didn't even flinch. In fact, her ice-blue eyes twinkled with mirth and she began to laugh. "It actually sort of tickles."

Relief washed through me, and I steadied my breaths, finally pulling the lightning back into me.

My lightning didn't hurt her.

And it wouldn't.

Never again.

The enchantment had worked. Sloan was my champion.

I stood there a moment, stunned between the comedown from Sloan's ministrations and the gravity of what we'd done. A small bead of reddish light flared from where we'd cast the enchantment. We watched, transfixed, as the bead moved through the tree, following along a branch until it dripped into one of the teardrop crystalline leaves, painting it a pale crimson.

I climbed forward, reaching up toward the crystal. The tiny facets sparkled, catching the light of the other crystals, illuminating the bark of the tree. This union—our union—frozen for eternity, adding to Celaria's power.

"Let's see if we can light it up more," I said, narrowing my gaze on Sloan, framed by a perfect cloud of pillows and blankets. She'd spent months unnerving me—I wanted to get my chance to unravel her.

I climbed back to her, placing my hand on her chest and pushing her down. She gave me a knowing smirk, and I ran my palms over the crest of her breasts, lathing them with my tongue. Teasing her nipples one at a time, I sucked in tiny pulses. She arched into me, clamping her thighs together, breathy rasps bursting between her lips.

Her skin was still misty, raindrops scattered in various spots, and I licked and kissed them away before stripping off the fabric scrap she considered underwear. Grabbing her by the waist, I lifted her hips, propping a pillow under them.

My hand drifted down, releasing tiny bolts from my finger. Sloan's body jolted, responsive to my electric touch. A tear ran down my cheek, seeing my powers giving life to the woman I loved instead of taking away.

I extinguished my bolts, fingers dragging over her halo of shimmering silver. She unclenched her thighs, parting them to let the heel of my hand press against her. She rocked her hips, taking initiative, showing me how she wanted to be touched, guiding my fingers into her. I reveled in how wet she was while I worked her over, watching her writhe. Continuing to curl my fingers, I sensed she was getting close.

She whimpered, nails raking my back. "Fuck, Ais."

I pushed the heel of my palm against her clit, giving her the extra friction her body sought. Taking my other hand that'd been teasing and lavishing her breasts, I released a few bolts, letting them dance along her nipples.

"Oh, *fuck.*" She pressed her back into the pillow, her gasps becoming urgent with the new sensation, hips lifting to greet me. She gripped me like I was her lifeline, and I drew on my power, unleashing a shock to her clit. Crying out a slew of curses, she shattered around my fingers, her body convulsing against me, and I continued to stroke her, decreasing intensity as she came back down to our treetop perch.

The crystal glowed above, a warm light casting down on us, as if the tree had drawn from our joining, turning it into energy—into power. I couldn't tell if it was just my imagination, but it seemed like the entire grove gleamed brighter than before.

My champion held me through the night, the bond settling in, making me stronger than ever.

Together.

46

DRU

*W*here am I?

How did I get here?

I couldn't see anything aside from my legs, part of the chair I'd been tied to, and a small sliver of floor in front of me. My eyes were dry, having been blindfolded for what felt like an eternity, and I was severely dehydrated. The skin on my lips had cracked, beginning to peel.

Left for hours at a time, I wasn't sure how many days I'd been here. The only thing that broke up the isolation was when I was given a bit of water and food and a cup to piss in. My blindfold and bindings were never removed, making the whole experience all the more humiliating.

I felt naked, my glove and shoulder strap confiscated when I was taken. Maybe if I was lucky, they'd left them in the room. If I figured a way out of these bindings, then I could grab my things and find a way back to Celaria. To Kyleigh.

She needed me now more than ever.

Kyleigh must have been a wreck with me missing. I'd

pictured making love to her underneath the illuminated Evergleam so many times since we'd decided to bond. Even now, stuck in the darkness, thinking of reuniting with her was one of the few things getting me through it.

I still couldn't believe she had chosen me as her champion.

She was more than anything I could imagine for myself. Ferociously protective of those she loved, stunning to the point it made me speechless, and stronger than she ever realized. And she wanted me.

Me. A null.

She could have chosen anyone to be her champion. The texts I'd found had said that men and women would line up a mile to be considered, no idea the dragon they sought to serve had so much more to them beneath their scaled surface.

I would do everything to protect her—to be a champion worthy of the title.

Straining against my bindings, I tried not to panic.

Panic wouldn't get me out of this situation and back to her any faster.

The lock's *click* pulled me from my thoughts, and I tried to focus on any sounds I could pick up that would clue me in on what was to come. Boot steps echoed off the walls. Peeks of brown duck boots showed through the gap in my blindfold, laces going up the middle with black rubbery material around the edges. From the watery sludge tracking on the floor, it must have snowed before he came down here to check on me.

"Hello, Dru." The deep growl made me pause. It was the first time someone had spoken to me since my capture.

"Did President Grymm put you up to this, Travis?" I rasped.

"My father doesn't know you're here," he said, smugness coating his tone.

Someone's impressed with himself.

He ambled in a circle around me, his footsteps pounding in my ears. Then he was behind the chair, ripping off the blindfold. "Now that you've had some time to yourself, we can chat."

I looked around at the room. The walls were beige and uneven, a few cracks snaking down to the concrete floor. It was completely empty aside from another chair and a table with a red plastic cup. If my mouth had enough moisture in it to salivate, it would have. I was parched. Unable to take my eyes off the prospective drink, I tried to think of a question to move the conversation along. "What do you want?"

"Well, it's pretty simple. You fucked up everything I've been working toward. Now you're going to help me fix it."

"Why would I ever help you?"

"You'll want to go back home at some point, won't you? To *her.*"

Of course. He knew about Kyleigh. About us.

The scraping of chair legs against the floor brought me out of my thoughts. Travis flipped it around to sit, resting his elbows on the back of it while he made his demands.

My eyes snapped to the black studded glove on his hand. *My glove.* I never let anyone else touch it, other than Kyleigh, and Aislin once, so she'd see I wasn't a power-hungry maniac attempting to steal their abilities from them. Trying to stay calm on the outside, I counted my inhales and exhales in my head.

"I merely want to hitch a ride." He talked like he was casually inviting himself along for brunch, not claiming an invitation to slide through a portal to another realm.

"No fucking way."

The corner of his lip curled up. "I mean, I can also just do it my way when she comes here."

"She's a person, not a key for you to use," I said, eyes flitting around the empty space. I needed to figure out what he'd done with the rest of my supplies.

"But what a beautiful key she is." He raised an eyebrow at me. "You can't tell me she won't be coming for you once she figures out you're here. Her champion to be?"

How did he know about that?

The ropes seemed to only pull tighter each time I fought against them, and my chest heaved as I gasped for breath from the exertion. "I won't let you hurt her."

"Well, that depends on you, Dru." Travis was calm. Too calm. "Figure out how to get Vindicatio Vis's members to the other side. Otherwise, I know what I did last time will work—"

"You mean sacrificing her?" My whole body tensed, gritting my teeth as I spoke. I wanted to be reunited with Kyleigh, but I hoped she was still too afraid of Vindicatio Vis and its Celaria-obsessed members to be bold enough to come through the portal. Besides, she'd have to find a way to it without getting taken by the Enchantress in the Silent Woods. She'd be in too much danger coming here.

I'm sure the Queen wouldn't allow it either. In fact, the Queen would probably encourage her to forget about me.

"Don't be so dramatic, Dru. Kyleigh's fine. Better than fine, if you ask me." He smirked to himself, and if I thought I could take him right now, I would charge the bastard.

"Shut up. You have no clue what you're talking about."

"You should be thanking me. I hear this glove of yours even lets you get a taste of her power before becoming her champion." He looked down at the glove, poking at the various compartments and gadgets as he clenched and unclenched his fist. "I can't wait to give it a spin when we get there."

"Kyleigh is much more than her power. And you have no clue how to use that thing. You'll probably hurt yourself trying. It actually involves a base level of intelligence that I'm doubting you even possess."

"We'll just have to see about that. And don't worry, I have no plans to hurt her—well, unless she's into that kind of thing. Is she?" he asked, cocking his head to the side. "If so, I could get on board with it."

"Fuck. You," I spat.

"I'm only asking you to use the same resourcefulness you used to create this glove to find a way to help those of us who want to go home. I'm sure there's a less...extreme way to do it," he said, smirking.

"How am I supposed to do that when I'm chained up?"

"Oh, I don't plan on keeping you here. I just wanted to give you some time to rest that pretty head of yours. Once you agree, I'll escort you to the archives where you'll stay until you've figured it out. After your little stunt letting Anna and Kyleigh down there, my father changed the locks and now he and I are the only ones who have access."

I knew that would come back to bite me in the ass.

"And how do you know I won't just thwart your plans?"

"That's very simple. Kyleigh will come looking for you, and I'm sure she will run into me before she finds you. If you don't want a repeat of the last time we tried to get through the portal, you'll spend every moment you can figuring out what needs to be done for all of us to get over there. We both know her blood activates the portal."

I stilled.

"When Kyleigh arrived at Halston, I knew her mom was the Queen of Arafax. Our families had been close for many years. After all, she was supposed to marry my father. If she had, their child would have unlocked the portal."

"She made the right choice," I seethed.

"Oh, I don't disagree with that." Travis shrugged. "Although, I wouldn't say that turned out so well for her in the long run. Maybe Kyleigh will learn from her mother's mistake."

"She's already made her choice."

"Maybe she did. But that was *before*. How do you think she felt when you didn't show up to your little ceremony?" Travis pouted, putting a hand on my shoulder, and I flinched, wishing my hands were free to rip it away from me. "Poor girl. I heard she was quite...distraught, being left once again."

She couldn't have honestly thought I'd leave her. "She knows I wouldn't leave her. That I love her. And she loves me."

"Kudos to you. You do seem like a lovable guy, in a nerdy, sweet, probably virginal way, but I also know she's powerful, Dru."

"And?"

"You really think you're the best man for the job? To be the champion of one of the most powerful creatures in existence?"

"She's not a creature. She's a person."

"We both know she's so much more than that," Travis said, swirling the red cup in his hand before holding it up to my lips. I was so fucking thirsty, but I didn't trust him, so I waited, denying the pang of dehydration that was gnawing at me. "At the end of the day, power can take you further than love ever will."

He picked at the studs on my glove, popping one off. "You're a null. Utterly useless."

"Maybe you're right. Doesn't mean she would ever pick you after what you did to her, though."

"I'm sure she's changed a lot since coming into her power." He reached out a finger, bringing my head up to look up at him as he stood over me. "Besides, if she's as wild with these new powers as I've been told, she needs a king who's got the balls to tame her, not some pathetic loser with nothing to offer her but some silly inventions. She's got the future of Arafax and her people to think of."

Travis was the biggest asshole I'd ever met—an entitled, arrogant, walking example of the Dunning-Kruger effect. I'd watched him over two years after I came through the portal, and my opinion of him never changed. Now that I was talking to the man face-to-face, it only solidified my prior assumptions. "You're a selfish prick, Travis. No one believes you're doing this for anyone but yourself."

He grabbed the chair in front of him and knocked it over on the floor, crouching down, leveling his face with mine. "You have no idea what I've given up to get my people to this point." He stood quickly, holding the hand sporting my most prized possession into the light, admiring the glove in taunt. Luckily, most of the interesting gadgets only worked in Celaria.

Keeping his gaze on the various studs, he pushed them. "If you love her and truly want her and Arafax safe, you'll refuse her request to be her champion. Are you so selfish that you'd keep her for yourself when you could help Celaria by letting her have full access to all the power she could gain?"

I said nothing. It was like hearing every worst thought that'd passed through my mind since I'd learned Kyleigh's true identity.

"You're a good man, Dru. But we both know you aren't ready to do what's necessary for Arafax." He grabbed the red plastic cup and guzzled down all the water within before crushing it in his gloved hand and throwing it at my feet.

"Stay away from her!" I shouted, kicking the empty cup away, pulling at my restraints.

He kept his back to me, slightly glancing over his shoulder at my outburst. "I'll try my best, but if you two are as in love as you claim, I think that's an impossibility."

He walked out of the room, pausing before the door closed. "Get some rest, Dru. You'll need that big brain of yours. We have work to do."

47

KYLEIGH

"You sure you want to do this?" Ox asked, face wrinkled, running a hand through his beard while he studied the plan I'd laid out after speaking to my mother.

"Yes," I said, confidence swathing my words, tugging at the leather jacket I'd grabbed out of Aislin's armoire. I figured she wouldn't miss something that was tucked away in the back. It was stiff, obviously never worn. It made me feel stronger. More badass. More capable.

I needed every ounce of courage I could muster to go back to Halston.

While I'd always planned to return to Vermont, I'd been putting off making anything concrete. The idea of seeing that school again—everything I'd worked toward, only to realize what a crock it had been—was something I wanted to avoid. Not to mention the prospect of running into anyone from Vis, especially their deranged leader, Travis fucking Grymm.

I'd learned from my mother that there were multiple

entry points to Halston's campus from Celaria. Each had a specific drop point. For a few different reasons, Ox and I couldn't go back the way I'd come. One, we would have to travel through the Silent Woods, potentially going up against the Enchantress, which we weren't prepared for. Two, its exit point would land us right in the middle of Vis's ceremonial chamber.

I never wanted to see that stone slab again.

Strategically, it would be better to have a location that would give us the element of surprise, which ruled out using the portal attached to the Sentry Stone. Appearing out of nowhere in the middle of Halston's Quad with a burly, seven-foot man would draw way too much attention.

Luckily, there was another option to get us to the Otherworld.

Ox looped his arm through mine, escorting me to an empty patch of dirt that dipped into the stream flowing along the inn's posterior. Stripping off his shoes, socks, shirt, and trousers, Ox stood there in just his underwear.

I was beginning to understand how he had such a steady stream of attention and conquests.

"Enjoying the view?" he taunted, tying his hair back.

I blanched.

Jerk.

I rolled my eyes, not dignifying him with a response.

He strode into the water, bending down and bringing his hands around his mouth and whispering into the current, like he was telling it a secret. Then he stood back up, waiting with his arms crossed.

The current continued to flow around my barely clad companion. After a minute, I let out an exasperated sigh. "Are you sure this is going to work?"

He ignored me, keeping his eyes focused on the water. The crystalline hues shifted, parting when iridescent purple and blue hair breached the surface.

Delicate hands slid up Ox's chiseled torso, a pair of mermaids literally climbing him. They swished their shimmering onyx tails playfully against the water, splashing me. Tucked into his arms, they pressed against either side of the giant, trailing their fingers over the planes of his chest.

I recognized the two mermaids from when I'd first arrived in Celaria. They seemed to recognize me, too, because once they realized I was gaping at them on the water's edge, they hissed, displaying their razor-sharp teeth as they possessively caressed the giant between them.

My cheeks heated, and I smacked my chest, coughing out my discomfort.

"What is she doing here, Fergie?" Opal asked, flipping her hair and splashing me in the eyes. I recognized her from when we'd been out flying. The other mermaid, with a darker complexion, remained silent, spearing me with her gaze.

Maybe getting their help wasn't going to be as simple as I'd thought.

"Just hear her out, ladies," he said, gliding his palms up and down their sides. I blinked the excess water from my vision, wishing I could be somewhere, anywhere, but here. It seemed like everyone was getting laid except for me, including the freaking mermaniacs. "She comes bearing gifts. And more than that, you'd be doing me a big favor."

Opal's friend ran her fingers through his auburn beard, bringing his lips to meet hers. He dropped his mouth by her ear, murmuring words that had her cheeks flush. As intrigued as I was about how their little ménage worked, I had a champion to save.

I shook my head, the mermaids and Ox suddenly staring at me like I was the oddity in this scenario.

"Opal and Aurelia, meet Kyleigh," he said, pointing to me.

"What are you?" the previously silent-but-deadly Aureila asked, her narrowed gaze skimming over me.

"It doesn't matter what I am. Just know it's extremely rare," I said, pulling two vials from my jacket. "These are yours in exchange for safe passage into the Otherworld."

The mermaids were out of Ox's grasp in an instant.

"Why would we want to help you?" Aurelia trilled.

Their attention never dipped away from the vials in my hand. I'd kept them strapped to me after grabbing them from Dru's room earlier—glad that he'd taken my blood. There was no way I could have done it on my own. The needles reminded me too much of the thin blades that the Vis members thrust into me like I was a life-sized pincushion.

I shuddered, the memory bleeding into my mind. I tugged at my jacket, tethering me to the present. This was about getting Dru back. I needed him—hell, Celaria needed him, considering no progress had been made in finding a way to take down the Enchantress since his kidnapping. Plus, I knew I would be at my best with him at my side.

"Your males will fight over you with some of this." Ox held up one of the vials. He talked me up like he was a used car salesman trying to showcase my features to prospective buyers, not mermaids who would be coating themselves with my blood to seduce a mermister.

"We have been wanting to settle down," Opal said to her friend, combing through her purple streaks with her pale fingers. A moment later, their white eyes intently focused on Ox.

"Oh, I'm so flattered, ladies. But you deserve someone you can build a nest with," he replied, somehow coming off endearing instead of like a total asshole that was trying to let them down easy.

Their lips curled into a frown as they waded over to me. I knelt at the edge of the water, holding out the vials. "Safe passage for both of us."

With a sigh, Aurelia glanced at her mersister who nodded. "Back in a splash."

They reached an arm up for the vials, and I pulled them back, attaching them to my belt. "Once you return."

"Fine," Opal said. The two mermaniacs dove away from us, tails slapping against the water, spraying Ox and me.

"You said you knew the mermaids, but you didn't say you *knew* the mermaids." I raised an eyebrow at him. "How did none of us know about this?" I asked. "They definitely want your not-so-little merbabies!"

He laughed. "Well, you all have been busy with training and with each other."

His words struck me. We'd been so wrapped up in dealing with the Enchantress and our own relationships, we'd shirked on our friendship, ignoring the man that had put himself in harm's way on our behalf. "I'm so sorry, Ox. I've been a terrible friend."

"Friendships have their ebbs and flows." He shrugged, wading out of the water and heading toward the inn to grab a towel that was hanging over a workbench.

"So you're really okay giving them my blood so they go find another male?" I asked.

"Oh yes. I don't have any intention of giving up these two

legs," he said, flexing his quads and giving them a playful smack.

I couldn't stop laughing. It had been far too long since I'd joked like this with someone. "Oh, Ox, don't ever change."

WHEN A CRATE SHAPED LIKE AN OVERSIZED COFFIN FLOATED TO the top of the stream, I took a step back, concern punching holes into the confidence I had in my plan.

Ox pulled it out of the water, taking it from Opal and Aurelia. A handful of mermaids had joined them. They all had the same white eyes and startling jaws, but these mermaids had different brilliant manes. One boasted neon orange, green, and yellow, standing out among the bunch. Another, pastel pink mixed with white. The last had deep crimson with rich-plum accents.

"Your hair," I said, in wonder. "Are you born that way or do you dye it?"

The mermaid ran her hands through the tresses that fell in crimson waves down to her waist. "We are born with it." She shook her head, letting her hair sway back and forth until a moment later it was dry. I was stunned.

"Alright, we've got to get moving." Ox tapped on the box that I had absolutely no intention of getting in.

"Seriously?" I watched him open the lid. "Isn't there another way? Like a small boat?"

"This is the only way *we* can get you to the Otherworld," the crimson-haired mermaid replied. "You're welcome to use one of the other portals."

But I knew that wasn't an option.

Bile rose in my throat. I hated enclosed spaces. The cell

had been enough. The idea of being stuck in this box, with Ox who'd take up most of it, terrified me. I grabbed my knees, bending over, holding a hand up while I tried to take some deep breaths.

Get it together, Ky. Dru needs you.

I slowed my breathing until it was steady again, squeezing my eyes shut to buy myself time. When I was a little more steadied, I peeled one lid open, half hoping I had been imagining we were traveling something akin to a coffin. I supposed it was fitting, considering it could be my final resting place. We were heading to Halston, which wasn't helping my anxiety either.

"And you're sure you can get us there discreetly without alerting anyone on the other side?" I asked the mermaids.

"Yes. There are no shipments due in the Otherworld for another week, so no one will be waiting at the drop point," said Opal.

I took my leather jacket off, afraid my nerves would make me sweat to death in its clutches. Folding it up, I placed it on the bottom of the container before pointing at the box. "You get in first, Ox. I'll try to fit in around you."

The giant climbed in, bending his knees a bit, trying to fit within the length of the box. Patting the small, empty space next to him, he grinned up at me. "Time to get cuddly, Ky."

The crate wobbled as I climbed into it, playing my own version of Tetris to fit around Ox. As I stared up at the Celarian sky from inside the box, I wondered what I had done to piss karma off.

I curled into a ball. "How do we know we won't drown?"

Two heads popped up over the sides of the box. Opal and Aurelia.

"That's what a mermaid's kiss is for," said Ox with a low chuckle.

"What!" My eyes went wide. They both smiled, their massive maws flashing piranha teeth in our direction. I gulped back the what-the-fuck rock lodged at the tip of my throat, then washed it out with a disturbing realization. Of course Ox would know about this, how else could he have survived sexy time with the mermaniacs?

Aurelia stuck out her hand, blocking Opal from diving toward Ox. "It's my turn."

"You said that last time," Opal countered, glaring at her mersister.

The crimson-haired mermaid cleared her throat. "Why don't you both do it?"

"Fine," Opal and Aurelia pouted in unison. They leaned over the side, each imprinting a deep, lingering kiss to Ox's lips. A pale-blue puff of smoke filtered up from his mouth, his lips turning navy—a stark contrast to the scruff of his auburn beard. It looked like he had lipstick on.

The crimson-and-plum streaked mermaid stared down at me. "Ready?"

I nodded, trying not to think about the terrifying teeth that would be so close to my jugular. I shut my eyes, and she kissed me, her cool breath sweeping over my tongue like the ocean's winter breeze. My lips and nose grew numb. I knew they must be the same navy color as Ox's.

"How long will it last?" I asked, detaching the vials from my belt and handing them to her, watching her pass them back to Opal and Aurelia.

She began closing the lid. "About two hours."

Stopping the lid, I peeked my head up. "And how long until we get there?"

"About two hours," the mermaid said, brushing my hand away.

The lid snapped shut, the crate's locks clicking into place, and the box shifted, slowly sinking into the water, some of the stream seeping into a small, open crevice in the corner. I placed my hand in front of the hole, trying to stopper it as the weight of the box dragged us down, down, down...

48

NEVE

"Kyleigh went where?" I asked, drinking wine with Isla on the balcony in her chambers. It had been decades since we'd just drank and talked, and for a moment it felt as if no time had passed at all.

She took a long sip, staring off into the distance. "She went to the Otherworld yesterday. To get Dru."

"And you let her go by herself?" My protective instincts were sinking in. Even though we'd only formally known each other the last handful of months, I'd cared about Kyleigh since her birth. The idea of my goddaughter out on her own, potentially dealing with Otherworld fanatics, scared me. Isla had warned me about them when we'd communicated to each other through the stones all those years ago. Now she was sending the person most important to her right to them.

"She has back up," she said simply. Taking another sip without saying more.

I shrugged. "That's something at least."

I didn't like it, but I supposed I didn't have a right to say anything about it. She was *her* mother and *my* queen. I may have had sway with her years ago, but we were basically getting to know each other all over again.

"She wouldn't have listened to me anyway. Her mind was made up," she grumbled, plucking a chocolate from the triple-tiered serving tray.

"Sounds like she takes after her mother," I huffed. I held my chalice out to her, and she clinked hers with it before we both took another long swig.

"I can't blame her," she said, tone low, holding the chalice to her chest.

The circles under her eyes had become less pronounced, probably due to the dream weaver that'd been visiting the fort. The weavers were strange. I avoided them. So did the rest of Celaria.

But I guess times were desperate, even for a queen.

"Nope." I placed my wine on the table. "You really can't."

She rolled her eyes. The motion one that I'd seen Kyleigh mimic perfectly without meaning to. "Look, I feel bad enough as it is."

I shifted in my seat to face her better. "Have you told her the truth?"

She frowned, bringing the chalice to her lips but not taking a drink before she pulled it back and placed it on the table. "I've given her enough of it."

"What's that supposed to mean?"

"It means not everything is my place to share, Neve." She circled a scarlet nail around the rim, ruby flames igniting from the inside. It was something we used to do for fun—her party trick when things got too dull or stuffy at grand balls all those years ago. Isla loved lighting people's drinks on fire, their faces usually panicking a moment before settling into awe.

I didn't like how much she was keeping from Kyleigh. It wasn't right. The girl had spent her whole life in the dark. If she was meant to one day rule over Arafax, to become a key power in Celaria, she should know everything. Until Isla was honest with her, they'd never be able to have a real relationship. At least not the one I sensed they each desperately wanted but didn't know how to move toward.

If anyone knew something about a relationship obscured by lies, it was me.

"Don't look at me like that," she said, my thoughts too intense to hide from my face. "I just want to get rid of the Enchantress once and for all so I can finally have my daughter back."

I pressed my lips into a firm line until the words spilled out of me. "She's been here for months."

"It's not safe for her to have a relationship with me yet."

"Keep telling yourself that," I replied, nodding my head. I knew better, but I didn't feel like getting into it.

She closed her fist, chocolate seeping between her fingers and pooling on the table. "What is that supposed to mean?"

"Is it *really* that it's not safe? Or are you too afraid of what you'll have to face when you can't use the Enchantress as an excuse anymore?" I handed her my extra napkin.

"And what would that be?" she asked, cleaning off her hands, avoiding my eyes.

The words came out of me before I could think them through. "That while you thought you were protecting her, you probably hurt her more than anyone else."

A line of ruby flames lit at my feet, trailing out the door. She didn't need to say a word. I stood, sidestepping her power writhing beneath us, following its path to the exit.

"I'm going to be up in my room reading. If you need to talk, you know where to find me."

———

A SHADOW DRIFTED INTO MY ROOM.

I sat in bed continuing to read, assuming it was Isla coming to have that conversation. When she didn't just walk in, I looked up, surprised to find Redmond standing in the doorway.

The ring of his thin crown perched delicately atop his dark hair, and he was dressed in charcoal from head to toe—Celaria's mourning color. I wasn't sure what he was grieving, though, at least not anymore. I was right here, alive and well.

Well, as well as I could be, considering I was looking at the man who had unknowingly held me captive the last decade.

"What's with the outfit?" I asked, turning my eyes down to the page in front of me.

"I have worn this color for over ten years," he said, pausing a moment. "If I wore something different now, it might raise suspicion. But, if you must know, I came to see the Queen to check if there have been any updates on Dru or the tome."

"Ah, yes," I replied, tone fully mocking, "wouldn't want that lovely fiancée of yours to suspect anything."

He sighed, furrowing his brows.

"Why are you *here*, Redmond?" I brought my attention back to my book.

His continued waiting in the doorway felt like a joke, considering he spent so many nights flying through the open balcony. He ran a hand through his dark hair, leaving it disheveled. "I wanted to check on you. See how you're doing."

Even if he claimed to be Arafax's ally—bringing intel and trinkets from the Enchantress's cabin of exile—I didn't see how he could be marrying her and still be on our side. I'd seen the bond mark, *her mark*, slung low on his hip.

They deserved each other.

I brought my eyes up from my book, straightening my spine. "I'm fine. Thanks for asking."

He shifted uncomfortably, the sapphire rings dangling around his neck clinking against the silver cage.

Our rings.

Ones we never wore.

"Are you planning to give it to her?" I glanced over at the delicate ring.

"No," he said, gripping the sapphire bands tightly in his fist. "Never."

He unclasped the chain and held the cage in his palm. Removing the smaller of the two bands, he placed it on the bedside table next to me before turning to leave. He glanced over his shoulder. "I know things between us are over, but I hope one day to earn more than your hate."

I picked up the small band, twirling it between my fingers.

When I snapped my head back up, he was gone.

49

KYLEIGH

Everything was dark, void of life other than the man breathing in unsteady increments next to me.

Ox's panting filled the small expanse of the container, and I shivered, sweaty palms pressed against the flat walls closing in, still plugging the tiny hole I'd found. Keeping my eyes squished tight, I unsuccessfully pretended we weren't stuck in a misshapen coffin, floating to our probable deaths.

A large palm met my shoulder. "It's okay, Kyleigh."

It would have been reassuring if his voice hadn't cracked.

"How is this alright? We are in a *tiny* box. Underwater. If there's a delay, we will fucking drown, and I might never see Dru again." I missed him so much, my heart beat wildly at the thought of being near him. Picturing his bronze skin and hazel eyes with golden flecks staring into mine, my body began to relax.

Ox didn't respond. He just kept holding me while trying to steady his own breaths. I had almost forgotten that, despite his intimidating size, he also had a somewhat irrational fear: the dark.

Reaching out my free hand, I fumbled for his shoulder, giving it a few pats once I'd found it. I needed to distract him. Hopefully that would distract me for a few minutes—ideally hours—until we arrived in the Otherworld.

"Tell me a story, Ox."

He let out a chuckle. "How dirty can it be?"

"As dirty as you can tell."

He paused a moment. "Okay, let me think...which one..."

I laughed, a comforting sound considering the circumstances.

"Well this one time, I met an illusion weaver from Alucinor in The Lavender's pub. Long, white hair, purple eyes, and an ass you just had to take a bite out of." I tried to hold back my laughter. "She took me upstairs and told me she could make my naughtiest fantasies come true."

"Could she?"

"Blazes," he said on a sigh. "The images she weaved..."

"Tell me." I was riveted, breaths slowing, the weight of my anxiety lifting more with his words. Whatever it was, it was going to be absolutely ridiculous. I'd expect nothing less from Ox.

"First, she created another set of me."

My eyes widened, not that he could see them—which I was glad for.

"Then I watched as my doppelgängers filled her..."

As I'd assumed, his story was the perfect distraction. I was certain he'd have enough tales to last us a few hours. Ox's presence helped me remain calm despite the heavy pull on my chest while the mermaids dragged us through the watery trenches. Every so often the container would snag, taking a moment to start moving again, but minute by minute, they pressed on.

"...They ran their wings along my body, painting me in strokes of sapphires, emerald, and ruby. Then one of them pressed their hands against the canvas wall while I drove into her. The other tongued and toyed with her clit until she was screaming louder than anyone else in the lounge, and that's when I pulled out and came all over their—"

Sucking sounds echoed in the tiny crate, and my body tensed until a few knocks beat at the side of the box, letting us know we were through the portal, nearing Halston's campus.

Ox had told about twenty stories. I now knew much more about him than I probably ever should, but I'd never been more grateful for my friend and the tales of his midnight snacks.

I held my breath, keeping my body pinned in place. It sounded like being inside of a rain stick as the portal swallowed us up. Pressure tugged at my insides, but I refused to move until I knew we'd fully crossed into the Otherworld. Our underwater coffin-carriage bobbed, my stomach lurching against the sensation of lifting higher and higher until it felt like we were gently floating above the surface.

Time to channel that inner badass, Kyleigh.

Time to go get your champion.

50

KYLEIGH

Last time I was here, I was leaping off a cliff, pledging a secret society I thought would bring me closer to my mom. In reality, they couldn't care less about making me a member. They just wanted a key into Celaria.

I guess, in some fucked-up way, pledging did get me closer to her, just not in a way I ever imagined. And physical proximity aside, I didn't feel like I knew my mother any better than I did back in August when I was last here.

When I first fell through the portal, I couldn't understand what the realm's connection could be to me or my mother. And while my questions had been partially answered, my mother felt like anything but the woman I'd grown up with. I needed to let go of the embellished memory of who I believed she was and accept who she'd ultimately become.

But I wasn't ready to.

I had to believe, somewhere beneath the dark and detached exterior, the woman who used to comb through my curls and tell me seemingly fantastical bedtime stories remained within.

Gulping down the earthy air, I stared up at the snow-dusted cliffs of the quarry. I shivered, pulling Aislin's leather jacket over my shoulders, the crisp smell of snow and frost serving as an immediate reminder of how cold Vermont got this time of year. It made me miss my dad and all the things we'd do together during the holiday season.

Part of me wanted to go see him, being this close by, but I needed to prioritize finding Dru and getting us back to deal with the Enchantress. An even bigger issue was what could I really say to him without sounding crazy? I'd have to lie. About me. About Mom. About where I'd been. Heck, showing up with a seven-foot, middle-aged man named Ox wouldn't thrill him too much either. Until I knew what deceits I was willing to live with, I couldn't see him.

I clenched my fists, ready to utilize Sloan's training if there were any surprises. Plus Ox was here, minus his mighty twins. I'd requested he leave those back in Celaria. It already wouldn't be hard for him to draw attention to himself, between his height and the permanent expression of shock on his face from being in a world completely different than the one he'd known.

Much like how I probably looked when I fell into his.

The grotto outside Halston's underground tunnels was shrouded in darkness, aside from the sliver of moonlight that sliced through the jet-black sky.

Ox walked ahead of me, fumbling around, using the glowing crescent to guide us. I wasn't sure if our journey in the crate had desensitized him a bit to the dark or if he was trying to be strong for me, but he kept moving—not letting his fear show if it was there. His head flitted around, eyes wide, taking in the surroundings. This was not much of a change in comparison to Celaria but seeing Halston's campus would blow his mind.

Luckily, once we made it closer to the tunnels, there were lights lining the walls. Instinct told me which path I didn't want to follow—the one that took us to Vis's ceremonial chamber.

I directed Ox the other way, taking us toward a fork in the underground corridors, wishing I'd memorized more of the map Anna and I had seen in the archives all those months ago.

"Please tell me you at least know where we're going," Ox said, looking back at me to see which path to take.

I shrugged. "Nope. But I think I know where a map is."

I had no idea what they had told Anna about my disappearance. I didn't even know if she had ended up using the map. For her sake, I hoped she hadn't. That easily could have gotten her expelled, even if her parents gave shitloads of money to the school. Maybe she still had the map. That would be our first stop, to better plot out where to find Dru within Halston's underground.

Doing an internal eenie, meenie, miney, mo, I picked the path to the right, and we followed it, selecting doors at random until a six-sided one came into view. I ran up to it, pressing my ear to metal, somehow thinking I'd be able to hear what was waiting on the other side.

Nope.

Ox nudged me over placing his hand on the circular lock. "Let me go first, just in case."

He turned the large dial, and the hexagon split into three triangles as it opened. I peered around his elbow, staring into the dark tunnel leading to faint light. Ox stepped through the door, and I followed, grasping along the wall until I found a switch and flicked it on.

Beams of dim light poured down through a few grates above us as we walked down the tunnel. At the end of it, a set of crude, cement stairs rose up to a six-sided grate latched to the ceiling. Peering up through its grid, I saw the streetlamps lining the Quad. This was probably the best place to exit and get to my old dorm without having to backtrack and wander around more underground tunnels.

Ox ascended the stairs, lifting the grate and peeking through the small opening.

"How busy is the Quad?" I asked, unable to see around him blocking my view.

"That big courtyard? It's mostly empty, other than a few people stumbling around."

It must be the middle of the night here.

Ox hoisted me up with one arm, keeping the grate open with the other. A few drunken students staggered across the Quad, and a couple was making out on the Sentry Stone. I stared at the giant rock, ignoring the action taking place on top of it. Where the story of my parents meeting used to be etched in my mind, the memory of being held down on Vis's matching underground slab echoed instead.

I'd wanted to come to Halston for so long. I'd made it my mission to emulate my mother—to live up to the legacy she'd left behind.

All of it was a fucking lie.

But the part of me that had idolized this school and coming here still felt the wonder of being on campus, even if the truth had tainted it.

"Blazes." Ox gaped, head spinning around the Quad.

"Welcome to the Otherworld," I said, arms wide. "First

thing we need to do is to go to my dorm and see if Anna, my old roommate, still has the map of the campus and underground."

"Uh-huh," Ox mumbled, still gawking at the view.

Tapping his shoulder, I continued, "Maybe once we see the map, we'll get a better idea of where Dru could be."

I pulled myself up on the sidewalk, keeping my eyes peeled for anyone looking our way. Watching Ox try to shimmy out of the hole was entertaining, with a side of terrifying. After a solid minute of thinking he was definitely stuck, he finally wiggled himself free. We walked down the Quad in the direction of the dorms, Halston's library planted in front of us.

I stared at its stained-glass windows. The first pane had a seemingly fairy tale world—purple sky, a floating castle, and dragons flying overhead. The second a clash of knights and swords wearing red and blue capes, a tall, white-and-silvery palace with four towers in the background.

Bile rose in my throat as recognition sank in.

The next had a few people, presumably kings and queens, shaking hands with their armies clustered in the background. The second to last had a man floating rocks in Dorset's quarry. And finally, the last window showed Halston with its purple knight standing at the forefront. Its Guardian.

Clever.

Halston's *real* story, hidden in plain sight where fiction lived and breathed. The college had been built as a haven for protecting both realms. Celaria's ancestors were sent here as an honor, their pride eventually transforming into bitterness, leading to the founding of the twisted secret society, Vindicatio Vis.

"Would you look at that?" Ox said, beaming as he moved toward the statue.

"You recognize it?"

"Of course I do." His head lined up with the knight's helmet, and he knocked on the metal statue. "It's my great-great-great-grandfather, the first Sir Fergus."

"So you're technically Sir Fergus V?"

"I am." He smirked. "Bet you didn't realize I came from such a line of renowned warriors? We've served Celaria for centuries."

"Why would his statue be here?" I stared up at Ox posing next to his great-great-whatever-grandpa. The statue was seven feet tall, too, life size of the man it emulated.

"Well, he was the one who advised we end the wars and find a more diplomatic solution. Arafax and its allies wanted to protect magic from harming this world. Some other rulers"—he indicated Inverno's blue banners and a few others I didn't recognize—"believed we should allow magic to flow freely between our worlds. That it would open up new territories to expand their reach. Arafax and its allies established Halston as a way to protect magic from going through and sent some of their people here as guardians."

"What?" My head hurt trying to process this history lesson. "You never mentioned that before."

"It never came up," he said, shrugging. "Plus, after the royal family—your extended family—were killed the night of The Blaze, I've spent my time trying to live up to the Fergus name. Some job I've been doing, though." He looked down, wringing his oversized hands together.

"Well, you're the best Fergus to me," I said, smiling and reaching up to place a hand on his shoulder. "But I get what you're saying."

If anyone understood trying to live up to some unspoken familial expectation, it was me.

"Now, let's go get that map."

"Lead the way," Ox nodded, following me toward the dorm.

———

THE DOOR FLEW OPEN, MY SHORT-TERM ROOMMATE SMILING back at me, her curly blonde hair mussed, lips swollen, and wearing a partially buttoned men's flannel shirt. "Oh. My. God. You're here!"

"I am." I plastered a smile to my face, unsure what Anna believed to be the reason I'd vanished without warning.

She stepped into the hallway, grabbing me in for a big hug. "Already on winter break?"

"Umm. Sure," I replied, trying to stay vague.

"How's studying in Ireland been? I'm mega jealous!" She looked up at Ox, tucking her wild hair behind her ears. "Who's this?"

Ox only nodded, probably too afraid to say something he shouldn't. I was shocked he wasn't trying to be suave.

"This is Fergus." my eyes darted around the hall while I tried to think. "We—uh—met during the program."

"Nice to meet you, Fergus." She stuck her hand out to shake his, then looked over at me, head cocked. "I didn't realize you were into the silver-fox thing, Ky."

He frowned, bushy brows merging at the top of his forehead. "Excuse me?"

"As fun as these introductions are, I was hoping to grab some of my stuff," I cut in, ready to find Dru and get back through the portal.

"Sure! Something specific you were looking for? I put together a box of some random things I found in the room that your dad didn't grab."

My dad?

The door opened behind her, and I stilled, my chest clenching at her choice of company.

Travis leaned into the doorway, jeans slung low around his hips, shirtless, his hair its usual mess of jet black. His green eyes lit in amusement, taking in Ox and me. "Hey, Kyleigh. Long time no see. Glad you've been having such a great time abroad."

He stepped toward me, and my body went completely rigid. Then he had the audacity to give me a hug, as if he hadn't tried to kill me the last time we were in the same room together.

I thought I would throw up right there.

Sensing my discomfort, Ox pushed Travis back a bit before sticking out his hand, inserting himself between us. "I'm Fergus. And you are?"

"Travis Grymm," he said, shaking Ox's hand. Travis removed his hand, holding it gingerly with the other one, glaring up at Ox. I don't think I'd ever appreciated my friend more than I did in that moment.

"I couldn't help but overhear you're looking for something?" Travis said, seemingly entertained, which only annoyed me more. "Why don't I walk you guys out and see if I can help?"

He gave me a knowing smile.

"Oh, that won't be necessary—"

"That's a great idea," Anna said, shuffling behind the door and handing the borrowed shirt to Travis a moment later. "I need to get some more sleep before my coffee date with Mitch later anyway."

"Who's Mitch?" Ox asked, suddenly interested in the conversation. I stepped on his foot, trying to end this awkward exchange. He didn't even notice.

She peeked out as she pulled a sweatshirt over her head. "Remember that gorgeous ginger from our first night here? The one at Books & Brews?"

"I do!" I laughed, thinking to that night when I'd met Dru and we'd escorted a very inebriated Anna back to the dorm. At least it didn't sound like it was serious with Travis if she was getting ready to meet some other guy.

"It was great seeing you guys. We should grab coffee while you're in town, Kyleigh."

"I'd love that." I went in to give her a quick hug. "But I'll need to see what my schedule looks like while I'm here first."

"Perf!" she said, pulling me back in with a squeeze. "Shoot me a text."

"Shall we?" Travis nodded toward the staircase, arms gripped around the only box of my possessions left behind.

I strode past Travis, Ox making himself an imposing fixture between us, and we headed back out to the Quad.

As soon as we walked around the side of the building, Ox pinned Travis to the corium with his elbow.

"Where is he?" I demanded.

"Who is this *he* you speak of?" Travis asked, shivering against the slab, making me wish my sparks worked in this world. His eyes dropped to where Ox's arm pressed into him.

"Where is he?" I repeated, and Ox twisted Travis's wrist until he cringed in pain.

"Where you'd expect." His evergreen eyes darted to the library's entrance.

My words slipped through gritted teeth. "Take me to him. Now."

"While I'd love nothing more than to satisfy your highness's demands"—he winked at me—"no one can get to him right now. Not even me."

"What do you mean?" I asked, ignoring his dig at my identity. How he knew, I didn't care. I had bigger problems to contend with than a self-important frat boy.

"Well," Travis said, looking around and making sure no one was within earshot. "I had locked him in the archives since no one really goes down there, but he somehow managed to tweak the locks. Now I can't even get to him."

"You locked him down there?" I watched Ox tighten his grip on his wrist. "Why?"

Travis cocked his head at me. "Why do you think?"

Me.

He was still after what he'd wanted all along.

"Planning to bleed me out again?"

"I wouldn't dream of it." He lifted his free hand to his chest with mock sincerity.

"You didn't seem to have a problem with it last time." Crossing my arms, I stroked the leather beneath my fingertips. I wouldn't let this idiot get to me. I wasn't the same girl that had gone through the portal all those months ago.

"Look, just because I was willing to do it, doesn't mean I enjoyed it," he said. "You just happened to be the answer to a problem I've been dealing with my whole life. You can't blame me for believing the end justified the means."

I rolled my eyes. "Are you seriously comparing yourself to Machiavelli right now and trying to make it somehow endearing?"

I nodded to Ox, and he released Travis from under his enormous weight. The green-eyed dumbass grabbed his hurt arm, stumbling back a few paces. He took a moment, adjusting the flannel shirt I'd seen Anna wearing minutes ago, his usual cocky expression filling his face.

"Hey, sometimes you have to be a little savage," he replied, as if that was justification enough. "If anyone should get that, it's you."

My hands clenched, fingernails digging into my palms. I was pretty sure I'd be shooting sparks right about now if we were in Celaria, and I immediately regretted not having Ox twist his arm a little more. "What's that supposed to mean?"

"Just because I'm here doesn't mean I don't have access to information about what goes on in Celaria."

My heart sank, hands unclenching by my side before I shoved them in my pockets.

He shook his head, giving me a smirk. "Don't worry. I broke the news to lover boy about your little...outburst. What's your body count now? A few dozen at least, right?"

No, no, no.

I didn't want to believe him, but there was no reason for Travis to lie about this. Would Dru forgive me for what I'd done, or just look at me as an out-of-control monster? Someone—some*thing*—to be afraid of. Like he'd looked at me in Inverno's dungeon.

No. I refused to let Travis get to me. I was in control here, even without my powers, and I needed to use every resource I could, including Travis himself. "What do you want?"

"I thought that was obvious?" he said, readjusting his shirt. "I want to get myself and a few buddies into Celaria."

"That's it?"

"That's it for now."

That sounded more like Travis. Always looking for a way to benefit himself. His agenda colored everything he did. "Out with it."

"Consider taking two champions." He leaned back against the corium. "I mean, I'd rather be the only one, but I know you're sweet for Dru, so I'm willing to compromise. It is possible to bond more than one champion in a single ceremony, you know."

Ox stepped forward, ready to intervene on Dru's behalf, but I shot my hand out for him to hold off. I could handle this on my own. Travis might see himself as the big man on campus, but to me, he was just a minor nuisance, an ant to crush beneath my crimson Chucks. I'd made a promise to myself that I would never let others have that kind of power over me again. It was a vow I intended to keep. "Never going to happen."

"Come on, Ky." I hated his casual use of my nickname. "Dru doesn't have the stomach for the darker side of what leadership entails. I'm willing to make a concession to keep my princess happy."

He walked over to me, placing a hand around my shoulder and pulling me close to him. It made me feel claustrophobic, like I was locked in that tiny box I'd traveled here in. Only this time I was with my least favorite person in the world.

Why didn't this guy get the hint he wasn't in charge?

I channeled my inner Sloan and lifted my leg, bending my

other as I stomped on the middle of his foot. Then I drew my elbow up into his nose.

Ox barked out a laugh. "Atta girl, Ky."

"Fuck!" Travis yelled, staggering away, holding his nose, blood spilling between his fingertips.

Sloan would be proud.

I stuck out my fist to Ox who stared at me, confused a moment before matching my movement, and I tapped our knuckles together. Turning to Travis, I gave him a hard pat on the back. "As I said, never going to happen."

"Our families were always meant to have an alliance. We could still have that." He wiped away the blood from his nose with the sleeve of his flannel shirt. "You can't tell me that wouldn't be helpful. Remember, I still have ways of knowing about everything going on in Celaria," he said, standing back up. "My father might not side with you, but I have more sway with Vis, and I'd be the one coming through the portal with *my* people."

He was probably full of shit, as usual. "So, you're promising me an alliance?"

"I am, and I wouldn't mind having some informal fun with it either," he teased, giving me a wink.

This guy.

"Of course you wouldn't."

"You make it sound like it's an awful proposition, but I promise you it isn't." He smiled, trying to come off charming despite his bloodied face. "Just ask Anna."

"Ugh," I shook my head at him. "You're disgusting."

"But only in the best ways." He chuckled. Ox joined him for a second—until he caught me glaring in his direction.

We already had a tenuous alliance with King Redmond,

what was another shaky détente at this point? There's no way I would ever make Travis my champion, but if an ounce of misguided hope got Dru and me back to Celaria, I could deal with whatever problems came with him. He was right about my body count, it had been in the dozens at this point, and Travis wasn't someone I'd lose sleep over if he joined their ranks.

"I'll get you and your...buddies safely through the portal. *My way.* Not your sadistic fucking way," I said, imagining blasting him with my sparks and feeling instantly more zen. "You take me to Dru, and we will figure out what's realistic and how many of your people can make the trip and when."

"And what about my other request?" He stepped forward, raking me with his gaze.

"Oh, I wouldn't come near you if you were the last man in all the realms." I huffed out a laugh, his body shrinking back in shock making it all the more rewarding. "But I do expect your people to be aligned with mine when we get to Celaria. You'll come with us to Arafax, and we will draw up the terms there. If you truly care about your people and want to bring them, you'll agree."

"That's fair," he said, sounding like a normal fucking person for once.

I started walking toward the library before I glanced over my shoulder to call back to him, "And Travis?"

"Yes?"

I gave him a wave of my hands. "Don't even consider betraying me, or I'll have no issues ending you."

He smirked. "I don't think I've ever been more turned on."

"Shut up, Travis," I said, giving him the middle finger salute.

51

AISLIN

*C*opper talons squeezed around my throat, the Enchantress's inky eyes boring into mine.

"Bring what I seek," she whispered through crimson lips, "or soon you'll be mine."

A hand gripped my shoulder.

Shooting up in the darkness, I pulled the amethyst dagger from under my pillow, holding it to the jugular of my assailant.

"Aislin!" Sloan whispered urgently. "It's me."

I unclenched my fist, dropping the blade onto the comforter, chest heaving from the adrenaline coursing through me.

It was our first night back at the fort since we'd been champion-bonded. Until we figured out a more permanent living situation, we had settled on staying in Sloan's room so I could be closer to Leigh if she woke up. Plus, it was more convenient with training.

I wasn't used to sleeping next to someone—in fact, I never had. The closest thing to it was when I shared a cell with

Kyleigh. Even when I'd gotten lucky during my days at the inn, the amors or guests had their own beds to go back to.

Sloan stared at the blade that weighed down the covers on her—*our* bed.

"Do you always sleep with a dagger under your pillow?" she asked, tying her shoulder-length hair into a ponytail.

"Yes," I said, confused by her reaction. "Don't you?"

She lifted the blade, crawling over me to place it on my bedside table. "I most certainly do not. It's too dangerous. You could have easily killed me."

"Don't make it so easy to kill you, then," I huffed, still pissed that I could have accidentally hurt her out of fear. As she shifted to go back to her side, I pulled her to me for a quick kiss. "Didn't you ever worry about being attacked when you slept during battles? It's better to be prepared."

I'd been surrounded by criminals I couldn't trust for the last decade, and if being an assassin that killed people in their sleep had taught me anything, it was that your opponent didn't wait for you to wake up to strike.

"I'm always prepared," she said, pointing to the throwing knives Dru'd engineered to attach to her bedside table. "But I don't sleep with weapons."

"I beg to differ." I grinned, sliding my hand over her waist, letting my lightning prickle lazy circles on her hip. "Speaking of, if you're waking me up for some naked sparring this morning, I'm a very willing participant."

"Unfortunately, the naked sparring will have to wait until later. I told Ox I'd handle Neve's training while he's away."

"Where is he?"

"He went with Kyleigh to the Otherworld. She thinks Flynt's men could have sent Dru there."

"What?" I asked, louder than I probably should have considering people were sleeping.

She planted a kiss on my lips, rolling away from me to get out of bed. In just a simple sapphire camisole and matching underwear held together by straps that crested over her curves, she looked tantalizing. I wanted to hide away in bed with her all day. "She didn't tell you?"

"No. She fucking didn't."

Sneaky bitch.

Despite the relief I felt knowing that she'd figured out where Dru had been taken, I was also annoyed. Why would she go without me? At least she wasn't stupid enough to go on her own.

I fell back against my pillow, crossing my hands over my chest and letting out a disappointed sigh. "Since you're getting up, I might as well get myself together and go see how Leigh is doing this morning."

"I'll come grab you after I finish up with Neve. Then we'll see what we can do now that we are bonded." Sloan slipped into a pair of gray trousers and a loose, pale-blue shirt that hung off one shoulder.

I watched her intently, memorizing every inch of her.

She walked over, straddling me before brushing her lips against mine. She was making it very hard to be motivated to leave this room and she knew it.

"Will clothing be mandatory?" I asked, trailing kisses along her neck, eliciting a satisfied moan from my champion. I held my ear level to her heart, loving the feel of the bond as it hummed in my chest. Every time we were together, it seemed to become stronger.

I kissed her again, savoring the scent of citrus and

jasmine enveloping my senses eliciting a moan of my own. Sloan's desire streaked through our bond at the sound.

"If clothing's not required, I'd be more encouraged to attend."

She ignored my request with a laugh. Slipping me one final kiss, she stepped out of reach before I could pull her back into bed.

<hr>

I WASN'T SURE WHY I WAS SURPRISED LEIGH STILL HADN'T MADE any progress.

The hope that'd begun to take hold within me was shriveling up more with each passing day.

I sat with her, in a sullen haze, until a honey-smooth voice came from behind me and a firm hand rested on my shoulder, our bond perking up at the touch. "You ready to practice?"

"Sure," I said, hesitating a moment before letting go of Leigh's hand. I did one final check-in with the healers before heading outside.

"When is your deadline?" Sloan asked, gliding along the labyrinth leading out to the arena. We'd walked this path so many times, knowing the way was instinctual.

"I still have about a week."

I wished Dru was here, then at least he could have told me if he'd thought of any ways around the deal. Thinking back to the vials in his room, I did have a way through this... But could I betray Kyleigh and Arafax? The alternative of becoming a wisp under the Enchantress's thrall also didn't hold any appeal—

"What kind of fighter do you anticipate the Enchantress is?" Sloan asked, cutting through my thoughts.

"Not a fair one, I'd guess," I replied, pulling my hair into a side-swept ponytail. "She's used to making deals. I'm not sure how much fighting she does, but I would guess she has a lot of power at her disposal. Including my own and the Queen's."

Heading into the center of the arena, Sloan rolled out her shoulders. I followed suit, stretching out my wrists and back before I spent the next few hours shifting in and out of my dragon form.

"Okay, so how do you want to do this?" I had no clue how to even start this type of training.

"Why don't we start with you still in your current form before you shift? That way we can see how your power works now that I'm connected to your magic." Coming closer to me, she put her hands up in front of her. She caught on to my hesitation right away. "Remember, you can't hurt me."

My mind went back to the other night, when my lightning had skittered over her skin. She was completely safe from my powers now.

Taking a deep breath, I mirrored her hands, bringing forth some bolts to crackle along my fingertips. Sloan moved her own fingers closer, grazing the electricity flowing from mine. Usually my bolts were white or purple, but pale blue tinged the spots Sloan touched. Tiny streaks danced along her hands and wrists, alternating between blues and purples.

I stared, in awe of what she was doing.

"Go ahead and shift," she directed. "Let's see what happens to it now that I'm holding onto some."

"Knew you'd try to get me naked for training. I'm on to you." I kept my eyes locked on hers, watching her play with my power. Removing my clothes, I threw them off to the side of the arena.

Sloan's rapt attention on my body sent shivers down my spine. Mox came into view, onyx eyes bulging at his master handling the bright, jagged light. Lifting away from the ground, scales burst through my skin, wings stretching out. Mox froze, growling before taking a few steps back, and I bowed my snout to him.

"It's okay, Mox," Sloan said. "It's just Aislin."

Just a badass, as usual.

I huffed. Sloan barked out a laugh and Mox shook his head with a lazy grin.

Wait, can they understand me?

"Yes, we can," Sloan replied, walking over and holding out her lightning-spun hand. I nuzzled into her palm, a tart taste on my tongue. Instinct kicked in, and I breathed out a cloud of gray smoke mixed with thin, iridescent strings of electric power. It encircled Sloan, creating a ball of lightning branches that flickered and twisted around her.

She tapped her hand against the edge, fingers pressing into the surface but not enough to burst it, the lightning from her hand merging with the orb around her. Taking out one of her throwing knives strapped to her thigh, she struck it, dragging it down and breaking the barrier enough to climb out. The slice stitched itself up behind her, and she threw the small blade at it, watching it bounce off the shell.

"Well, that's helpful," she said, standing back and looking appreciative. "Now if I can just figure out an easier way to get in and out of that shield... It would be great to have Kyleigh practice with us at some point, too, once she's back. She could test its impenetrability."

She turned back to me, smiling. "What else have you got?"

It was the strangest feeling, giving over to the instincts that ran through my veins. I threw back my head, letting out a roar, barbs of lightning reaching the sky. Rain began to blanket the arena in tiny droplets. I knelt, bowing to Sloan in invitation, and she ran to me, using her momentum to propel off the ground and swing her leg up on my back.

Taking to the clouds, we headed into the storm above—one that I wondered if I'd somehow managed to summon. I glided and dove, dodging the strikes of lightning I'd conjured, so Sloan could get acclimated. She stroked the jagged scales along my back before patting me. "I'm going to try to stand, okay?"

I was nervous, but I remembered seeing my father on his dragon—my mother. He maneuvered with such ease, which I now understood was partially from his own ability, but it was also combined with a heady dose of the bond that existed between them. Sloan felt like an extension of me, the delicate cord of our bond becoming more entwined with each passing day.

Try to use my lightning.

She gathered herself up on my back, testing her balance, and I focused on staying steady, flying through the rain. I heard her longsword unsheathing, and I craned my head so I could see her. She gripped the hilt, face pinching as if trying to make something happen. "Argh! I don't know what I'm doing."

Picture the lightning and how you want it to appear. Sometimes thinking of something that makes you blissfully happy or completely pissed off helps.

Her icy eyes reached mine, and it was as if I could see the light glow behind the pale blue. Lifting her sword above her, she wobbled a moment, causing me to hold still as much as I could, slowing the beat of my massive wings against the rainy breeze.

Jagged streaks crawled up the hilt, making their way toward the tip of the blade, and the bolts flashed, curling around the sword. Bringing one foot forward, she sliced her electric claymore through the air, sending lightning into the vast clouds around us. A loud *boom* crashed as the blade struck wind.

I let out a proud hum.

"Let's head back," Sloan said, sheathing her sword, the lightning dissipating. Sitting down, she rubbed my scales, and we descended toward the arena.

Once we landed, I roared again, reeling in the storm. It felt a bit like wrestling it, lacking finesse since I'd never worked with my abilities in my dragon form. Sloan bounded off me, coming around to pepper kisses along my snout. "Why don't we see how your dragon magic works with Mox?"

Okay.

I bent low, letting the snow fox come closer. His tail was held tight, eyes pinched, sniffing me curiously. He bowed his head, looking up at Sloan, who gently placed one hand on his furry, white snout, the other on mine. I huffed out a few bolts of lightning, and Sloan caught them in her hand before tossing them to Mox. He bounced them off his nose and into his mouth, licking his black lips.

He blinked at me a few times. Sloan, still poised between us, pulled forth my lightning, letting the strand stretch until it floated over Mox's head as well as my own.

I snapped my lids shut, feeling a strange pressure tickle my mind.

"Open your eyes."

When I did, my vision split into two horizontal perspectives, stacked on top of each other. The top view was the arena directly in front of me. Beneath it was Mox's, peering up at Sloan. It made my head instantly dizzy, trying to distinguish where to look.

Freaky.

"You have no idea." Sloan laughed. "When we bond our familiars, everything they see and hear, we do as well. At first it can be nearly impossible to function, so we had after-school lessons to learn how to handle our new senses. I threw up often that first month adjusting to Mox, especially since he loves to roam and run through the woods."

Understandable, I huffed.

"Eventually, the dual vision became easier to control. Now I can summon it at will."

Show off.

I laid my head on the ground, trying to steady the whirling sensation of seeing through both our visions. Mox grunted, seemingly unimpressed by how I was handling our newly formed connection.

Sloan walked up and petted my snout. "Why don't we work on that later, when you're less tired?"

Who says I'm tired?

"Well in that case, why don't you shift back and we see what other things our magics can do?"

I huffed, black smoke billowing from my maw.

Already wanting to see me naked again?

Reeling back my wings, my body cracked and bent until I stood there, naked and grinning at my champion. I stretched out my arms, arching my back and reacquainting myself in this body again. Sloan moved toward my clothes.

"I was promised naked sparring," I called out as she reached the pile strewn on the ground.

"We won't get any training done if you stay like that." She tossed me the clothes, so I purposefully only put on the camisole and underwear.

Sloan raised an eyebrow at me.

"I can't make it too easy on my opponent," I said, placing my feet wide and bending my knees. "Now try to send some lightning at me."

Sloan held her arms out like mine, tensing her body repeatedly and getting more and more frustrated. I pulled forth some lightning, arcing it toward her to catch. We spent the next few minutes sending it back and forth between us. Then I grew a ball of electric energy and sent it toward her. She caught the sphere between her hands, hurling it at the wall, cracking it on impact.

It seemed that when I was in my normal form, my power couldn't harm her and she could manipulate it but not summon it on her own like she had when I'd shifted.

We continued to play with different drills and techniques the next few hours, running through various defensive and offensive ideas of how we could handle the Enchantress if a fight became necessary. The connection between us making it easier to work together, syncing our energy as we practiced.

When the moon's glow began to fade into night, I took Sloan's hand, leading her back to our room, uncertain what tomorrow would bring but determined to make every moment count.

52

KYLEIGH

*K*nock, knock, knock.
Knock.
Knock.

My fist shook, pounding against the door to the library's archives. With each crash of my hand against the wood, my body shook more, the force of my blows and increasing fear of rejection overtaking me.

"Dru?" my voice cracked. "It's me. Ky."

Click.

The door groaned open, Dru poised with a dusty trophy held up behind his head. Ox had Travis detained behind me, wrists pinned to his back. As soon as Dru saw Travis disarmed, the silver trophy crashed to the ground.

His eyes shot to my clothes, and I gave him a nervous smile. "Different?" I injected into the silence, hoping he wasn't freaked by the new attire.

He reached his arms out, thumbing over the neckline of my jacket, using it to close the distance between us. His hands shook as they caressed my cheek, then he combed his fingers through my hair. I bit my bottom lip, and his eyes instantly tracked the movement. He brushed his lips in a whisper over mine, "You look incredible."

"Touching little reunion," Travis said, giving a smug grin, a few smears of blood still staining his face, "but there's a lot to do before we head to Celaria."

"We?" Dru moved to step in front of me.

"Yes." I kept my hands on Dru's shirt, pinning him in place. I was too afraid that if I let go of him, this reality would fade away. Dru was here. With me. And I would never let him be taken from me again. That is, if he still wanted me. "Travis will be bringing some of Vis's members along with us in exchange for your release. I told him we'll take them as long as it's done on our terms."

Dru eyed him suspiciously. "How many people is he looking to bring?"

"How many can we take?" Travis asked.

Dru grabbed a sheet of paper and started jotting down calculations. "I think the safest amount we can handle is about a dozen people before the portal will need to be closed."

"Yes, we must keep our princess safe above all else," Travis said, smirking at me. "How soon can we leave?"

"Tomorrow?" I asked Dru, eager to get back where I had access to my powers before I had to deal more with Travis or his Vis goons.

"That should be doable," he replied, scribbling some numbers that didn't mean anything to me. He looked up at Travis. "I'll need to start drawing her blood now, though. With the amount necessary for these numbers, she'll need ample time to rest before we go through."

He grabbed another sheet of paper and jotted down a few

supplies, then he folded it up, tossing it to Ox who caught it with his free arm. He gave Travis a little shake, still in his grasp. "I'll keep an eye on this one and make sure we get the necessary supplies for our trek."

I met Travis' gaze, glaring and sending intangible sparks in his direction. "Gather your people and meet us thirty minutes before sunrise at the Sentry Stone. We're not using the one you tried to bleed me to death on."

***

DEEP CRIMSON FILLED THE VIAL IN FRONT OF ME, NEARING THE top before Dru gracefully swapped in the next one. We'd need one for each person going through the portal, plus a few extras in case it wasn't quite enough. I tried not to flinch when Dru switched them out, still not a fan of needles, but more tolerant of them since he'd been stockpiling some of my blood to use for enchantments.

"Sorry," he said, softly running a hand up and down my forearm. I leaned into the touch, starved for it. For him.

He cleared his throat, flicking the vial in front of him before placing it into the holder.

"It's okay. I just want to be done with this." I took a deep breath, trying to push down any feelings that threatened to ruin our reunion after what felt like one of the worst weeks of my life. And that said a lot, considering *everything* that had happened this year.

"The Sentry Stone will take us to Arafax's castle," I said, glancing back at the dusty trophy cases. How simple things had seemed when I was last here. "I actually flew there when I was searching for you."

"You went up there?" He stilled before swapping in the next tube. "What was it like?"

I looked down, voice just above a whisper, not wanting to think about all the bodies we'd had to move. "Sad."

A tear trailed down his tawny cheek, and he quickly wiped it away with his shirt. "My parents were left there."

"I remembered you telling me they worked in the castle." I placed a hand on his, keeping my gaze trained there. "We brought the remains down from the tower. Gave them a hero's send off."

"Thank you," he said, pressing a kiss to my temple.

He screwed the lid on the last vial before removing the needle from my skin and bandaging the area in neon pink. Grabbing a juice box, he tore off the straw, punctured the foil, and handed it to me. "Look, Ky, I—um—know Travis wants more than just to go to Celaria—"

"I'm not going to be with him, Dru. Even if you don't want me anymore. Even if you think I'm a monster after everything that happened," I said, my insecurities tumbling out of me. "I'm not going to make him my champion instead of, or in addition to, you. Not ever."

"Thank the stars! There was no way I'd willingly share you, especially not with *him*," Dru admitted, running a hand along the five-o'clock shadow trailing his jaw. "I could never stand by and see you with him after what he did to you."

"He's horrible, but honestly, Dru, do I even have room to talk at this point? After the things I've done. Even if Flynt wasn't trying to force me into completing the ceremony with him—"

"He did what?" Dru's hands tensed at his sides. "I have a newfound appreciation for what Travis said you did to those men. Remind me to thank Aislin when we return."

"That's if she's even talking to me then," I said, staring down at my crimson sneakers, accidentally shooting juice through the straw of the box in my hands while I tried to get the words out. "Leigh came out when everything happened. Flynt used her to protect himself and I... She... She got hurt. Before I came here, she still hadn't regained consciousness."

"I know you'd never hurt her intentionally. And I'm sure Aislin will forgive you. She just needs time." Dru slid to the ground, moving in front of me, taking my juice box and placing it on the table next to us. "Once we are back, I'll go check on her myself. I'm sure something can be done. There's always a way."

Resting his elbows on my knees, he stared up at me, nothing but devotion and golden flecks swirling in his hazel eyes.

"Thanks," I said, not fully meeting his gaze. "I hope what happened doesn't change how you feel about being my champion..."

"I'd be honored to be yours in every way," he said, bringing my hand to his lips and kissing my knuckles. "But Travis isn't completely off about your champion. You could find someone more advantageous a match for your station. Someone with abilities—"

"Dru, I don't care about some fancy ability. Don't you see? The fact that you don't have powers—*that* is your strength." I pulled him closer to me, our mouths crashing with so much unexpected force that for a second I forgot to breathe.

"Celaria needs you," I murmured between kisses, my body becoming warm against his. "I need you."

He kissed me without hesitation, like he knew the heat between us wasn't the kind that needed to be stifled like it had been back in Celaria. Standing up, I took him with me, giving him a gentle push, and backing him up against the archive shelves.

Removing my leather jacket, I let it drop to the floor before working to unbutton his black shirt. I kissed along the strong panes of his chest, continuing to fumble with the buttons.

When I leaned into him, his cock pressed against my hip, making me salivate. I'd been thinking about this moment for what felt like ages, but fear always held one or both of us back.

Fear of my powers. Dru's fear of his perceived lack.

We'd let our insecurities rip us apart instead of realizing we were united in our self-doubt. And we really didn't need to doubt anything. At the end of the day, we both wanted this.

"You were right." Dru paused, hands resting on the hollow of my hips, our chests heaving. "Some things can't be explained away through logic, and I don't want to try to anymore."

"Fuck logic." I laughed, drawing my palm down to the band of his trousers, lingering where he strained beneath them.

"You sure?" he asked, eyes dropping to my hand drawing up and down the length of him.

I was ready to cross the line that we'd been blurring for far too long, but he restrained himself, waiting for the confirmation I was beyond eager to give.

"Never been more certain."

53

DRU

My hands captured her waist, and I gripped her close, flipping us around and pressing her against the shelves. She let out a surprised yelp, probably not expecting me to take the reins, but nothing was holding me back.

Not now. Not ever again.

She deserved all of me. Nothing less.

I lifted her tank top over her head, then reached for the clasp of her bra, fumbling a moment until I found the hooks. Kissing her jaw, I traced down her neck and chest, taking one of her breasts into my palm and rolling the nipple between my fingers, sucking the other into my mouth and flicking the bud with my tongue. She arched into me, emitting a sultry moan that shot straight to my dick.

Her hands skimmed the top of my pants. Biting her lip, she unbuttoned them with tortuous precision, pulling them down, along with my boxers. My dick popped up, eager for her. It wasn't the first time she'd seen me, had seen how much I wanted her. Nothing had been left to the imagination during our time at Renovo Falls. But this was the first time I didn't have to smother my desire.

Her pupils dilated, watching me fist myself in one long stroke. A glistening bead formed at the tip, and her fingers brushed against mine, nudging away my hand to replace it with her own. She gripped me tightly, twisting in delicious sweeps that made me shudder.

Swiping the beads that had accumulated, she brought her finger to her mouth, and I groaned when she sucked it clean.

How did I end up so lucky that this woman, who could have her pick of anyone in all the realms, wanted me?

I didn't know the answer, but I'd spend the rest of my life showing her she'd made the right decision.

Slowly trailing kisses down her stomach, I knelt, wanting to worship every inch of her. Unzipping her pants, I tugged at them in earnest, Kyleigh stifling a giggle from above. It wasn't as smooth of a transition as I would have liked, the leather happy to stay snug against her, but I eventually wrestled them down.

I teased her with my lips, my teeth, my tongue, kissing her through her underwear, coaxing the wetness building there. She gripped my head, groaning in frustration, hips jerking into me. I let out a breathy laugh before removing the final layer between us.

Completely bare against the shelf, she leaned back, sending a few books clamoring at our feet. Instinct had me wanting to put them back, but nothing was going to get in the way of this moment. All the texts could catch fire and it wouldn't stop me.

I moved in, devouring her—nudging her legs wider so I could fully lick up her slit. She tasted divine: a mix of tangy, sweet perfection. I lapped her up eagerly, starving for her pleasure, satisfied with the knowledge that I was the one giving it to her. The one she'd chosen time and time again.

And I'd choose her every time. Above all else.

Working my tongue up into her, she whimpered, body jerking. Her hand clutched my hair, tugging to the point of delicate pain, the other grasped at the shelf behind her.

She was nearly where I wanted her.

I replaced my tongue with my fingers, curling them in as I latched to her clit, listening to her scream out, hips convulsing. A few more books scattered on the ground, her body quaking against the shelves, riding her orgasm.

The hand that had dug into my scalp ran lazily down my cheek before seizing my chin and pulling me to stand. She kissed me. "I love how you taste with me on your lips."

I kissed her back, running my nose along her cheek. Her hand wrapped around me and gave me a long stroke.

"Ky," I rasped out. I could easily come any moment from her touch, especially after watching her taking pleasure from me. I wasn't ready for this to end, but before I completely lost my head..."Hold on. I need to grab some—"

She held a finger up to stop me, gliding over to the heap of leather on the ground. Reaching into a pocket, she grabbed a vial filled with peridot liquid.

I raised a brow at her.

"What? It's always good to be prepared," she said, shrugging and walking back over.

Great minds.

I lifted her leg, placing it on the second shelf from the bottom, knocking a few books out of the way. Continuing to stroke me, she pulled my body closer to hers, lining me up with her center. "I want you. Now."

I'd never seen Kyleigh like this. So sure of herself. Of us.

Her newly evolved confidence shimmered over her like a radiant second skin.

It only made me love her more.

"As you wish." I brought the elixir to my lips and drank it down. It bubbled on my tongue, tasting like licorice and mint —not a great flavor combination, but I couldn't care less about that right now.

My body trembled, anticipating the bliss I was finally going to have with the woman I loved more than anything. The first feeling of family—of belonging—I'd had in ages. We were both beautifully broken, brilliant and flawed. But there was no score to keep, no secret tally when it came to the heart.

She gasped as I edged myself into her. Pulsing, plunging deeper with each stroke, giving her time to adjust.

"*More*," she pleaded, her body primed for pleasure.

It may not have been our champion ceremony, but when I was fully seated in her, our bodies unable to get any closer, it felt like the most magical thing possible. I held her there a moment, wanting to savor having nothing between us. "You feel incredible."

She rolled her hips, hand gripping the back of my neck, the other pressing into the shelf above her. Eyes shooting downward, she watched me twirl her nipple between my fingers. Watched the thrust of my hips inching in and out of her. I ached to fill her, but instead I slowed down, studying her body's response, not wanting to miss a single one. I was in no rush. I'd waited my whole life for this feeling, and I was determined to learn every way to make her writhe around me.

Heat rippled through our bodies, and she clenched me tighter.

I gripped her thigh, hitching it higher, knocking off a few more texts when I changed angles.

A surprised whimper escaped her lips as I hit the sensitive spot that had her clamping around me.

Bringing my hand down between us, I toyed with her clit. Her eyes widened, gaze spearing to the ceiling, breath coming out in short bursts.

"Hold tight," I rasped against her cheek as her body shook between me and the bookcase.

Nodding wildly, her fingers clamped around the shelf, and I picked up the pace.

"Dru!" she cried, shattering into a million beautiful pieces. She was breathtaking—cheeks and chest flushed, gray eyes pinned to the ceiling, her nails stamping crescents into my shoulder.

"*Blazes!*" I grit out, hips punching a few more times before I detonated, spilling into her.

My body went slack, our heads pressed together, my mind soaring above the clouds.

I wished more than anything to never come down from this high.

54

AISLIN

"Yes!"

Sloan clutched the comforter, writhing above me, her thighs trembling on either side of my face. I slid my palm up the hollow of her hips before rolling her nipple between my fingers. My tongue strummed her clit, lapping in shallow strokes while I increased the pressure. Back arched, silhouetted in moonlight, she seized the headboard, bracing herself through her third glorious orgasm.

I smirked beneath her, proud of my handiwork.

"*Oh*, isn't she exquisite."

My body froze.

Copper-tipped fingers crept over Sloan's shoulder, brushing her silver, sweat-slicked strands out of the way. Another set of claws glided down her belly.

Poised behind my champion was the Enchantress.

She licked up the column of Sloan's throat, holding my gaze. "I've never taken from one with familiar magic before," she whispered, her lower hand drifting dangerously close to Sloan's center.

I tried to struggle, to kick, to release my lightning. *Anything.*

But nothing happened.

Sloan leaned into the Enchantress's touch, soft moans drifting past her plum lips, hips rocking over my face. Pinned beneath her, I was unable to do anything about it. Shadowy wings unfurled from her back, each tendril wrapping itself around my champion, a few coaxing her into another orgasm.

"That's four, isn't it?" the Enchantress purred with a smile, showing off her elongated canines.

I couldn't move. Could barely breathe.

She stroked Sloan's cheek, then raised her claw. Slashing through her throat, she spilled my champion's blood onto me, its iron-rich scent drowning me.

Sloan's body flopped forward, vacant eyes penetrating mine. Blood soaked through the comforter, painting the white sheets crimson.

Tears sprang from my eyes, mixing with the ichor splattered on my face.

"This isn't real," I said, spitting out some blood that had seeped its way into my mouth. "It's a dream."

"This may be a dream, but the message isn't any less real."

"And what message is that?"

The Enchantress lowered herself until her chest was flush with my own, licking up my blood-covered cheek before whispering, "I'd hate to bring her into our deal if you try to wriggle out of it somehow."

"She has nothing to do with it," I seethed, turning my face away from hers, only to find Sloan's icy, dead eyes. A chill streaked through me.

"You think that matters to me?"

I struggled against her, gaze darting around the room, looking for anything that could hint at a way to wake myself up from this dream, to get out of her clutches.

"Tick tock, sweet Aislin, time's running out." She snatched me in for a kiss, slithering her tongue past my lips.

I gagged, sputtering out a series of coughs, waking up with my dagger clasped to me, still tasting the Enchantress.

A spear of moonlight illuminated Sloan fast asleep next to me.

It was just a dream.

This may be a dream, but the message isn't any less real.

I wriggled into my leather pants and tunic, securing my amethyst blade into its holster at my hip. Looping through my straps, I tightened the belt so it was snug against my chest. Tiptoeing toward the door, I slowly twisted the knob, pulling it open only enough to slip through.

After Sloan had fallen asleep, I'd spent most of the night contemplating how we could take on the Enchantress, but one thing got in the way every time—we had no real clue how powerful she truly was. The small glimpse of what I'd seen when I'd met her wasn't reassuring considering she'd easily drained my powers to the point I was barely alive.

If we went there together, I couldn't guarantee Sloan's safety, and I wouldn't be able to live with myself if something happened to her. She was the one good thing that had come into my life in as long as I could remember. Sweeney was a prime example of how you never got over someone like that. He'd never moved on from loving Pierce.

Besides, I had a way to keep my end of the bargain. Even if I didn't like it.

Slinking into Dru's room, I stalked over to the fridge, feeling around for the vials and holding them up to the moonlight to find the one I wanted. Pouring the crimson liquid into the copper vial, I attached my shot at freedom to my chest strap before leaving.

I could be more powerful if I wasn't so afraid of what that would mean for me. If I had taken all those lives when my powers were just a whisper, I couldn't imagine how devastating they could be—especially in the wrong hands. That reason alone was why I needed to free myself from any connection to the Enchantress.

I knew Sloan would be angry I was doing this alone. She wouldn't agree with it. But it was better to beg for forgiveness than chance having her ripped away from me by an enemy I still didn't fully understand.

My boots crunched against the floor of the Silent Woods, and I focused on the pain radiating from the nape of my neck through my shoulders and chest. Swirls of dusky bodies curled around me, urging me forward. The Enchantress's wisps didn't attempt to glamour me. They simply floated alongside me, escorting me to their mistress.

She knew I was here to make good on my deal.

I turned my eyes to the sky, sending a silent apology to the stars above for what I was about to do.

Hoping above all else that it would work.

55

TRAVIS

"Brothers and sisters, it's time."

I peered through the slats of my wolf mask to the shadowed group gathered around the Sentry Stone, a peek of sun rising in the distance. Kyleigh had said thirty minutes prior to sunrise, so I'd had our group meet an hour ahead of time. We weren't going to miss this moment, and I wanted to give it the pomp it deserved.

My father and I had reached out to our network to notify everyone that it was happening and the first eight to respond would be allowed to go. Of course, I'd given a heads up to my dearest associates, ensuring I'd have allies with me in Celaria.

I couldn't remember the last time I'd felt so alive. My heart pounded in my chest. I'd spent years working toward this, and now I'd finally get to learn the real truth about the mysterious realm we'd been cast out of. The generation before us had founded Vindicatio Vis, trying to get back, but I was the one who lead us to this moment.

Many of the first people sent to this world were from one of two camps—Celarian misfits or Arafax's most powerful who could help build Halston and protect the Otherworld from magic's interference. The plan seemed fair at the time, but how could you ever feel at home in a place you were told you never belonged, knowing you had so much unlocked potential waiting for you somewhere you weren't allowed?

My father never wanted me to forget what I'd been born into.

What I'd been born for.

There was never another path for me. I'd been given life on that stone, and I was tied to it by fate, knowing I'd either die on it or on the other side.

Thankfully, I now knew which side fate's coin landed.

"Today we descend as one," I said with quiet determination. We were standing on the Quad for fuck's sake. I had no idea why we weren't using the ceremonial chamber, but I wasn't going to be choosy when Kyleigh had been so agreeable to our passage to Celaria. She must've been desperate.

A massive figure padded into view, two smaller ones trailing behind him.

"It's time," I announced to my Vindicatio Vis brothers and sisters.

Kyleigh paused for a moment, gripping Dru's hand tightly in hers before moving through the crowd. Considering some of us had stabbed her the last time she'd seen us, I couldn't really blame her apprehension.

"Did you have to wear the fucking masks?" she asked, her giant companion and Dru helping her onto the stone.

"It is how we always meet," I said, shrugging, my voice slightly distorted by the mask.

She cocked her head, such a different woman than the timid girl whose body I'd painted beneath the stars at the start of term. "Even on the Quad before sunrise?"

"All the more reason. If someone sees, they won't know our identities. They'll probably just assume they're still drunk."

Dru seemed a little more confident this morning, smirking at me. Pretty sure they fucked in the archives last night. Nothing else could have boosted that dude's confidence in my presence—other than the knowledge he'd gotten a taste of something I hadn't. *Her.*

She had turned down my proposition of an alliance. One that included sharing with her plain ol' Jack and his—what I could only imagine to be—tiny beanstalk.

Meanwhile, I couldn't help but think about the things I could do to her. If she only knew...

But that was secondary to me getting to Celaria. Once I was there and she saw my power, it would be an easier sell to ensure an alliance against whatever had her scared enough to let us through the portal in the first place. Until then, I'd bide my time and play nice.

Well, as nice as I possibly could.

Her new clothes hugged her in all the right ways. Definitely not the girl I'd met in August. She pursed her lips at me, like she could hear my thoughts.

"You ready?" Her leather-clad tone was laced with annoyance.

"I was born ready," I said, never believing the words more in my life.

Dru was counting to himself, "—seven, eight, nine." His brows furrowed.

Kyleigh glanced over at me. "I didn't realize you had so much trouble with math, Travis."

"What do you mean?" I looked over the group, counting, realizing they were right. Somehow, an extra had shown up.

Had I sent reply emails to too many members? I pulled out my phone, starting to scroll my messages.

"Don't worry about it," Dru said. "Kyleigh provided enough blood to handle one more. But don't think about any more surprises, Grymm."

I placed the phone in my back pocket, not that I'd need it much longer.

A single light popped on in the main administrative building, my father's silhouette in the window, watching.

He'd opted to stay here, knowing the sudden disappearance of the president of the university would rouse suspicion with no one to take over. No need to worry the board members. I'd send updates once I got settled in Celaria. Maybe one day he'd join me there. I hoped he wouldn't, though. After waiting a lifetime to be out from under his thumb, it only felt right that I'd get to by doing the one thing he never could.

I'm sure the cocky bastard was patting himself on the back right now. Proud of himself.

Fuck him.

I'd gotten here in spite of him.

The seven-foot mammoth helped everyone onto the stone before climbing up himself. Pressed against each other, my senses keyed into the increased heart rates and panting breaths of everyone around me. Ruby vials were passed around the group.

"Spread it on your chest," Dru instructed.

I smeared the cool blood over my pecs, watching Kyleigh's throat bob in disgust.

"Just following your boyfriend's directions," I whispered to her.

She stilled, eyes clenched tightly while Dru sliced her

palm, her fingers covered in the copper faerie blood we'd brought from his list now mixing with the crimson of her own. She knelt and touched the corium, Dru nestled low beside her.

The stone crumbled into tiny grains of sand, slowly sucking us down. I caught one final glimpse of my father's silhouette before the light flicked off and everything around us disappeared.

I shut my eyes, welcoming fate.

BLACKNESS SURROUNDED ME.

I'd made it. But where the fuck was I?

I didn't see anyone else, only a few beams of light reflecting on the stone beneath me.

Did I somehow get redirected?

Booms echoed and the ground shook, sending me bouncing a few feet over the floor. I closed my eyes, trying to decipher the blaring noises. When I opened them, the world finally less distorted, I realized I wasn't peering through my wolf mask. Where was it?

"Whhhhhaaaaaaatttt happeennnnnneed toooo Travvvvviiiiissss?" The muffled words clamored around me.

Suddenly, the darkness lifted. Massive feet circled me as an enormous hand pulled away the wolf mask.

Kyleigh's hand.

A dozen gigantic faces gaped down at me, a shit-eating grin plastered on Dru's face. His eyes shifted to Kyleigh who was stifling a laugh.

What's so funny?

Why was everyone so big? Even the giant seemed more ginormous. If that were even possible.

Odette, my black swan beauty and occasional fuck buddy, lowered her hand, and I jumped back, afraid she was going to smash me. She left it there a moment, presumably waiting for me to climb on.

It took a few tries, but I finally swung my leg over her fingers, my balance feeling off. She brought me level with the faces of everyone around me.

No one said a word.

My back buzzed, a strange whirring sensation humming behind me. I glanced over my shoulder to see a set of iridescent wings beating wildly, decorated with intricate zig-zag patterns shimmering in the light. I strained to see where they came from, fumbling over them with my hands.

Two buds jutted out from my shoulder blades, anchoring the fluttering wings.

Holy shit.

Kyleigh's glowing silver eyes were the size of two illuminated moons, waning a bit while she squinted at me, confused. "What is he?"

Her gaze snapped to Dru's, searching for answers.

He gripped his chin, rubbing the stubble, taking me in before he spoke in a hushed tone. "A faerie."

What the fuck?

56

SLOAN

An icy shock whipped through me. My eyes snapped open, the moon glowing against the violet sky. Rolling over, I found Aislin's side of the bed empty.

Where is she?

Wiping my eyes, I sat up, pulling the sheets aside. I tucked my hair behind my ear, heading into the bathroom to get ready so I could find Aislin and drag her back to bed, or wherever I could get her, really. It had taken months for her to give in to what we both knew was inevitable—what we'd denied since she'd met me from the other end of my sword, spelling me with her courage and hypnotic emerald eyes.

Memories of last night swam in my mind: her slick body wrapped around me; making her come in rippling waves; the steamy bath water lapping around us while we let our mutually competitive natures rise to the surface, seeing who could wring more pleasure from the other.

It was the best kind of battle.

After a night like that, what could have pulled her from our bed at this hour?

Reaching out to her through the delicately woven strands of our bond, I sent some lingering desire, feeling a brief pull of determination on her end before it went silent. Intentionally silent.

I turned on the sink, splashing my face with water, trying to push away the uncanny feeling that nagged at me. A ghost-like sensation crept along my skin, goosebumps following its path.

Descending the stairs, I headed to the infirmary in case she'd gone to visit Leigh.

The room was dark, and I whispered, trying not to wake any sleeping patients, "Aislin?"

No response.

A rumbling growl rolled through my chest, and I staggered back, startled by my familiar—the thick rope of our connection pulling taut.

Mox?

What could have him so on edge?

I could always rely on Mox's intuition. Even when I couldn't figure out exactly what Kaeghan and the other guards had been up to, Mox had been on to him all along. If only we had known before Neve had gotten hurt.

The first time Redmond had gone to visit the Enchantress, he'd growled out, the feeling vibrating through me while I was in the middle of bathing. It was an alarm—Mox's way of letting me know I needed to watch. Knowing what I did now, it was probably when Red was roped into his father's old deal.

Now Mox was telling me something else was happening that I needed to see.

Something important.

I closed my eyes, letting his vision coalesce with mine.

THE CABIN LOOMED OVERHEAD, MOX'S LARGE, WHITE SNOUT pointing the way. Wisps flew in and out of the open windows, the scene bobbing up and down. He scampered to a windowsill. A wisp blew past, and his head whipped over to the pile of husks strewn behind the cabin.

I didn't understand what she gained from draining people until they were a gray, translucent shell. The Enchantress didn't nourish herself with food.

She nourished herself with power.

It's one of the reasons I had kept such a careful eye on Redmond going to visit with her. What would stop her from one day discarding him with the hundreds of bodies that littered her yard? Whatever she had planned for those husks, it wasn't good.

Mox's snout lifted, trying to peek inside the cabin. A coven of wisps blocked the view through the kitchen window. One wisp among the group flitted over with a few pieces of bread and discreetly dropped them on the windowsill, then quickly returned to its coven. None of the others seemed to notice the exchange.

He sniffed a few times, inspecting the offering, then his long, pink tongue snuck out, munching the bread before lapping up the crumbs.

Mox's satisfied purr rumbled through me. I sighed, trying to stay focused despite my frustration with the huddled wisps obstructing the view. I still wasn't sure what he was trying to show me.

Two quick claps jolted his head up, looking for the source of the sound. The wisps swirled, dissipating from their spectral cloud in a flurry, moving about the cabin, searching for something.

When the area cleared, my heart stopped.

"I'd love to give you a reward for showing up early," the Enchantress *said, sprawled across a black chaise. Streaks of purple light twisted about the room, wisps dodging the bolts bounding in all directions. The Enchantress lay there with a clawed hand, the lightning feeding into it while her onyx eyes shimmered maliciously. "I'm glad you made the smart decision of following through on our deal, though I will miss visiting those* enlightening *dreams of yours. I could teach you and your knight a thing or two, I'm sure."*

Bringing a finger to her mouth, the Enchantress swirled the lightning on her tongue before sucking it down.

"Mmm," she groaned, "you taste even better than last time. That bitterness that tinged your powers has been replaced with something much more decadent. Yes, something has changed..."

Excuse me? The only one who should be tasting her is me.

"N-nothing's changed," Aislin said through chattering teeth. She was clenching her fists tight, trying to fight the pull of the Enchantress's power as it took from her.

"Don't lie to me," the Enchantress said, licking her crimson lips. "We both know that tongue could be put to much better use."

Possessive heat flared in my chest.

I needed to get to Aislin.

"You'll never be so lucky," Aislin said, face pinched in pain. "I'm a one-woman kind of gal."

"That's a shame," the Enchantress pouted, her copper claws releasing Aislin. She fell to the ground, wincing as she clutched her wrists to her.

The gossamer tether in my chest pulled taut. Our bond.

The sensation was still new to me, and it was weakening, but I still felt it there. She needed me.

Her champion.

Sprinting out of the fort, I headed toward the Silent Woods. I kept watching on the events unfolding through Mox's vision, begging the stars that I'd make it to her in time.

Pressing up onto her elbows, Aislin reached for her chest strap, unhooking a small, translucent copper vial from it, crimson liquid sloshing within.

No.

She wouldn't.

Just yesterday she'd said we would do this together. What had changed her mind? What was the point of being her champion if she didn't trust me to take on our foes as a team?

Aislin held the vial out to the Enchantress who gave her a satisfied smirk, elongated canines peeking from her lips. The shadowy tendrils of her wings enveloped Aislin, one of them taking the vial while the others lingered against her arms and legs. Lingered too long.

Stay the fuck away from her!

Aislin heaved, trying to catch her breath, pushing away the wings caressing her body. Her hands gripped her knees, whole body shaking.

"I must admit, I'm disappointed I won't get to have more fun with you," the Enchantress purred, walking back to a hallway and disappearing her from view, "but you've kept up your end of the bargain."

The click of her heels grew louder, the Enchantress coming into view again. She gripped Aislin's shirt, claws ripping the fabric as she lifted her to stand. "Now leave before I take more of those decadent powers of yours. Whatever has changed since the first time we met, it makes you all the more delectable, and I don't know if I'd be able to stop myself from taking things too far."

A pair of stark claps rang through the cabin, and the wisps pulsed their wings, closing in on Aislin. Her pupils dilated, watching them, entranced. They slid their ghostly forms along her body, caressing her, herding her. Following their hypnotic lead, she walked out of the cabin's door and out of sight.

If she gave the Enchantress the vial, gave her what she wanted, then Aislin had just betrayed Kyleigh, endangering the alliance between Inverno and Arafax. Endangering Celaria.

Pulling away from the window, Mox trotted toward the humming sound, trailing behind Aislin and the wisps she followed so obediently.

Eventually, they led her away from the cabin, leaving her in the middle of the woods. Blinking tears away from her eyes, she ran her hands up and down the sleeves of her jacket, taking slow, deep breaths. Walking farther away from the Enchantress's home, Mox stalked quietly behind her until she stopped abruptly.

Jumping to face him, her dagger out, she was ready to attack.

"Fuck!" she croaked, sounding more dejected than startled once she recognized who'd been shadowing her. Mox cocked his head at her, turning the vision sideways. Aislin bent down, and he lifted his snout while she scratched under his chin, eliciting a purr from his chest.

Stop worrying about belly rubs and focus on keeping her safe until I can get to her!

The growing frustration and anger in my chest unleashed itself as a growl coming from my familiar, aimed at its intended target. Aislin.

She pulled back, realization hitting her.

"You're watching, aren't you?" she asked, staring into his eyes, already knowing the answer. "I promise I'll explain when—"

My boots crunched against the dead tree branches and debris littering the underbrush, and Aislin's head snapped in my direction in Mox's vision.

I closed my eyes a moment, pausing to clear out my familiar's view.

AISLIN'S EYES WERE THE FIRST THING I SAW, TWO GREEN beacons that tugged at my core, the tether of our bond relaxing with each closing step.

The grip on my chest loosened, senses flooding when I saw her, knowing we would soon be out of the Enchantress's reach. But I was also angry, terrified of what the cost of this freedom she'd gone to secure would mean. For us, for Kyleigh, for Celaria. We still didn't possess the knowledge to stop the Enchantress if she used that blood to free herself from exile. One dragon-champion pair and a handful of disorganized magic wielders wouldn't be enough. Inverno's army would help, but was Redmond ready to provide what he'd promised when he'd requested an alliance?

A mix of seething frustration and relief pierced through me, seeping into my words. "What happened to dealing with her together?"

"I know," Aislin said, breathing out heavily, looking suspiciously over her shoulder as if she expected the wisps to be trailing behind her. "But I couldn't put you in danger. She would have overpowered us."

I claimed her mouth with mine, not waiting for an invitation. It had been close, *too damn close*. And I was livid. She'd have to learn her lesson about keeping me in the dark, but that would come later, when I'd edge her into oblivion, making her beg for release.

Right now, I was just glad she was safe and here with me.

My heart pounded, hands trembling in anger. In fear. I hated feeling helpless, stuck watching what was happening to her.

"It's going to be okay," she rasped over my lips, kissing me with an intensity she never had before.

I felt our bond's tether weaving tightly together, strengthened through our love. We knew the bond would grow, would need to be tended to and nurtured, but I was just starting to understand what that really meant.

I never wanted to feel the raw, taut fragility of it again.

Aislin pulled down her jacket and moved her shredded tank over, showing me the spot of her heart-shaped bond mark—the one that kept her in the Enchantress's grasp. The lines had already begun to fade, blending into her skin. "Is it going away?"

"It is."

She sighed, a smile peeling up at the corners of her beautiful mouth. It made me want to kiss her again, but right now I wanted to get far away from these creepy woods.

I held my hand out to her. "Don't do that ever again. We'll figure out what to do next, together."

She nodded, taking my hand and walking toward the edge of the dark forest. She gently ran her fingers against my palm, tiny pulses of lightning tracing it, sending shivers down my spine. Her other hand stroked the spot where the bond mark had once been, and she let out a sigh at the bareness of it.

Mox growled, teeth bared.

We stilled, surveying the area for any sign of the wisps or their mistress.

"What is it, boy?"

I blinked a few times, making sure I was seeing correctly. Mox wasn't staring at an outside threat. He was snapping at Aislin.

"Wha—"

The hand clasping mine changed textures. Like grains of sand it began to slip away. Aislin's eyes shot down to it, then back to mine.

"What's happening?"

Her hand floated through mine, the woman I loved disintegrating slowly in front of me.

"I don't understand."

My chest clenched, the seams of our bond starting to fray.

No, no, no.

Panic shone in her eyes, a solitary tear grazing her cheek. "I'm sorry."

"Sorry for what? What's going on, Aislin?" Heat flared through me while her body drained of warmth.

"Promise me," she pleaded, her emerald eyes dimming. "Don't come for me without the others. Not until—"

She continued to fade, her skin's warm glow dissipating into an ashen haze.

"*No!*" I shouted into the barren woods, only to be greeted by silence.

This can't be happening.

That's when I heard their low hum, calling to her.

Aislin floated in front of me, a translucent silhouette, wings unfurled from her back, fluttering wildly. Her body moved erratically, frantically trying to navigate her new form.

A shadow wisp.

"No," I cried, tears spilling from my eyes, taking a step toward her. "Our forever has only begun."

The coven of wisps swarmed around her, their darkness swallowing her up.

I screamed, a fiery ache clawing up my chest as our bond stretched, strained...

Snapped.

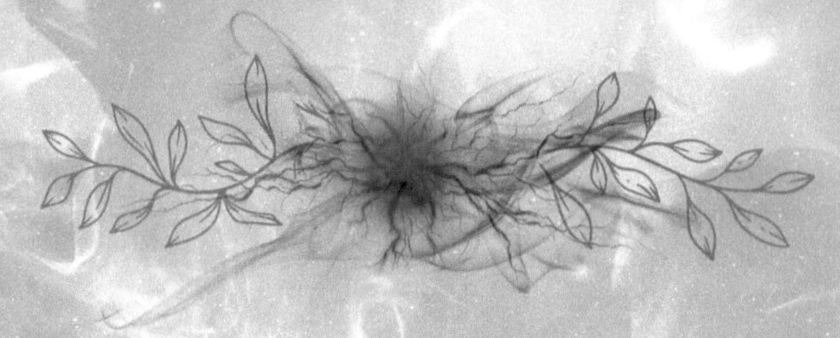

EPILOGUE
THE WISP

Clap, clap.

The winged king bowed to the dais, straining against shadow bindings.

Doesn't he know there's no use resisting her?

Our Queen brought out the box, slipping the chain over his head.

He curled onto the floor.

Screaming.

Grasping for something I couldn't see.

Holding someone who wasn't there.

Our Queen loved watching him.

Enjoying him.

Breaking him.

Sticking a spiky boot to his chest, she told him his punishment was over.

Time for his reward.

Clap, clap.

I floated by the shelves.

Red fire.

Black feathers.

Blue powder.

A beating heart.

That one's important, the one who moved mountains whispered.

A glowing jar. Lightning.

I wanted to touch it.

I flitted forward, wrapping a shadowy wing around the glass.

Warmth.

Our Queen chuckled behind me.

"We are going to have so much fun together."

I went rigid at her words. Her gaze.

Violet streaks danced across her fingers.

She smirked, bringing her hands together.

Clap, clap.

I gazed at the pile of husks.

Used and discarded.

For now.

A flash of green crossed the sky.

I flew out the window to see.

Black trees blocked my view.

I moved up, up, up.

Scaling the treetops, I hit the barrier of my invisible cell.

A huff echoed from a green scaled snout.

Its emerald orb winked before the creature jolted away.

Out of reach.

Clap, clap.

I couldn't remember much.

The things I did clung to my attention like static.

I felt its stare. Like it never left.

I flitted near, but not too near the window, glimpsing a white snout peeking over the edge.

Watching me.

I hummed, flitting closer.

Another, the one who erased them, dropped some bread on the windowsill.

The white fox sniffed, then lapped it up. Pink tongue snatching every crumb.

Its eyes were kind. Pitch black.

Familiar.

Clap, clap.

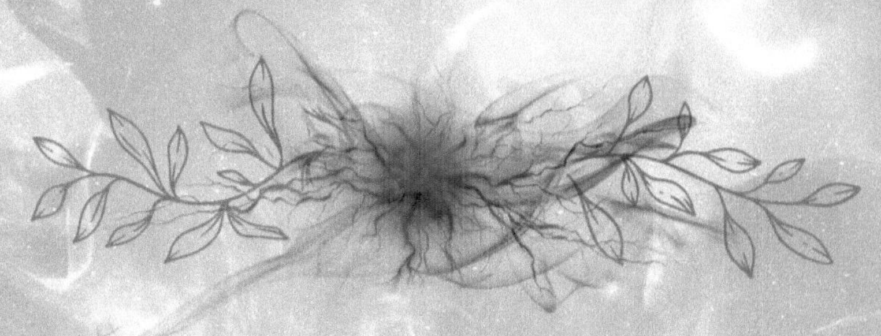

THE COVEN

Time ebbed and flowed.
Hours.
Days.
Decades.

Moments between.
Pain throughout.
With only three rules:

Obey.
Enchant.
Destroy.

THE JOURNEY CONTINUES...

If you have thrown your book across the room, I apologize. Thank you for picking it back up to get to this point.

Whether you just started reading or have been following along with me since before I published my debut novel, Descend—I appreciate you taking the time to escape with these books.

If you have a moment to leave some stars and a review, they are such a help for fellow readers to find indie authors and their work. Even just a few words makes a big difference!

This book for me was such a joy to write, getting to dive deeper into these characters and share more of the incredible world of Celaria.

If you're curious about the Enchantress, her origin story, *Pitch*, is now available and you'll want to catch up before moving onto Book 3 in the series, Ascend.

As a special treat, there is a short story included after the acknowledgements called Rise of a Champion. This story takes place prior to the events in Descend and features cameos from some of your favorite characters. I hope you enjoy it!

452

ACKNOWLEDGMENTS

Thank you to my parents who have cheered on this series since its inception. I love you both more than you'll ever know.

To my amazing husband who is working his way through these books and has supported me since I said I wanted to start writing—thank you for showing me through your own example the power of hard work and persistence.

Jennifer A. Vodvarka—the best critique partner I could ask for. Thanks for always pushing me.

Chinah—working with you on this book was nothing short of extraordinary. Thank you for never shying from asking more from my writing and for helping me shape this book into something truly beautiful.

Jo—you've been rooting for Aislin and Sloan from Day 1. Thank you for all your advice, encouragement, and for loving these two as much as I do.

Brittani, Angelique, Emmaline—thank you for your time in reading and giving feedback to help get the most from this book. I appreciate it more than you know. You are all simply the best.

The Book Tour Gals—you are all amazing women who are beautiful inside and out. Thank you for for all the love over the last year with preparing to release this series. Vanessa- a special shout out for letting me talk your ear off about these characters.

To my fellow indie authors, it's not an easy journey but it is certainly incredible alongside you guys. Sarah A. Parker, Ann Denton, Vanessa Rasanen, Tati B. Alvarez, and Brittany Ann—thank you for always inspiring and encouraging me.

Finally, thank you to all the readers who have taken a chance on this series. Every time you message or tag me in a post, it fills me with so much joy to see the books out there in the world and loved.

RISE OF A CHAMPION
A BLAZE LEGACY PREQUEL NOVELLA

INTRODUCTION

Rise of a Champion is set in *The Blaze Legacy* world and takes place decades prior to the events of Book 1, Descend. You will see some familiar faces and meet some new. I hope you enjoy a taste of more to come in Celaria by a brief visit to its past.

PRONUNCIATION GUIDE

People

Caden - KAY-duhn

Ciaran - KEER-on

Desmond – DEZ-mund

Isla - EYE-luh

Laoise – LEE-shah

Laisren – LAS-rain

Moira – MOY-rah

Reynard – RAY-nard

Rianna – REE-anna

Places

Alucinor: ah-LOO-shin-or

Arafax: AIR-uh-fax

Celaria: SUH-lair-ee-uh

Inverno: In-VER-no

1

Swords clang, their echo ringing through me. I swing both of mine at Graham, but he blocks them with his shield. The scrape of blade against steel electrifies my insides, a thrumming reminder that this is what I train for. Live for. Thrive within.

"You can do better than that, Caden!"

I spin toward him, knocking him off balance before I stick my armored boot out. He stumbles over it, puffs of dirt rising around him when his ass hits the ground. Sweat beads across my brow, and I shake my arms off, huffing in satisfaction.

Victory is mine.

Graham scrambles backward on his palms and I charge forward, twisting to slice down my blade.

He lifts his shield, stopping it. "Ha!"

Graham is far too cocky during these training sessions. Good thing I'm here to keep him humble. I angle my sword and knock the shield away, chuckling when it bounces between Pierce and the knight whom he's currently dodging a blow from, Desmond. The pair shoot me a glare, and I shrug with a smirk. Turning back to Graham, I cross my swords above his throat, holding a moment to signify my win before tossing them off to the side and helping him stand.

Heavy footfalls approach along with the prideful rush of wings beating against the wind. The cacophony of sparring settles. Thibauld and Owen stand stoically behind King Laisren, whose golden crown glints in the morning's shine. Without a word, we all kneel before Arafax's ruler, King of Embers, Guardian of the Revered. Our chests heave, adrenaline coursing through us from training, our energy thrumming with nowhere to go.

"Rise." King Laisren waves his hand lazily. "I came to remind you all that The Gauntlet starts at moonshine tomorrow."

How could we forget? It's all that's been talked about in the territory for the last three months.

"Tonight, all those competing for the prestigious position of champion will be expected to attend the welcome banquet as our honored guests. There will be nobility from throughout the realm in attendance, so please be on your best behavior."

"Tibbs better lay off the home brew," Graham teases.

From behind the King, Thibauld's amber eyes narrow, his lips pulling into a firm line. We've never seen him drink. Ever. In fact, he could be the most straightlaced of all the royal guards. It's also the reason he's usually assigned to escort Arafax's eldest prince, Ciaran. He's there to keep him in line. It's a fool's errand. He's the last choice for any of us to be stuck with. Pierce is the only one who doesn't seem to mind it, but he doesn't count because he likes everyone.

"How many champions are to be selected?" Desmond asks, tucking his sweat-soaked sable strands behind his ear. He's my greatest competition if only one of the two unbonded Revered chooses a champion. While the King selects The Gauntlet's winner, the dragon can choose not to go through with the tethering ceremony. But no one's been told what's involved with that, though the current champion, Aveena, knows. She's pushing seventy but is no less lethal on the back of her Revered than she was forty years ago, from what I hear.

Every time we've asked her about details, she plies us with whiskey and bows out of the conversation. Soon I shall know for myself, though.

"As of right now, there are two Revered without champions. One has signaled their intention to bond this year. Hopefully, the other will be encouraged to as well."

I hope so. That would give Desmond and I both a shot at champion, turning my greatest competition into my greatest ally. The line between is finite, and at the end of the day, as much as I want this, we are all fighting for the same cause:

A radiant and thriving Arafax.

My gaze climbs the purpling sky to the glints of gold radiating from the floating castle above us. Heart thudding wildly, anticipation cuts through my nerves like a freshly sharpened blade. In just two days, I could be named champion.

A huff comes from behind me, the Revered watching us all from under their snouts. The navy one with golden flecks splattered across its scales, like metallic paint tossed on a canvas, is lazing in the grass. Aveena leans back against him, her gray hair braided tightly to her head in a series of wavy coils. They mimic the flaming sigil stamped on her golden armor. She smirks at us, her voice a commanding rasp. "Good luck. And don't be idiots."

The ruby Revered roars appreciatively at that. A few of us stumble off balance as the arena floor shakes beneath from its vibrations. Aveena and her Revered chuckle at our expense. Meanwhile, the emerald dragon sits quietly. I've heard that one's the most headstrong of the three beasts. Steadying myself, I hesitantly meet its gaze, not missing the slight lift to the corner of its maw.

2

After we're dismissed from the arena, I wave off the others as they head toward the fort. We are allowed to take residence there if we wish, so many of the single knights do, including me. It makes it convenient enough to get to training, and I like being close to the castle. After all, every decision I make is one that can bring me closer to becoming commander one day.

It's something I've wanted since the first time my father put a sword in my hand, and it's why I'm signing myself up for The Gauntlet. Not that being a champion is necessary for the position, but it's hard to argue against promoting someone a Revered has chosen. Much about the connection is unknown, though many of the dragons and their champions are able to harness each other's abilities to some degree. While I do not wield any element, my strength and formidable battle tactics would certainly give Arafax an advantage.

Not that we are at war, but all it takes is a momentary

shift, a decision that someone is no longer your ally, to tip over that blade's edge. With The Gauntlet bringing in people from all over Celaria, it isn't beyond me that it could turn into something much more lethal. It's why we've rotated our training sessions to ensure the royals are safe and always guarded throughout the event.

There hasn't been one of these in more than three decades. The Gauntlet isn't a necessity, but for whatever reason, King Laisren announced that there would be one this year.

Roar!

As if on cue, the ruby beast takes to the sky, sharpened scales glittering like they're covered in a thousand gems when the moon's light hits them. Two large wings flap slowly with its ascent, a slightly paler shade than the rest of its body with opalescent veins streaking across their leathery hide.

In a few days, I could be bonding with that magnificent creature.

"Already imagining your win?" A voice calls from across the lavender field. "Aren't knights supposed to be humble?"

I can't see anyone over the thick rows of purple clusters, but I'd know that chuckle anywhere.

I crouch and begin to skulk between the flowers. A bunch of blooms rustle a few yards away, moving toward Arafax village. Black tresses whip with the breeze as she bolts out of the field, the skirts of her dress clutched in her hands.

"Just remember you started this, Moira!" I yell after her.

She glances over her shoulder, a wild smirk on her lips. The decades may have passed, but this game of chase never gets old. I'd run after her anywhere.

She zigs and zags between houses. We've done this so

many times, I don't even have to guess where she's headed, so instead of increasing my speed, I veer right and take my secret shortcut.

When Moira reaches the clearing, she collapses on a toppled tree trunk, laying across it on her stomach and kicking her feet back and forth. Waiting.

"Going to keep hiding?" she asks, green eyes sparkling between the trees surrounding her.

I hold my breath an extra moment before I peel out from behind a wide everwood, and she shifts on the bark, making space for me to plop down. Her hands are stuffed into her pockets and her chest is puffed out defiantly. I lean over her, but she doesn't move. "Miss me?"

How many times have we done this dance? In fact, only two years ago I had sat on this same trunk, offering my heart to her. Asking for her hand. It was two days before I was sent off to my first posting, patrolling the Grymm Mountains. I knew it was a leap, but I took it anyway. We'd never discussed our feelings, though they'd hung between us for years, like a star within reach but too precious to touch.

Moira had said it wasn't the right time, that I should wait and ask her when I returned. It could have been the recent passing of her father before I left. It'd been too soon for her to think about—but when I came home, something had changed. Her mother had also passed while I was gone, from a broken heart—or so Moira claimed. Whatever had happened, it was like a wall had been drawn up between us. So instead of asking to build a home with her only to be rejected again, I'd moved to the barracks and focused on the next steps in my military career.

But even now, I can't distract myself enough from

wanting her. I suck in a breath, drinking in the sight of her right by my side. Moira bites her bottom lip, and it takes every ounce of self-control for me not to dip down and bite it for her. I have before, during reckless moments that are embedded in my soul. But I won't push her.

She's my best friend. I could map the freckles scaling her cheeks and nose by memory. I remember when each one appeared, darkening with the warmer seasons. She was someone I believed could be so much more. *Everything.*

My pulse riots while I watch the slow rise and fall of her chest. She hadn't even let me kiss her one last time before I left for the mountains. Would she now?

Something flashes in her stare, but her lashes drop before I can really look at her. An elbow meets my side.

"*Oof*, I know your musk is supposed to attract the opposite sex, but have you considered the wonders a bath would do?" Moira chuckles but keeps her gaze away, like she can't stand to look at me. It's an expression I recognize all too well from when I first returned.

"I'm sorry my rugged aroma offends you," I tease her in kind before clearing my throat and cleaning my mind of any misread signals. "Just wanted to stop by before I get ready for the banquet tonight."

She groans, her hands raking down her cheeks. "I can't believe you're participating in that barbaric practice."

"What's barbaric about a competition? You win, you become one of Arafax's champions. It's very straightforward, if you ask me."

"I wasn't asking you," she snaps, then clamps her mouth shut, exhaling loudly.

I arch a brow at her. She's been on edge ever since The Gauntlet was announced. I'm not sure if it's out of worry for me or something else. Her mother was a champion...maybe it hits too close to home.

"I just don't understand why you're so focused on it."

"One day I'll command Arafax's forces."

The crease between her brows hardens. "You don't have to be a champion to do that."

"I don't," I agree, looping a wayward strand of her raven locks between my fingers and tucking it behind her ear. Her gaze traces the movement before dropping to her lap where her hands fidget with her apron. There are clumps of lavender poking up from the pockets.

Whatever's got her upset thickens the air between us, and I try my best to ease the tension. "I'd sure look good on the back of a dragon, don't you agree?"

"You're insufferable," she says, her tone filled with utter annoyance, but she chuckles.

Victorious once again. "And you love me all the more for it."

"Shouldn't you be preparing for tonight's festivities, *Sir* Caden?" she asks, batting her eyes.

I'm pretty sure it's meant to be an insult, but it doesn't have the intended effect. In fact, my mind goes to all sorts of scenarios where I could draw that title from her lips.

I blink myself back to reality, my trousers a touch too tight. "Is it so bad to want to spend time with you first?"

Her voice softens. "I suppose not."

"How's the village garden coming along?" I ask, trying to change the subject. Moira works at the school, teaching young wielders how to hone their skills.

"I've been reminding the children to water the plants every day instead of doing it myself." She sighs. "I'm realizing patience isn't my strong suit."

She's definitely not patient, but she's amazing with them.

The times I've caught her at work, watching her with them—it used to fuel my visions of a life with her. One where she'd nurture our little ones the same way. I try not to dwell on it too much anymore, though the ache in my chest lingers with the lost dream.

"I was grabbing some lavender for lessons tomorrow."

"What are you teaching?"

"The earth wielders wanted to learn more about the language of flowers."

"Ahh." I point to her overstuffed apron. "So what's lavender mean?"

She pulls out a few twigs, twirling them between her fingers before she hands me one. "It can mean different things: calm, grace..."

Moira's always loved flowers, it's why she's been so keen on working with her students to build the garden at the heart of our village even though earth isn't her specialty. "What's your favorite meaning, then?"

Her eyes slice up to meet mine. "Devotion."

My throat dries. I swallow hard enough to get out a simple "I see."

The woods are so quiet I can almost pretend there's nothing here but the two of us. That there's no fancy celebration to attend tonight. No challenge to face tomorrow. Even my desire to be commander softens from a pounding need to a gentle hum.

"Think if I bring some lavender to the Revered that it'll be enough for them to choose me?"

"Maybe." She shrugs, picking off the tiny violet buds and collecting them in a pile on her apron. "Can't say it'd work on me, but I'm happy to give you enough to make a small bouquet."

"Well, good thing you aren't the giant beast I'm meant to win over."

"Yes. Good thing." She reaches into her pocket and plucks out a small bunch, along with some twine, tying it together. Her hand brushes mine as she hands it to me, the touch gone before I can savor it. Then she stands, waiting for me to do the same.

We begin walking in the direction of the castle side by side. "Moira?"

"Yes?"

My hands clutch the lavender like it holds all the devotion I could ever want. "Will you be there tonight?"

"I may stop by." Her expression betrays nothing.

"You should." I nudge her with my elbow. "I'll save you a dance."

"A dance?" Bringing her hand over her heart, she shifts her tone, mimicking some damsel in distress that we both know she's not. "*My, how generous of you, Sir Caden.*"

"Seriously, though. Come." I can't help but chuckle with her, but then the laughter ebbs between us, and I halt, waiting until she looks at me. "Come to all of The Gauntlet, won't you?"

Her spine straightens. "Why?"

"Because I can win if you're with me. You're my good luck charm." I flash her a crooked smile, and her disposition softens, shoulders lowering a tad.

She's never been one for big get-togethers. Normally skips them all. But when she starts to roll her eyes and groans, I grin wider, knowing I've won.

"I'll see what I can do."

"Good girl."

Pink stains her cheeks, her scattered freckles dancing

above her blush, somehow making her even more striking than usual. I hope she'll join me tonight. That she'll be there for it all. Not just for The Gauntlet, but far beyond the days and years to come.

3

I meet Desmond and Graham at the base of the stairs. Each rocky step hangs midair, held in place by our wind wielders' magic, and like every time before this when I've had to climb them, I remind myself that they've never fallen, not once, in history.

While the official Gauntlet doesn't begin until moonrise tomorrow, we all know better than to think tonight isn't a test in itself. The banquet would have all of Arafax's nobility, plus possibly high-ranking officials from the other territories. They didn't always accept the invitation, but it was extended as a courtesy.

We cross the courtyard, passing rich red roses that climb the walls of the castle. Their thorns are stark against the cream-colored towers, all of which are tipped in gold. Each spire curls toward the sky, creating Arafax's flame when seen from afar—the pinnacle of Celaria's power.

Our boots clamor against the marble floors with its golden streaks as long as lightning bolts reaching along either side of the crimson carpet leading down the Great

Hall. Clusters of Celarians are huddled on either side, eyes darting our way as we approach. It's hard to go unnoticed in golden armor and deep-red dress capes, a beautiful reminder of the bloody battles we've fought and won through the centuries. Gilded flames and leaves adorn the silk, much more luxurious than our usual attire.

"Is it bad if I say I'm ready to go home already?" Graham whispers to us.

Not at all. What I would give to have a quiet night in the glade of the Serene Woods. I hate how I left things with Moira. A pair of glittering green irises pierce my vision, along with an ache between my ribs that only worsens when I realize she isn't here.

"Want to win The Gauntlet?" Desmond replies between gritted teeth before his lips pull into a perfectly bright smile. "This is just as important as the trials."

He isn't wrong, but most soldiers don't want the extra bullshit that comes with the job. We crave the taste of battle, savor victories amidst our brothers—the bonds that connect warriors when you've repeatedly soldiered, suffered, and sacrificed alongside each other.

Rianna, heir to Arafax's throne, sits poised next to her parents on the dais in a lush chair tufted with crimson and ornate gold accents. The corset of her gown hugs her sumptuous curves, and layers of chiffon fall from her skirts in a dazzling cascade that seeps onto the floor.

All three of us halt in place when she spots us.

Her blonde hair glimmers beneath the candelabras floating throughout the room, and her golden eyes spear us, pinning us to her very presence.

Desmond clears his throat. "Shall we?"

I nod silently, and we continue forward until we reach the

base of the dais. Knee dropping to the ground, I pull a hand across my chest, the rampant pulse of my heart beating beneath my fist.

"Sir Caden, Sir Desmond, Sir Graham, so glad you came. You've all decided to participate in The Gauntlet?" the King's voices calls over us.

"Your Majesty," I say, Desmond and Graham echoing the sentiment. Glancing up, gaze darting between the King and Queen, I add, "We are looking forward to proving our worth."

"Good. That's what your king wishes to hear."

I suck in a breath, knowing what's coming next but unprepared for the sting, regardless. Flames etch themselves around my wrist. The Gauntlet Cuff. The official mark of committing to the trials. If a competitor were to run now, the flames would continue to rise until the deserter was covered in their shame.

Not that I'd ever do such a thing.

I twist my wrist, taking in every line with pride. Once I complete the trials, they will disappear, but for the duration of The Gauntlet they will be a badge of honor. A sign that I'm devoted to my kingdom, eager to claim championhood and serve Arafax.

"And who do we have here?" the King asks, looking past us. The princess's attention diverts as well, and I follow her gaze to a tall stranger, his brown hair hitting his bronze shoulders. If he's from Arafax, he isn't someone I've ever met.

"Zavier," he says with a kneel.

The King's gaze narrows, and I'm unsure if it's curiosity or displeasure painting his face. Either way, he shakes it off quickly. "Where have you visited us from, Zavier?"

"The south." It's an odd response considering there are

only two known territories below Arafax, and this man looks like he hails from neither of them. "I'm here to compete in The Gauntlet."

"Welcome, Zavier." Princess Rianna's silvery voice sweetens any sourness filtering from her father. Her gaze turns toward the King, expectant.

Zavier's eyes never leave King Laisren's, not a wince or show of pain in them as he's marked. In fact, their like pools of ignited copper, something unspoken swimming in their depths that I can't quite put my finger on. He clenches and unclenches his hand a few times, then smiles, as if he's been given a precious bracelet and not a cuff of scars.

"That was...odd," Desmond huffs under his breath as we walk away from the dais.

"I agree."

Out of the corner of my eye, I spot Pierce and Thibauld. The latter subtly nods for us to come over, so I bring my hand to the back of Graham's arm and direct us toward them.

When I glance at their wrists, they're empty. "Have you entered into The Gauntlet?"

"No. We aren't," Pierce says, shooting Thibauld a furtive glance. "We were, er...ordered not to. Not that I had any interest in losing my lunch on the back of a dragon anyway."

He laughs, and we join in with him. Thibauld says nothing, his gruff exterior no different than usual. I did notice him tuck his hand at his side, though, as if embarrassed he couldn't participate.

"No one can order you not to compete in The Gauntlet, Tibbs," I whisper to him while the others take to the dance floor. "By right, any Celarian is allowed to enter."

"Yes, but what is the point if you know you will not win?" he grumbles under his breath.

"Why would you say that?" While the royal family did announce the champions, all contenders have to prove their worth to the dragons.

"You do this long enough, you understand better how these things work."

Pierce straightens as Prince Ciaran enters the room, his red velvet coat falling almost to the floor. He looks about as interested to be there as the children prancing about the corner of the room—the ones earning stern glances from guests who I assume to be their parents.

When the prince waves them over, Thibauld turns to me, giving a resigned sigh. "That's our cue."

"Leaving already?"

"Yes. The prince isn't staying. He has other plans for the evening. Duty calls."

As soon as they reach him, the three leave swiftly, somehow managing to keep the prince from getting detained by too many eager guests eyeing him with glints in their gaze.

"Lucky bastards," Desmond says with a shake of his head. "Another night spent in Faerie Hollow."

"Why would he go there?" The faeries live in Faerie Hollow, tucked within the majestic Everwood Grove. Their king was known to entertain all levels of debauchery within the Hollow, invite-only soirees. Just the kind of thing the prince enjoys. But during a formal celebration when the nobility of Celaria are present? That seems...strange.

"He's meeting with their king." Desmond guards the prince sometimes, but I know he's grateful to not have him as his main assignment. He's had his sights on guarding

Princess Rianna since he was promoted to royal guard. Of course, I do spend most of my days with the princess, and while I can't deny her captivating beauty, she does not stir my attention.

The next few royal children to enter the throne room are the twins. Their chestnut curls have been trained to stay perfectly in place and freckles pepper the tops of their cheeks. They walk immediately to where the other children are gathered, spinning around until they're stumbling and giggling.

I bet they want to be at this party about as much as I do.

Finally, the youngest daughters make their entrance. The taller one, who's about fourteen, has platinum hair pulled into a tight braid that hangs down the middle of her back. Her blush gown billows out like curls of smoke behind her, nearly eclipsing her petite frame. Her brothers wave at her, but she continues on, seemingly not wanting to be bothered.

"Douglas said she's been getting more miserable to keep track of. Snuck out three times last week to try to meet up with some squires," Graham whispers to me with a chuckle.

The youngest of the Arafax royal siblings follows behind her slightly older sister, eyes downcast at her feet the entire time. She clings to the scarlet folds of her gown, striding down the long carpet toward the dais. Her face only comes up at the end, glancing over at her best friend, Neve, who's wearing a golden gown that highlights the amber hue of her eyes. While I've only met Aveena's granddaughter a handful of times, she's often invited to castle events, usually stirring up mischief with the youngest royal.

Princess Isla's silver eyes dart around the room, her chestnut curls pinned partially atop her head. She gives a small smile when her parents greet her, then pulls her skirts to the side, rushing off to meet her friend.

"Guess we'd better head to the dance floor," Desmond says. His eyes are pinned to Princess Rianna, who's whispering to her father, gaze scanning the crowd.

I groan, knowing he's right. It's not that I hate dancing, but attempting to not look foolish clad in our heavy armor is more difficult than it may seem. With each clank against the marble, my eyes search for Moira. At least if I look like a fool dancing with her, she'd just laugh alongside me rather than at me.

Desmond departs from us, not missing his opportunity with Arafax's heir. Princess Rianna gives him a gracious nod, extending her hand as he escorts her to the dance floor. The other women watch with eyes glittering at the pair. They're beautiful together. Even King Laisren's lips quirk. But that's why we're here, isn't it? To present ourselves as candidates to be in the upper echelons of society. As a champion, we'll be expected to attend these affairs indefinitely. There's no retiring from this, only an honorable death alongside your Revered.

"Sir Caden," a delicate voice chimes from behind me, "may I have a dance?"

A grin spans my jaw when I spin around to find Princess Isla smiling up at me. "Of course, Your Highness," I reply, bowing for her before giving her my arm. She places her hand on my elbow, a giddy skip to her step as we stride to the center of the floor.

"Didn't want to dance with one of the boys?" I scan the room, nodding toward the blue-clad huddle. "Perhaps Inverno's Prince?"

"Eww," she said with a wince. "Don't be ridiculous. He's far too young for me."

She glances unimpressed at the young prince with dark-brown hair and navy eyes playing hide-and-seek with a few other children behind the wide skirts of some of the guests' ball gowns.

I bark out a laugh. "Well, I'm much too old for you."

"Yes, but watching you dance gives me a form of entertainment, Sir Caden." Her gaze drops to my golden boots barely moving on the floor. I hate the sound of their clacking, drawing unnecessary attention to myself.

"Hey, I take offense to that," I say, releasing the hand on her upper back to clutch my wounded heart. "My dance skills have much improved since the last banquet."

"If you'd prefer I stand on your feet so you can pretend you're helping me, like we did when I was younger, I'd be happy to oblige."

That silver tongue is going to carve out some boy's heart one day.

Isla's my favorite of the royal siblings, but she doesn't need the level of protection that her elder sister does as the heir. It made it all the more fun to see her when the family was all together on occasions such as this one.

As I spin the young princess beneath my arm, a glowing-green gaze strikes me from behind a crowd of silver-clad knights with blue capes. When Moira walks between them, they all take notice. Purple fabric drapes across one shoulder, leaving the other exposed, the material clinging at her waist and pooling around her feet. You'd think she was royalty with the way she holds her chin high, ignoring their gawking.

But she doesn't need a crown to be the queen of my heart.

"Ask her to dance," Princess Isla's whisper creeps into my ear.

"I will." *At some point.*

"Uh-huh." The princess twirls away from me, swinging her gown from side to side like a trying to flag down my attention. "Would you like to pretend to keep dancing with me or does standing in the middle of the dance floor staring at her from afar seem like a better option?"

"Hush!"

She's not wrong. In my mind, I'd been moving this whole time, but my eyes drop to my heavy boots cemented beneath me. All I need is the courage to walk over there, to ask Moira to dance.

"Go. Ask," the princess repeats, her tone regal and commanding, even at twelve.

I lift my boot to stride in Moira's direction, but hesitate when Sir Desmond steps in front of me and escorts her to the dance floor. He moves her with fluid grace despite the heavy armor. Her raven curls bounce and spin as they waltz in circles around the room. Tossing her head back, she laughs, pink blossoming over her nose and cheeks.

Breathtaking.

"Don't be foolish, Sir Caden." Princess Isla's soft hand slips into mine, leading me across the polished floor. "Follow me."

I try to keep up, dodging the dancing duos pirouetting and swaying along the path toward Desmond and Moira. The two are moving in unison, but the princess doesn't hesitate, placing a hand on the knight's shoulder and halting their promenade.

"Sir Desmond, mind if I cut in?" She tilts her head to the side, flashing him a brilliant smile.

Clever girl.

"Er." His eyes flare to Moira quickly who nods before he replies and offers his arm. "Of course not, Your Highness."

She takes off with him, leaving Moira standing alone for a moment. She turns to leave, but I catch her wrist. Her eyes flash brighter than usual, but she doesn't meet my gaze, blinking the expression away.

"May I have this dance?"

Her emerald gaze meets mine as she curtsies. "Of course."

She lets me lead her into the center of the dance floor, and I set us into position. Knights receive formal training for these things, but I've found dancing takes more than logic and counting.

Unfortunately.

My palms grow sweaty beneath my gloves as I try to glide with the ease I know she's capable of. I'm regretting Princess Isla getting me into this.

Moira doesn't miss a beat, though. She's smiling and enjoying herself, despite my skills or lack thereof. "I thought you weren't going to be here tonight?"

She cocks her head to the side. "Disappointed that I am?"

"Not at all." *I've hoped every moment since I arrived that you'd come.* "Surprised."

"Well, you made such a compelling argument for my attendance. I had to see you stumble over your feet for myself." She chuckles and the sound vibrates through my golden armor, humming through every part of me.

"Any chance I can convince you to change your mind about The Gauntlet?" Her voice quiets, all prior mirth vanishing in place of something serious. Lifting my hand up with hers, she inspects the marks wrapping my wrist. "Nevermind... I see I am too late on that front."

"You are, not that it would change my mind."

Moira opens her mouth as if to say something, but instead swallows the thought. I walk her off the dance floor, past the throng of onlookers, and back out into the Great Hall. People appear on the dark-gray stone, portals twinkling beneath the crystal chandelier dangling in the middle of the room. Pools of gold form into formidable beasts, a celebration of the Revered on display for all who enter the castle.

The dragons themselves are resting tonight, away from prying eyes, but it doesn't stop guests from sneaking glances out the large windows, hoping to catch a glimpse of them.

"What's going on, Moira?" She won't even meet my stare. I hook my armored finger under her chin, lifting it until her eyes are blazing into mine. "You're my best friend. You know how much being commander one days means to me. Don't you want that for me?"

"Of course I do. I wish for you to have all that you desire." Her hand lifts to her throat. "I just..."

"What?"

"It doesn't matter." She wraps her hands around my wrist, frowning at the mark. Her lip wobbles, and she blinks a few more times before rising onto her tiptoes to kiss my cheek. "I have every faith you'll win The Gauntlet and be chosen."

I shrug. "Winning The Gauntlet is one thing, winning over the royal family and a Revered? We shall see."

"Well, you've already won over Princess Isla. That counts for something."

"Ah yes. I'm sure she will have the most sway over my standing in the competition." I chuckle. Moira does too for a moment.

And then the comforting sound is gone just as quickly as it came.

"You truly want to be stuck coming to all these events the rest of your life?"

"If that's what duty demands of me, yes."

"Well, *Sir Caden*, let me be the first to tell you that you will need some tutoring on your dancing skills if you are to make these events a regular occurrence," she teases. We exchange smiles but they're hollow, void of all the words unsaid. Before I can fill the space, tell her why I need her to believe in this—in me—she's retreats a step.

"Better go make our rounds." She doesn't even wait for me to extend an arm to escort her before she strides past me, greeting guests along the way.

We don't talk the rest of the night, merely existing in the same space. Two ghosts passing each other from different planes. What she doesn't realize is that on any plane, she's the only one who truly haunts me.

4

The nerves that charge through me when I walk into the arena on the morning of The Gauntlet only intensify when I glance over the sea of opponents. There have to be at least fifty men and women vying for a spot as champion. Many I recognize and some I've never seen before. Though, that could be because everyone had been dressed up at the banquet last night and my mind had been stuck on Moira and her icy treatment most of the evening.

Roar!

The audience's chins all lift, gazes trailing skyward until they collide with the magnificent beasts above. It doesn't matter that we're surrounded by them each day and spot them on patrol at night, there is something inherently mesmerizing about our dragons. You can't deny their majesty. Even King Laisren's eyes twinkle as he watches them, transfixed.

The arena shakes with the staggered landings of the two Revered. The ruby one sits proudly on its hind legs, maw pointing upward, silver eyes scanning over us all. Next to it, the navy dragon lays down, Aveena resting on its back with her hands behind her head, as if silently letting us know they're ready for the show. The crowd's attention is still cast toward the clouds.

Waiting.

Waiting.

Waiting.

A minute later, King Laisren finally sits down on his throne, his voice booming over the crowd. "It's time to learn who our next champion will be!"

Champion. Not champions.

The emerald dragon is nowhere in sight. While it wasn't guaranteed both of the unbonded Revered would be interested in a champion, I can't help the disappointment that strikes my chest. Graham and I exchange furtive glances. While I believe I have it in me to come out victorious, the odds have just bolstered the competition by double.

"At least the ruby isn't as wild," he offers. "I've heard the emerald tends to do as they please."

I've heard that, too. Saw it for myself when I'd been stationed in the mountains, watching them patrol its edge. They were supposed to do it nightly, but there were many evenings when I watched for all three, only to spot two. No one knows where the dragons camp out when they aren't assisting Arafax. There are rumors they have a hidden home among the clouds, not too far from Arafax's castle. Others believe they live out on the untouched islands in the far south, past where the mermaids swim.

Thibauld and Pierce walk through the competitors, handing them small stones. Portal stones. They are time-consuming to conjure, so I am shocked to see one given to each challenger. King Laisren smiles at his fellow Celarian leaders, obviously pleased with this display of luxury. Thibauld drops the copper-painted charcoal stone to me. It's cool against my palm, and I stare at the symbols and numbers etched into it with faerie blood.

The King stands to address us, and the crowd silences. "We'll start simple this morning with some sparring to narrow down to our final six competitors. Place the stones in your hands on the ground in front of you. Once I've said the incantation, smash the portal stone. You and your opponent, who's been selected at random, will land in your sparring zone."

Thin lines etch into the ground, dividing the arena into squares.

"Remain in your sparring zone and beat your opponent. Fall past the line and you are disqualified. Stay grounded for more than six seconds and you're disqualified." The King's attention is pinned to the pocket of us clad in golden armor. It's no secret that while he cannot control the Revered and their choice of champion, he and the Faerie King, who holds claim over the bonding lands, still have some influence.

The King does not want an outsider claiming champion of his Revered. It's why so many of us are competing, though there are many, like Graham, who have no desire to ride on the back of a dragon. Of the fifty competitors, maybe a dozen are from other territories. They would be stupid not to toss someone into the arena on their behalf—most would kill for the chance to have a Revered tie them to Arafax. From the cluster of large blue-caped warriors in the corner, King Reynard of Inverno is definitely aiming for a shot. The last handful are all clad in different garb, some not even wearing armor, looking like they've never held a weapon before, including Zavier.

He wears black leathers, a thick chain tucked into the breast pocket of his jacket and a glittering braided rope hangs from his waist unlike anything I've ever seen before.

King Laisren chants the incantation. I'm not good at translating them, so I only catch every other word. Something about *stone* and *reveal*. After the third time, he nods to us all.

I toss the rock onto the ground and lift my boot. Giving Graham a quick glance, I take one last deep breath and stomp down.

***

THERE ARE NO RULES ABOUT MAGIC USAGE DURING THE Gauntlet, so I'm not surprised when the swirls of grays and browns clear away and I'm staring at a blue-caped soldier from Inverno with his familiar. What I am surprised at, however, is that it's a small hedgehog. Someone might consider the creature nestled atop his shoulder cute, but the malice shining back at me through its beady eyes won't allow me to attach that pleasant description to it.

I swallow, hard, feeling wholly unprepared to deal with them despite my years of training.

"Sir Caden," I say quickly with a bow, bringing a fist across my chest.

"Ridgemont." He nods down at his tiny evil companion, the spikes along its back glinting like silvery blades that will happily slice me up. "This is Laoise."

More like lethal.

I scan the crowd, hoping to spot a pair of green eyes

looking back at me. That Moira is here, my good luck charm. But she's not.

A roar echoes through the arena, the ruby Revered giving the signal to begin.

The arena erupts in a symphony of steel and shouts.

Ridgemont surges forward, crashing down on me with his sword. I twist back, dodging the attack and nudging his blade away with one of my own. We stand apart for a moment, and I cross my swords in front of me. He holds out his longsword, and I suck in a breath, ready to unleash, but I'm stopped in my tracks when the hedgehog springs from his shoulder, tucks herself into a ball, and rolls down the blade.

What in the—

Its tiny body thunders toward me. I don't want to kill this soldier's familiar, but I also can't ignore the searing pain slicing through me when her silver quills meet my cheek. I stagger backward with a hiss. Shouts and screams ring around me, mimicked by the rowdy audience, and I nearly tip over the thin line with my boot.

I drop to the ground, scanning for Laoise. Somehow, she's already next to her master. Lunging at them, I strike forward and low, getting a shallow cut into Ridgemont's ankle. His knee buckles and he drops just as I stand, holding my swords above him.

A smirk draws across my lips.

But the moment is cut short when spikes clear my vision. Laoise is clutched in Ridgemont's gloved hand, meeting my face with a sharp punch. The arena spins and I clench my core, one sword slipping from my grasp.

This is it. Bested by a hedgehog.

My face itches and heats. Bringing my palm to my

stinging cheek, I glance over at Ridgemont. From the pleased expression on his face, something is visibly wrong with it.

"Ready to yield?" he asks, scooping up his familiar and tossing her onto his shoulder, pride glimmering in her eyes.

"You wish." I grip the one sword I have with both hands, ignoring the prickling in my face as I slash and swing with all my might.

Ridgemont believes he's won, but he's mistaken.

His eyes widen when I charge for him, the current of a million dreams swinging the sword for me. I came here to win. To ride the wind on the back of a mighty dragon, to lead armies and vanquish enemies.

Yield is not a word I'll ever use.

But he will. Now.

My next moves are all fierce conviction and trained instincts, sending Ridgemont scrambling backward until he's gripping the ground behind him for a weapon, only to turn and find his hand reaching past the thin, pale line in the dirt.

"*Fuck.*" He shakes his head but bows it in defeat. The sign of a worthy opponent. I extend my hand out, helping him stand. Laoise watches me warily.

"Sorry 'bout your face," Ridgemont says, though I can tell he's really not sorry at all. I can't fault him for that. At least he can say he got a few swipes in—or Laoise did, rather.

The ruby dragon tips its maw to the sky and roars, drawing my attention to the rest of the arena. It was easy to forget that it was more than just me and my opponent. That there's a full audience and an arena full of challengers vying for one spot of honor.

Champion.

I scan the arena. Most of the challengers are kneeling or being carried off on stretchers toward the fort's infirmary. I spot Desmond and Graham on the opposite end of the arena, chests heaving. Desmond's body is ignited, the expression he gets after he's warmed up and is ready for the battle to begin. Graham, on the other hand, looks shocked. His hands shake and there's a large pool of blood at his feet, a body being dragged onto a stretcher. I want to run over to him, to make sure he's okay, but I already know he isn't.

"Our final six have been culled. Congratulations, Sir Graham, Sir Desmond, Sir Caden,"—the King's voice loses its bravado—"Zavier, Freya, and Malakai... Now it's onto the final task." His molten gaze rakes over me before moving to the other golden knights. He doesn't have to say anything. We already know. If the champion is not from Arafax, then we have failed him. We have failed our kingdom.

Graham is still quivering in my peripheral vision. Desmond's hand clutches his sword possessively, like the fight hasn't ended for him. And in a way, it hasn't.

Six of us may remain, but there can only be one champion.

5

We stand along the fort's entryway waiting to be called in, one by one, to be seen in the throne room. The spectacle of the morning was for the masses to enjoy, but this is just us and a small, undisclosed group of people. *A final evaluation* is all we've been told.

I know how to fight with hands and weapons. Whatever this challenge is... Do I have what it takes to face it?

The doors groan open, Zavier yawning before striding down the long red carpet. He takes his place in the row of challengers, a lazy grin spreading across his face. Like he's in on some joke we don't understand. It makes my fists clench.

Pierce looks back into the room, waiting, Thibauld holding the door his opposite. Pierce turns around finally, calling out, "Sir Caden."

What have I gotten myself into?

The walk feels much too short despite how long the carpet is. When the doors shut behind me, it takes a few moments for my vision to adjust to the dimly lit room.

"Welcome, Sir Caden," King Laisren says from the front of the room.

Upon the dais, he sits on his throne, Princess Rianna on one side, Prince Ciaran on the other, and Aveena next to him. The last person on the dais surprises me most of all. It's not someone I recognize per se, but from the violet of their eyes glinting in the candlelight and the long, dark tresses...they could only be one type of magic user.

Weaver.

The weavers are a very private people who only come into Arafax in small groups for short visits, always scurrying back to Alucinor, the peninsula where they hail from. My throat dries, and I wonder what kind of mind magic this one would be spinning today and how it would be a test for me. A strange skittering sound filters through the room.

Is it just in my head?

Are they already combing through my mind for whatever they're looking for?

When the princess shifts uncomfortably in her chair, I know it's not just me.

The King gestures to my left. "You are welcome to watch with us or face away if you prefer. This just helps us get a sense of the kind of champion you may be. A glimpse into all that you are."

"Where's the Revered?" I ask.

"Verre here," he gestured toward the weaver, "has a counterpart with our Revered. They are still able to see through their network."

I swallow the unease lodged in the back of my throat. "I see."

The weaver clutches a crystal hanging around their neck,

and there's a faint scraping at the back of my mind. They are in there. Looking. Learning.

A dozen glittering bulbous bodies with eight tiny legs hang above the sheet of what I now realize to be spider silk. I shiver where I stand, not a fan of...bugs. I've already had one critter run-in today with Laoise. Between events, I had to go to the infirmary to get balm put on my half-swollen face. A red rash still remains, and I'm grateful I'm unable to see myself right now. I'm certain I look abysmal.

Colors merge on the silky backdrop, filling the blank space with familiar visions that tilt my world.

My parents bending down to play with me.

Training with my father at the fort.

Running through the lavender fields with my mother, watching her tend to the blooms, growing them from beneath her palms. Across the way, a little girl stares at me, a long, black braid hanging over her shoulder. Emerald stars glint in her eyes as she clutches her mother's skirts. I've known that face at every age, with every new freckle.

The memories fly in and out like birds on the wind. Snippets of my life, the good and the bad. I watch my father become too ill to train with me then witness my knighting, barely holding on. Somehow, even just seeing it I feel the frail touch of his hand, his final strained breath.

There's something about seeing your life in flashes, presented to you like you're not part of them. Logically, you've experienced them. You were there. But each moment carries a hundred thoughts, a dozen smells, that forever transports you back to that time.

That's when I realize how truly brutal this evaluation is. No blade can slice like these memories do, cutting to the core of who I am and setting it out as if on a platter for everyone else in the room to examine and feast upon. I'm becoming smaller as Moira rejects me, saying goodbye to her as I leave for the mountains, my heart breaking all over again when I return to find her here but somehow a million miles away.

I'm served to everyone watching from the dais. A few times I note a brow raise or the pursing of lips. But other than that, they show no sign to let me know if I'm passing their *evaluation*.

"Thank you for your time, Sir Caden," the King calls, and I'm being escorted toward the door, still in a haze. I've been laid bare and consumed.

Judged.

And now I have to hope that showing them everything is enough for me to be called champion. For me to one day be called commander.

I'm going to be sick.

Slinking against the stony wall, I take a few steadying breaths with my head between my knees. Graham is called in next, and I pray that his shaking hands from the fatal blow they accidentally landed earlier aren't replayed. That he doesn't return looking like how I feel.

Maimed.

One by one, the others go in and come back out looking like they'd aged more in that room than they have since I've known some of them. We're brought refreshments while the committee deliberates, and I have no idea how much time passes because my whole life has just been hurled out in ten minutes.

"Sir Caden." It takes me a moment to realize everyone is back out and leaning against the wall next to me. "Time to come back in."

I slowly make my way down the carpet, clutching the

small lavender bouquet from Moira in one hand. I'd tucked it away with my things today, just in case I made it this far. Each step is agonizing, having to face these people again much too soon.

This time the room is lit and everyone is gone except for the King. Kneeling low, I bring my hand across my chest in a bow. He returns the gesture, then waits for me to stand. "I wanted to congratulate you myself on being selected as one of Arafax's esteemed champions."

It takes me a moment to comprehend the words. "Really?"

King Laisren chuckles. "Don't act so surprised, it's unbecoming of your title and of your experience. I had no doubts you'd be a champion, though I would have seen things maybe going differently..."

He trails off with a shrug.

"What do you mean?"

"No matter," he says, waving off my question. "Just know that it was a very tough decision."

"What happens next?" I ask, trying to rein in my surprise.

"Go meet your Revered at the arena. Your bonding ceremony for this evening has already been relayed to the Faerie King. There should be no...interference."

"Does that happen?"

"It has once before." King Laisren clears his throat. "Though, the Faerie King seems to prefer to exercise his power just to show he has some. Prince Ciaran has assured me there will be no issues."

I did it. I'll be champion.

One step closer to commander.

"Remember, Sir Caden, the Revered and everything that comes with being a champion is a closely kept secret. Very few are privy to the things you will be. It's both an honor and a burden." I'm still in my haze, heart pounding with excitement for all that's to come. The King calls down to me, dragging my attention back. "Do you understand?"

"I do." I nod, giving a final bow of respect.

"Then go forth, and may you have a blessed ceremony."

"Thank you, Your Majesty." My voice is nearly giddy and I have to tamp it down, not wanting to sound unprofessional.

"I look forward to seeing you serve many years alongside your Revered," the King says as I exit the throne room through its back entrance leading straight to the arena.

Once I bonded the dragon, what would we work on first? Flying tactics? Combat? Would we be able to communicate somehow? There were so many things I wondered and now I would finally find out.

I'm bubbling with excitement by the time I reach the arena. Nodding to the ruby dragon, I extend out my arms, clutching the lavender so tight that I wouldn't be surprised if a few of the stems are bent. With a huff, the dragon's gaze flits to the flowers before it turns its nose up and shoots into the sky.

Shit. Did I do something to offend my Revered?

That's when I spot someone else on its back. I squint, trying to make out who the rider is, but they're speeding away far too quickly.

What's happening?

A growl echoes through the arena, snapping my attention from the clouds. There, in the center of the arena, the emerald dragon glares at me through narrowed slits.

6

What are you supposed to say to the dragon that's chosen you but also looks like it's heavily weighing the option of ripping your throat out?

While the ruby dragon glitters from the sky, the emerald's scales look like they are composed of crushed shards of sea glass, mostly green but some slips of aqua where the light hits. Its big eyes glow but remain unblinking, watching me carefully.

Warily.

Unsure how to proceed, I toss the lavender at its claws and kneel, tucking my chin to my chest and bringing my fist across my breastplate. "I am honored by your choice, Revered one."

It merely blinks at me then the lavender before turning away to lie down. Huffing at me, it shifts its hind legs a bit, and I realize it's trying to tell me to get on its back.

"Oh," I say, standing quickly and grabbing the bouquet. I tuck it into my armor, then scramble to hoist myself onto the dragon's front leg, using the ridges along its scales to pull myself up. Once I've settled behind its neck, I take some deep breaths, trying to calm my nerves.

I'm sitting on the back of a dragon. My eyes drift up to the sky. *We're about to go up there.*

My hands shake against the green scales reflecting my face back at me like a tinted mirror. Despite the swelling having gone down, half my face is still an angry shade of reddish purple, tiny gashes cutting across my cheek. Good thing my looks weren't a necessary factor in the evaluation.

Fucking hedgehog.

The initial ascent has me gripping tightly, basically hugging the giant beast's neck with my head tilted to the side so I can see Celaria's full expanse below. The clouds rush past us, and while I'm tempted to touch them, I'm too frightened to reach out. I remind myself that once the bond is in place, things will get easier. We will have a lifetime of riding together.

Stars, this is incredible.

One day I'll be a silver-streaked old man, lounging lazily on the back of my beautiful emerald Revered, like Aveena has done for decades with her navy one. My children will watch me from their bedroom windows, eyes twinkling with pride. That vision, that future, is a treasure that sparkles with each flap of the mighty dragon's wings. I watch its body push and pull the wind, as if it's in charge of the breeze and not the other way around.

We land with a soft *thud*, and I'm grateful to see the blades of grass within reach. The dragon tilts its body to the side, and I slide off its abdomen. We aren't near the ancient grove where we're meant to bond tonight. In fact, we are in a spot I recognize all too well.

Before I can utter a single word, the scales on the dragon's body begin to shake, shrinking down in a rippling wave until they are hidden beneath flesh.

Beautiful flesh. Full of freckles I'd recognize anywhere and a handful I've never had the opportunity to discover before.

Moira is naked before me.

"Y-you..." I blink rapidly in case this is some illusion the weaver spun—that none of this is real and I'm still back in the second trial, losing my mind.

"How?" I ask, my mind zipping through every moment we've had together. How did I not know about this? "I thought—"

I clamp my mouth shut before I finish the sentence.

"What?" She wanders over to our trunk and drapes across it like this is a usual day in this clearing. Like she didn't just turn from a massive dragon into the woman I've loved my whole life. Like she isn't taunting me with her bared beauty right now.

I'm a man who's wandered the desert far too long, the feel of her skin against mine the refreshment I'm desperate for.

I'm desperate for *her*.

Have been for as long as I can remember. But— "If you're Revered... If you could choose me, why did you let me enter The Gauntlet?"

"I've never *let* you do anything. You made your intentions very clear. And, for your information, I wasn't planning on choosing someone from The Gauntlet." She huffs out an exasperated sigh, legs kicking back and forth. A tick, I've realized, she does to steady her nerves. I wait for her to continue, ignoring the ache to pull her close, shake her, and ask why she never said anything to me about this. Then maybe pepper kisses up the curve of her shoulder blade...

"What if you had lost? What if you'd won but were chosen by the other Revered... Princess Rianna? As royalty she'd get preferential treatment over whomever she selected."

So that's who the ruby dragon was... She'd been in the evaluation, had been there the whole time. Curiosity pricked at the nape of my neck. "Who did the princess select?"

"Select might be a bit strong of a term, but Sir Desmond."

"Not Zavier?"

"No. Though, knowing her, she'll never let on that she didn't end up getting much say in the decision." She yawns, as if she's the one who's been through grueling trials all day. I should be exhausted, but I'm a live wire, electrified by everything I'm discovering about my future.

Our future.

"Even though it wasn't her choice, I'm sure she won't mind bedding him again when they bond," she adds with a chuckle.

"Again?" *That sneaky fucker.* Not that I care that they've been seeing each other, but it definitely means I need to have better royal guard instincts. I had no clue. Then my mind trips— "You mean that part of the bonding is—"

"The bonding is a merging of magic as much as it is one of bodies." She says it so casually, like she's inviting me for tea. *Naked* tea. I can't stop myself from devouring every inch of her with my eyes. My heart thuds to the point where I wonder if it will burst up and out my throat.

"I hope you're not disappointed." Her voice cracks on the last word, like she truly believes I'd be disappointed by this. By her.

"How could I be?" I'm genuinely confused because I'd made it plain that I wanted us to be together. But maybe she's the one who's unhappy. She didn't want to deal with The Gauntlet after all. "Are *you*...disappointed?"

She kicks her feet a few more times before standing up and walking toward me. I drink in every fluid curve of her body, the fullness of her hips and breasts. I want so badly to reach out and trace each line with my fingers, brushing along the soft skin that minutes ago was a collection of thick, glassy scales.

Moira hesitates a moment with her palm lifted, and I nod, unsure what she'll do but desperate for whatever it is if it means she'll touch me. When her palm cradles my stinging cheek, I don't even wince, too entranced by her. "Not at all. I want this."

"Then why did you say no to my proposal before I left?" My words are drawn like swords, defensive and ready to attack. "Why do you want me now?"

She brushes along my cheek and combs through my hair. "I had just become what I am when you asked me. I didn't know if I was ready to tie you to all of that yet. To everything that comes with being a champion. But it's always been you. I just wanted it to go a bit differently."

"And how's that?" I asked, voice softening as I lean into her touch.

"You know..." the corner of her mouth peels up mischievously, "swoon-worthy romance."

I dip my head lower, until our lips are nothing more than a wisp apart. "Are you saying I'm not swoon-worthy?"

"Not at all." Her eyes glow, searching mine, and I almost catch my mind playing tricks on me, believing her irises have split into slits before retreating back again. This will definitely take some getting used to. "I just wanted to make sure there was *mutual* swooning."

"There is," I assure her, pulling a few lavender twigs from the battered bunch I brought with me and tucking them behind her ear. My palm slides around her waist to the base of her spine. "And I plan to romance you plenty now that you're mine."

"I've always been yours." Moira's truth sinks into me as her lips crash with mine. This isn't our first kiss. There were a few playful ones when we were young, a few more reckless ones when we were a bit older. But this kiss? It strikes me between the ribs so deeply I'll never be the same. *We'll* never be the same.

It's the kiss of knowing, of wholeness, of *devotion*.

It's coming home. It's reverence.

It's *us*.

"Then what are we waiting for, champion?" Moira whispers against my lips. The smile on her face matches my own.

I could do this for hours. And I intend to.

I press a slow kiss to her forehead and my fingers skim over the scales marking her side. "We wait for nothing, Revered. Forever waits for us."

ALSO BY L.R. FRIEDMAN

The Blaze Legacy

Descend

Scale

Pitch

Ascend

Fall

Soar

Celestial Haven

Wicked in the Pines

Midnight with the Hexed

Hallowed Harbingers

Etched in Frost

Inked in Bloom

Death's Songbird

ABOUT THE AUTHOR

L.R. Friedman started writing in 2021 after spending a decade putting "write the book" on her five-year plan. Her first book published in August 2022.

The girl that grew up trying to find a hidden realm in her closet, she now spends her days curled up with a cup of coffee, playing matchmaker for her morally grey characters.

All of her stories include LGBTQ+ leads, mental health rep, and are set in worlds that are dark, sexy, and whimsical.

Her immersive and character-driven stories are full of emotional healing and relatable characters, meant to both entertain and empower her readers.

She lives in Virginia with her husband and three children.

For updates about upcoming releases, please visit http://www.lrfriedman.com, and sign up for her newsletter or join her group on Facebook at Books & Brews with L.R. Friedman.

PLAYLIST

Every Little Thing She Does is Magic - The Polic

Bruises - Lewis Capaldi

Animal - Neon Trees

Play with Fire (ft. Yacht Money) - Sam Tinnesz

Bad Dreams (stripped) - Faouzia

Sorry To Me Too - Julia Michaels

Self Sabotage - Ruelle

Kiss or Kill - Stella Cole

Daisy - Ashnikko

Girls girls girls - FLETCHER

Beautiful Creature - MIIA

Champagne - Lia Marie Johnson

Legends Are Made - Sam Tinnesz

Without You - Boyce Avenue

Fallible Creatures (acoustic) - Scott Quinn

Monster in Me - Little Mix

Thick and Thin - Faouzia

Wicked Game - Daisy Gray

Big Bad Wolf - Roses & Revolutions

A Little Bit Dangerous - CRMNL

Figure You Out (remix) - VOILA

Queen of Peace - Florence + The Machine

Feel About You - Aislin Evans

Lost - Dermot Kennedy

Minefields - Faouzia, John Legend

CONTENT &
TRIGGER WARNINGS

Content:
Explicit language, alcohol and magical drug use, mental health themes, on page sexually explicit scenes (MF/FF pairings)

Triggers:
Themes of grief and mental health including ptsd, physical violence and on page death